A TELLING of STARS

CAITLIN SWEET

PENGUIN
CANADA

PENGUIN CANADA

Published by the Penguin Group

Penguin Books, a division of Pearson Canada, 10 Alcorn Avenue, Toronto, Ontario,
Canada M4V 3B2

Penguin Books Ltd, 80 Strand, London WC2R 0RL, England

Penguin Putnam Inc., 375 Hudson Street, New York, New York 10014, U.S.A.

Penguin Books Australia Ltd, 250 Camberwell Road, Camberwell, Victoria 3124, Australia

Penguin Books India (P) Ltd, 11, Community Centre, Panchsheel Park,
New Delhi – 110 017, India

Penguin Books (NZ) Ltd, cnr Rosedale and Airborne Roads, Albany, Auckland 1310,
New Zealand

Penguin Books (South Africa) (Pty) Ltd, 24 Sturdee Avenue, Rosebank 2196, South Africa

Penguin Books Ltd, Registered Offices: 80 Strand, London WC2R 0RL, England

First published 2003

1 3 5 7 9 10 8 6 4 2

Printed and bound in Canada on acid free paper ∞

National Library of Canada Cataloguing in Publication

Sweet, Caitlin, 1970–
A telling of stars / Caitlin Sweet.

ISBN 0-14-100740-0

I. Title.

PS8587.W387T4 2003   C813'.6 C2002-903576-7
PR9199.4.S95T4 2003

Visit Penguin Books' website at **www.penguin.ca**

*For Alison Frances Shand
and Brent Arthur London—absent, present, beloved.*

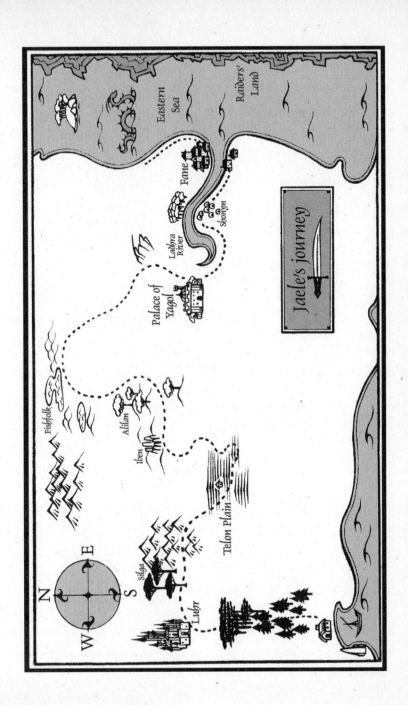

PROLOGUE

"Telling is magic": she hears this somewhere, before or after, as sparks coil.

Speak to us of sunlight, they say now, bending so close to her that she feels the cool breath of their horns and talons. *We have told you how long we have been prisoners, bound beneath the world. Please: speak to us again of the bright places you have seen. Tell us the turnings of your mind and steps.*

I will try, she says, and as her voice falls into the darkness, they listen, straining to catch the words and make them sun. She speaks in this deep place, with earth and stone above, and forgets her hunger and her skin. Spaces of sky and sea and desert. Giant, fisher, weaver, dancer, boy. A tangle of words, but she sees them all, feels each in her mouth like sorrow.

My home, she says, before or after. Shell's curve of beach, and wind that turns the sun to water.

BOOK ONE

HOME

CHAPTER ONE

Jaele was six years old when she met Dorin. He was nine or ten; she never knew for certain. They met for the first time on the beach below her parents' hut. This beach stretched in a wide crescent around the water, which was so green near the shore that it looked like crystal, or the shine of a serpent's back. Farther out, near the cliffs, the water was blue. Beyond that it was nothing, only a hazy line below the sky.

Jaele was running on the day she met Dorin. She liked to run when the sun was up and blazing on the sand; the soles of her feet burned then, but only if she was slow to lift them. She ran through hot wind and sunlight that was almost white.

She stopped running when she rounded a towering rock. Her father had told her that it was a club, all that remained of the giant whom the Warrior Queen Galha had killed long ago, when there was only sea and no beach. There was a pool of water here—clear, neither green nor blue—and a large collection of snails of all sorts. But today there was also a boy, and Jaele frowned.

He was looking out across the water. A cloth bundle lay on a rock beside him. He was very small—smaller than Jaele—and had light hair, while hers was as black as deepest water. He did not turn round, even when she coughed loudly. She frowned again and moved to stand beside him.

"Who are you?" she said. "Why are you in my private place?"

The boy looked at her and she saw that his eyes were pale—grey or light, light green. His voice was high and measured. "I am Dorin. I have left my home."

"I am Jaele. Why did you leave?" she demanded, and thought that he looked very sad, even though he was not crying.

"The Raiders attacked my town, and the elders wanted all the children to learn fighting. I didn't want to, so I left."

Jaele was suddenly excited. Her words trembled a bit when she said, "Raiders? The Sea Raiders that Queen Galha conquered?"

The boy glanced at her; now *he* was frowning. "I suppose so."

"Did they have webs between their fingers and toes?" she went on, stretching her own fingers wide as if to show him.

He nodded. "Yes. But there weren't very many of them, and—"

"You didn't fight?" she interrupted, bouncing from foot to foot. "You *left*?" He turned his head away, and she said, "I would have stayed. I would have protected my land just as Queen Galha did."

Dorin was silent. Jaele almost asked him if he was a coward, but something in his face frightened her a little. She stood quietly beside him. White-and-black seabirds called high above them, and it sounded like weeping.

"So you're alone?" she said at last.

Dorin nodded. "I'm going to see the world. I've heard there are golden sea snakes and trees as tall as the sky."

"This is the Giant's Club," Jaele told him, pointing to the huge stone beside them. "Queen Galha killed him, and the water swept away all but his club, which got stuck in the bottom of the sea. This is it."

Dorin smiled, and his face softened. "I like those stories."

"So do I," said Jaele. "My father tells them to me when he's weaving. Let's race," she said abruptly, wanting him to smile again.

She ran past the rock and along the beach without looking back. At the beaten track that led to her hut, she stopped and turned. Dorin was not behind her, and he was not at the Giant's Club when she ran back to look. She could not see him anywhere along the beach or on the forested hills that rose behind.

She was angry, and later just sad. As the years passed, she forgot what he looked like; sometimes she even forgot that she had ever met him. But even though she did not remember that his eyes were light and his face was sad, she did remember that there were golden sea snakes somewhere, trees as tall as the sky, Sea Raiders who still hunted across the water.

Jaele's father often told her the story of the Sea Raiders, especially when the sky was dark above the sand. "It was long ago," he would begin, leaning close to the single candle so that his shadow leapt and twisted. "The land was beautiful, and those who lived in it were happy, for Queen Galha ruled with wisdom and kindness. But one day," he said, his voice dropping as he bent to catch her eyes, "one day in midsummer, strangers came from across the sea. They killed the people of the coast, who were not expecting such an attack. They pushed on into the desert, where Queen Galha awaited them. She had called together her Queensfolk, the strongest men and women in her realm. These Queensfolk had until that time been explorers, teachers; now Galha gave them bows and swords and named them Queensfighters. And although she was a queen of peace and gentleness, she rode with her warriors to face the Sea Raiders." Jaele huddled deep into her blankets, knowing what was next.

"The Raiders were strong and many in number, but they were also of the sea, descended from the fishfolk who breathe water as if it were air. Queen Galha knew this when she saw their hands

and feet, which were webbed like a seabird's. It was obvious that
they were able to live in the earth and air for long periods of time,
as the fishfolk could, but the Queen guessed that they could not
be separated from water forever, so she held them in the desert
and filled in all the wells. These Raiders fought and killed many
Queensfighters, but slowly they began to sicken, for the water
they had brought with them was gone.

"The final battle was fought at the very gates of Luhr, the
Queen's City. Queen Galha was strong and proud, sure of a
victory—and so she sent her only daughter into the fight, wanting
the desert people to see their next ruler." Her father paused and
looked into the candle flame; Jaele watched the light shivering in
the blackest part of his eyes. "The Princess Ladhra rode proudly,
her dark hair shining, and with her own bow she killed many of
the enemy. But at the very end of the battle, as the sun set along the
sand and the Raiders fell back, one of them crept up to her horse.
He gripped her ankle and pulled her down, and her mother, sitting
at the head of her victorious army, saw the man thrust his dagger
into the young princess's heart." Usually Jaele's mother, Lyalla, was
listening now as well, standing in the darkness by the window with
baby Elic breathing softly in her arms.

"With that one thrust Queen Galha, whose love was peace,
became the Warrior Queen. Leaving her consort at Luhr, she
pressed the Sea Raiders back toward the Eastern Sea. She drove
them through desert and mountains, plains and hills and finally
desert again, following the rising sun. Many died as they fled, and
the Queensfighters slew many more who were too weak to keep
pace with the main Sea Raider army. Nonetheless, when the Raiders
at last reached the river they had been seeking—the great desert
river that has since borne the name of the murdered princess—they
swam, strong and swift." Jaele would shudder as her father spoke
these words, for she almost understood the Sea Raiders' underwater strokes, long with hope and relief.

"Even in the great ships that awaited them, the Queensfighters could not overtake their enemies. When Galha and her army swept downriver with the tall houses of Fane—that glorious port city—on either side of them, she found that the Sea Raiders had already swum from the river into the sea. The Queen and her troops followed in their ships, accompanied by the boats of humble fishers such as ourselves. She pursued them to the edge of their land, which was green and lush and shining with the water of many rivers and lakes. She looked on this beauty of water and growing things, and in her heart was the desert and the blood of her daughter. She ordered the Queensfighters to hack down the trees and fill the lakes and rivers with earth. She herself set fire to the tall grass and tore at the vines that hung thick from the branches of trees.

"At last, when all was scarred and dry, she called upon her mindpowers—mindpowers which could be summoned only in direst need. She cursed the land of the Sea Raiders. Never again, she decreed, would water come to them in lakes and rivers, but only in trickles that would barely sustain them. Never again would green things grow in abundance, but only in small, ragged clumps that would hardly keep them alive. Oh, they could sail across the sea if they wished, and they could gaze at or even swim in the water of other lands—but a taste would bring instant death. They could eat the fruits and grains and meats of other lands—but without water they would inevitably perish. They would live in misery, either in their own seared land or travelling away from it, and their webbed hands and feet would forever remind them of water and green and the girl they had killed."

In the silence that followed, Jaele would hear waves sliding onto the sand outside her hut. The stars would be out, and it would be difficult to tell sky from sea.

"Will they come back?" she whispered each time, and each time her father murmured, "It is said that they often return by night and in silence, to little children who have misbehaved . . ."

"Reddac!" Jaele's mother would say, coming into the circle of light with a smile in her voice. "Enough! I wish you wouldn't frighten her so," and every time Jaele would cry, lying, "I'm not frightened!" For during the day, as she played Queen Galha under the sun, she was very brave—but at night she was small in her bed, as she listened for the grinding of boats and the hissing of webbed feet on the sand.

Jaele's father told her stories as his loom clacked and his fingers flew over sunlit wood and cloth. Her mother taught her the sea. When Jaele was very small, her feet chubby and unsteady on the earth, Lyalla rowed her out into the bay and showed her the fish that wound like her father's threads beneath them; she showed her green and blue water, and water that prickled sharp stones. She taught her how to swim just below the surface and how to dive until deep-growing plants trailed along her skin. Jaele collected some of these plants to eat while her mother gathered fish in a net Reddac had made. He called Jaele and her mother his Sea Loves, and he always smiled as they pulled the boat onto the sand, their hair glowing dark and wet. The baby would be bouncing on his knees, chortling excitement, and when Lyalla bent to him, she said that he too would be a child of water.

Jaele dove and watched her father's colours twining and taught baby Elic how to paddle. She was not lonely, although after her encounter with the boy Dorin she felt an ache that she did not recognize. Every rising of the full moon she and Reddac, bearing swaths of woven clothes and blankets, rode their donkeys to a nearby town; there was always music at the inn in their honour, and Jaele forgot her solitude as she danced.

She dreamed of Queen Galha and desert-churning horses and swords singing air, but she was not restless. Elic was soon old enough to be her groom or manservant. She trained him to brush her steed's mane and sides, and to bow to her so that his forehead touched his knees.

"If you continue to order him about so much," her father said to her once, "your servant may become annoyed and seek out other employment."

"He will not," Jaele answered firmly. "I am the Queen."

And so she and Elic played and grew, until he said, on a day of sun and silence, "I want to be the Prince."

She turned to him. They were standing throwing pebbles from the rocks that jutted and tumbled into the sea. "No," she said, surprised but unconcerned. "You can't. I am the only ruler."

Elic's pebble danced once, twice, then sank. He did not look at her. "You're *always* important. I never even have a name."

"I'm ten," she explained, "and you're seven."

"Doesn't matter," he retorted, and then he did turn to her. "We should have a test to see who can be in charge. We should see who's brave enough to open Father's box."

Jaele gaped at him. "The dagger?" she said, and he nodded. Eyes wide and full of sky.

"But we're not to open the box. Father made us promise not to. He said he wouldn't lock it if we promised." She glanced over her shoulder at the hut. Smoke drifting, door open, no sounds of loom or voices.

Elic straightened his shoulders. "*I'm* not afraid. And if you are, you don't deserve to be Queen." He paused. "And he's in the forest," he said. "And Mother's fishing."

They walked across the sand, Jaele a few paces ahead. When she reached the door, she stopped, and a moment later Elic stood beside her. They gazed at the box, which sat on a shelf above the loom: a box of smooth light wood, with two hinges and a lock that looked like gold (but weren't, Reddac had told them).

"He made us promise," Jaele whispered as her brother stepped toward the loom. She was very still as he climbed onto their father's bench and reached up until his fingers grazed the wood. She was still as he returned, clutching the box against his chest. Only when he passed her did she move, crying out his name. Then they ran, stumbled giddy and terrified to the rocks.

"Put it down," she said, attempting in vain to sound queenly.

"I will," he replied, "but remember it was me who got the box. Me."

"Yes—but I'll open it," she said as he bent and placed it carefully on the sun-warmed stone.

He did not speak. They blinked as the golden metal caught the light. A warm wind rose and stirred the water and their hair and the trees beyond the sand.

"I'll open it," Jaele repeated, and waited for Elic to challenge her. He did not. Shrugged instead, and looked at her, steadily and in silence.

She was breathing very quickly. The box glinted. She knelt before it, traced her fingers over its wood and clasp. Then, because her brother was waiting and everything was too quiet, she threw open the lid and grasped the dagger's hilt and lifted it shining toward the sky.

There was a stillness—a boy and a girl, rocks by the sea, a gentle wind—but only for a moment. Red and blue jewels flashed. Jaele leapt to her feet and cried, "I am the Queen!" and Elic turned and ran. They laughed as they slithered over the stones onto the beach, laughed as she chased him into sprays of water and back to sand. "You cannot escape me!" she shouted, and lunged forward so that he tripped and carried her with him to the ground.

"No, no," he giggled, squirming.

She sat up, declared, "I have won!" and raised the dagger again into the sun.

"Give it to me."

The dagger fell, though Jaele did not feel her fingers loosening. Reddac's shadow slid over them as he picked it up. Then he stood, very tall; the light was behind him, and they could not see his face.

"Jaele. Elic." A new voice—not for singing or laughing or even for telling stories in darkness. They did not look at each other, did not look at him. "Never again. Do you understand? *Never again.*"

He turned and strode away from them, following the damp, curving wave-line until he was small, on the bank across the bay. They saw him stop, saw him turn his head toward the open sea. They watched him, and he did not move—not even as the sun tugged shadows long across the sand.

Jaele and Elic stayed on the shore in front of their hut. Elic hollowed out holes with his bare heels; Jaele wrapped her arms around her drawn-up knees and tried not to shake. When their mother's boat appeared at the mouth of the bay, they glanced at each other but still said nothing. Lyalla's boat stroked toward the beach and Reddac began to walk back. Elic and Jaele rose and waited for them both.

"What . . . ?" Lyalla asked after she had waded out of the water, her fishing traps and nets heavy behind her. She looked at Reddac, only paces away. At him and at the dagger in his hand. "Reddac," she said quietly, "what has happened?"

"Let us all go inside," he replied.

Jaele thought he sounded very tired, but not angry. Because he did not seem angry, she ran back to the rocks, picked up the empty box and returned to where they were waiting. She held it up to her father, who took it and smiled at her—tired, sad, his face veined with sun-dried salt.

"Tell your mother what you did," he said when they were in the hut. He and Lyalla sat on the loom bench, Jaele and Elic on the ground.

"We . . ." Jaele began, staring at the carpet beneath her. "*Elic* said we should take it—"

"Because you're always the ruler!" She heard his tears before she turned and saw them. "It was part of our game," he went on, struggling, clenching his hands against the tears. "To see who was brave enough to rule. So I . . . got the box, and Jaele opened it. *I* never touched the knife."

She leapt to her feet. "But it was your idea!" she cried. "I didn't want to do it." Her own eyes filled, stung, as if the wind had blown sand against her face. "I *said* I was sorry."

Elic yelled, "You never did! You never said anything until right now!"

She was silent for a moment. "No," she admitted at last, and looked at her parents. "I meant to, though. I did." She paused, then continued in a rush, "But in stories there are Queensfighters and battles, and we were only playing . . ."

Lyalla shook her head slowly. "Stories, yes. But you two are not Queen or Queensfighter—"

"Yet," interrupted Reddac with a small smile. Jaele felt weak, dizzy with relief.

"Yet," agreed their mother. "For now, you are children who imagine only. You do not need a real knife for that."

"Why do we have it, then?" Jaele demanded, and Reddac turned the dagger over in his palm once, gently.

"Because it belonged to my parents, and it is beautiful . . . And it would serve to gut a fish, if all of your mother's knives were somehow lost at sea."

Elic giggled and sniffed. Lyalla turned to Reddac with raised brows. He raised his in return, and grinned—an exchange so familiar that Jaele felt her own smile aching on her lips.

He was not smiling when he said, "Both of you promised, before, that you would not open this box. Must I lock it now? Or will you promise again, and truly?"

"We promise," Elic and Jaele said together. Elic added, "Truly," and sniffed again.

"Very well," Lyalla said briskly. She took the dagger from Reddac's hand and placed it back in its box of wood and gold.

Later, Reddac sat between his children's pallets and spoke into the darkness. He did not tell of the Warrior Queen but of the girl Galha. She had lain in her bed, ill and afraid, and listened to the song of an iben seer—a song of gentleness and light and comfort, words of future lulling until she slept. When the story was done, Reddac kissed Jaele and Elic on cheeks and foreheads, and Lyalla came in from the doorway and bent to smooth their hair.

"Jaele," Elic whispered when they were alone.

Jaele shifted and groaned. "Go to sleep."

"No—wait," he hissed. "I wanted to say . . . that we're both brave."

She rolled onto her side and looked at him, his pale face against the blankets. "Yes, we are," she said. "And," she added after a moment, "I think you can be a Queensfighter from now on." He did not answer, though she knew he was awake.

Jaele heard Elic's breathing and her own, twining, slowing to sleep. She heard the waves against the shore, and the wind against the waves. And she heard her parents' voices, laughing and murmuring, steady as singing or the beating of her heart.

Jaele was eighteen and alone and far, far beneath the cold slate surface of the water when her world shifted.

Fog had gathered over the harbour at dawn that day; by afternoon the air was frigid and thick, the water invisible. Jaele and Elic were arguing and tossing bits of cooking rock at one another. The loom sounded louder in the dimness. As the wood thundered and their voices rose, Lyalla cried, "Jaele, Elic—quiet!" They turned to her. "Elic," she said in a low, dangerous voice, "there are fish to be cleaned. Jaele, we need some seagreen. Go, both of you, and give me some peace!"

"Excellent," Elic muttered as they walked out onto the beach. "Now I'll stink of fish guts and you'll freeze to death."

Jaele snorted. "I will not. And you already stink."

They laughed and parted and did not look back.

Jaele's skin rose in shocked bumps after she had draped her cloak and outer tunic over a rock. When she dove, even the oily paste she had rubbed over herself did not entirely blunt the chill. She swam close to the surface for a time, circling until the water was almost warm. When she was ready, she drew in a chestful of ice-sharp air and sliced down and down, and the grey sky faded into darkness.

She gathered seagreen strands until they billowed behind her, but she did not return immediately to shore. She cut deep, around the black rocks and into the stretch of water that lay outside her own. By now she was warm and effortless, guarding the breath in her lungs more easily. She swam and swam, unwilling to go back to the sullen sky and the noisy hut. And so she was many strokes away when the boats slid silently through the moss-thick fog and cold water of her bay.

She gasped as she surfaced at last and her mouth opened on air. She rubbed a hand over her eyes to clear away black spots, tiny fish that trembled in and out of her vision. As her heart pounded and her muscles relaxed into aching, she looked through the darkening sky toward her home and saw torches.

She swam with her head above the water until she reached the pile of black rocks nearest her hut. As she drew closer—silent strokes, barely a ripple in the sea—she saw two boats, large and strange and resting on the beach like terrible creatures, water-slick and waiting. There were people—not many—some dressed in ragged skins and a few in thick leather armour. Steel glinted in the fog-blurred light. Jaele's fingers wrapped white and sea-tender around the pitted rock when she saw the knife at her mother's brown throat, the arm that held her brother thin and small against a stranger's body. Her father was free: he was standing very still, facing the tallest of the men in armour.

"Please," she heard him say, clearly and without shaking, "do not harm us. We will give you whatever you ask. Please—let my family go."

The big man turned so that she saw the sharp bones of his face and the shadows of his eyes. He spoke to a woman next to him in a rough, halting language. The woman answered him and he looked back at Jaele's father. Jaele watched the man's hand clenching around a dagger handle. He spoke, and her father shook his head.

"I'm sorry—I don't understand you." He held out his hands, palms up and pale. "I have no weapon . . ."

Jaele sobbed. As she thrust her fist into her mouth, she saw her mother's eyes shift quickly toward the rocks. No one else had noticed. There was no way that Lyalla could see in the stone darkness, yet she looked at her daughter, eyes wide and torchlit and commanding. *Don't give yourself away, daughter. Stay.* Commanding, Jaele told herself later, over and over, as she remembered how she had huddled against the tumble of rocks and done nothing.

More strangers emerged from the hut, carrying sacks, a pile of Reddac's weaving, cook pots, sleeping mats. They shouted to the leader as they threw their armloads into the boats. Others began to walk toward them, putting daggers back in belts. The tall man smiled and stepped forward. His arm moved, so quickly that metal and armour blurred. Reddac's eyes widened as his throat opened dark beneath the dagger. Lyalla screamed and writhed. The leader called out, and the man holding her stared at him in fear or disgust. After a moment he drew his own dagger across her neck and let her slip to the ground.

Jaele was watching the sand darken in rivulets beneath her parents when Elic moved. Perhaps his captor's grip had loosened; perhaps he, like the other man, had thought to defy his leader; perhaps he had merely underestimated the thin boy in his grasp. Elic twisted free in one fluid motion and lunged silently, reaching for the man who was twice his height and blood-eyed. Jaele saw a flash of blue and red; some breathing part of her remembered an unlocked box and a promise. But Elic gripped the dagger now, and thrust it under the leader's armour, hard and sure below his heart. The man cried out, and his own dagger shone up and into the boy's chest, and both fell limb-twisted to the sand.

Later, Jaele remembered sounds: the yells of the attackers, the pounding of feet and the heavy pull of bodies, and afterward her own screams, ringing white against her skull. She did not remember watching her parents and brother being thrown into the hut; she did not see how the leader was also tossed inside, except for an arm which sprawled out the door. She did not see the man who had cut her mother's throat standing still, shaking his head as the others milled around him and shouted. She did not see him fall, struck hard by a club; did not see his body lying crumpled where waves met shore. What she did see, at last, was torchfire in the thatch, red-gold streaking along the walls and up against the sky; the Raiders leaping into their boats, faces wrenched and hands scrabbling; the boats smaller, smaller and shivering below the first stars. And the torches, graceful wingfishes, falling slowly into the sea.

LUHR

CHAPTER TWO

The leader's hand was webbed. Jaele stared. Fingers joined by tiny
fans, flesh like a seabird's.

She was very cold. The fire was gone, burned down to black
rubble and stench. She had looked for them while the flames still
roared; she had looked and cried out their names until her voice
had bruised to silence. They were not on the beach or in the shallow
water—and she remembered, as she cried, that she had heard the
dragging of bodies on sand. She gazed up at the hut and the fire,
saw the long smooth tracks that led to the place where the door had
been. They were there, within. Coursing, dissolving, curling away to
bone. They were there in the heart of the fire, far beyond her sight
and her hands and her voiceless keening.

Then she had seen the outflung arm. Had found that she was on
her knees in water, and that her father's dagger was beside her,
almost buried in tide-wet sand. She had wrenched it free and
turned again to the arm. The leader's—she knew this from the
armour. She did not notice the other body by the shore: the fire was

too bright; she was nearly mad; she saw only that one arm and moved toward it. She had hacked at the arm while the heat battered her, hacked until the hand twisted off in her own. She held its fingers, wiped it clean of blood. She retched, suddenly, water and bile—then shook until her bones and teeth had ground into sand and she lay with her face turned up to the dawn-white sky.

It was blinding noon when she woke. There was terrible pain, a blade drawn along her muscles and skin and behind her eyes. She sat up carefully. Carefully she folded a cloak that had been dropped by one of the Raiders—her father's cloth bright and soft—and put it in the sack she had almost emptied of seagreen. She removed the swimming paste from her pouch and attached the empty pouch to her belt. She did not look at the hut, though she could smell it behind her, acrid and blackened. She brushed fire ash from her face and saw more blowing out over the water. She turned her father's dagger over in her hands, slowly, seeing it without colour or edges. Blood still smudged her skin wet; she washed blade and flesh in the shallows and watched the blood dark coiling as smoke between her fingers. She dried the dagger on her tunic, then wrapped it in the folds of the cloak in her sack. The wind was thrusting the smell toward her. She picked up the Sea Raider's hand and held it, stared at its webs and its short, ragged nails. Then she threw it arcing into the sea. Birds descended instantly and she looked away—away, and into the face of the man who had killed her mother.

He was standing a few steps to her right and slightly behind her—white-faced, a smudge of blood across his forehead; swaying slightly, so that some part of her knew he had only just stood up. His eyes were narrowed and dark, and his lips were curled, snarling without sound. He looked at her, and she at him. The wind was still blowing; though she did not take her eyes from his, she could see leaves and smoke stirring behind him. The wind made no sound. She heard nothing but her own blood.

Only when he took a step backward did she think of the dagger. Her fingers were stiff as old dry wood on the mouth of her sack. She glanced down, the blood a roaring now, as if she were diving too deep. A glance—but when she looked up again, he was gone, running toward the wooded hills, leaving a trail of blood and webbed prints in the sand. She followed, her whole body wood now, unbending, splintering with every sleep-slow step. He disappeared into the trees and she whimpered—far behind, staggering, her sack dragging like stones.

When she finally reached the forest, the path before her was empty. She stood for a moment, panting, leaning on a lightning-shorn trunk. The earth was dark and firm here, swallowing blood and footprints. No trail of his—only this trail, which wound among the close-set trees. She ran on, more quickly this time. At first her feet recognized the path: she had wandered here before, over the fallen leaves and needles. She had never wandered far: there was a heavy, closed silence about the deeper forest, and she had always turned back to the sunlight and the beach and the open sea. But now she ran on, on, following the track further into a dusk of trees. Following him. When she could no longer see the way, she sat at the base of an oak; she wrapped her arms around her knees and was very still. The hollow rasping of her breath calmed, but she did not close her eyes. A howl rose high among trunks and branches; she did not move, did not blink. She sat until a muddy grey dawn lit the path before her—then she rose and ran again, her fingers wrapped tight around her father's dagger.

Days and nights swam together, and Jaele could not count them. She walked or ran. Occasionally she slept, curled against bark, drifts of leaves, earth damp from a river she never saw. It was a shallow sleep that did not relieve the dry burning of her eyes; shallow because she listened for him always—his steps, his breathing, his voice calling out words she would not understand. Sometimes she thought she heard him, thought she saw a shadow slipping away ahead of her. She would leap forward, scrabbling and panting, and run until long after she knew she had been wrong. She smelled her mother's blood, and his, and ran, ran.

She noticed rain once or twice, but the limbs above her were woven close as threads: the rain was a distant murmur, and only a few drops fell cool on her skin and hair. Sometimes she found water pooled in stumps or among roots; she drank, head down like an animal, and tasted ancient green.

Days and nights; latticed sun and shadow. She stumbled on, among trees that were no longer forest: the bark was raddled, and the leaves bent huge and curving to brush moss-sprung ground. She smelled earth and oozing decay that was jungle-rank—her own warm salt smell above and beneath. She ate fruit that had fallen and split, spouting seeds; she tore at fungus that bloomed like sickly yellow flowers from stumps, not thinking of poison or illness or living. Thinking only of him: blood-streaked skin, narrowed eyes, forearm corded muscle across her mother's throat.

She could not run here; she staggered, and now and then she crawled, when the path was slick. Shapes—always him, never him—twined around the edges of her sight. There was no night, no day. The hissing and cackling of beasts she could not see filled her ears, and she moaned in fear or relief. Suddenly she *did* see: there was something looming, panting, on the track ahead of her. Something too enormous, too misshapen to be him. She fell to her knees and swayed. Then it surged toward her and she slipped with a cry into darkness.

"Close your eyes." A whisper. Jaele feels her little brother breathing sleep against her cheek.

"Luhr is the most beautiful city in our world. Queen Galha made it so, when peace was upon the land. She built it tall with towers and twisting spires that glittered in sunlight like pearl. The walls were stone without mortar, and they stretched smooth. After the Sea

Raiders shattered Queen Galha's peace, she built a silver portcullis
where before there had been no need of a gate, and it shone and
burned the eyes of those who gazed upon it.

"But Queen Galha's greatest pride was Luhr's market, for there, in
a space below the palace itself, gathered folk from all parts of the land.
The fishfolk—who have always been good and wise, unlike their
Raider kin—whistled out of their small mouths as they sold the green
fronds and shining orbs of their lakes and seas. The half-giants of the
eastern islands stamped their feet and clacked their great teeth
together as they showed their pots of dark clay and eels' scales. The
iben seers—who had horns on their heads and talons instead of
fingers—sang of the future in voices so beautiful that people who
heard them wept in fear and joy. These iben can no longer be found at
Luhr's marketplace; they stopped making the long journey from their
mountains and have not been seen by Queensfolk since. But the others
are there still. There are booths and carts and tents and wooden stages,
as there have been since Galha's time.

"You may travel to Luhr when you are older; you may follow the
long path from our beach through forest and jungle. You too may hear,
weaving through the other noises, the bone piping of the desert
nomads, that high, sweet sound of red wind and sand."

She is slipping into the sand and it is just like water, and she hears
the piping, far away—or perhaps it is her father's voice.

When Jaele woke on the edge of the jungle, she saw a wide and
empty road that led into the desert; she saw bushes and clumps of
rocks and grass; she saw the spires and walls of Luhr, soaring into
the sun. It could not be real, of course. She remembered fainting,
remembered half waking to find damp fur beneath her cheek.
There had been a rolling motion like waves, and breathing that was
not her own. *I was carried,* she thought dimly, and remembered
dreaming her father's voice as she lay slumped and almost sleeping.
And now, somehow, she was here, sitting propped against a tree.

When she peered around it, she saw only other trees, still and silent. She turned back; the spires remained. Everything was painfully vivid: the plants' leaves, curling wrinkled veins and brittle; the rocks, shining crystalline, whorled with black and pink; the road, stretching flat and red beneath the cloudless sky. She sat and looked and was empty.

When at last she stood, a dull pain bloomed in her head and up her back, and she wondered again what had brought her through the jungle. She moved onto the road, very slowly (days and nights of running, stumbling, needles and thorns); she walked and looked only ahead, at the water-glint of Luhr. She did not think of an ash hut, blood-clotted sand, ache of nails on stone; she thought only of the Sea Raider, and this city. One path through forest and jungle; one city only in this great desert. *He will be hungry,* she thought; *he has come here as well.* Certainty rose in her like tears. As she walked toward Luhr, Jaele's hand closed around her sack, and her fingers traced the cloth-fattened edges of her father's dagger.

She walked alone for a time, but as the city grew large, other paths met the main road, and figures trembled out of the heat to join her. *He is already in the city,* she thought again—so sure—as she looked at them. There were green-robed Devotees with their bats concealed beneath black-draped cages; children in wagons hung with tapestries and baskets full of tiny mice; Queensfighters with curved bows and tall desert horses. These last Jaele saw with a sudden sting of memory: she had played by the sea, Queen Galha on a donkey, legions of Queensfighters massing behind her on the sand. Her father's voice and her mother's shadow against the wall. Elic's breath. Jaele saw the riders and forced it all away, the images and stories, and the terrible softness beneath her skin.

There were songs and laughter on the road, and the sound of languages that were not hers. She listened carefully and felt safer. She glanced down after a time and saw a desert child walking beside her, swathed in white except for her eyes. Jaele gazed into the gold-flecked black of these eyes and smiled brittle glass. The girl danced in small light steps, and whirled so that her robes rose and fluttered. When Jaele smiled again (from a place far away and almost warm), the girl reached up and took her hand. The child's hand was small and dry; Jaele clung to it. When they reached the steep and seamless walls of Luhr, they passed together beneath the silver portcullis.

Trees towered silver-green, growing from impossibly dark earth that lay like an arrow in the middle of the gleaming main street. Other streets branched off into the city. Jaele saw houses of shining stone, fountains where children laughed and drank, shadowed archways where old people sat. Then she looked ahead and saw the palace: the heart, the home of the arrow, the tallest and slenderest of the spires and arches. She and her companion stopped where the road widened to form the great sweep of marketplace that stretched around the palace. There was a roar of noise and colour. People, animals, creatures she had never seen before—and somewhere, him. The little girl tugged at her hand and she walked forward.

After a few paces they came to a red-tasselled tent, and the girl left her there with a swift hug and a flashing of black-gold eyes. Jaele watched her swung up off the ground by a tall veiled woman, and for the first time heard the child's voice, high and laughing. Jaele turned away.

A young man crouched beside her, bent over the shards of a broken pot. She knelt in front of him. "May I help?" she asked, her voice rough and jagged. Words and kneeling because she did not know, now that she was here, how to begin.

He looked up. She knew him at once, even though she had not thought of him for so long. His eyes were as light as they had been, but his hair was darker, more like golden sand, now, than sunlight.

"Dorin," she said. He frowned and sat back on his heels. "Dorin," she said again, then continued in a rush, "You don't remember me, of course; we met a long time ago. On my beach. You had just left your home."

"Ah," he said, beginning to smile, "the girl from the beach. There was a big stone there—the Giant's something . . ."

"Club," she said.

"Club. And you are . . . Jaele. Yes?" He was smiling broadly now. She saw that his smile still lit his face, and that he was still sad.

"Yes," she said.

"You must forgive me for not recognizing you right away. It *has* been a long time—and you are a bit more grimy and tangled than you were then."

She did not realize she was trembling until her head was on his shoulder and his arms slipped around her. They crouched among the glinting clay pieces, and he rocked her and she shook but did not cry.

"Dorin," she said at last, lifting her head, "the Sea Raiders came to my beach, just as they did to your town. They killed my family. One ran. I chased him, but I couldn't catch him, he was too fast . . . I am sure he is here. You know what they look like. Please, please, say you have seen him . . ."

He made a low sound and took both of her hands in his own. She clung, nails pressing, skin white. "No," he said quietly, "I have not. I am sorry. I am so sorry, Jaele."

They knelt for a moment more, silent in the shouting and singing of Luhr's market. Then he said, "I will take you to a safe place," and he helped her rise, slowly, gently.

He led her through stalls and tents. She held his hand and watched her dirt-crusted feet moving over the ground. He stopped in front of a large wagon stacked high with pots and dangling jugs. There was a little room at the back of the wagon—red-gold cloth attached to wooden posts—and Dorin and Jaele ducked inside. A woman was sitting there, with a potter's wheel before her. She did not look up when they entered; Jaele saw only her stooped back.

"She's deaf, and she can't speak," Dorin said, but there was something in his voice—a smile, a wink.

He touched the woman's shoulder and she raised her head. Her face was wrinkled, her eyes dark and piercing, and when they turned to her, Jaele felt a bit afraid.

"This is Jaele," he said as the woman watched his lips. She nodded and smiled. "Jaele," he went on, one hand still on the potter's shoulder, "this is Serani."

They sat together on the ground, smooth and light as the road outside, surrounded by wide-lipped bowls and sweeping-necked jugs and pots of bright glaze. A small, round-doored oven stood in one corner of the room; two narrow reed pallets lay at either end. Sunlight streamed thick red through the cloth roof and walls; Jaele watched the colour shift and fade with the drifting of unseen clouds. She felt suddenly dizzy and Dorin, looking at her, said, "I'll get you some food, and then you must sleep. Do not think of him—not now."

They ate slivered cheese and fleshy pink fruit and bread full of tiny holes, and she did not remember the green water, the fungus that had cracked in her hands.

After she had eaten, Jaele peered at Dorin, who looked dim and soft in the light. The noise from outside faded. She blinked and moved her head, trying to shake off sleep. "Dorin," she said as she at last curled up on the ground, "you went away. I went back to look for you, but you were gone."

He turned away from her. "I couldn't stay," he said. Sad—a boy's eyes, his smile, so sad. "Now rest, Jaele. No more talking."

"Mmm," she mumbled, and closed her eyes. He sat beside her, humming softly—voice rising, falling, sending her to darkness and forgetting.

Jaele woke to red light and the piercing, wild sunsong of the desert nomads. She lay still, at first not recognizing the shapes and colours, the sound of voices outside or the soft whirring near her head. After a few moments she remembered—a rushing like water—and knew that the whirring was Serani's wheel. She sat up, slow with bruises, and watched the old woman. She was sitting on a low stool at the wheel, head bent over a lump of clay that was spinning into curves before her. Serani looked up and smiled at her with her dark eyes, and Jaele felt herself smiling back—safe, in silence, from the raggedness of her new voice. As she stood, Dorin's head appeared through the folds of the doorway.

"So," he said with that grin that Jaele already loved, "the sleeper returns to us."

She followed him through the hanging cloth and into the shade of the wagon. Pots and jars swung and stood cluttered; some of them, sun-lanced, shone brilliant red, blue, yellow. Jaele stepped out beyond the awning and looked up at the sky, huge and empty except for spires and mist-thin traces of cloud.

"I must look for him," she said.

"First you'll wash," Dorin said from behind her. "And you can wear one of Serani's tunics while she cleans yours. Then we'll take a walk—I'll close up for a while." He motioned to the marketplace around them. "It's a hundred worlds, a thousand. I'll show you— and you can look for him."

And so—after sun-warmed water on her skin, and cloth that smelled like clay—they walked together through the heat and noise of morning in Luhr. They watched the half-giants clacking and stringing eels' scales; sun-black nomads polishing the bone and sand of their pipes; acrobats dangling from their own long legs. Jaele slowed as they passed the tasselled tent of the desert tribe, but she did not see the little girl with the black eyes. They walked over carpets and rushes and cobblestones, around urns and stages and prayer mats. They did not see anything more than once, although she felt as if they were going in circles. A four-armed starfish lay on its back in a tray of water, juggling snail shells, and she looked at it with a stinging dryness in her chest. "It's beautiful," she said to Dorin, then walked away quickly, quickly, as he turned to her.

She craned to see faces, hair, eyes, hands. Tall men glimpsed from behind, or walking toward and past her made her blood roar as it had on her beach, when she had looked at him and the wind had moved silently in the trees. But these men were strangers. Most, she saw when she drew closer to them, did not resemble him at all. *Be calm,* she told herself as Dorin led her among the changing shadows of the spires. *He is here; there will be time to find him.*

They ate spongy sweetmoss and watched a play. Jaele could not understand the words, and Dorin said, "The actors are from the north. They live mostly underground; see how small their eyes are?"

Jaele looked at him, remembering the boy. "Did you ever find the golden sea snakes?" Her words slipped out, away; she heard them, echoing and strange, even as he said, "Or trees as tall as the sky?" and smiled slightly. "Not yet. We'll see."

They returned to Serani's wagon as the sun climbed higher. Around the marketplace, tent flaps slapped shut and sleeping rugs were unrolled. Jaele could not sleep. As Dorin and Serani rested, she sat among the pots and jugs and breathed in lungfuls of hot air. She watched coloured cloth moving in the dry wind that rose and fell, carrying the scent of the desert. She looked up from the pots and cloth, to the palace towers and the balconies that belled like blazing fishing nets against the sky.

The market stirred again as shadows lengthened. Jaele and Dorin sold Serani's wares, paid for with shells, coins, arrows, flowers, while the potter stood beside them. Darkness, when it came, was deep blue. Jaele remembered looking up from beneath water that was golden-green in the sun and blue-dark at night. She thought she should be wet; she could almost feel the scarred rock beneath her fingers.

"It's like the sea, isn't it?" Dorin asked quietly from beside her.

Jaele blinked, looked at him. "Yes. I was thinking that." For a time they did not speak. Then she said, "Dorin . . . they did the same thing to you, to your village. You must still be angry, even though it was so long ago."

He turned his face away and wrapped his arms around himself. The wind was blowing night cold. "They did not do the same thing to me," he said. "I didn't tell you that."

"But," she said, "you told me that the Sea Raiders had attacked your town—you left—I thought that your family had been killed."

He bit the inside of his cheek. "The Sea Raiders came, yes. Ten of them, in two boats. They stole some livestock and burned some houses and struck down a woman who tried to stop them. I do not know if she died. I left the village the next day, while the elders were giving speeches about the necessity of improved preparation and defences." He paused and drew a deep breath. "I had no family. I had been planning to leave before the Raiders came. So, no—they did not do the same thing to me."

"Oh," Jaele said as emptiness spread through her like cold. *I am alone,* she thought. She gazed at him and wanted to grip his hand again, until hers was white.

They stood a while longer in the marketplace, which was silent except for the wind, and very dark. The only light was from the palace, fire that shivered in the highest towers. "Let's go inside," Dorin said at last, quietly, and she nodded.

She lay awake for a long time as he sang softly into the cold and the stillness.

The next day, when the sun was high and Dorin and Serani lay sleeping, Jaele left the wagon with her dagger in her belt. She walked among the empty stages and booths, looking at the others who were sleeping and at the few who, like her, were not. She was calmer in this bright silence. She walked and looked and waited, the dagger firm against her hip.

A bend, another bend, and she could no longer see Serani's wagon behind her. She stepped around a cushioned bench and over a wall of round green stones, and then she heard water. A splash, a creak of rope, a murmur of voices. She walked more swiftly, until she came to the fishfolk who were also awake in the blaze of afternoon.

They were not like the Sea Raiders; she saw this immediately. Their bodies were green and blue scaled, their eyes round and white and nearly unblinking. But though they were not like the tall, sharp-angled men who had killed, she stood with her heart stilled, then frantic. The fishfolk were Raider kin; they were also—like the Queensfighters, like Luhr—words spoken by her father. She watched them at their well, drawing water, which they poured dark over their scales and mats. She watched them weaving green sea fronds together into shapes that were fluid or tangled. Jaele stood unmoving, until at last one of the fishfolk approached her.

"You have been here for a long time," it said, speaking her language with a hissing and bubbling of breath, and Jaele smiled uncertainly.

"Yes," she said.

"Would you like to purchase something?" it asked. She shook her head and the fishperson made a sound. "I did not think so. What is it you want?"

"I . . . I lived near the sea," she began, and her voice went soft and steadied. Not the words she had expected, but she spoke on. "It is wonderful to see you here, with your water." Again she felt the strangeness of speaking. Suddenly, standing with the fishperson who also loved the sea, she thought that words could not be the same without loom or oars or the deeds of Galha and her groom. She forced the thought away, and since the fishperson had not replied, she continued, "It must be so difficult for you to be in this place."

The fishperson's little mouth twitched, and Jaele hoped it was smiling. "Indeed," it said, and glided back toward the well.

A moment later it returned, carrying a plait of seagreen. Jaele took it in her hands and bent her head. She could almost feel it, unbound and billowing against her skin in cold grey water.

"The greens you eat," it said, "as you know."

She nodded, knowing also that she would not—could not—eat them. "I must ask you something," she said quickly, ready now. "I need you to tell me about the Sea Raiders. Please."

It gazed at her, its white eyes steady on her face. *Please,* she said again, silently, and then it spoke.

"We swam together, long ago, when the seas were one and there was no land. Then the land rose above the water, and our strokes parted. They lived more and more above, and we remained beneath, though we did know each other still. But they became strangers, as time passed. Their desires for land space were not clear to us." The fishperson blinked. "The rest you have heard, I think. All Queensfolk have."

She nodded and looked away briefly. *I have heard. I have seen.*

Then it said, "Strange, that you ask this now," and Jaele turned back to it.

"Why?" she asked, though she knew what it would say. She shivered, and her hand gripped the hilt of her dagger.

"It has been many generations since we fishfolk have heard talk of those you call Sea Raiders—longer still since we have met them. And yet here you are, and only days past a Raider came here to us. A male," it went on as Jaele saw the blood, the face, the body bent and disappearing into trees. Days past. "Wearing a torn tunic. He stood and stared at us as you did today. When I went toward him, he fled, even though my hands were empty before me." It looked down at its hands, turned them over so that the webs and scales glinted in the sunlight.

"It is not chance," Jaele said softly. "A group of them destroyed my home. He killed my mother, and I followed him inland. I lost him on the jungle road—but when I came here, I knew . . ." She closed her eyes against the shine of spires and scales. "Why is he here? Why did he not return with the others?" she asked, and opened her eyes when it said, "Of course I cannot answer with certainty. Perhaps he did not want to return; perhaps the others did not want him to." It paused; she heard its breath gurgling, deep in its throat. "There are tales of others of his kind who tried to live for a time in this land, eating foods rich in juices in order to survive. These tales say that they soon turned east, even though they did not want to. In their walking and their swimming they followed the old path of their ancestors, who had been pursued by Galha. They were pulled by their history and their sea. Those who resisted died. He will feel the same pull, and he also will die, if he does not heed it. Of this I *am* certain."

There was another silence. Jaele was still clutching the dagger, her fingers wrapped numb and nail-ground. "So he will go east," she said at last, "when he leaves here."

The fishperson touched her lightly, on the hand that held the dagger. "He was seen yesterday," it said, "on the road. Riding alone, away from the city."

Yesterday, she thought. *While I was telling myself that there would be time to find him.* She said, "Then I too will go east."

"She drove them through desert and mountains, plains and hills . . . following the rising sun." Her father's words; Galha's army. Now there was only one Sea Raider, and Jaele, and an ancient rage. "I will go east, and I will find him," she said, and a new certainty bloomed hot within her.

The fishperson gazed at her without blinking. "He may die in this land, without water, before he reaches the sea. He may try to live with food only, as those others did—but soon he will be very sick. Perhaps you do not need to find him."

She shook her head and thought that she might laugh, or weep. "You do not understand," she said. "I do need to. It is more than need."

The fishperson stood before her a moment more. "Wait," it said. Again it glided away from her and back, this time bearing a polished red stone, the kind she had collected at the edge of the tide. It pressed the stone into her hand. "This may be used to enter our waters," it said, "if your strokes lead you to us."

"Thank you," she said, curling her fingers around the stone's coolness as the fishperson slipped away, water-streaked, through the sunlight.

"He was here. Dorin—he was here."

Dorin rubbed his eyes with his palms. "What?" he said, blinking. Serani had already returned to the booth; Dorin had been slower to wake, despite Jaele's grip on his shoulder. "He," he repeated, "here . . ." and then he understood, and gaped at her.

"Until yesterday—one of the fishfolk told me, he saw him—and someone else saw him leave the city, riding. He will go east. Dorin," she said in a different voice, as she looked at him, "you didn't believe me. You didn't think he was here."

He pulled his fingers through his hair, did not raise his gaze to hers as he said, "You were so upset. I thought . . ."

They sat without speaking. The marketplace outside was stirring again, with music and laughter and footsteps. Jaele closed her eyes and was still.

"What will you do?"

She opened her eyes. He was looking at her now. "I'm going to find him. I will follow him east." She spoke in a voice that was hard and glittering as the daylit spires. "I will find him as Queen Galha found those others, even if I have to follow him to the Ladhra River and Fane. Even if I have to follow him across the Eastern Sea."

"And if you do not find him?" Dorin asked quietly. A gust of wind blew the red cloth inward, and Jaele saw his fair hair move across his cheek and back again, to lie against his neck.

"I will," she said. "I will walk in Galha's footsteps and I will find him." A breathless pain pressed against her flesh from within; she was stretching, glowing, with the joy of it.

Dorin arched his brows and said, "An epic plan, Jaele. But Galha had an army. Fighters, horses, ships. You will be alone."

"Not alone," she said quickly. "I could go to Queen Aldhra and tell her that the Sea Raiders are back; she might send some Queensfighters with me. Her family was wronged as well—"

"Yes," he interrupted, "a long, long time ago. Perhaps it is only a story. Whether story or truth, Queen Galha had her revenge. Queen Aldhra will not see the need to send *her* fighters across the sea. Especially now, when they are required to battle the northern tribes, who are many—and very, very real."

"But the Sea Raiders are also real," Jaele said, voice leaping high, "and they have killed her subjects. There will be fear along the coast now."

"Will there?" he asked, and she flinched beneath his eyes. "Did you hear of fear along the coast after they attacked my town, so many years ago? Did you run and tell anyone in the town near your home? There will be rumours. Stories told at night, as always. And the Queen will certainly not waste her troops and time pursuing rumours—not when she has so much else to attend to."

"If I went to her, though, and told her," Jaele said, but without the eagerness of her first proposal. "If not Queensfighters," she went on slowly, "then others. Companions I will meet as I travel—people who will understand my need." She gazed at him until he glanced away. "Dorin—come with me." She remembered his words the night before; remembered also her own grasping emptiness. *Not alone,* she thought.

"I have already told you," he said, "that I do not have your anger. I cannot pursue this man—these people—without it." As she opened her mouth to reply, he added, "Serani and I were intending to leave soon, in any case—and we will be going east. You could travel with us for as long as it suits you. But please—do not expect me to share your fight. Things are different for us, Jaele."

"You say that now," she said after a moment, "but you may not, later. I will travel with you and Serani—and perhaps someday you will travel with me."

The red-gold hangings parted then, and Serani looked down on them. She smiled and gestured at the wagon outside, and Dorin nodded. "Yes," he said, "it is time to leave."

Before noon that day the tent was dismantled and the pots were packed away, and Jaele rode with Dorin and Serani through the marketplace and out beneath the gleaming portcullis of Luhr. They first stopped at the communal stables for Serani's horse—a bedraggled, muddy-hued creature that Jaele regarded with suspicion.

"What did you expect?" Dorin asked with a grin. "One of Queen Aldhra's war stallions?" To the horse he said, "I don't think she likes you much." The horse blew his breath out in a sound like a sigh. "No matter, Whingey—she'll change her mind." Jaele snorted and climbed into the wagon.

The sun rose and set; the moon narrowed and broadened again to fullness as the travellers skirted the deepest, cruellest part of the desert. Dorin told Jaele that they were heading for the mountains that blotted the horizon like green-patched fingerprints. *The mountains Galha crossed,* she thought. "*Pursuing an army; following the rising sun.*" She watched for another horse, a tall rider who would be urging it forward, straining east. But the land lay empty except for sand and stunted trees, and later small brown bushes.

Jaele and Dorin began to race each other every morning in the cool before dawn, while Serani still slept. Jaele loved the sunless stillness, and the sound of her sandals and Dorin's, muffled in sand or sliding noisily down slopes prickly with stones. They would return to the wagon as the sky lightened; Serani would smile at their flushed faces and give them water from a bag to cool themselves. Dorin laughed often as they raced, even though Jaele

was always half a stride ahead of him. The sadness in his eyes
seemed to flicker and pale.

At times she found her own pain slipping loose in happiness and
cold mornings. But an image would come to her—her mother's
eyes, the man's eyes, blood dark on sand and skin—and she would
shrink from the pain, then cling to it, knotting it hard and sore and
tearless. At night she slept with her sack beside her on the ground.
She did not unwrap her father's dagger, but she knew its shape and
the bumps that were jewels, and she remembered its darkened
weight in her palm.

The mountains grew larger and clearer on the horizon, and the
grizzled brush gave way to trees which stood defiantly in dry and
rocky soil. "Willows," Dorin said one day. "We'll follow them, since
they grow over underground springs. They'll lead us to water, and
the mountains."

Jaele began to wake at night; the sound of wind in the trees was
not the desert silence to which she had become accustomed. She
would sit up and look at the black shadows of trunks and hanging
leaves, and at the blacker shapes of the mountains. Often she
noticed that Dorin was not there. At first she was concerned, but
she woke every dawn to his hand on her shoulder and his smile.
They would run, and she would forget the worry.

The food they had brought with them from Luhr began to
disappear, in great part because of Whingey, who, though scrawny,
ate anything given to him and frequently munched quietly on the
others' portions while unobserved. Serani showed Jaele which
plants had leaves that could be boiled into soup. She also, with a
serious look and a hand on the girl's arm, warned her which were
poisonous. It was Serani who gave Jaele her first taste of herb water,
a drink of hot water and steeped sweetleaves taken from plants that
grew in shade, close to the ground.

One night Jaele woke to find Dorin sitting beside her with his
arms wrapped around his drawn-up knees. She mumbled sleepily

and struggled to sit up.

"We're almost there," he said.

"Oh?" she said, rubbing a hand across her eyes. She heard the rustle of the wind, the low murmur of a night bird, the faint crackling of the barely red cook fire.

At last he said, "Tomorrow we'll reach the mountains, and the silga. The mountain folk."

"Good," Jaele replied. "Then we'll be able to get more food. That horse of yours might have driven us to starvation." She did not speak of her sudden excitement—the quick thrill of her plan shaping, like Serani's clay. The silga, who might have seen him, who might understand.

Dorin was silent for a moment more, then said, "I have something for you." He opened the pouch at his belt and drew out a small object. Grinning, he held both his hands behind his back. Jaele laughed and grasped both his arms, shaking him. He pressed the thing into her right hand, saying in a rush, "I saw you looking at the starfish and the shells, and I know they remind you of your home."

Jaele opened her fingers. She was holding a small shell shaped like the top of one of the mushrooms Serani had shown her. She held it up to her eyes and saw that it was light, perhaps blue, marked with a darker thin spiral line. There was a tiny hole in it. "I thought you could put a thong through the hole, to wear it around your neck," Dorin said.

Jaele did not speak at first. She slipped it carefully into her own pouch. Then she leaned over and put her arms around him. "Thank you," she said. He stiffened, and she drew away. "I'm sorry," she said. "I'm just . . . happy."

He nodded but did not look at her. She saw his eyes as he rose to return to his pallet; they were dark. He did not wake her before dawn to run. That day, sitting in the wagon while he walked silently beside it, she felt a heaviness in her stomach and limbs that she later knew was fear.

SILGA

CHAPTER THREE

Serani, Dorin and Jaele reached the foothills at dusk. Jaele gaped up at the trees: they were huge, towering darkly green and gold. "These are the ones!" she said to Dorin excitedly. "As tall as the sky! Aren't they?"

"No," he said with a small smile. "No."

There was a path between the trees, just wide enough for Whingey and the wagon. The ground was soft with fallen leaves and moss, sharp with needles. Once beneath the trees it was very dark, and Jaele saw only patches of sky, grey and blue spaces shifting among the boughs. The path climbed slowly; when they came to a clearing, she wondered at how far they had walked. The scrub stretched away below them, and the white-capped peaks were not far above. As they turned to continue on, they heard the horns.

Jaele saw later how these were made—from ore hacked and smelted and moulded in the deep places within the mountains—but now, standing in the clearing above the trees, all she knew was that this sound, so high and lonely and wild, frightened her.

"We are expected," Dorin said dryly as the notes faded. "As usual." Jaele noticed that Serani had put her hands against a tree trunk. Dorin said, "You can feel the sounds: they make the trees tremble."

They went a bit farther along the path, walking so that Whingey would be able to pull the wagon up the slope. Jaele tried to imagine Sea Raider and Queensfighter armies surging up this path, and could not—though one man, yes: again she could almost see him, his shape in the trees before her. Her breath began to whistle, and her head felt full of air. Just as she was certain she would have to stop, Dorin pointed ahead. There were lights, flickering high up among boughs and leaves. Horns sounded again, much closer. She noticed that smaller paths branched off the main one, and that huge holes gaped beneath spreading roots. "What . . . ?" she asked, and Dorin replied, "You'll see."

Serani, Dorin and Jaele halted before the widest, most pitted and gnarled trunk. Serani turned to Jaele, putting a hand on her arm. "Don't be alarmed," Dorin muttered. "We don't enjoy dealing with the tree silga, but we need—"

Three silga stood before them; Jaele started, for they had come so silently and gracefully. They were very tall. Their skin was so white that she could see their veins, criss-crossing and dark. Their hair was long and, depending on how the light struck it, brown-green. Their eyes were large and round and yellow.

"Serani," one said, and his voice was low and rough. The old woman nodded at him but did not smile. "And the youngling," he went on, looking at Dorin.

"And this is Jaele," Dorin said quietly. "She is travelling with us."

The silga man looked down at her. She felt tiny, a twig on the ground, a sprig of moss. He said nothing to her.

"We will purchase the goods tomorrow," he continued, looking again at Serani. "Your customary lodgings have been readied."

Dorin led Whingey away, and Serani walked behind them. Jaele followed slowly, trying not to look back at the silga. Instead she looked at the holes beneath the trees. She began to see indistinct shapes moving within them, and was certain that there were eyes gleaming from the darkness. She blinked, and hurried to catch up with the wagon.

They came to another small clearing. Here the trees seemed younger, and there were no holes. Torches had been lit along two low platforms and beside the steps that had been let down below them. "I didn't see steps or platforms anywhere else," Jaele said, glancing up into the trees.

Dorin smiled grimly. "They don't need them."

"How do they live up there?" she asked.

He shrugged as he began to lift packs out of the wagon. "Perhaps in huge nests of leaves? Perhaps hanging upside down? No one knows."

Later, lying next to him on the lowest platform, she said hesitantly, "I thought I saw creatures under the trees. In the holes."

"Mmm," he mumbled, rolling over and folding his cloak into a pillow. "There are the tree silga and there are also the earth silga; you'll probably see soon enough. I'm tired."

Jaele lay awake a bit longer, looking up through the dark masses of boughs and leaves and creepers above her head. She thought she heard the horns again, very far off, and was more sad this time than frightened. She fell asleep. She was lying on a boat, surrounded by a gently shifting sea.

Jaele woke to the sounding of horns nearby. She sat up and found herself covered in spots of sunlight which danced as the leaves above her fluttered. Dorin was leaning against the trunk below her, panting and mopping his forehead.

"You ran without me," she said.

He shrugged. "You were sleeping so soundly; didn't want to wake you."

"Ah," she said. The hard, sharp weight in her stomach had returned. The horns sounded strident in the green sunlight.

Serani was sitting on a boulder by the wagon. She looked resigned, as if she were preparing to taste something she knew would be unpleasant. Jaele stood above her. She looked questioningly at the old potter, who grimaced and gestured toward the entrance to the clearing.

The same three silga were approaching, led by the tall male. In the daylight their hair was green and shining, and their skin looked even more transparently white. Their robes seemed made of leaves. "I trust you slept well," he said, gazing down upon them. No one answered him; he did not seem to notice. "We have come to purchase your goods." He turned to the two behind him and spoke to them in his own language. Jaele gasped at the beauty of its sounds, fluid as wind or water. Not words, but images of sunlight and shadow and deep green smells.

Dorin handed Serani a number of pots and jars from the wagon. All were squat and broad-necked and unpainted. The head silga turned them over in his hands, then passed them to the others. They produced—Jaele did not see from where—pine cones and acorns and a jingling handful of silver.

"Many thanks," the head silga said, inclining his body slightly toward Serani. "You may stay two more nights." And then they were gone, dissolving among the trees.

Dorin saw Jaele's frown. "Rude, aren't they?" he said. She nodded, thinking too how very beautiful they were.

Serani set up her wheel beneath a tree and went off to fetch water to add to the raw clay they had transported in large covered vats. She took water sacks as well as her sifting pails and spades. Dorin and Jaele ate bread and cheese, sitting cross-legged on the platform upon which they had slept. They were silent during the meal, but when they finished, Dorin sprang to his feet.

"Come," he said, holding out a hand to pull her up. "I have a place to show you."

She followed him along a narrow, twisting path, up through the trees. After a time he called back, "We're leaving the path— take care."

The trees grew very close together now, and branches and vines slapped at her face. The ground had become springier with moss, softer with dark, damp earth. Dorin led her up and up; at times they scrambled on all fours. Except for their muffled steps and the rustling of branches, there was a deep, deep silence; wind and sunlight were still among these trees.

At last she heard him stop, and she came up behind him a few paces later. "Ready?" he asked. She looked sidelong at him; his face was lost in the tree shadows. She felt him take her hand as they stepped forward between the trunks.

Sunlight struck her eyes; she threw up a hand to shade her face. When the blindness had passed, she said, "Oh!", low and incredulous.

They were standing at the edge of what was almost a clearing. The trees were spaced farther apart; all were massive, and no branches swept downward. Among them were strung shining threads and cords. They were woven into webs of intricate or simple design. Some stretched away out of sight, some hung tiny and trembling between leaves, others rose above them like glittering domes. "Spiders?" Jaele whispered after a time, remembering the small webs she had seen in spaces between the boards of her hut.

"No," Dorin answered quietly, pointing up. "Birds." And there they were: spots of colour—blue, red, green as the water of Jaele's harbour—their curved beaks flashing silver.

"How?" she asked.

"From their feathers," he said. "It takes them a very long time."

He gripped her hand very tightly. As soon as she felt the pressure, it was gone. "This isn't all," he said, and walked out into the clearing with Jaele behind him.

They went carefully among the webs. She knocked one with her elbow and halted in fear, but the birds paid her no heed. "I think they know friends from foes," Dorin said, "and that's probably why the tree silga don't live here."

They stopped at the base of a particularly huge tree. Its trunk was covered with large round growths like wooden knots. Dorin said, "Stay close to me, but not too close," and put his foot on one of the growths. Jaele watched him begin to climb.

"Dorin . . ." she said uncertainly.

"Come on!" he called, already a good way up the trunk bottom. "Nothing to be afraid of."

She grasped a knot and followed him, willing herself not to tremble with the fear that was spreading through her limbs. After a time the climbing took on a rhythm, and she stopped thinking. Dorin began to sing. Jaele could never remember the tune afterward, only phrases like "a chameleon sat on a brocade chair" and "my favourite hat is brimless." She giggled, clutching the trunk and keeping her gaze on the striped wood in front of her. Just as she was considering wrapping her limbs around the trunk and becoming part of the tree, she felt Dorin's hands on her wrists. He pulled her up gently to stand on a wide, flat branch. Jaele's arms and legs quivered violently. He held her, and she listened to his heart thudding beneath her right ear. "Just a little farther," he said with a smile. She felt the smile—his mouth moving against her hair.

When her legs could support her, they walked along the branch. It was like a road, broad and firm beneath their feet, sloping steeply upward. At the top of the bend it levelled out again. The leaves here were smaller, and light green instead of the dark silver-green they had been lower down. "You can look now," Dorin said. "Just climb up here."

Jaele stepped up in front of him. For an instant, sky and forest reeled, and he grasped her shoulders. They were at the very top of the tree, looking out over the mountainside, which fell down and away from them in waves of green and gold and silver. The webs close to the treetops glittered, and the sky was open and vast above them. Beyond the trees was the plain, and beyond that a shimmering blue which Jaele knew was the desert. She almost expected to see the spires of Luhr, shining like day stars in the distance.

"Breathe in," Dorin said, and she did. The air was cold and thin, and her head felt weightless. She exhaled slowly. He was smiling at her. The sunlight made his hair white-gold.

"Let's sit," he said. "We'll still be able to see."

They were silent for a long time. Jaele watched the wind stirring the leaves that rose and fell like water below the sky. "Tell me about the silga," she said at last, and Dorin sighed.

"You've met the tree silga: tall, beautiful, arrogant. But there are others who live in the earth. I haven't seen them yet, but I know Serani has. They never come out of their tunnels; they spend their lives in the service of the tree silga." He cupped his hand around the tiny blue of a winged insect. After a moment he let it fly out, sparkling, beyond the leaves. Jaele felt eagerness again—companions, need, the man who was ahead of her.

"So," she said quickly, "these earth silga are slaves. They will be angry. We could help them, and afterward some of them could come with us—with me."

Dorin turned his head away from her. He traced the veins of a leaf with one finger. "No," he said, "I do not think so," and a windy silence fell again between them.

Shadows of the small leaves around them slanted across their laps. Blue deepened slowly to purple. The sun hung huge and round, red above the western mountains, and everything around Dorin and Jaele grew rich and briefly, dazzlingly bright. Horns rang out below them; the sounds rose and drifted over the trees. It was then that Dorin saw the thread.

A web had been strung from the top branches long ago; now only this one strand remained, stretched between two twigs. He plucked it free and held it in his palm, then handed it to Jaele. It was smooth and strong, water-clear but tinged with green within. She turned it between her fingers.

"Jaele," Dorin said, "keep it. You could put your shell on it; it's thin enough."

She looked at him. His eyes seemed firelit. She drew the shell out of the pouch at her belt and handed it to him with the thread. "Please do it," she said.

He bent over them, into a patch with no shadows. She saw tiny hairs, touched golden, on the back of his neck and hands; the shape of his fingernails; the curve of his eyelashes. He was biting the inside of his right cheek.

"There," he said after a few attempts. "Turn away from me—I'll tie it." His fingers brushed her neck and she shivered. He laughed and did it again, and she reached back to bat at him. The thread was cool and light against her skin.

"Now turn back."

Jaele glanced down, just able to see the shell below her chin. When she raised her eyes, Dorin was looking not at the necklace but at her face. He was no longer smiling.

"Tell me about your town," she said, wanting him to speak. "Or where you went after you left my beach. Tell me anything."

He shook his head slowly. "No. No—I can't."

"Why not?" She leaned forward to touch his hand, but he drew it back. "What is wrong?" she asked, and he closed his eyes before he answered.

"It is difficult for me sometimes—being with you. With most people. I have never . . ." Then, in a different voice, "We should leave." His eyes open, sliding over the leaves. "It will be dark soon."

He climbed down and she followed, swallowing around a dryness in her throat. He did not sing, or make any noise at all. "Jump now," he said when she reached the bottom. She jumped. She did not look at the sundown-burnished webs around them; she saw only his back.

"Hold on to my belt," he said when they came to the path, which was now in absolute darkness. Jaele did, and they stumbled through the trees and vines. By the time they reached their clearing, there were stars dancing in and out of the branches.

Serani was sitting by a fire; a cauldron was propped above it, and Jaele smelled herb soup. The old woman looked sharply at them, then offered a soup bowl to each. Dorin walked past her to a platform that was far away from Jaele's. Serani's black eyes were steady on her, and Jaele drew an uneven breath.

"I don't know what's wrong," she said. "He's so sad, maybe angry, but I don't know why . . ."

After she had eaten as much as she could, she stood at the base of the tree Dorin had chosen. "Dorin," she called, and cringed at the raggedness of the word. She looked up into the branches but could see nothing. "Dorin, please tell me what's wrong."

The silence was so long that she turned to walk away. "I'm sorry," Dorin said, his voice distant and muffled, "but I can't explain. Please leave me."

After a moment she said, "Thank you for showing me the webs and the tree. And thank you for singing—here and in Luhr." She walked off, climbed up to her platform. His bundle of clothes was still lying there. She put it to her face; it smelled like him. When he held her against him at the top of the tree, she had breathed him in: sun-warmed skin, clay and water, other scents she did not recognize. She clutched the bundle and fell asleep.

She dreamed Dorin's tree-climbing song; it came to her, asleep, as it never would again, in every note and word. Then it began to fade. She tried to catch at it as she swam toward open spaces. She woke as it died completely, and sat up groggily. Dawn light was filtering through the branches. Dorin's bundle was gone.

Jaele crept up the steps to his platform and peered over the boards. "Dorin?" she called. "He's gone running," she said to herself

later, as she walked around and around the clearing. "He'll be back."
Whingey watched her with sad, wide eyes.

The light changed from grey to gold. Horns sounded. When
Serani rose, Jaele was sitting on a root of the tree where Dorin had
slept. The old woman put a hand on Jaele's shoulder. Jaele shook
her head from side to side and did not look up. "No," she said, "no."
A moment later she stood. "Serani, take me to the earth silga."
Serani gazed at her; Jaele could not see herself in the woman's black
eyes. "Please—show me which tree to go to. I need to meet them.
Right away."

The old potter took one of Jaele's hands in both of her own. Her
fingers were thick-knuckled, with tips dry and cracked as clay left
too long in the oven. She held Jaele's hand for a moment, then led
her down the path. They stopped at one of the holes which gaped
below twisted and arching roots. Serani pointed down into the
darkness.

"Thank you," Jaele said. Serani squeezed her hand once, tightly,
before stepping back.

Jaele had to crawl at first. Once she had ducked into the hole, she
saw a tunnel sloping away before her; its walls glowed a light green.
After she had crawled a short distance, the tunnel deepened and the
ceiling grew higher. She stood up, brushing grit off her hands. She
walked for a long time, down and down, until the earthen walls
became stone, beaded and glistening with water. The water too
shone green, and she heard its steady dripping against the stone.
She was trembling and raw.

Soon there were other noises—distant clangings and ringing
blows. Jaele walked on until the sounds were nearer and a light
began to grow ahead of her, dimly orange and flickering. Against
this light appeared a dark, stooped shape. It advanced toward
her, casting a distended shadow on the walls. Jaele did not think
to be afraid. *They are angry—they are slaves,* she thought, and her
steps quickened.

They stopped a few paces from each other. She gazed at the creature, and he gazed back at her. He was a silga, but his skin was not white and he did not tower above her. He was dark and gnarled, covered in dirt and hair. His back was bent, coiled like a root. He regarded her with black, orange-dappled eyes.

She waited. After a moment he said in a rough voice, "Murtha," and pointed to himself.

"Jaele," she said. Her voice sprang from the rock walls, and she cleared her throat. "Please," she continued, more quietly, "could you show me your home? I am from far away, and would like to see it."

Murtha nodded and gestured down the tunnel, toward the light. "Down here is where we live. Follow," he said, and she did.

After a few moments of silence she asked, "Did you know I was here? Did you hear me coming?"

He looked back at her over his humped shoulder and replied, "We hear, yes. Steps, and changes in the air."

"Do people like me come here often? Strangers?" She remembered sunlight in Luhr, the dazzle of fishfolk scales. Certainty rising like tears in her throat.

"No," he said, but he slowed and moved so that she could walk beside him on the path, and she knew he would say more. "Not many, until these latest days. Now you, and that other before you. That one did not speak the Queen's language, so I fed him berries and he went away. With you I can talk."

Jaele stopped walking. He took a few steps more, then turned to her. "This other," she said, "what was he like?"

Murtha held up his hands and spread his fingers, and she felt a chill like fever aching in her flesh. "Fingers with more skin, here. He was tired. Very hungry. He looked long at the water on our walls, but he would not drink when I gave him a cup. *You* want food? Water?"

"No," she said, walking again. *He was here,* she thought, shivering as her feet touched the ground. *Here where I am, as in Luhr—I knew.* And she too looked at the water, trickling green from mountain stone. "How long ago?" she asked, and the earth silga glanced at her.

"Long ago?" he repeated, and she said, "How long ago did that other come here?"

Murtha shrugged. "Eight sleeps, perhaps. Nine. I am sorry to not know."

Jaele took a deep breath and smiled at him. "No—do not be sorry. Thank you for telling me. Now please—tell me more about this place."

He pointed ahead and said, "There is a place of metal where we work. I will show you."

Moments later the path ended at a rock ledge. Jaele stood with Murtha and looked down on a huge cavern, blazing with fire and heat, and ringing with the sound of hammers on metal. The clanging made her blink; sparks shone red behind her eyelids. Earth silga milled below them, hunched over enormous vats of bubbling green liquid, carrying pots, beating strips of glowing metal.

She did not realize she had become accustomed to the noise until it stopped. Hammers fell silent; the earth silga were suddenly still among the vats and flames. She saw Murtha's hands clench at his sides, saw a look of waiting in his eyes, which he did not turn to her. She understood a moment later, when her own eyes fell on three tree silga. They were tall and unbowed, pale as moon against the dark earth and stone. Graceful and slow, they walked through the cavern, pausing to examine the liquid and the strips of metal, and turning, sometimes, to speak to each other. They did not speak to the earth silga, Jaele noticed—not even when one of the tree silga grasped some tongs and hurled a rounded bit of metal back into the fire; or when another tipped one of the vats so that the bright molten liquid flowed away down a trough. Although they were not instructed to, the earth silga who had been standing by the vat and holding the discarded metal crept away into corridors at the edge of the cavern, bent low, eyes downcast, shuffling among the other earth silga, who made way without looking at them.

When they came to the last of the fires, the tree silga slipped away into darkness, their backs curving only briefly beneath the low doorways. The noise and motion resumed almost immediately, and again Jaele flinched and blinked. *The earth silga are strong, and they must yearn to leave this place.* Her companions, when freed, standing with her in wind and light by the Eastern Sea?

"Murtha!" she cried, and he peered up at her. "Where did those earth silga go?"

He motioned toward the tunnel and they stepped back; the clamour faded as soon as the cavern was out of sight. "Away," he said. "Not forever."

She shook her head. "But that is terrible! Why do you allow the tree silga to command you this way?"

He frowned a bit. "Command?" he repeated, then said, "They are apart, from above. We are here." He regarded her calmly.

"That is . . . that is not . . ." Jaele began, but fell silent as she looked at him. "Please," she said after a pause, "could you show me more?"

She followed him into another tunnel, which plunged even further down. New sounds began here: sharp blows, crumbling stone, high singing. She thought she recognized the language of the tree silga but was not sure; there was a difference.

They came to another opening. Smaller tunnels branched around them. Earth silga hacked at the stone walls with picks and hands. Children helped; Jaele saw that their backs too were stooped. She also saw, leaning against the walls, some pottery jugs that were most certainly Serani's, and she smiled. The earth silga's voices rose and fell, and did not falter when they looked at her. The green walls glowed; the rocks that were sorted into pushcarts and taken away shone green as well. Murtha picked up a small piece and held it close to his eyes. Then he put it into Jaele's hand.

"Oh," she said, hearing her voice crack and leap high. "I thank you."

He took her to a workroom, where she saw what these silga made with their molten green. There were rows of horns of all sizes, clear but still shadowed with colour. Some were one loop; others were twisted into two or three; still others were straight, flaring slightly at the end. Earth silga examined them, heads bent, fingers running lightly over the metal. Singing quietly.

"May I hear?" Jaele asked Murtha, pointing at the horns. "Could you play something?"

He looked at her. All of them looked at her with what she imagined was sorrow, old and heavy as root or stone. "No," he said. "Never here. Only above." *They yearn to leave this place,* she thought again, and her heart began to race with the words she would speak to them.

Jaele and Murtha sat in the chamber and watched as the earth silga inspected the horns, watched as new instruments were carried carefully in by children. One of these children held up a horn. Someone looked, pointed to a bubble or fold, and turned the child gently back to the corridor. Feet scuffed and hands smoothed and children smiled; time passed, beyond circling of sun or moon or stars.

The soft hiss of Murtha's indrawn breath jolted her back. This sound was the only one; feet and voices had suddenly gone silent, as the hammers had done, before. All of these earth silga, like those others, were still, looking at the doorway. Jaele knew what she would see.

A tree silga was standing in the entrance to the chamber. He had to stoop beneath the low ceiling, yet even stooping, his long fine hair was dusted with earth. He looked down at them and they looked at the ground. He did not glance at Jaele, though her nails dug into her palms as she waited for him to do so.

As in the cavern of fire, the earth silga waited. He walked slowly among them, examining the instruments. The colours of his clothing blurred, like leaves in wind. He came to where a woman was standing with a child, each holding one end of a horn. He looked at it, though not at them, then took it from them. It was a slender, delicate thing; he twisted it easily in his hands until the mouth-tip snapped and fell to the dirt at their feet. The child made a sound— a sob, Jaele thought—and the woman took his hand and led him from the chamber.

"Wait!" Jaele's voice leapt from the rock and she cringed at its loudness, even as she stood before the tree silga. "What have you done to them? Where have they gone—and those others from the cavern?" *I will not hide. Not now—not this time.*

He did not blink. "You," he said, "will not know. You will leave this place."

She was small again—a leaf on the ground, or a twig. She stared at him in a moment that lengthened and stretched. She was not hiding—but it did not matter. He did not speak again.

The tree silga left—ducking and straightening in a rustling of leaves—and she swallowed. Time to speak now, while the earth silga were quiet and her anger still burned.

"Murtha," she said carefully, and he smiled at her, very slightly, "do you hate them?" Murtha's smile slid away, and he gazed at her with his head cocked to one side, like a bird. "Because I will help you," she went on. The other silga were watching intently, but there was a thread of singing twining once more against the green. "I understand hatred. That other stranger who came here before me—he is my enemy, as the tree silga are yours. I am following him east because he murdered my mother. I will wound him as he has wounded me." She paused, willing her voice to harden into the shapes of her words.

"I will help you," she said again. "We will go above together and fight the tree silga. I have a weapon; surely you could make some.

But we can decide these things later. Afterward you could come with me to the Ladhra River and Fane and the ocean, if need be, and you could help me in turn. We hate—"

And then she stopped speaking, for Murtha held up his hands and said, "No." His eyes were full of stone darkness. "No," he said once more. "We live here. We do not know the sea. And you do not know the silga."

Jaele cried, "But you must hate them, and this place so far below the earth!" Her throat was thick with unshed tears.

Only Murtha was looking at her now; the others were bending to work, singing and touching the cool green horns. He shook his head and smiled again—his small, sad smile.

They might have sickened, she thought then, breathing the tears away. *They might have died on the journey, and they are so misshapen, not formed for fighting.* She forced her anger to dissolve and nodded at him over the regret that remained, like bile. Her fingers closed tightly around the green-hearted stone in her hand. "I will leave now," she said quietly.

Murtha guided her back to where the tunnel began to slope upward. The orange light leapt and flickered behind them. "Farewell," he said. "Jaele."

"Farewell, Murtha," she said, not looking at him. Then she turned and walked up and up, until daylight shone above her and she heard the wind in the leaves.

Serani was sitting in the wagon when Jaele reached the clearing. Whingey stood patiently. The pots, wheel and fresh clay had all been packed away. Jaele took the bundle from her platform and climbed up to sit beside the potter.

"They were not what I expected," Jaele said, glancing from the trees to the trail before them. *"Eight sleeps, perhaps nine";* he would be far from this forest now—but still ahead, where her feet too would fall. "Not what I had hoped for. Thank you, anyway, for taking me to them. And," she added, "I would be grateful if I could travel with you for a time—if you are still going east."

Serani nodded. She touched Jaele's hand lightly.

Whingey drew them down the path. The tall, beautiful silga did not appear, and the holes beneath the roots were dark. Later, as the sun began to slant and the path left the silga's trees, Jaele heard for the last time the horns singing piercing and lonely over the mountains.

CHAPTER FOUR

Serani guided a melancholy-eyed Whingey northward, up a new path. They rode over slopes where few trees grew. The air was shockingly cold, like deepest water, and their breath hung suspended before them. They came at last to a gorge, a stretch of shadow between walls of mineral-whorled rock. Whingey shied at the entrance to the pass, but Serani laid her hand on his neck and he went slowly forward.

Jaele shivered as she looked up at the bare mountainsides, and drew her woollen cloak more closely around her. She watched Serani, who was sitting very straight, with a light growing in her black eyes. But mostly Jaele stared at the rock, waiting for a wisp of colour she could make into Dorin—running back along the sandy earth to the Giant's Club, reaching to touch her shoulder at first light. Dorin or the other one, the man without a name. She sank into silence and did not think to yearn for words.

Bundled in all their blankets and cloaks, they slept beneath ledges of stone. Two nights passed in the cold darkness of the mountains.

Jaele slept soundly and woke each morning to pale, chilly sunlight, and the quick throb of remembering, and Serani's smile. "What?" Jaele finally demanded on the third morning. "Why are you so happy? Where are we going?" The old woman only smiled more broadly and climbed into the wagon.

On that third day they came suddenly to the end of the pass. The stone walls fell away, and the path sloped sharply down and into sunlight that was strong and warm. The sky soared above them; Jaele felt light. Below was a plain, rippling golden-green in the wind. *The mountains and now the plain. My footsteps in Galha's.*

She turned to Serani, whose eyes were round and blinking with tears. At last Jaele understood. "This is your home," she said when the potter looked at her. "This plain is your home." Words of pain—a lost place, memory like a wound. Serani took her hand and held it tightly before she sent Whingey trotting down the path.

That night they slept in grass that rose high above them and cut at the sky. Jaele listened to the wind hissing in the grass; it sounded like water rushing in foam to the edge of the sand. She tried so hard not to remember, tried to think only of a path to the rising sun.

Serani urged Whingey on almost without halting, and the horse drew them swiftly over the flat earth. Jaele learned then to love the feeling of wind whipping around her face and through her hair. But even as she exulted in this wind and in the grass parting before them, she imagined Dorin and that other appearing, running, riding over the shifting ground beside them.

They spent one more night alone on the plain. Jaele woke twice, and both times saw Serani standing looking northward. She was small and straight beneath the sky, which was bottomless in the dark and the endless stars.

That day they came to an expanse of wheat and corn, and Serani left the wagon to walk. She held the fronds of grain to her face and

closed her eyes. Jaele remained in the wagon. Shortly after this they
came to a hut. It was small, made of stones of all sizes, and Jaele
knew instantly it was Serani's. She watched her walk up to the
wooden door; she laid her forehead against it, then pushed it open.
Jaele did not follow. A few moments later Serani put her head out,
smiled and beckoned her in.

The first thing she noticed was the table. It was a flat, round
stone, close to the packed earthen floor. It was set for three, and
strewn with flowers—pink, blue, yellow-hearted white. A large reed
pallet lay in a corner below a window, and it too was covered in
petals. The room danced with scented light.

Jaele knelt before one of the glazed plates on the table, and
waited. Serani sliced the bread, peeled the skin off a ball of smooth
white cheese. The silence was even deeper about her than usual.
When a shadow fell across the table, she looked up steadily.

He was tall and thin and a bit stooped. His skin was black and
only slightly wrinkled, although he was very old. His eyes sparkled
green beneath an uneven swath of white hair. He bowed deeply to
Jaele. "Greetings," he said in a voice full of twinkling, and turned
to Serani.

For a moment she stood in the petal-coloured light, hands
outstretched. Then she was up and whirling, and the man's laughter wrapped round them both as he spun her.

"I am Bienta," he said to Jaele afterward. "Welcome," he added
with a grin and a sweeping gesture. "Serani has no doubt told you
all about me." He looked at Serani, and she at him, and Jaele looked
at her plate of bread and cheese.

She learned, that afternoon, that if Serani was silent calm,
Bienta was flood. "We built this house ourselves when we were
young, young—you should have seen us—Serani was as beautiful as a wind in the corn—not, of course, that she is not still as
lovely—what was I saying? Ah, the house . . ." He moved,
always—touching Serani's hair, dancing in small light steps

through the deepening shadows. Jaele relaxed beneath his words, for none were expected of her—and she smiled, although she did not know it. She looked from Serani's eyes to Bienta's and felt an ache.

"My, how I go on," was one of the last things she remembered Bienta saying. "Put your head down, like that—good—now sleep, my dear."

Jaele woke to darkness and chill and distant laughter. She rose and stood at the window. She saw the wheat and tufted corn stroking black against the sky; and she saw Bienta's tall shape and Serani's slight one, circling and dipping in the silver grass.

Jaele stayed with Bienta and Serani for one more night and two windy days. There was rain at first; Bienta drew her out of the house, crying, "The rain on Telon Plain is one of the wonders of this world! No one must sit inside—come, come!" Jaele stood with her face upturned, her eyes narrowed: the water was grey, more like silver, and cool and smooth as the underside of a shell.

The rain passed in the wind, and when the plain was again golden, Jaele saw the stream that wound dark and clear behind the house. She saw the kitchen and the large oven beside it, already burning and lined with bowls. A cat, small and orange, rubbed around her ankles and mewed cheerfully, and Whingey huffed contentedly, despite his wet hair. Jaele picked up the cat and buried her face in sun-scented fur.

She ate bread, sweetmoss and pinkfruit from a cellar below the kitchen, and slept in the grass by the stream. Rustling and buzzing and golden warmth: she did not dream.

At dusk, Serani and Bienta came to sit beside her. Serani pointed to the sky that hung low over the wheat. Bienta said, "Sunset here is quick. If you look away, it will elude you." Jaele watched the colours sweep up from the grasstops: gold, scarlet, green and orange, then a rush of darkness.

"Another wonder of the world?" she said to Bienta, and was shocked at the edge of anger in her voice. He looked at her, but said nothing.

She sat by the stream well into the night. When Bienta came to her, one of Jaele's hands was wrapped around the shell at her throat and the other rested on the cat in her lap.

"I see you have a siri bird thread from the mountain forest," he said quietly.

She glanced at him. "Have you seen the place?" she asked, and he smiled.

"No. But I have heard that it is very beautiful." They were silent for a moment; the water gurgled, and the cat's purring rumbled around them. "Jaele," he said at last, "Serani has told me about Dorin."

"Oh," she said, not thinking to ask how Serani had told him this. She was squeezing the shell so tightly that she felt its tiny grooves pressing into her palm. "Have you met him?"

"We laughed together," Bienta said, "and he seemed happy here. But Serani and I knew at once: he is a fleeing one. I knew he would not travel with her for long. He needs to run."

"I run," Jaele said in a small, muffled voice.

"Yes," Bienta replied, "but why? and where to?" He paused, then said softly, "Serani has also told me another, larger thing: that you are seeking to avenge your family, and that you are searching for people to join you."

"Yes," she said, turning to him, "I need help, and I thought that he would come with me, since the Sea Raiders attacked his town as well. And then I thought that the earth silga would help, but . . ." Her voice sank into the dark pulsing of the river.

"I am sorry," Bienta said, "that *I* cannot help you. I am old— though still much as I was as a young man, I must add."

She said quickly, "No—you and Serani aren't too old—you are both hale, and could be of great help to me. And I would enjoy your company."

He shook his head and smiled. "Thank you, my dear, but we are most definitely too aged to go hurrying east with you. And most definitely too aged for fighting, except with each other."

"I do not need to hurry," Jaele said. "It is something I have thought about since Luhr. I am certain I will find him—but he is already well ahead of me. I am not sure how far, any more. I may have to travel all the way to Fane and then across the sea. I will need companions for this. I will need them more than I need haste." Part of her cried out in denial: *No—go now, go on.* Another part (shuddering alone by a burned-out fire, walking alone round a clearing) clung to safety. *"Companions who will understand my need."* Rage and fear, twinned.

Bienta said in a slow, careful voice, "I do understand your pain, and your desire. But I think, Jaele—and do not be angry with me for saying it—that this journey may be yours to make alone."

"No," she said, "that is not true. I will have others."

"Perhaps," Bienta replied, and Jaele bent her forehead into the lacing of her fingers. She felt his hand on her shoulder. "Sleep," he said, "if you can. Much comes clear in daylight." After a time she did fall asleep by the stream, with the cat curled around her head.

The wind woke her. The cat was gone, and the sun was up and shimmering. For a few moments Jaele lay without thoughts; then she remembered Bienta, and what he had told her. She rose and walked over to the hut, where he and Serani were waiting.

"I must leave," Jaele said, eyes darting to the table, the window, the flowers. She did not say: *You will not come with me, so I cannot stay. Dorin has been here, laughing and singing, so I cannot stay.* But when she did look into their eyes, she saw them smiling, gently.

"We understand," said Bienta. "Where will you go from here?"

"East," she replied. "I have told you this. If I do not overtake the Sea Raider soon, I will find the Ladhra River. It will lead me to Fane."

She saw Serani glance at Bienta. He said, "East is a large place, Jaele, and the Ladhra River is far away. Where exactly will you go from here?"

"I do not know," she said, and looked at her feet. "That must seem ridiculous to you; it does to me now. But I have found my way this far, and I know where I want to be." *"Mountains and plains and hills": my father's words will guide me.*

Bienta went to the high shelf near the door, touching Serani's hair lightly as he passed her. "It does not seem ridiculous," he said as he took down a folded piece of parchment. "Perhaps what is ridiculous is the querulous worrying of two old people. In any case," he continued, turning back to Jaele and holding the parchment out to her, "here is a map. An ancient map—many towns will be missing. But the rivers are there, and so is Fane, and so, of course, is the sea."

Jaele unfolded the square and held it carefully; it trembled a bit in her hands. At first she saw only a tangle of ink, lines black red blue green, bright upon the faded honey of the parchment. Then Serani put a finger lightly on the paper and Jaele saw the palace of Luhr, the empty space of desert, the jagged points of mountains.

Bienta too was beside her. "Telon Plain," he said, pointing at ink strokes like bending grass, "though you will not see its name. There are no names at all here, only images of each place. Perhaps the person who drew it could not write. But see how clear it is: here is the path of the sun; here is the land of scrub and stone beyond our plain; the lake country and the red desert. And here," he said, "is your river."

A broad, curving stroke, blue-black, swept across the desert scarlet, widening and widening again until it met the edgeless green that was the Eastern Sea. Where river and ocean merged, there were rows of scratches: houses, Jaele saw when she looked more closely. Tall houses with steep roofs. Tiny ships in a sheltered harbour. "And there is Fane," she said, and it was so close and so distant that she trembled again. "There is nothing after the sea," she said after a moment, and Bienta shook his head.

"No. An ancient map, drawn by someone who only set down places known and seen."

Jaele swallowed and turned away from Fane and its river. She found Luhr and the jungle, the forest—then the shore of the Southern Sea. An empty shore, whose shape she did not recognize: no Giant's Club, no echoes of children laughing, loom clacking, oars dipping. She closed her eyes.

"It will not be harmed by water," Bienta said. "The parchment has a smooth finish that keeps it dry. I do not know how this was done. But it may be important when you reach the river."

"Thank you," she said after a long silence. "Now I am truly ready."

"Take good care, my dear," he said as they stood in front of the hut.

She smiled as she closed her hand around the sack of food Serani had prepared for her. "I will," she said.

Serani laid her cheek against Jaele's, then took her face in her hands; her fingers were hard and cool against Jaele's skin. Bienta squeezed her until her bones ached. And then, before she could speak or sit down or stay there forever, Jaele set off alone in the wind, with the grass stretching like a road before her.

IBEN

CHAPTER FIVE

Jaele walked for days, almost without halting; the noise of her thoughts dimmed and she soon knew only that her legs were moving. The grass became shorter, coarser, and flat grey rocks appeared with stunted trees growing out of their fissures. Her feet, bare since Telon Plain's soft, springy earth, now fell on prickly lichen and plants with dagger tips; she did not put her shoes on, and the soles of her feet grew thick and criss-crossed with lines. She saw a mountain range in the distance—a dark smudge along the northern horizon. Every morning, she took the map from her pouch and bent over it. *I am here,* she thought each day, as if she could see herself in the ink. *And he?*

The moon swelled red and huge over the rock, then shrank again to darkness. The grass was replaced by slate and moss. Nights were whitely cold, and the wind sighed among the stones. Jaele's food was gone, and there were no longer field plants or roots to eat. She stumbled on in exhaustion too great for fear. Somewhere beside or behind her, Dorin sang.

At last, when the moon was black, Jaele came to the barrows. It was a cold, cold night. Rain was slicing the air around her, falling and leaping off the rock, twisting like folds of cloth in the wind. Lightning flickered, turning the rain to silver and the stones into looming white shadows. She was running, her head bent against the water. She was weak and bone-weary and ill, and did not realize where she was until everything—the rain, the wind, the lightning—stopped.

She was standing within a circle of eight stones. At first she did not realize they were stones: they towered over her, carved into shapes that glowed faintly red. These stones ringed a moss-covered hillock. She looked out beyond the stones at the storm, which she could see but no longer hear or feel. As she looked, a figure appeared. It drifted, blew like smoke toward the stillness of the barrows. Jaele saw hair, black streaming in silent wind; she saw a wildly flaring dress or cloak. And she saw horns, two of them, curving above the hair. Lightning forked: the horns were closer, and talons flashed. A memory, quick and clear, of her father's voice: *"The iben seers—who had horns on their heads and talons instead of fingers—sang of the future in voices so beautiful that people who heard them wept in fear and joy."*

Jaele fell to her knees as the iben woman slipped within the ring of stones. *Oh, Father, she will tell me—she will speak to me of my journey's end.* The thought was slick with terror and relief.

The woman's talons were cool and smooth on Jaele's arm. Jaele rose, supported. The woman led her to the tallest of the stones, then laid her palm upon the lightning-lit surface. There was a rushing—wind or water or blood—so loud that Jaele closed her eyes. She felt herself falling then, spinning down into darkness too deep for shadow. She screamed—but the talons gripped and guided her, and she met the ground softly. Lay whimpering, in black silence.

"I can't see," she said at last, and her voice rasped. "Please—it is too dark."

The talon touch returned, this time on her forehead, and she shut her eyes again. "No light may be here," said a low voice. "It is pain. You will see, as well—now and after. We will give you sight."

And all at once Jaele did see: the night-haired woman with horns and cool, smooth talons, smiling infinite tenderness and safety; seven others around her, faces hidden but smiling.

"How . . . ?" Jaele asked, and the woman said, "We have lived so long in darkness—we have learned how to see, as if in sun. It is a thing we can share, so that there will be no fear."

"You are iben," Jaele whispered. "Why are you here? My father told me you lived on mountains."

The woman's face turned away. "We are iben, far from our home. Captives, far from our home. So far—and still we must be, in darkness dreaming of sun."

"Why? Why captives?" Her own voice pulsed away from her like a line of waves.

All eight were silent, breathless, until the woman said, "We cannot explain—we must wait, only, without explaining. Perhaps we will be free."

"How will you be free?" Jaele asked, and they answered together, their voices twining like roots beneath the stone.

"Our freedom will be spoken without knowledge. A gift of air and footsteps, our beginning from an ending."

Jaele shivered; earthen walls and talons bent to warm her. "You have seen your own future, then," she said. "My father also told me that your people are seers. There was a story—you helped Queen Galha when she was just a girl, sick and afraid. And in Luhr's marketplace you sang of time to come and people paid silver . . . Please—I need . . ." Her voice disappeared again in the strange dark light. *Sing of my journey. Tell me I will find him.*

Talons on her brow, stroking her eyes until they closed. Silence, then a sound like sunlit rain, falling, dancing around her. The iben sang, and Jaele strained toward the words. She heard birds and waves and the heavy hum of darkness beneath ocean. Seagreen billowing, fish blurring, her own limbs weaving among them. She sank into the sounds, still straining; they swelled and slowly subsided. Her own ragged breathing echoed.

"No," she said. "I do not understand. I heard the ocean but nothing more, nothing *important*. Please sing again, in words that will help me."

The iben looked at each other. The one who had led her down turned to her and said, "We are sorry for your sadness—sorry we cannot help you in the way you desire."

Jaele turned her face away, to root and earth. "Let me go, then. Take me back up so that I may continue my journey."

The iben woman said, "Yes—I will do this, when the storm has passed. But now *you* can help *us*."

"Oh?" Jaele said, hardly noticing the eager stirring of the iben. Her sudden hope pressed away by cold and bitterness.

"We need your eyes," a man said, quick with yearning. "So long not to see; only Llana sees, when the moon is dark above. She walks above, beyond the circle of our prison, but there is skylight sometimes, and she has to return. She cannot tell us fully. You tell us your eyes."

Jaele felt a surge—understanding or future, streaks of sky and leaping. "My eyes," she repeated, and the feeling ebbed. *Later,* she thought, *know later*. She did speak into the darkness, though at first the words were awkward and reluctant. But then they came more smoothly, faster, and her bitterness dissolved in longing. She spoke about the water of her bay: green as a serpent's back near the shore, blue by the rocks below the sky. How this water, from below, smudged the sun so that it could almost be looked at. She spoke about voices and a single candle, brown hands on woven cloth, a baby laughing in the sea. Very slowly she spoke about strangers and her mother's eyes, steel and blood and torches dancing into dark water, a man running into shadow. Her voice grew thick and dry.

"Calm," the woman Llana crooned as she faltered. "Calm, child."

"Llana," Jaele said when she knew she could not yet tell them more, "I am so tired—please tell me of *your* home . . ."

For a time their own strange language lit the cavern. Jaele slept as hours, days spun above the stone. Woke again and heard, ". . . but our families are many in number, almost countless members, and each print in the grass is known. So many, leaping and climbing, close to the face of the sky. So many voices, raised together in singing. Now we eight only are family. We speak to see again the faces and running of our kind; our songs too seem so briefly to bring us light. But our speaking alone is not enough. Not enough, though beautiful."

They sang. Jaele heard dawn and cold, the white-green of meadow frost. She heard the mountain peaks of jagged rock and dazzling, windy heights of sky. Heard the sun, burnishing horns and talons and ice-limned pools. She shivered at the yearning, the glow of beauty and remembering.

They bowed their heads when the song was done. She looked at them, and spoke through her own sorrow. "Long ago your people travelled to Luhr. I too have seen it." The spires, stretching blue-white among scatterings of cloud. Then sunrise over sand, and sunset over dancing stalks of grass and corn. She faltered a bit. Suddenly she felt her eyes, and the emptiness of her body. "Yes," they urged her, "yes, you are nearly finished—be strong," and she spoke of root tunnels and wet, singing stone, of threads spun among branches and tiny, sun-pricked hairs on the back of a neck.

"And the house, the cat . . . the lapping blue river. And that is . . . all, only the lightning on the slate and stones. I ran, and I was so hungry . . . the rain was like ice, and I pushed against it until I was within the stones and . . . there was silence. Silence, then Llana and here, beneath . . ." She felt the weight of the darkness and of her hunger, and cried out.

"Please," she said when the pain had passed. "Sing to me of where I am going. I am sure that you could tell me more. I *beg* you to tell me."

Llana said, "No, little one: it is for you to tell. For us to ask you— what is next?"

Jaele remembered Bienta, who had asked the same question in a room of sunlight and flowers. "My journey," she said at last, over the sting of regret and fear. "Like Queen Galha's. I have a map: I will find the Ladhra River and the Eastern Sea, for he is going there. The Sea Raider . . . I will find him." She was dizzy with sleep and words.

"Now this part is done." Iben voices far away, rich as earth. *This part?* Jaele wanted to say. *I still do not understand.* "Go, Jaele, and we will wait." Before she slipped away beneath Llana's song, she heard sighs, rippling joy and tears.

ALILAN

CHAPTER SIX

The sun was round and golden above the slate when Jaele opened her eyes. She was lying down; two of the twisted barrow stones rose above her. She blinked, squeezed her eyes shut against the light. Far up in the green-blue sky a bird called.

The air was clear and sparkling now that the storm was over. Shadows stained the rocks: dark wet patches, leftover rain. Jaele sat up, hearing her bones, her blood, feeling her skin, warm and aching against the air. Turning her head, she saw a bag of grey cloth lying beside her bundle on the stone. It was full of berries, roots, green fronds that smelled of spices. She remembered darkness and cool talons, singing that had told her nothing of time to come. She clutched the cloth in her hands.

Dusk gathered, and still she sat on a rock outside the barrows. The moon rose full and red, and when she saw its light on the stones, she knew that Llana would not come. Jaele did not sleep: she was vividly awake, almost in pain. She twined her dark hair between her fingers, waiting for dawn.

When she set off eastward in the sunlight, she did not look back at the red-stained stones. "I have seen the iben," she said aloud—and again the feeling, the almost-knowledge of a return and more words beneath the earth. "Dorin," she said, and longed to tell him.

She walked for days over the slate, knowing from her map that she would soon find the hills. She began to see tiny flowers among the moss, and more small, warped trees. The sun rose before her and set behind, and the night rain fell cool and gently. She filled her empty grey cloth again with roots and yellow berries, thinking of Serani. And when the sun hung deep in the sky, she ran, bare feet falling on grass and soft earth.

The moon dimmed from full to crescent to sliver, until one night there was only star-lined darkness. For her, though, it was not just darkness. *"You will see, as well—now and after,"* Llana had said—and on that night without a moon Jaele discovered the truth of these words. She saw shapes and details in the black, as she had beneath the iben stones, and she did not stumble as she walked. In the days that followed, this iben-sight came to her only in complete blackness; the merest hint of dawn would rip it away, leaving her eyes awash with tears. Gradually it strengthened, until on nights and days that came much later—in shadowed rooms and tunnels, and beneath the sky—it was no longer as sensitive to the light of flame or moon. On that first moonless night she thought, with wonder and tenderness, *Oh, Llana*—and, immediately after, *Not the help I wanted—not what I* needed . . .

The moon had waxed and waned several times when Jaele came within view of the hills. They rose tall and rounded out of the grass; they were covered with trees that shone scarlet, orange, yellow, silver-green. When the first line of hills grew close, she ran—ran until she was standing in the fragrant shade of the trees. For the first time since leaving the mountains, she heard birdsong and the rustling of leaves.

The light filtering down around her deepened to bronze. She wandered among the hills, breathing in earth and cool shadow.

Then, when dusk had finally fallen, she smelled wood burning. After a long moment she followed the smell, iben-sight leading her around trees and over roots. The scent grew stronger; as it did, she heard a steady pounding, and voices, many of them, raised in shouts and laughter and singing. She hesitated, especially when she saw the orange of the fire flickering through the trees. But then, as the laughter echoed, she walked ahead and into a clearing.

At first, as her iben-sight was wrenched away in light, she saw nothing but tear-blurred colour—flurries of colour which gradually sharpened into bright skirts flying wide, flashes of copper arm and neck rings, brown skin, white kerchiefs and billowing shirts. Drums sounded; bare feet flattened the grass; limbs wove through the sparks of the fire. Hands clapped in time with the feet and drums, and horses stamped.

As she stood, blinking and overwhelmed, one of the dancers spun into her and sent them both sprawling. Jaele struggled to her knees and found herself looking into the flashing-eyed face of a girl.

"What were you *doing*, standing here like a sunstruck horse? You've ruined my dance! Who are you? Can you speak?"

Jaele gaped, her throat too dry and constricted for words. The girl's face was thin and dark brown, and she had a decidedly turned-up nose covered by a smattering of freckles. But most striking were her eyes, which shone a clear, bright blue.

She was rebraiding her black hair, which had come undone in the fall. As her fingers flew, she said, "Perhaps you *don't* speak? I'm sorry. My name is Alnossila, but everyone calls me Nossi. Maybe you could write your name in the earth with a stick?"

Jaele laughed. Nossi, after the shock of hearing her, laughed as well. As the dance ended, Jaele took a gasping breath. She picked up a twig and, as she traced letters in the ground, said, "I am Jaele."

"Well, Jaele," Nossi said as they wiped at their eyes, "are you hungry? Thirsty? You can nod: it is quicker and easier than writing in the earth."

Jaele chuckled. "Yes," she said, "to both."

Nossi led her among the fires and Jaele looked at them, at cook pots simmering, at the young people, polishing daggers, who clustered around the horses. She saw wagons standing among the fires, wheels large and still and crusted with earth. "This is my family's wagon," Nossi said, gesturing. "And over there is our fire. Let me take you to them—I will introduce you."

"No," Jaele said hastily, "please—could we just sit in your wagon for now? I am . . . tired." Noises and people still too beautiful, too strong after solitude.

"Tired as well as hungry and thirsty," Nossi said, and smiled. "Very well. Come inside."

They ate bread and soup and laughed again, and Jaele felt a fullness like tears, warming, spreading into spaces of loneliness. When she had finished eating, she looked up through the lantern-lit darkness at the wagon's ceiling. It was painted in greens and reds: twisting ivy and grass and licking flame.

"I suppose," she said after a silence, "that you want to know why I am here, alone."

Nossi shrugged. "We Alilan say that there is a time for every telling. You do not have to tell me this now, if you do not want to."

Jaele thought of the young people outside, with their horses and daggers. She thought of the wagons and the drums and Nossi's quick laughter. Jaele said, "But I do. I do want to tell you now."

Nossi leaned back against the wall across from her. "Then I will listen," she said.

Jaele remembered the words she had spoken beneath the barrow stones; now she spoke them again, sitting in a wagon as Alilan danced outside. Nossi listened and did not move, except to roll the end of her braid over and over between her fingers. Jaele felt a familiar weight settling in her stomach—the bruising and tears which she clenched her fist around. When there were no more words, she too eased herself back against the wagon's wall.

She could see out the open door to the sky; the moon was just a fragment, a silver-blue curve among ribbons of cloud.

"Telling is magic," Nossi said after a moment. "Any Alilan will swear it. You will be free. But first," she went on, leaning forward so that shadows leapt, "first you will have your revenge. This is something I understand. My own parents . . ." She turned her face away, eyes and lips closed tight. When she looked back and spoke again, her words were firm and even. "My own mother and father were killed in a battle with our ancient enemies, the Perona. They are a cruel desert tribe. I long to meet them again, to avenge myself and my parents, whom I hardly remember."

"I am so sorry," Jaele said, and Nossi smiled at her.

"You see why I understand you. I feel your need."

"Yes," Jaele said, and she knew, suddenly and with joy, what Nossi—already, unbidden—would say next.

"I will go with you," Nossi said in a low, urgent voice. "I will share your journey. But," she added as Jaele also sat forward on her bench, "I think that this revenge should be a larger thing than you have said. It is not one man only who should suffer."

"No," Jaele said—light, dizzy, trembling. She understood. All words, all meetings, had led to this. "You are right. Queen Galha did not take her revenge only upon the man who killed her daughter. Of course not—upon a people instead. She cursed all of them." She breathed deeply; the smoke outside was sweet, clean in starlight. "I spoke to Dorin once of asking for Queen Aldhra's aid against them—but I was not really thinking about *them*, only about that one man. The Sea Raiders—all of them—were too big a thought, after that. I never dared . . . Nossi," she said more slowly, "we would only be two."

"No," Nossi said, "not two—many, for all Alilan understand revenge and honour. Others will come with us; I am sure of it. I must get my horse and dagger first, so you would have to travel with us for a time. But when I do have horse and dagger, we will all ride east; we will overtake the Sea Raider and then go on to the ocean." She paused. "Will you wait for this? Can you?"

"I . . ." Jaele began, then bit her lower lip. "He may die. The fish-person in Luhr told me he would sicken. If I wait with you and he dies and I never see him, never find him . . . Nossi, he cut my mother's throat. I need *him*—*his* blood."

Nossi nodded once, quickly. "Of course. If I had to choose between avenging myself upon the very ones who killed my parents or upon all the Perona, I would hesitate. The first choice would be so just, so satisfying . . . but the other, Jaele, would be so much larger—so much more daring and lasting and *great*." She smiled again. Jaele thought she was glittering, her eyes and teeth and hair, the planes of her skin and the copper at her throat and wrists. "You would be glad of the larger choice in the end. And in any case, your Raider may not die. We may find him; your circle may be completed. And," she said, "you should not be alone in this. Please wait for me. For us."

I will find him, Jaele thought, certainty swelling in her as it had in Luhr. *We will find them.* "Yes," she said. "Oh, Nossi, yes: I will wait for you."

"Well, then," Nossi said. "We will ride together to the ocean, and we will fight these Sea Raiders for the honour of your family."

Jaele closed her eyes, which were dry. "Thank you," she said. She smiled as she opened them again. "You are very . . . passionate."

Nossi grinned back at her. "Yes. That is the goddess Alnila in me. She is fire. Her twin, Alneth, is earth; she is the stubbornness in me."

"Tell me more of these goddesses," Jaele said. She wanted Nossi to talk, wanted to listen in this glow of flame and hope.

"Alnila is the beginning and the end," Nossi said, rolling her plait. "Fire burns in a body struggling for birth and in a body struggling to leave at death. So fires are always tended at a birth, and the dead are always burned to ash. Alnila is this fire; she surrounds our livingtime. Alneth is Alnila's sister. She is the solid earth to Alnila's fire. She is the other half of birth: all the plants, all the animals, come from her and are fed from her. She is the other half of death: her soil holds all that has turned to ash. Alneth is the twin shaper of our livingtime."

Jaele thought, briefly, that she had sensed images beneath Nossi's lilting words: earth and sparks, damp ashes blowing and then still. She shivered.

"Ah," said a new voice, "the story of Alneth and Alnila." A young man was leaning against the door frame beside Jaele; she had not heard him come. He looked down at her and smiled. He was tall— would have to stoop to enter the wagon—and his blue gaze was the same as Nossi's. Jaele noticed a scar, a thick white line that cut through his left eyebrow to the bridge of his nose. The flickering light turned this scar from white to gold.

Nossi rolled her eyes. "Another timely entrance," she said, and to Jaele, "This fine example of Alilan manhood is my brother, Aldreth. Aldreth, this is Jaele, who is also a traveller."

He smiled at her again, and she felt herself flushing beneath the flames and ivy. "Jaele," he said, "it is good to meet you. And now I must add to Nossi's excellent account of Alnila and Alneth by telling you that we always worship these goddesses. We love fire: we love battle and passions of the body, we love the spinning of dance and drink. And we love all this with the constancy and stubborn weight of the earth."

And so, Jaele quickly discovered, they did. In the morning the Alilan rose with clamour: shouting, singing, a clanging of pots. Daggers were drawn and used before dawn; the healer's wagon was quickly surrounded by a collection of grim-faced youths nursing assorted cuts and bruises. The wagons began their daily journey slowly; children ran around and beneath them, screaming with laughter or challenge. The young women and men with their own horses, Aldreth among them, rode ahead, straining to best each other in speed and grace. And as soon as night began to fall—at the slightest hint of long shadows and thickening light—the wagons halted and the fires were lit. There was eating then, and storytelling, and of course dancing, that whirling and leaping through the fall of sparks.

"Alnila's tears," Nossi's grandmother, Alna, told Jaele, nodding at the orange-white sparks. She was smiling her toothless smile, stamping a brown and gnarled foot as the others danced. Jaele smiled back at her and turned again to the dancers.

I was hungry for the sight of them, she says, much later. *As hungry as all of you are, still, for my words of sunlight and freedom. I watched them: so many people, and so bright. I thought of Bienta and Serani, dipping, spinning in the wheat and corn; I remembered them, and felt so far away from Telon Plain.*

The wagons soon left the hills and rolled into the marshes beyond—northward, Jaele saw when she looked at her map and at the sun, hanging behind cloud. This land was a muted brown, dusted in the early morning with crackling white frost. The cold made the ground firmer than it was in summer; the horses walked without fear over peat that sank only slightly beneath their hoofs. Chunks of peat were thrown on the fires: the flames hissed and smoked and gave off a dark moist scent.

North, not east. A longer journey, but I know it is right. I am as sure as if the iben had sung it to me. Their voices gentleness and comfort, lulling fear to sleep.

"What is that?" Nossi was standing above her.

Jaele looked up and smiled. "A map that shows where I want to go. The east."

Nossi frowned at the map as she sat down beside Jaele. "You plan to use *this* to find your way? To find the river and the sea?"

"Yes. There is much on this map that I do not need or plan to see. But look—there are the hills, and here are the marshes. We are here . . . and this is where we want to be."

Nossi shook her head; the braid hanging over her shoulder swung back and forth. "It is pretty, I suppose, but we Alilan do not need such things. We could take you to that river riding backward on our horses."

"You know how to get there?" Jaele asked, and Nossi snorted.

"The wide river that begins in the desert? Of course we do! Put this map away. When it is time, we will find the river for you." She stood again and gazed at the campfires around them, glowing, coiling smoke into a low and sunless sky. "I think," she said, not turning to Jaele, "that you should speak of your journey to the others now. I have mentioned it to some; they are eager to see you, to listen to you. As many as possible should know—especially the young ones. Then you will be sure of your army, though it will not ride for a time. Aldreth!" she called, and her brother's head emerged from the doorway of their wagon. "Could you ride through the camp and tell everyone that Jaele would like to speak to them here?"

"I—" Jaele began, as Aldreth sketched a bow with mock gravity and intoned, "But of course: I am ever in the service of She Without a Horse." He ducked to avoid the clod of earth Nossi had thrown, and chuckled as he jogged away from their fire, toward the line of horses.

Jaele looked down at the map in her hands but did not see it. Saw instead her own brother's face, and heard his laughter and hers, their scoffing, with waves and wind beneath. *No,* she thought. *Stop.*

"What were you going to say?" Nossi was still standing, and Jaele rose beside her.

"I do not know if I can speak," she said. "To so many people, that is. This is what I have been wanting, but now . . ."

"Then I will speak for you," Nossi said. "If that would be easier. If you would not mind your tale coming from my mouth."

Jaele smiled. "No—I would not mind. All words sound stronger when you speak them."

Moments later Nossi climbed the wagon's steps and turned to look out over the whispering crowd that had gathered. Jaele sat at her feet. She also looked at the Alilan, all of them young, only some of them familiar to her.

"Thank you for your presence here," Nossi began, and the whispering faded as gently as foam sinking into sand. "I am speaking now for my friend Jaele, who has come to us from a great distance." Jaele nodded once. All the faces were blurred now, except for Aldreth's. He smiled at her from his place in the first ring of people, and she willed her eyes, at least, to smile back at him.

"Jaele is a traveller because her family was murdered by Raiders from beyond the Eastern Sea. These Raiders are the ancient enemies of her people, whose warrior queen, Galha, was known to our own ancestors. Jaele is alone. She is journeying to the sea now, following the same path of vengeance ridden by Queen Galha so long ago." Jaele was biting the inside of her cheek; she tasted blood, warm salt dark, and swallowed convulsively.

"We Alilan understand vengeance. It has been many seasons since we battled the Perona, yet our hatred only burns more strongly, and we yearn, always, to meet them in their desert of red and stone." A murmur rose; the Alilan shifted and seemed to lean forward, straining toward Nossi's words. Jaele did not move. She felt hot, as if the sun were blazing from an empty sky, as if there were sand beneath her bare feet. She shook her head and heard Nossi say, "We are many; Jaele is but one. Her desire and her courage are plain to me, and I wish—need—to aid her. I have promised that I will join her once I have my horse and dagger, and she has said that she will wait for me." She gazed at the assembly for a moment; she was fierce in her stillness and her silence.

"Who will come with us? It will be a long journey—but we Alilan journey every day for all our days. Jaele's rage is hers alone—but rage has ever been the wood beneath our fires. Also," she said, and her smile flashed, "it would be glorious. A tale Told by generations of Alilan. Who, then? Who among you will journey with us to the Eastern Sea?"

Wood snapped and spat; a horse whickered. Aldreth was the first to step forward, lifting his dagger high above his head—and then other blades were drawn and held against the sky, and torches as well, so that many suns shone above the wagons and the cold grey marsh.

"No," Jaele protested feebly to a group of youths the following morning, "I don't dance, really I don't. I just watch. The only thing I do is run." There had been an inn once, smoky and candlelit, with a scarred wooden floor that buckled upward so that it felt as if it were moving as she danced. Her father had held her, laughing. She shook her head, and the memory—another too warm, too near—melted away.

"Ah, you run!" Aldreth slid from his horse's back, and Jaele flushed and stared at the ground. "If you run," he continued, "you can also dance: it's all in the way the soles of your feet meet the ground. But let's see you run. A race to that rise, beyond the wagons?"

As the people around her cheered, Jaele flushed more deeply. "Let's go!" Nossi cried, leaping from foot to foot. "I'm ready! Anyone who dares, line up here. Alila, you give the signal."

Jaele found herself between tall Aldreth and his taller friend Alnon. They looked at one another knowingly above her head; at that moment her panic slipped away and into defiance. She tensed as the girl Alila raised a white kerchief. When the cloth came down, fluttering against the grey sky and orange-sputtering fires, Jaele hardly felt herself move. She sensed the men beside her launching themselves forward, and she heard the yells of the spectators; but she herself was stillness as soon as her feet began to fly beneath her.

She was alone by the time she reached the rise. Aldreth was well behind her, and Nossi and Alnon were behind him. Jaele stood on the hillock, squeezing her toes into the springy peat, and watched them come. The stillness was about her yet when Aldreth arrived, panting, eyes wide.

"By the Twins," he said, doubling over but lifting his head to look at her, "I can hardly wait to see you dance."

And that night, despite her resolve, she did. Aldreth and Alnon sat at grandmother Alna's fire ("Well, well," Nossi had hissed, clutching Jaele's arm, "Alnon has come too. Isn't he handsome? I will fight beside him someday"), and they brought with them a burning drink of honey and spices.

"To the winner of the race," Aldreth said with a grin, lifting his wooden goblet. "May she dance as lightly." Jaele drank. The liquid was sweet and smooth, and slid warmly down her throat to her stomach. Somehow her goblet was always full after that, and she drank until the flames blurred and the drums were her own pulse.

Dimly, she felt Nossi tug at her hand. She stood and whooped at the mad tilting of the earth. People were already spinning and clapping, and Jaele saw Nossi join the widening circle. She had watched her friend dance every night, and each time had felt full of yearning as Nossi's limbs and braided then unbound hair became river and flame. But this night Jaele too was fire, and Aldreth was beside her, laughing; she leapt past him and into a fall of sparks.

It *was* like running, except that there were so many people, so many voices and bodies which she sensed, even when her eyes were half closed. She danced on her own; later she danced with Aldreth, turning in the circle of his arms. She heard Nossi's laughter over the drums and stamping, and saw her wiry friend Alin leaping head over heels around his own small fire. But these faces swept by; the next day Jaele remembered only the flames reaching into the darkness, and the heart-thud of earth and drums and blood.

After the race and Jaele's first dance, Aldreth and Alnon came often to sit by Alna's fire. Nossi's eyes would flash and her hair would toss, black waves in the light. Alnon braided it; Jaele watched his fingers stroking and drawing the strands apart, but she could not watch for long. The next day the boy Alin would wag his finger at Nossi, mock severe. "My dear," he would say, "you are breaking my heart. If Alnon weren't so big, I'd knock him right off his horse's back."

Jaele watched them; she listened to them fighting with smiles in their voices, and saw their faces when they looked furtively at each other. She was awake the first time Nossi stole away in the darkest, stillest part of the night, and she woke again when her friend crept back at dawn. And though she tried to laugh as Alin did, all she felt was a spreading emptiness. Dorin returned to her then.

"Jaele," Nossi whispered one night, many days after the race, "I was wrong about your being mute, but I *am* sure that you're blind."

"Oh?" Jaele said, watching her breath curl smoke into the darkness. "How am I blind?"

Nossi half rose and leaned on one elbow. "Don't be such a misery! Open your eyes and look away from Alnon and me for a change. When you do, you'll see Alnila's flame in someone else's eyes." There was a silence. After a moment Nossi lay back with a thump. "You're as stubborn and fiery as we are, Jaele, the way you love Dorin. But he's not here, nor is he ever likely to be."

Jaele closed her eyes and began to breathe slowly and deeply. Nossi growled, "Alneth bury you, you foolish girl! And," she hissed, "I know you're not asleep."

The next day the two avoided each other. The sun was shining, though not warmly; the sky was thick and grey. "It will snow soon," Aldreth said, coming up quietly behind Jaele as she stood outside the cluster of wagons. When she did not reply, he smiled. "Come with me—I'll take you for a ride on Nilen."

"No," Jaele protested as he led her to the horses, "I haven't had much luck with horses—I don't think they like me." Within moments they were galloping away from the fires; moments after that, Jaele was laughing.

"Nossi told me you fall more than you ride," she said to him later, shakily, as he slid off Nilen's back.

He snorted and held up a hand to help her down. "She's just jealous. What else has she told you that I can clarify?"

Jaele sat down on a pitted boulder. Although she attempted to stop them, her legs were trembling. She still felt the pounding beneath her, against her thighs and up into her stomach.

"Well," she said as Aldreth sat below her, "this is perhaps too serious a response, but she hasn't told me much about what happened to your parents. Just that they died when she was young, in a battle with the Perona, and that she doesn't remember it very well."

As soon as the words were said, she cursed silently. Aldreth looked away from her, the tendons in his neck standing out suddenly as if in pain. But he spoke, staring at the thin lines of smoke rising from the fires that lay behind them.

"The battle happened when Nossi and I were children; she was six and I was eight." His voice had deepened and hardened into edges. "The Perona are cold and heartless wanderers of the eastern deserts. They ride horses as we do, but cruelly, with metal and whips. The beasts bleed and foam, and their eyes roll back in terror. I remember this. I hid beneath our parents' wagon with Nossi and watched the horses come together. The Alilan fought with daggers, and the Perona with their three-pointed short swords. Swords like stars, I remember," he said, and Jaele closed her eyes.

"The battle was short and terrible, but we triumphed. So I am told. There were many dead on both sides, of course, and one of them was my father. He was laid beside our wagon, and Nossi screamed. He was covered in dirt and blood, and she did not recognize him. The blood was from his chest, torn by the three tips of a Perona sword. Our mother knelt by him, with her hands in his hair, and cried while Nossi screamed. I will never forget her face—my mother's face."

There is a fire—huge, roaring, filled with dissolving shadows. The desert air is cool: the flames climb into a stream-clear sky. The drumming is slow, and feet shuffle as people circle the smaller watch fires. The bodies of the dead blacken and tremble among Alnila's tears. Suddenly there is a scream, torn high and breaking. A woman runs from a watch fire, away from a boy and girl who stand and do not move. Dark hair flying around her, mouth gaping wide, she runs into the heart of the fire. There are cries—some almost silent—and the wide liquid eyes of the children. No one follows her. After a moment the shuffling grief dance begins again, quiet and slow. The fires burn.

Jaele blinked and shook her head to clear it of the sounds of flames and grief. Aldreth was still staring back at the smoke. He was rubbing at the scar over his left eye, gently but steadily.

"I'm sorry," she said, her words thick and blurred.

He looked back at her. "No. I'm sorry it all came out like that. I forget, sometimes. Are you all right?"

"Yes." She could not speak of the sickness that had risen into her throat. Flames, flesh blackened, curling. "I feel," she went on, "as if I've been sleeping—confused, I don't remember what you said."

"No," he said, "you wouldn't remember exactly. You probably saw images, heard sounds, maybe even felt heat or cold?" He moved so that he was turned toward her. She watched his eyes and thought they were sad, but not like Dorin's. "I have an ancient Alilan . . . gift. In our caravan only Grandmother Alna and I have it. We Tell and our words become real for a moment, sometimes longer, depending on the story and our skill."

"Does it hurt?" Jaele asked. The sickness was subsiding now, as she breathed and looked at him.

He smiled, very faintly. "Yes, but in a way that is almost impossible to describe. It is pain of distance and vanished things. It is as if I exist among layers—I could call up any one of them, but I feel lost doing it. I belong nowhere when I Tell."

"Does Nossi have a bit of this gift as well?" Jaele asked after a time. "Because when she was explaining the Alilan to me, and then again when she was speaking about my journey, I thought I felt something—just a bit, like a shadow of colour. Heat, also."

Aldreth nodded. "Yes, she has a hint of it. Our mother had it too—I remember her images so clearly. She used to fill the air with stories at night: sometimes I fell asleep still caught in a Telling."

"Yes," said Jaele, and closed her eyes briefly on candlelight and baby's warmth and imagined footsteps on the sand.

"Jaele," Aldreth said, his face very close to hers, "sharing your journey will be so important to me. Revenge is something I understand even more keenly than most Alilan: my Tellings are sometimes so vivid that I emerge blind with rage and blood-need." He touched his scar again, lightly.

"It will be important to me as well," Jaele said, and added quickly, "I also will fight these Perona, if we encounter them." He smiled at her and she flushed and turned her face away. "This Telling—can you use it in battle? To confuse your enemies, or to frighten them? To hurt them?" Beginning to hope—until Aldreth shook his head.

"It is forbidden by the goddesses, who spoke to the first Alilan Teller. To use words as violence is a terrible crime. It did happen once, long ago, but that Teller's deeds and name cannot be known. And that," he went on in a lighter voice, flexing a muscular arm, "is why we are so handsome and strong!"

They rode more slowly this time, returning to the camp. She was aware of his stomach, flat beneath her hands, and of the feel and smell of his rough tunic as it brushed her cheek. She hardly looked at him when they dismounted, and she walked away before he could speak.

"Nossi," she said when she found her friend at their cook fire.

Nossi glanced up at her. "Well!" she said. "Look at you. Been riding, have you?"

Jaele groaned. "What can I do about him?" she asked. She felt herself smile, felt the heat in her cheeks, and wanted to groan again, because it could not be so simple. "Please tell me."

"Oh," Nossi said with laughing blue eyes, "do whatever you want! But," she added, wagging a finger at her, "I warn you: do not break his heart."

Jaele did nothing, for a time. They travelled through the frost until there were trees again, tall and bone-thin against the sky. She stayed away from Aldreth. She remembered his tunic beneath her cheek, his stomach beneath her hands; she remembered Dorin's arms around her atop a mountain tree. Both memories stung her with need and confusion. After a few awkward attempts to sit with her, Aldreth no longer came to their fire at night. She watched him, though—watched as he rode with his body straining forward above his horse's head, as he leaned over his dagger, polishing it, as he danced tall and graceful in the darkness, against the bodies of other girls. Soon he did not look at her at all.

"Alnila's Night is coming."

Jaele turned to Nossi, who was leaning over a soup pot, stirring and tasting and sprinkling herbs from a small clay jar. "Oh?" Jaele said. "And what is that?"

"A celebration of flame's victory over winter, Alneth's sleeping time," Nossi replied. She set the spoon carefully across the pot's rim and looked at Jaele with narrowed eyes. "You *may* enjoy yourself. This celebration involves even more drinking, dancing and passion than usual. Or," she went on, shrugging, "you may just want to sit and tap your feet with Grandmother Alna."

"Nossi," Jaele said slowly, "I am sorry—I wish I could explain myself to you, or to Aldreth, but it's so confusing. *I'm* so confused . . ."

"Shush," Nossi said, picking up her spoon again. "I know I should not tease you—but he is my brother. Try some of this. Too spicy? Too rich?"

The day of the festivities dawned bitterly cold. Shivering in her layers of cloaks, Jaele watched men and women tending huge cauldrons and gathering wood for the evening's fires. Children ran shrieking and laughing. There had been numerous fights already about who would dance with whom. The older youths wheeled their horses among the trees, calling to each other. Jaele could not see Aldreth.

With dusk came a silence. Families gathered around their wagons. Without words the eldest of the groups lit the fires, one by one. "Ah," Nossi breathed beside Jaele. Perhaps the flames were the same as always; perhaps the cold was no more biting than usual. But the fires bloomed like winter flowers in silence, and the air was white.

Jaele drank a good deal, very quickly. She ate, but not much. She did not speak; no one did. At last Grandmother Alna stood, gripping her staff and drum. Aldreth rose beside her. He bent over her briefly, then straightened and laid a hand on her rounded shoulder.

It was Alna who began. I will never forget the first touch of her Telling voice: a great wave, all the water and thunder of the world as it had been once, before words. It was like your singing—but different, as well. I wish that my *words could make you hear it.*

There was a scalding, roaring wind, and fire, and slowly, slowly, green and breath and footsteps in the rich dark earth. Jaele closed her eyes against the cooling wind and heard a thread like river water, another, gentler voice calling the first Alilan to their wandering. And so she listened to Alna's ancient Telling and Aldreth's young one, and something within her began like a tide to recede.

The twin Telling ended in winter cold, an image of flames rising huge and blistering over snow. Jaele's cloak slipped to the ground. She spread her arms wide and saw herself and all the Alilan whirling in the fire as they themselves were Told.

There was a long silence afterward. Jaele was sitting by the small fire, breathless and burning-cheeked as the images bled to stillness. She looked up at Alna, who stood with her eyes tightly closed; then at Aldreth, who gazed back at her from wild, faraway eyes, and smiled.

Alna finally moved. She brought her gnarled hand down on her drum, again, then again, as the other elders joined in with their own drums and feet. People began to rise and dance, still slowly. Jaele saw Nossi lifted up by Alnon, saw her twine her arms and legs around him and open her mouth to his, saw his hands drawing her hair down around them both. Alin touched Jaele's hand and she rose to him.

The dance grew faster. Cloaks flew off, and overskirts, and shirts. Jaele saw old Alna spinning, white hair unbound. Alin's hands held her; she felt them run along her arms. And then, suddenly, Aldreth was there.

He lifted her, held her face so that she was looking into his eyes. "Yes," she heard herself say, and she put her hands in his hair and kissed him wet and drink and fire.

They were on his horse; they were riding, threading their way among the trees. For a time there were others around them, but soon they were alone. She was lying on the ground with her head turned toward him; he was making a fire with swift fingers. She was sitting facing him. She touched her clothes and they fell away; she watched the skin puckering in bumps along her breasts and arms, but did not feel cold. He kissed the curve of her collarbone; she bit his shoulder and knotted her legs behind his back and there was dagger pain and then a rush of crackling joy as he strained and strained and stilled in the weaving of her body. Then the tears—her tears—hot sparks searing her cheeks black, and a terrible wound ripped from its hiding, her voice calling blood on the sand and Aldreth's voice matching hers, Telling of a forest of light and peace where he would hold her wrap around her until she fell asleep by his heart.

CHAPTER SEVEN

Jaele woke to pale grey light and the smell of burned-out fire. Aldreth's head was on her left breast, and her arm was around him. She felt his breath, steady and warm on her skin. Snow had begun to fall; she watched it melt in his hair. She was so cold that she could not move her fingers. Her eyes felt like sand.

After a time he stirred, lifting his head and shifting onto his elbow. His face was smudged with sleep; he smiled like a boy when he saw her. He bent and kissed her, smoothing his fingers across her cheeks. She almost reached up to touch the corners of his eyes and the scar that she knew would be soft. But she did not; and when he tried to draw her against him, she said only, "No." His face changed; he sat up and drew on his clothes.

"Nossi told me about Dorin," he said as he laced his boots, his back turned to her. "Is that it?"

She touched her shell. She felt the knot within her again, and forgot that it had ever dissolved into forest and tears. "Yes," she answered, amazed at the strength of her voice. "I'm sorry." Not enough, she knew.

They stood at last, facing each other. She tried to speak and could not. He smiled crookedly at her. When he put his arms around her, she pressed her cheek to his chest and heard the pulsing of his blood. "You know my heart," he said roughly, into her hair, and she nodded.

They rode back through the thin, pale trees and falling snow. She wound her arms around his waist and closed her eyes against his gently moving back.

The camp was very quiet that day. Children lay curled up around fires as their parents and siblings stumbled back from the woods to sleep inside the wagons. A line of girls and women gathered around the healer's wagon to drink a sour concoction of roots and berries; they would bleed and cramp for a bit, the woman told them, but there would be no babies. Jaele found Nossi there. The two smiled wearily.

"I see you enjoyed yourself after all," said Nossi with a half-hearted arching of her brows. Jaele shook her head and looked away. Nossi said at last, "We'll soon be in the lake country. It's beautiful, even in winter. Maybe things will be easier there."

Jaele could not say, *No, I don't think so, there's so much unfinished in me.* She said, "Maybe."

The lake country *was* beautiful. The Alilan entered the hills when the snow was thick and soft; their wagons left deep furrows, and the horses sank up to their knees. The lakes among these hills were not entirely frozen: black water lapped around tooth-shaped blocks of ice.

"Cold," Jaele mumbled, shivering.

Nossi chuckled. "Just wait until we get to the desert. We'll be going from well to well, parched and blistered. Remember this place then."

They stood in the doorway of their wagon and gazed at the lake below. Their breath smoked and thinned. "I've heard there are fish-folk here," Nossi said, and Jaele turned to her.

"Oh," she said. A single word, hardly more than a sigh; a sweep, within, of spires and marketplace, the glint of desert sun off scales, a webbed hand and a red stone.

"I nearly mentioned this to you before," Nossi went on, "when you first told me of your journey—when you talked about Luhr, and meeting one of these fishfolk. But I was afraid that you wouldn't be ready; that you wanted to tell then, not hear. And in any case, they have not been seen since well before my birth. They may no longer be here."

"If your strokes lead you to us," the fishperson had said in its voice of hiss and bubble. "I will find out—I will go to them," Jaele said quickly. "I must. I didn't ask the fishperson in Luhr for aid; it was too soon and I didn't think to. I will ask now. We will have companions to the sea."

Nossi nodded. "That would be wonderful, of course . . . but how will you find out if they are there? Surely you don't intend to leap into one of the lakes?"

"Why not?" Jaele said, and smiled at her friend's expression. "I have swum in cold water before, Nossi. This could not be so much colder."

Snow had begun to fall. Jaele looked up at the heavy clouds and remembered another sky, endless above a sea of trees. Her words to Dorin: *"Tell me about the silga."* Tunnels beneath the earth, lined with green stone and singing.

"Murtha did not understand revenge," she said to Nossi. "The fishfolk will. They have hated the Sea Raiders for a long time." She watched the black water, as if she would see the darker shadows of limbs beneath. Then she stood. "I will seek them out *now.*"

"Jaele," Nossi said slowly, as if to a child, "do not be foolish. You may have swum in cold water before, but not this cold. Imagine what it would feel like." She spoke more swiftly as Jaele moved down the steps. "Listen to me. You'll get sick, you'll die— oh, *wait,* you stubborn girl. Let me at least get some blankets—"

Moments later they both walked down to the lake, through the gusting snow.

"I may not surface right away," Jaele said as she unclasped her cloak and stepped out of her skirt. "Don't worry. I can hold my breath for a very long time, and I'm an excellent swimmer. Do *not* leap in after me." She grinned at Nossi, who was holding extra blankets and cloaks tightly against her chest.

"Very well," Nossi snapped. "But I wish to say that I did not swear to join you on a long journey to the east only to lose you now, in a freezing lake, looking for scaly people who may not even be there. Now go—and may the Twins guard you."

The water was much, much colder than in her bay. Jaele flailed and lashed. She saw nothing but murk and could not tell, after the first thrust of her dive, which way she was facing. She waited for her iben-sight to bloom, but it did not. The only light she saw was from the fishfolk stone clutched in her hand: a thin, crimson glow, dribbling between her fingers. She spun and kicked, already numb—and then there were webbed hands on her arm, wrapped tight as oceanweed, tight as talons in another darkness.

The fishperson did not draw her up to the air and the teeth of ice; down instead, and down. At first she struggled, but the hands were strong, and she stilled the thrashing of her limbs. Farther down, and farther. *Nossi was right. I will die here—I* am *a fool.*

Suddenly, as though she had come over the rise of a hill, there was light and warmth and a vast space. Jaele watched the bubbles of her scream trailing above her. When she looked down, she saw this new place through the familiar water-weaving of her hair. She saw arches and spirals of living coral—red, pink, brilliant blue. Lakegreen rose like mountain trees; silver-flashing snakefish slipped through the fronds, leaving sinuous paths. The light, golden-green, seemed to be coming from the water itself. Jaele had swum through the sand-thick water near the shore of her bay; she had gone deeper, into water that was clear and laced with distant sun. But never had she seen water such as this. She felt its warmth against her skin, and breathed—*breathed* it, like air.

When she had become accustomed to the water-air, she looked for the first time at her guide. "Mmmff," she said, in another rush of bubbles. The fishperson nodded at her, white eyes unblinking, and released her arm. Then it swam. After a moment Jaele followed it through a blue arch of coral. She felt excitement blossoming, filling her as it had when Nossi said, *"First you will have your revenge."* She thought, *The Alilan on their horses and the fishfolk in the river—all of us sweeping down to Fane.*

The fishperson led her to an enormous slab of stone. There were many fishfolk here, gliding in and out of the cave that lay below the overhanging rock, and among them swam wingfish, swallowtails, blue skimmers. A very large fishperson held itself upright in the cave, running strands of lakegreen through its webbed hands. Jaele's guide stopped before it and it turned. She unclasped her fingers to reveal the smooth red stone that had been given to her by the fishperson in Luhr. The creature before her bent and touched it, then straightened and nodded. It raised its hands and sketched sharp spires, flat desert. Jaele bubbled, "Yes," recognizing the Queen's City. The two fishfolk looked at each other, and she thought that they were sad, passing between them a vision of woven pallets lying by a well beneath a blistering sun.

Small fishfolk leapt and wheeled around her. One of them gave her a ribbon of lakegreen to eat. Everything was sparkling and indistinct. She was so warm—it was inconceivable that above this water of honey and forest sun there was black and cold, and above that wind and snow. She thought she heard singing; she remembered the earth silga, and her need to speak to these fishfolk was as piercing as a blade.

"You?" the largest fishperson motioned. "Where?"

She swallowed and lifted her hands. Slowly, carefully, she began to sketch her own lines in the water: webbed fingers and toes (not fishfolk), boats, the sea. She saw with another stab of excitement that they understood. They were very still, and their wide eyes slipped from her hands to her face and back. Murtha and the earth silga had also watched her silently, in their chamber of green horns. There she had not spoken clearly enough of hatred and revenge. *Take care,* she told herself. *This time must be different.*

"Daggers and blood," she said with her hands. "Bodies falling. My mother, my father, my brother. Sea Raider boats and daggers and fire. One of them left behind, running, always before me. Me— walking, swimming. Carrying my own dagger to the ocean in the east, Alilan riders around me. Sea Raiders, me; blood and bodies falling."

She paused and breathed the golden-green. The largest fishperson nodded once; the others shifted in a rippling of scales and lakegreen. Her hands opened and closed, then swept out again. "Alilan riders—and you. The Sea Raiders are your kin—but you are so good, not like them. You must hate them as I do. Come with me, above; or travel by lakes and rivers, and find the place where the largest river meets the sea, at the tall houses of Fane. Come with me. Please."

She held her clasped hands before her for a long time. She felt their eyes, their stillness. Nothing rippled now—until the largest fishperson moved its head back and forth, back and forth. *No beneath a mountain; no beneath a lake.*

Jaele shook her own head. "Why?" she shaped, hands savage in the water. The warmth of Alilan understanding receded before an older bitterness. "You *must* hate them, you should . . ." The large fishperson shaped separateness, two halves drawn apart long ago, and she interrupted, sketching the spires of Luhr as it had, sketching a queen and a princess who had also lived long ago. "Long ago, but that does not matter: I understand them, they make me *feel* . . ."

Then the fishperson drew the Sea Raider, and she too was silent. The Sea Raider—seen by other fishfolk, farther south. Beneath a different lake, a moon ago. The Sea Raider swimming, his strokes steady, though his steps on land were slow. Following the path of his ancestors. *"He will die"*—she heard the liquid voice of that other fishperson as this one said with its fingers and palms, "He will die without help from you or your dagger. Leave him. Do not follow."

I cannot wait after all, she thought; *I must follow him* now. For a moment she saw him so clearly: paces away from her, his lips drawn back, his forehead bloodied. His blood? Her mother's? Rage and need returned to her for the first time since she had met the Alilan. She felt cold, weak, borne up only by golden water. Then she thought of Nossi and Aldreth and an army, blood among the stones of the Raiders' Land. *"You should not be alone in this,"* Nossi had said. Jaele lifted her hands with difficulty—suddenly tired, trying not to tremble. "It is not only him—it is all of them. I must find them in their land, where Galha cursed them before."

No. No. In the silence that settled then, the fishperson who had led her down placed its hand gently on her arm. She spun away from it, exhaustion gone as quickly as it had come. She spun away from their eyes and their shaking heads, and pushed herself upward, kicking at the many hands that called after her. This time she swam alone in hard, straight strokes, up toward the darkness. The golden-green faded; she took one last water-breath and entered the black and airless cold of the winter lake. She met sky and snow with a cry and floundered for a moment, hearing the wind and Nossi's calls from far away, and another voice much closer.

"Hold on to me—here—arms around my neck—Jaele, look at me." She blinked away tears of air and daylight and saw Aldreth's face, and she watched it as he pulled them both through the water and over the tooth-shaped ice, toward the shore where Nossi was waiting.

"Jaele," Nossi cried, bending over her, reaching for her hands and then her frozen hair, her cheeks, "I had to get him—I was so worried, you were gone for ages—not even a *fish* can hold its breath that long—have I mentioned that you're a fool? A stubborn fool? Aldreth, hurry, get her to the wagon, and I'll build up the fire . . ."

Nossi knelt beside her later. She and Grandmother Alna had stripped Jaele's clothes away and dressed her again, then piled blankets on top of her. "So," Nossi said, "you were gone a very long time, as I may already have mentioned. Does this mean that you found them?"

"Yes," Jaele rasped. Her eyelids were heavy, drooping; she was shivering only sporadically now, easing into sleep. "They heard about the Raider. From other fishfolk somewhere . . . south of here. They will not join us. They do not hate . . ."

"Hmph," said Nossi. "Well." She added after a moment, "Perhaps this will be for the best. We will ride much faster than they would have swum."

Jaele wanted to laugh. Instead she slept, and dreamed of golden-green and rage.

CHAPTER EIGHT

Winter passed as the wagons turned south again, following the ancient Alilan path to the desert, where youths tamed their horses from the herds that ran wild. The desert where the Ladhra River was born. Aldreth wheeled and laughed in the sunlight beyond the first wagons. Jaele watched him, although she did not want to, and she occasionally looked up from Alna's fire and saw him standing in the darkness nearby. He had hardly spoken to her since the day at the fishfolk lake; she sometimes thought she must have imagined him holding her there. Excitement crackled as the wagons rolled on: young Alilan thought eagerly of their first horses and dreamed of skirmishes with the Perona beneath a sky-round sun. Jaele dreamed of an ocean she had never seen.

She rose one morning and stood at the foot of the wagon's steps. She gazed eastward, squinting into dawn light.

"Well?" Nossi was beside her; Jaele saw her breath before she looked at her.

"Well?" Jaele repeated, arching her brows.

Nossi scowled as she wrapped her arms around herself beneath her thin spring cloak. "You know well enough what I mean. What is wrong? You've been so much quieter since the fishfolk lake. So distant."

Jaele turned to the wagons that ringed theirs. She watched morning smoke, morning light on painted wood and horses' harnesses. "Under the lake," she said slowly, "when the fishfolk told me the Sea Raider had been seen, I wanted to run after him. I wanted this so suddenly and strongly—it was like a pain. But then I remembered you and Aldreth and our army, and the desire left me."

"And now it is back?" asked Nossi. "You want to follow him again?"

Jaele drew a long breath. "I keep thinking about how much time is passing. He is so real to me again—I can see him, with that blood across his forehead . . ."

"Jaele," Nossi said, leaning toward her as she had in the wagon, that first night among the autumn trees. "He is still alive. Just ahead—one man, walking, while you and I are travelling with horses and wagons. We will find him. I am so sure of this—it is as if the goddesses had shown me our future. On our horses we will reach him before he reaches the sea." Jaele, looking east again, felt Nossi take her hand and squeeze it. "Do not leave us, Jaele. I would miss you too much."

Jaele smiled, though Nossi shimmered through tears that had risen in her eyes. "I will not leave," she said. "How could I?"

"Good," Nossi said briskly. "Good. Because I think we will need you too. This may be the Season—we may meet the Perona again. And I will have my horse and dagger, and Aldreth will Tell the battle by Alnila's light, as he will Tell the Raiders' Land someday."

"No, child." Alna was standing behind them with a cook pot in her hand. She placed her other hand—root-bent—on Nossi's arm. "Do not be so certain of these Tellings, or of your desire for them."

"But you're old, Grandmother," Nossi said. "You probably don't remember—and battles must be frightening for people who can't fight."

Jaele looked at Alna, and she remembered Elic and her father and a sunlit beach. *"Never again,"* Reddac had said, grinding words, then strode away from them along the edge of water. Never again. And yet there had been a running man and a blood promise and a desert of three-pointed stars.

The wagons were rumbling through scrub and red, blown dust only days from the sea of sand when Nossi danced with a man who was not Alnon. It was a huge empty night, and a dry wind was stroking the fires tall. The dancing was slow; men and women moved in a cooling of sweat and stirring hair. Jaele was dancing with Alin, whose knees were like jutting stones against her thighs. Nossi was with Alnon, at first, limb-wrapped as always. After he slipped away, she stood alone for a moment, head upturned to the wind. When Jaele looked at her again, she was smiling at another young man, one who rode with a group Jaele hardly knew. He put his fingers to Nossi's hair, twining out of its knot. She looked quickly around before she stepped into his arms. They were swaying close when Alnon returned. Jaele saw him start and raise a hand in a small, helpless motion. Then he gripped Nossi's arm and pulled her roughly away and into the night beyond the fires.

Nossi crept back to their wagon much later, and Jaele started from a dream in which she had been awake and waiting. "Nossi," she said thickly, and the girl looked at her with black, glinting eyes. "Nossi," she repeated, and sat up.

Nossi turned her head away. The wind was still grasping at her hair, lifting it like seagreen billows in water. "I have never seen him so angry," she said, and her voice tore on the words. "He thinks this may be the end for us—imagine! Just once I dance with someone else—and was it so terrible? Was it?"

Jaele rubbed a hand across her eyes. "Well, you were very close to him, and Alnon wasn't prepared—"

"And why should it matter?" hissed Nossi, leaning forward until Jaele saw herself—thrusting head and fading body—suspended in the darkness of her eyes. "I am an Alilan woman. I am Alnila's daughter, wild, free, bound by no man. I am young and beautiful, and tonight I was happy, differently happy."

Jaele put a hand on her friend's shoulder; she was trembling. "But you love Alnon," she said, and Nossi made a sound like laughter.

"Oh, yes," she whispered, "yes. And there's something else: the healer's herbs seem to have failed." She did begin to laugh then, softly, the drone of insects or grief. "A baby!" she said at last. "A baby! By the Twins, I am lost . . ." Jaele reached for Nossi's hand and held it tightly as her laughter turned to tears. "Tell me a story," Nossi said at last. "Something that has nothing to do with us or this place."

"Well," Jaele began, "this may remind you of Alilan custom, but it is an amusing tale. About Galha and her horse, a creature everyone had claimed could not be ridden. But long before she was a queen, when she was just a girl, she set off to tame this horse, taking with her only an apple and her own hair comb . . ."

Nossi chuckled and sniffed, then quieted. She turned her braid around and around in her fingers. Jaele smiled and kept talking. She finished the story even though she knew that Nossi was asleep.

Jaele was not prepared for the desert. "It's terrifying and ugly and glorious," Nossi had told her once, and Jaele had nodded absently, thinking of the Ladhra River. "It seems," Nossi had continued, "as if the desert will never end, as if there couldn't possibly be any other place. That is why it is wrong that on your map it is just a small red patch." Only when the Alilan wagons halted atop a stony ridge and the desert lay beneath them did Jaele understand Nossi's words.

The sand here was not smooth and golden like the sand on her beach; this was angry crimson, thrust into ridges that buckled and jutted against a sky which was also red, and endless. *The Ladhra River is near and we will find it together, soon,* Jaele thought, and could not believe it, though her heart pounded with excitement. She squinted but could see no horizon, only a frenzied shimmering, far away where earth and sky bowed together. The sand was pierced with rocks, squat and defiant, scarlet, orange, laced with blue. When the Alilan drew nearer to them, Jaele realized that some of these rocks were towering, unbearably slender; she thought of the iben, and Luhr, and yearned for water.

The Alilan set up camp beside the first in a string of stone-marked wells that would lead them across the desert. They draped white cloaks and blankets among the wagons, and sat in shade that could not dull the thick pulsing of the air. "And now?" Jaele asked, with breath that was squeezed dry and small.

Alin grinned and drizzled sand from his fist onto her leg, slowly, like snow. "We're here," he said. "This is the place. It's the same every Season: we make camp at this well, close to those rocks that form a narrow passage—"

"And we wait," Nossi interrupted, ducking under the sand Alin tossed at her. He was with them more, now that Alnon was not. "It won't be long: it's as if the horses know we're here. We'll hear them before we see them. We'll have to sleep very lightly, because if they come at night, it's very dangerous."

"And then," Alin resumed, "we young Alilan climb the rocks and leap."

Jaele sat up. "You leap?" she asked, narrowing her eyes at the jagged stone outcroppings nearby. "From those? Why didn't you tell me this before? Are you all sunstruck? Are you not afraid?"

Nossi laughed, but her blue eyes were quiet. "I *am* afraid—people die every Season—but when I imagine it . . . They say the dry, windy fall is almost beyond Telling, but Aldreth will Tell it. It's what comes after that is never Told: the joining, the taming ride. These things are so sacred that they are silent."

Jaele felt Nossi's words glistening, briefly, into golden water that slipped through her fingers and hair. She closed her eyes and heard a piece of cloth flapping, and the steady, tired murmur of voices.

The horses found them at dawn on their third day in the desert. Nossi shook her from sleep. "Wake up," she hissed as her fingers dug tiny moons into Jaele's flesh, "they're coming." *And we will go afterward—my army will ride,* even half asleep, Jaele thought this, and trembled.

It was still dark. A silver mist clung to the sand, the wagons, the bodies moving like shadows toward the black rocks. Jaele blew hot breath into her hands as Nossi whispered, "Listen." At first, nothing: cold desert silence and sand footsteps. Then, as she rose to follow Nossi, a tremor—far away, like the unseen ripple that becomes a wave. By the time they reached the foot of the rocks, it was closer. The Alilan elders had climbed onto a low stone and were drumming, and the two rumblings joined and ached against the soles of Jaele's bare feet. She stood beside Nossi as the mist shivered into gently reddening sky. When she put a foot to the notched cliff face, Nossi touched her arm.

"No," she said, "I'm sorry. This is ours."

"Ours?" Jaele repeated, then understood. "Wait!" she cried as Nossi began to climb. "Nossi—I meant to ask before—what about the baby? What if you are hurt?" Her friend looked down at her with glittering eyes.

"I am with the goddesses," she called back. "I do not care."

Jaele felt cold as she watched Nossi's plait swinging dark against the stone. Her eyes burned and stung; she stumbled to the rock where the other Alilan were gathered. Someone grasped her wrist and pulled her up to stand among the drums, above the shaking sand.

Just before the horses appeared, she looked around desperately— for a face, a hand, a voice that would call her "ours." She saw

strangers, smudges in the red light. She saw Aldreth standing with
Alna pressed against his right side, and their eyes were dark mirrors
before the Telling that would come with the hoofbeats through the
stones. Jaele turned away from them and dove into green ocean
while her brother called from the shore and her father's loom sang
threads and her mother laughed in the boat that she could see if she
looked up toward the light. At last, here, the full and twisting
warmth of memory. Tears coiled slowly down her cheeks, but she
did not feel them.

At first the horses were water or blood, pouring black over the
dunes. Then the lightening sky struck their flowing manes copper,
their flanks slick, their nostrils open wide as mouths. The sand was
spray rising thick beneath hoofs; Jaele saw their glint, like dagger
steel, and her beach receded in a great sweeping of fear. She looked
away from the pounding, rippling sand, toward the highest rocks.
The young Alilan were standing dark and still, so close to the empty
space of air and falling.

The sun rose suddenly, pushing crimson from the curve of dark
sand, and the white Alilan tunics blazed as the horses streamed
toward them. Jaele looked for Nossi's shining braid and could not
find it: the girls had bound their hair close to their heads so they
would not be caught and dragged. The drumming was behind her
eyes, scraping along her bones. She could see the horses' foam and
sweat and gleaming, flattened ears, and she looked again for Nossi
and saw her at last, poised above the entrance to the pass. Then the
horses were between the stone walls and Nossi was falling still a
dancer into the golden light and others fell around her until the air
was white and even though it seemed so slow their bodies met the
horses in a moment and were joined.

Nossi landed on a red-brown back. She scrambled, wrapped her
arms around the thick-veined neck and clung, and moments later
she was almost sitting, one hand raised to the sky. Jaele saw long-
limbed Alin lying backward on a silver horse; somehow he did not

fall. But even as she gasped in relief, she heard screams and saw blood against white cloth and sand, and she watched as hoofs passed over bodies and left them motionless among the stones.

Jaele sat alone and stared at the camp, the bloody sand, the distant place where the young Alilan and their horses had slid blindingly in and out of her vision and then disappeared. She saw the limp bodies being wrapped in red cloth and carried away. She saw the Alilan taking wood from the wagons they had stocked before entering the desert; they laid it out away from the rocks, in silence, as a hot, breathless wind began to stir the sand. Someone was weeping.

Jaele did not eat that day, and she smelled no cook fires below. By midday she was sun-blind; by nightfall she was shivering. Only when she heard the thunder of returning hoof beats did she crawl down the stone. She lurched back to the camp and stood with the Alilan who were waiting for the riders. She watched them approach through smoke as the blood roared in her ears.

Nossi was one of the first. Her hair was unbound now, flowing above her horse's mane. She was not smiling, but her eyes were bright, glittering, and Jaele looked away. The horses were shining with foam, and their eyes rolled white when they halted. A few reared, front legs churning, but soon all were calm, their breath blowing mist against the sky.

The Alilan elders stepped forward and extended their hands, and the youths slipped quietly from their horses and onto the sand. When the elders turned, the others followed with the horses. Jaele walked behind them all. They went out beyond the stones, into the dunes hissing wind and invisible night creatures. The horses stepped silently, and the sand closed over the shell marks of their hoofs. The Alilan halted at the wood that stood tall and dark; the young dead were there, still and glowing gently red beneath. Jaele heard weeping again, choked and dry.

Aldreth and Alna were standing on a dune above the unlit fire. Alna's head was bent, but Aldreth was lifting his face to the wind, eyes open wide. When Jaele looked at him, she felt a sudden ache. *Dorin,* she thought.

The Telling began in darkness. Alna's words of desert cold and fear, of bodies huddled together below rock, shrinking as the earth shook. The first Alilan in this place, lost in edgeless sand, footsore and thirsty even in the bone-stripping air of dawn. And the sound pounding closer: they did not know, yet, what would come, the slashing legs and teeth and blood. But then they saw the horses, and suddenly shadows rose, young and defiant, and they crawled up the rock, two, four, eight, until the sky was stroked liquid white. Aldreth's voice joined Alna's—Jaele strained toward it, to hold it in cupped palms or open mouth—and the horses approached as light broke, and it was both the beginning and this day, for there was Nossi, standing at the edge of the rock. So many youths, stretching like wave foam back into the breaking light, and horses streaming thick, too many horses, and the leaping. Jaele's breath was ripped away as she fell, and the air filled her eyes and ears and mouth as she screamed wild terror and ecstasy.

Light blazed, and the voices—spouted words with fire—looped tails and the desert flowed away in spinning colour as Jaele clenched her hands around hot, coarse hair. She saw daggers and wind-blown sparks and incandescent manes, young limbs gripping and trembling blood—and beneath the glow, a current like music. She closed her eyes against the light and felt the horse's heart and the earth, and as the words grew softer and faded, she cried out.

She swam up through darkness and flame. Drums were sounding, and the scarlet bodies of the dead were rippling, blinding soft curves and slowly black. She swallowed over rising sickness and looked at Aldreth, who was kneeling on the sand with his head bent. Alna stood very tall above him; for a moment Jaele did not recognize her straight back and long white hair. The Alilan were rising to their feet, the old ones quiet, the young ones whooping and laughing and thrusting their new daggers toward the darkness, stretching out their arms to the horses that stood calmly fire-dappled nearby.

The dancing that night was endless, grief and celebration and flying, stinging sand. Jaele watched from the shadows; she saw Alin leaping, Aldreth moving in graceful silence, Nossi dancing alone with her eyes closed, and Alnon standing apart, gazing at her. Jaele watched and did not move, and no one came to her. After a time she rose and returned to her tent shelter. She sat for a while with her bundle on her knees. Without touching it, she felt her father's dagger warm against her flesh, and the shapes of red pebble, green rock from beneath a mountain forest. *I have stayed because of Nossi, because of an army. I have waited*—and again she remembered the Sea Raider's face, and his body disappearing into forest. Again she wanted to run, despite vows of vengeance and aid—east, in his footsteps, in a queen's. She thought: *Nossi will not miss me after all. I will go: the river is nearby, I will find it alone.*

She lay down on her side. Too weary for flight; too empty, suddenly, for rage or grief or memory. She fell asleep near dawn as the drums sang and the sparks fell like stars.

CHAPTER NINE

"Wake up, Jaele! Come with me and meet Sarla." Nossi's face smiling above her was so familiar that Jaele smiled as well before she felt the stab of returning memory. It was already hot; the red sand throbbed and she closed her eyes. "Are you coming or not? She's beautiful—I never could have imagined her so perfect."

The horse was pawing in the shadow of the rocks. When Nossi reached out to touch her mane, she lowered her head and whinnied softly. Jaele hung back until Nossi guided her hand to Sarla's neck. She thought of Whingey—sad-eyed on the silga mountain, contented and bony on Telon Plain—and her hand pressed against Sarla's glossy warmth.

Nossi did not notice Jaele's silence during the morning meal. She talked of battle and wind and steel, and her eyes darted over the heat-bent camp. When she rose and said, "Now I have something else to show you," Jaele followed her, still without speaking.

Jaele heaved herself clumsily up onto the horse's back and put her arms around Nossi's stomach, which tightened and strained when Sarla burst away. Jaele clamped her thighs and felt a surge of power which was not Whingey, not even Aldreth's Nilen. The desert flew scarlet around them, and the hot air battered their cheeks and eyes; Jaele's skin breathed and glistened and ignored her strangling fear. Nossi's voice cried words Jaele did not understand, and the dunes sharpened into peaks higher than mountains. When the horse's pace slowed, Jaele heard her own ragged breathing and Nossi's laughter.

Sarla reared and snorted as Nossi urged her to a stop. They were in a hollow place among the drifts: waves frozen at the moment before thundering, shifting only as the slow wind stirred sand along crests and down slopes. Jaele slithered off Sarla's back and her legs crumpled under her. Nossi spoke into her mount's cocked ear and rubbed her lathered neck. She turned to Jaele with a new smile. "She's amazing, isn't she? Now wait while I find it."

She looked carefully at each dune, then moved swiftly toward one as Jaele wobbled behind. Nossi dug at the sand wall until black stone gleamed beneath the red. "What . . . ?" Jaele asked, although she had not intended to speak.

Nossi grinned at her over her shoulder. "Yes: the only black rock in this whole ocean of sand, as far as I know. This is a special place. Now help me get the sand off." Jaele scrabbled too, until her fingernails stung and bent against the rock.

After minutes of digging, a door emerged. It was very low, and imbedded in it was what looked like a golden claw, its talons pointing toward the ground. Nossi pulled on the claw, her feet buried and pushing, and the slab swung slowly outward with a gusting of cool, dark air. Jaele's legs trembled again, but she followed Nossi beneath the doorway, her body bent almost double. The door gaped open behind them.

Small steps led down, and the desert light that had shivered around them inside the doorway faded as they descended. Nossi went forward slowly, but after only a moment Jaele saw the fissured walls and the uneven stairs and the layers of darkness. Again she remembered the sorrowful dreaming voices of the ibén, who had somehow given her this gift, this vision in black places. Her breath caught as she thought of their talons and stones, then of the green tunnels of the earth silga; for a moment she remembered when she had wandered alone. Remembered also that she had almost run, last night. Alone.

"Nearly there," Nossi said as the steps ended. They walked stooping along a short corridor until they came to another door. Jaele saw the glint of Nossi's eyes as she put a hand to the golden claw. "At first it won't look like much," she said, "but I'll show you."

Beyond the door even Jaele, with her iben-sight, saw only darkness. She stepped forward onto cool sand and heard Nossi pull the door shut behind them. There was a wind, and Jaele felt a tendril of her friend's hair brushing sun-warm along her arm. She took another step and Nossi murmured, "Find the walls and draw your hands over them." A few more paces and there was stone beneath her fingers—cut shapes, smooth and jagged, which stretched from floor to curving ceiling. As she touched the shapes, they seemed to warm; a moment later the darkness began to glow blue. At first it was faint—fingerprints of thin light—and she closed her eyes and opened them again. "Don't close your eyes," Nossi said from across the room. "Keep touching the walls, and watch."

Colour bloomed beneath Jaele's fingers. It caught at cracks and peaks and spilled onto the sand. She and Nossi turned to each other in the trembling underwater light.

"It's beautiful!" Jaele said. "How . . . ?"

"I'm not sure," Nossi replied, standing on her toes and easing her hands along the ceiling. "Something to do with stone and warm skin perhaps. Aldreth and I found this place together, and it's still exactly the same: the buried door, the claws, this room."

It was like the water close to the shore: clear, with darkness underneath and beyond; cool, but not cold and lung-crushing as it was farther out, past the rocks. Jaele touched the stone; it was wet. She watched the blue slip through her spread fingers and the long ends of her hair. She heard the muffled silence—pressure on her ears, the echoed sweeping of her limbs. She sank until the sand drifted over her toes and ankles and held her still.

When she opened her eyes, she was sitting, and Nossi was beside her. "Jaele," Nossi said quietly, "we haven't talked for a while, not really. I've missed it. Talking to you. Falling asleep while you're talking to me. I feel a bit mad. Please ask me something, tell me something."

"Well," Jaele said, "you could tell me what it's like to feel your horse below you for the first time, or how it is that, when you return after that first ride, the horses aren't wild any more—or are you not allowed to discuss this with me?" She felt slow, beneath the bitterness. She kicked her feet and reached into the blue, but it was out before her, darting away.

Nossi turned to her. Her eyes were round and dark, even in the fluttering air. She did not speak. Jaele whispered, "I'm sorry—truly, truly. When you turned me back at the stone and said 'ours,' I suddenly felt so alone. For the first time since I met you."

"No." Nossi's voice was distant; she was facing away, her cheek on her drawn-up knees. "I shouldn't have been so careless. I didn't mean to say you were different."

"But I am!" Jaele cried, laughing, crackling. "I am. I am not one of you. I am alone, and have been since I ran after the Raider, away from my beach. Since Dorin left me in the mountains." She was shaking, gripping her own ribs hard as rows of tiny frozen waves.

Nossi slid across the sand and drew her close. Jaele shook violently, then more slowly, then not at all. Nossi stroked her hair.

"The terrible thing," Jaele said at last, "is that I should be asking how *you* are. Alnon, and the baby. Sarla. I do want to know. Please tell me." She smiled a bit, and felt Nossi chuckle. Sand filling in a footprint, softly and silently and mostly unnoticed.

"I don't know where to begin," Nossi said as they drew apart. "Sarla you know about. My only joy, now."

Her face was turned away again—Nossi, whose voice changed only in darkness, when her eyes could not be seen. Her fingers were flying, plaiting in the blue light. "Let me," Jaele said, and sat behind her, weaving and separating the strands herself.

"I miss him," Nossi went on. "I looked for him, when I was standing on that ledge. I couldn't see him, and it was horrible, cold."

"And the dancing?" Jaele asked softly.

Nossi laughed, and glanced at Jaele over her shoulder. Her eyes were filled with smoke shadows. "It was thrilling. Another body— seeing myself in his gaze like a stranger. My skin felt different. I was so aware of it: the air on it, the fire warmth, his hands. But I miss *him*. I can't even speak his name."

Jaele said, "He watches you, you know. All the time. He's sick, wanting you. And you haven't even told him about the baby."

"I know. I know. I can't seem to say anything; it must be Alneth's stubbornness in me. But I *will* tell him. And he'll have to apologize too, by the Twins!"

"Apologize?"

Jaele and Nossi started. When the door opened, they scrambled to their feet. The blue wavered against the darkness of the passage, and they saw the two tall forms very clearly. "Apologize?" Aldreth said again, more loudly this time, as he and Alnon stepped into the chamber. "I don't know what my friend Alnon will think of that."

Nossi and Alnon stood motionless. Jaele could not look at their eyes. She looked instead at Aldreth, who was smiling at her slightly, gently, like a question—or perhaps it was the weaving of shadows and light. She turned back to her friend.

Nossi slowly shifted her gaze from Alnon to her brother. "I think," she said in a low, dangerous voice, "that *I* will ask him what he thinks. Alnon," she went on, and Jaele, at least, heard the softening, "come outside." They did not touch each other as they left. The door closed behind them.

"Shall we sit?" Aldreth was no longer smiling. They sat paces away from one another.

She was surprised when she spoke first. "Your Telling was beautiful," she said, and felt her words stumbling, rushing. "I saw such wonderful images—wild ones, colours, the sky spun . . ."

"Thank you," he said.

She touched the wall beside her: more blue, more light against his face. A fear dissolved as she looked at his sad, bright eyes, at the dark branches across his cheeks and the line of his neck.

"You didn't dance, last night," he said quietly. "I looked for you."

She felt warmth and did not knot it away. "No. I was . . . very sad. I even thought about leaving."

"Why didn't you?"

"The desert would have buried me," she said. "I wasn't that sad." They smiled. "And I promised I would fight beside you, and you promised you would fight beside me." She paused. "And."

She stood. She watched him as she walked to where he was, sitting against the landscape of stone and light. She slipped down so that he was behind her and his arms were wound around her chest, her ribs, tight and still.

They did not speak. She felt the softness of his lips, his breath, his hair on her neck. Legs and stomach, skin over blood she could sense, beneath. The blue water-air. And it was not now *her* water, *her* sand, *her* rocks and seagreen; it was new, and theirs. She closed her eyes and slept in the silence.

"Jaele." Aldreth was shifting his arms and legs. "I didn't want to move," he said, "not ever. But I can't feel my legs."

They sat facing each other again, though closer this time. "Let's not go out," Jaele said. "The sand will blow over the door and we'll stay here." She spoke quickly, layering words over regret and silence and the sudden, surprising shape of her leaving *(No—he will come with me, to the river and beyond; they will all come with me . . .).*

He lifted his hand to rub his scar; she put her fingers there first. The skin soft and cool, a puckered ridge.

"You do this often," she said, still touching. "When you're sad? Worried?"

"Or tired," he said, smiling. "Also when I'm pining for a girl who pines for someone else."

"How did you get it?" she asked—not only to cover his last words.

"Alnon," he said. "He told me he would court Nossi someday. We were only about twelve. I told him he wasn't good enough, even though he was my best friend. I defended her honour and he defended his—with his mother's dagger, which unfortunately had been left nearby." He chuckled. "He cried and I fainted. Mighty warriors, even at twelve."

He did touch his scar then, twining his fingers with hers. "You're worried now?" she said. "Or sad?"

"No," he said. "Yes."

After a moment she said, "Aldreth—no matter what—"

There was a knocking then, and they turned to the door as it opened. "Excuse us," said Nossi's voice from the corridor, and Jaele heard her smile.

Aldreth rolled his eyes and murmured, "Thank the Twins, it is done."

Jaele was the last to leave. She looked back at the room. It seemed that the blue was flickering fainter, coaxing the stone into darkness. After she had closed the door, she laid her hand on the golden claw; it was cool. Aldreth kissed her neck lightly, and she took his hand—fingers warm and dry—and led him up the stairs, her iben-sight clear in the black. When she felt the sunlight and heat shimmering against her eyes and skin, iben-sight and silence poured away and she ached again, although she turned to Aldreth and smiled.

They did not ride immediately back to the camp. Alnon and Nossi unpacked bags of food and water, and they sat in the shade of a mountain dune. Nossi bent over Alnon with bread and sour-spread; she drew her fingers through his hair. When she settled herself beside him, he put his big hand against her stomach and she laughed cool into the scorching wind.

"Goddesses smile on you," Aldreth said with a wink, "—all three of you."

Nossi looked at him accusingly. "How did you know? I only told Jaele."

He reached over to tug gently at her ear. "I know things, sister," he replied. "I am a man of considerable wisdom. As you should know." He raised his water bag. "Joy," he said.

After they had drunk, Nossi said, slowly, "Jaele—I don't know how to begin . . . that Alnon and I—that we are sure—"

"You will not be able to come with me to the Raiders' Land," Jaele interrupted, though she did not realize it until she spoke. "You must stay and have your baby."

She and Nossi gazed at each other, remembering words, vows, ribbons of cloud lit by a slender moon—a sudden blaze of hope and friendship. "That is absolutely as it should be," Jaele said at last, over this new sadness. "You must have your child and tell her all about me. So that she will know me when I return."

Nossi grinned, though her eyes still seemed laced with smoke. "Well, well," she said. "When you return. We seem to have made an Alilan out of you after all, Aldreth and I."

"And Aldreth is still planning to take you to the river and accompany you to the Raiders' Land," Aldreth said to Jaele. Their clasped hands were lying on his right knee. "I don't believe we'll even notice the absence of my sister." She turned her head and they smiled at each other, even as they heard another name between them. But smiled, because of the blue room, the unborn baby, this long, lovely day.

"And," Jaele said, looking again at Nossi, "I will fight with you, remember, if the Perona come. I will not continue my own journey until we are past the borders of their lands. This I still promise."

"May the Twins smile on you also, Jaele," Nossi said.

The sun swept overhead and dune shadows stretched along the sand. They talked more and ate more. Alnon plaited Nossi's hair; when he was finished, she unbound it and laughed and said it must be done again. As the light turned red-gold, they stacked a few pieces of wood and Alnon struck flints into sparks.

The flames shivered, bending against a fresher wind, and as the last twistings of colour faded into deep blue and stars, the fire breathed higher and they danced. Jaele wrapped herself around Aldreth's body and felt herself smooth, her hair whispering around them both. Nossi sang and spun, and Jaele remembered watching her, so long ago—her grace wild and frightening. *"You can't speak? Write your name . . ."* She held Nossi's hands and they danced until sand and sky were joined.

After they had all collapsed onto the ground, Aldreth and Nossi beat at the fire until it died, black wood and billows of ash. Jaele looked away. Alnon smiled at her. The starlight was so bright that she could see herself in his eyes. "People will be worrying perhaps," he said. "But such a day. One to remember when our wagons are sunk in snow and our grandchildren are dancing by the fire."

"Yes," Jaele said, "I will remember."

Nossi and Alnon sent their horses flying over the sand. Aldreth and Jaele rode more slowly behind. She thought of snow and bone trees, and lifted her face to the desert sky. The fires of the camp appeared, caught among the black, jutting stones. Voices, drumming, children's shouts; she strained to hear, but could not understand the words. Aldreth pulled Nilen to a stop near the first fire, and he and Jaele jumped to the ground.

They stood close together. She ran her fingers slowly down his chest and he squirmed, laughing. She slipped her arms around him and they were still. When at last she drew away, he kissed her, hands tangled in her hair. Afterward he said, "Jaele, in the blue chamber, just before Alnon and Nossi returned—what were you going to say?"

She looked at him—eyes and mouth, dagger scar—and smiled. "No matter what happens," she said, "you know my heart."

They turned then, and walked together toward the voices and the flames.

At first the riders were only clouds of dust on the horizon—blurs that could have been far-off windstorms wavering against the sun. Nossi looked up from where she was standing, brushing Sarla's sides. Imagine everything shining: the horse's hair, the copper rings around Nossi's arms, the crystal veins in the rock. How you yearn for this light—while I remember it and feel only sorrow.

"Look," Nossi said to Alnon and me, pointing at the distant clouds.

"Hmm," Alnon said. Jaele said, "A storm?" as Sarla's large velvet lips curled around the wrinkled sourfruit in her palm.

Alnon frowned, shading his eyes with his hand. "I don't think so. Not dark enough."

They all looked away.

They heard the horns later, when the sun was directly above. It was a low sound, like the rumbling of water far underground. Silence fell in the Alilan camp. Slow wind against cloth, slithering sand. A moment only—enough time for Aldreth to touch his scar once, lightly. Then he leapt to his feet and shouted, "Perona!" and Jaele felt her insides coil. Nossi cried out beside her and Alin gripped them both, his long sharp fingers bruising, and daggers sang against flint.

"And now?" Jaele asked, although she knew.

"We fight—what else?" Nossi answered, and looked at her with strange bloodless eyes. "And you with us, Alilan-friend."

Jaele left them and ran to their wagon. Grandmother Alna did not speak as Jaele passed her in the doorway. Her hands shook as she opened her bundle—layers of woven cloth, her father's colours unfolding beneath the flame and vines. The dagger fell to the floor, and its jewels glittered like eyes against the wood. She curled her fingers around its haft. Her brother's silent lunge, the outstretched arm, the seabird's hand she had thrown into the water of her bay. Smouldering.

She thrust the blade into her belt. Refolded her father's cloak and placed it again in the seagreen bag, which she tied to her belt. She would carry these pieces of her home into battle. Just before she stepped into the heat and clamour, Alna laid a knob-twisted hand on her arm. Jaele saw tears pooled in the brittle creases of her face. "Be safe," said Alna, and her voice was deep with echoes of Telling. "And know that there is choice for you, child."

Jaele felt a need to stop, to stay and listen to Alna's words until she understood—but Nossi was outside calling her. She bent and kissed Alna's cheek, brushing tears and sun-beaten paper skin. "I'll see you soon, Grandmother," she whispered, and was gone before she could see the old woman's eyes.

Aldreth caught her hand as they ran to the stones. This time she climbed with them, up to where the young Alilan had waited for their windy leap. The indistinct shapes in the distance had become larger: light flashed on metal, and plumed heads rose and fell in waves.

"They use their horses' tails to adorn their own heads," Nossi said, her voice shaking. "They are barbarians. They use metal and straps to bind their animals and make them bleed. Twins," she breathed, "thank you. At last they have come to us—to me, after so many Seasons."

Jaele said quietly, "Your vengeance is also mine. You know this." Nossi had turned to her with wide dark eyes. Jaele smiled and was full, breathless with strength.

They waited together above the crimson sand. As the horns shrieked again, Aldreth held up his arms and cried out words Jaele did not understand. The Alilan flowed down the rock toward their waiting horses. She went with them and stood as they vaulted up and leaned to whisper into their animals' ears. Alnon and Nossi stretched toward one another and clasped hands. Aldreth reached for Jaele and clutched her silently before they sprang away and she retreated from the churning hoofs.

Aldreth and Alnon and Nossi were among the first to go. Jaele watched them bending low over their horses' heads, moving as one person and one animal, pounding through sand that hung in the air like sunlit sparks. She watched until all the riders had passed her, then slipped the sandals off her feet. When she began to run, she did not notice the burning of the sand, and she did not feel herself breathing through heat-sore lungs. The sun was lying bloated and red behind the fighters; she ran toward it. She ran until there was blood on the sand and horses reared above her. She saw swirling shapes, Alilan and Perona; she saw long cloaks billowing around sun-dark skin; she saw eyes surrounded by cloth and narrowed against blowing sand. She remembered the little desert girl she had walked with on the road to Luhr—her eyes gold-flecked black against white cloth—and the veiled woman who had swept the girl up outside a tasselled tent. *The same people?* Jaele thought, confused.

As she hesitated, she saw the Perona's weapon. They had the three-pointed swords Aldreth had told her about, but she did not notice these; she saw only the fire. The cloaked riders held torches, blazing white against the sky: somehow there was wood and flame. They swept their torches in shuddering arcs, and the Alilan shrank on bellowing horses from Alnila's breath. Some were already burned. Jaele could see cloth flaming, falling black from bubbling

flesh. She took a few steps back—not sure if she was screaming—
and sought out her friends.

Aldreth and Alnon were fighting together, leaning close to
their enemies so that they could not use their swords. Jaele saw their
knives darting, blurred with sun and speed. As she watched,
Aldreth's dagger sank into his opponent's chest; she saw him twist
it deep, until the two seemed joined by flesh. He jerked his hand
free and pushed the man off his horse in a shower of blood. Alnon
slashed again and again at the throat of the Perona rider beside
him, first with his dagger and then with the rider's own sword. Jaele
saw the veiled head snap back and off; it landed on the sand and
was kicked away by a horse. The body swayed slowly, as if in sleep.
The horse reared and its rider fell like a diver into water, gently
backward. Aldreth and Alnon had already pushed on.

Nossi's hair was the first thing Jaele saw of her; it was unbound
and streaming. Jaele could almost feel it in her hands, shell-smooth
and hot as the sand. Sarla was tossing her head and pawing at the
air; Nossi was urging her closer to a Perona woman. She was almost
upon her, Sarla moving more smoothly now, when the woman
looked away, only briefly, and gestured to a man nearby. Jaele saw it
happen so slowly—it seemed that there should have been time for
her to run and shriek Nossi's name. Instead, she stood very still, as
she had in dark water by a tumble of rocks, her nails digging. The
woman reached up and caught the torch the man had thrown. Jaele
stood still as the woman's arm swept out and touched Sarla's mane
with fire. The horse screamed—Jaele heard it, soaring above the
other noise—and as Nossi bent forward to smother the flames with
her hands, the woman rose up in her saddle. Jaele saw Nossi's eyes
and mouth as the fire caught at her tunic. She heard her cry, and
the death in it, and finally, finally, began to run.

Alnon reached Nossi moments before Aldreth and Jaele did.
Jaele had darted among horses, heedless of blades and fire. A space
had appeared around Sarla, who was stretched flailing and blazing

on two legs. Nossi was falling, her clothing and skin and hair alight. Jaele halted, Aldreth behind her on Nilen. Everything had stopped—even the screaming, even the swollen throbbing of the sun. Into this quiet burst Alnon.

He was on his feet, straining as he ran. He reached his hands into the fire and grasped Nossi's arms. She was shimmering like a body reflected—no longer made of lines and edges. As he bent his head into the flames, a Perona man rode up behind him. He leaned down and drew one blade of his three-pointed sword sharply across Alnon's throat.

Suddenly there was no space, no frozen silence, and Jaele's eyes were filled with red. She heard Aldreth scream and saw him thrusting forward. (She later remembered his cheek—the clear, sluggish wend of tears through the blood—and his twisted lips.) Her dagger was warm in her palm as she moved toward the rider who had killed Nossi. The Perona woman had turned to face Aldreth. Jaele held her in her eyes, and a cold passed through her limbs, although the red remained. It was so slow—like running through waist-high water, the dragging pull—but she was beneath the horse, whose mouth glistened foam and blood. Before Aldreth could strike, she pushed her dagger into the horse's chest—pushed until it was up to the hilt—and slipped it out as the animal flailed and bucked. The Perona woman looked down as she fell. Jaele watched her eyes, dark inside the fluttering cloth, and saw them widen until they were rimmed with white. Jaele's knee was against her ribs, and her hands tore at the cloth until it came loose and there was a face beneath her. She stabbed and ripped. The brown throat opened and the eyes rolled up and she heard a bubbling of air and wetness. She felt bone and thrust so that it splintered like driftwood. She was red, red.

Her hand slowed, and as it did, she heard Aldreth's voice rising like a bird over the battle noise. Through the thickness in her head she remembered him saying something about Telling, about how it was a crime if used for violence—but the memory was gone, swept away by the soaring of his words. They were wailed and hollow, huge quivering drops of blood. The sand lifted and rock shattered and the Perona riders fell back and turned their eyes desperately to the sky.

When Jaele stood, her legs shook and she fell again to her knees. She crawled toward pure light, silence, an escape from the words that were tearing her. As she reached the edge of the battle, the earth shifted and she saw Aldreth's face among the hoofs and curling smoke, and then something slammed against the back of her head and she lost sight of him and everything else in the darkness that rushed through her eyes.

THE PALACE OF YAGOL

CHAPTER TEN

Jaele woke a few times to confusing glimpses of sky and metal. She was lying crumpled; being dragged face down; bent double over someone's shoulder. There was one long moment when her eyes opened and she heard herself whimpering. The sky was dark blue; she thought she should be able to see her face in it. There was pain, somewhere, a feeling of clotted emptiness. And then there *was* a face, distant at first, later looming. "Dorin," she wanted to say, and the face came closer, lowering itself into the hollow of her neck.

"Jaele," said Dorin, and the darkness returned.

Jaele opened her eyes. She was lying in a high bed vivid with pillows and sunlight, in a room of red stone. There was a table and low chair, and on the table a row of tiny glass vials. A double-headed axe hanging on the wall above the table. A carpet of green vines woven together. A window, tall, open, overlooking a garden where trees bent with flowers, blossoms floating pink and blue among leaves and grass.

She saw all this in a moment that was empty except for breath. Then she breathed again, again, and remembered.

"Jaele?" Dorin's voice was far away, but she heard it. She opened her eyes. Saw his hands—bones and skin, nails blunt and sand-grimed—covering hers on the yellow sheet. She tried to turn her head to look at him, but pain clawed at the base of her skull. She heard herself whimper.

Suddenly a man was bending over her, and she whimpered again. He was huge: his ears, nose, hands, chest, his head, which was brown and smooth as burnished wood. Around his neck was a wide band of polished black—perhaps stone, perhaps metal. She looked at his eyes but could not see them: they were hidden by a shelf of bone and shadow.

He leaned toward her. One of his hands cupped her head. She writhed in the bed and Dorin squeezed her hands. "No, Jaele—it is all right. This is Keeper, Guardian of the Palace and the Princes of Yagol. That is where we are now," he went on as Keeper drew his hand back. Jaele saw that he held a piece of cloth—wet crimson that had been white. Dorin said, "You and Keeper and I—only we three. It's a place of beauty and strangeness and power. You'll see, when you're better. Keeper sewed your wound up. Be careful not to move too suddenly: it's not nearly healed yet."

She blinked as Keeper bowed his head slowly to the coverlet. "Keeper serves," he said in a voice that was dark and time-deep, flames and waters roiling far below the firmness of earth. "The Two Princes and the One Wife. The creatures of the garden. All who enter here. Keeper is Bound."

Dorin held a clay cup to her mouth. She felt water but did not taste it. Keeper retreated, vanished from her sight. Her tongue felt swollen as she moved it over her lips, tasting blood.

"How long?" she said. Blood and words, tangled. "How long since the battle?"

Dorin sat on the edge of the bed, still holding her hands. "Many days. You've been unconscious for a long time."

"I must see the battleground."

"No." He was shaking his head, gazing out at the blossoms and the green. "No. I went back the day after, but there were only bodies. And burned wagons and . . . birds. Nothing—no one."

She swallowed. "Tell me how you found me. What you saw."

"Keeper told me about the battle and we both went to see. I don't know what I expected to do. And there you were at the edge of the fighting, about to be set on fire. Keeper dealt with the man who was holding the torch. He carried us both back."

"How did it end?" She watched his mouth as if he would speak in colours and heat. As if she would feel these things.

"I'm not sure—we left after we found you. There was a lot of fire when I first saw it from a distance. I wondered how, in the desert . . . And after I caught sight of you, I heard a voice—and there were noises, terrible, unnatural ones, and blood oozing everywhere, and I almost turned back. It seemed as if the ones with swords were fleeing—but there was such chaos that it was hard to tell. And I was looking at you." He glanced at her and smiled, very slightly.

"The voice—did you see whose it was? Did you see what happened to him?"

His hands slipped away from hers. She was vaguely surprised at how warm they had been. "No. He was . . . important to you?"

Jaele turned her face to the wall. Cracks in the red stone, spreading like web or net. "And where have you been all this time?" she said, when she knew her voice would not shake.

He was silent. "Everywhere," he said at last. "And nowhere. As usual. I came here quite a while ago, in a storm. Keeper found me and brought me in."

She felt his fingers looping a strand of hair behind her ear. "Are you hungry?" She did not reply. "Rest again, Jaele. You are still not well."

She closed her eyes. Would have laughed (bitterly, salt like blood) if she had not been so dizzy, so wrenched by pain and memory.

Dorin hummed softly and she slid quickly, thankfully away.

The sand sloped smooth before the Palace of Yagol. Jaele wrapped her hand around the latch that held the fortress's stone gates shut.

She had woken alone, minutes or hours ago. Had risen from her bed, clutching the edge of the mattress. The blood had howled in her ears, and the chamber had faded for a moment to grey, dappled with white and black spots. She had breathed deeply and waited. After a time colour and sound had returned, and she had taken a short step, then two longer ones, and reached the door. She had bent there—slowly, each movement a breath held—and lifted her pouch and bundle. She saw, as she stooped, that there was a waterskin by the door as well, and a purple kerchief. She put the waterskin—full, gurgling—in her bundle and tied the kerchief just below her wound. *Keeper must have left these things,* she thought. *He knew, somehow, that I would need to go into the desert.* She had left the chamber and walked into the corridor, into the many corridors of the palace, despite weakness and fear and the blood that still seeped around knotted thread and skin. She had walked along twisting garden paths, following the towers she could see above the red walls.

Now she leaned against the doors, listening to birdsong and insect drone as her own breath rasped. Her pouch on her belt; her bundle tied, hanging heavy against her thigh. She gazed through the small barred window at the empty land and sky. The doors were massive but opened easily; she thought of Keeper oiling the hinges, dusting off the stone. She pulled the doors closed behind her, turned, walked slowly out into the desert.

She stumbled as she descended the gentle slope. She watched her feet, knowing she would fall if she did not. When the ground was level, she looked up. The fortress was already difficult to see: red against red, only the towers showing, with the lighter sky behind. The sand in front of her was rock-scattered and silent. The sun hummed around her.

The towers had vanished the next time she looked back. She stopped walking. A moment later she sat down. *No*, she thought. Dizzy again, her head and neck throbbing. *I cannot.* A helplessness too great even for grief held her still.

Dorin had said there were bodies. Charred, blistered? *A hut woman man boy, burned beyond seeing.* Birds gouging, insects burrowing, bloodied cloth lifting in wind. *Sand soaked black beneath webbed feet.* Hoofprints and spent torches. *Long sliding marks of boats like sea creatures.* Wagon tracks weaving among and then away. *Alone, running through jungle—alone.* She drew a breath that was wrenched like a sob. *I cannot. Cannot look, or find. I do not even know where . . .*

She was lying on her side. Staring at her fingers, which were smeared with blood. "Dorin," she murmured, and curled around longing old and new.

He bent over her, as he had before. "Jaele—oh, Jaele, you did not know where to look—why did you not ask me?"

"I thought," she said, words slurred and strange, "that I might remember, maybe," and then she closed her eyes.

A fall of black hair, grandmother Alna weeping. Snow spinning, and sand, and bodies lit by sparks. Aldreth, Alnon, Nossi, their daggers and their blood. A scar, white and puckered and soft. A chamber rippling blue. An army broken, scattered. Riders who would never stream down to the sea—not without Nossi to hold them, to bind them with her fierce smile. Her laugh quick beneath painted flame and ivy.

I murmured their names, over and over. I wept, and tore at my stitches. Dorin and Keeper held my arms and I screamed at them, into the emptiness where my hope and joy had been. I screamed and bled and burned with fever. Perhaps you have done the same, in this darkness so far beneath? So far from your own joy.

Darkness and light shifted against the cracked walls and the plants of the garden. Dorin sang and laid cold wet cloths against Jaele's face and cheeks. She dreamed and woke, sweat-soaked, whirling with faces and her own arms reaching into void. The room lifted and tipped and she retched into a bowl that was tiny in Keeper's fingers. "Sleep, my dear, rest, my dear, sleep and cool and rest are near," Dorin sang, and she clutched his hands as she had in Luhr.

One day she heard rain and opened her eyes. The room was still and solid. She blinked and rolled her head carefully on the pillow. No Dorin, no Keeper—but she saw a woman standing by the open window across from the bed. The curtains were lashing blue, and the woman's dress, and rain was blowing like silver against her skin and the flagstones. Jaele made a sound and the woman turned, and Jaele saw that her skin was the colour of Keeper's neckring and that her eyes were blazing.

"I must wait!" she cried, holding her hands out to Jaele. She was shining with rain. "They do not return, and the town falls to ruin. But I must wait. How long? Can you tell me how long I have been waiting?"

Jaele tried to raise herself on an elbow but could not. "I'm sorry," she said in a rough voice, "I don't know . . ." but the woman was gone somehow, between blinks. The curtains billowed with wind

and rain against the red stone. Jaele slept again, restlessly, muttering names and sometimes laughing.

The next time she woke, her head felt like clear water, and she
was alone. The rain had slackened and was sliding in noiseless,
golden-clear trails along the glass. She was gapingly hungry. She
lifted herself slowly out of the pillows and was not dizzy. She slid
off the bed and stood. The stone was warm against the soles of her
feet. She noticed that someone had dressed her in a blue tunic
which hung in long folds. She remembered the woman and
wondered if Dorin had slipped the tunic onto her as she slept or
tossed in fever. Before she opened the door, she put a hand hesitantly to the back of her head. She felt the wound-ridge there,
rising from one ear almost to the other, knobbly with dried thread.
No, she thought as the emptiness of loss began again to bloom. *Do
not remember—not now.*

She went out into the corridor that stretched away in arched
doorways on one side and sunlit windows on the other. These
windows looked onto a different garden—lusher, greener, more
tangled, bright with wings and eyes that blinked and disappeared
among the vines. Jaele walked slowly, half in sunlight. When she
tired, she leaned against one of the doors, and with a rush of air it
opened.

She heard the crying first: a thin infant wail, choked breath and
rage. The room was huge, thick with tapestries and golden vases
that caught candlelight, and sculptures whorled in black stone that
shone only dully. She could not immediately find the source of the
crying. As she stepped onto the carpet (soft as fur, covering her bare
toes), she saw that the candles were burning against darkness: it was
night beyond the windows. She hesitated for a moment, her head
and blood throbbing with confusion. Then she stepped forward
again.

There were two babies. They were lying together in a high bed
bounded on all sides by writhing wooden carving. They lay with

their dimpled arms around each other, straining their heads upward as they wailed. They were dark-skinned, shiny with saliva but not tears. Jaele bent to touch a cheek, a black curl—but before she could, there was a splintering crash and a hissing of blown-out candles. The crying stopped. She could not see or feel the bed, could not see anything at all. *My iben-sight?* she thought as she groped her way through the darkness. Her hands met stone. She fell into the sunlit corridor, where Keeper was waiting, towering against the garden.

Jaele cleared her throat, but when she spoke, her voice still shook. "Those babies—who were they? Why was it night, in that room? Please tell me what's happening."

"Keeper serves," he said, and again her heart beat strangely at the sound of his voice. "He serves," he repeated, pointing at the door, "when time flows backward and around."

"So," Jaele said slowly, "I am seeing other time? And you do not want me to? Should I not go into these rooms? Might I cause some harm, or be hurt myself?" When he did not answer, she went on, "Was it you who made the woman disappear, so I wouldn't keep talking to her?"

Keeper bowed his head. "Keeper serves," he said, and moved off down the hallway.

She followed him. He did not look back at her. She trotted along, four of her footsteps to one of his, glancing only briefly at the doors and windows they were passing. She was still dizzy, feeling in the centre of a circle turning into a spiral, folding in on itself. She kept her eyes on Keeper's back, which hardly moved with his strides.

They came to stairs, so huge that Jaele had to slide from one to the next. As the stairs wound down like the inside of an empty shell, the sunlight faded and was replaced by darkness that smelled of forest floor. Keeper still did not turn. Torches flickered from brackets in the wall; she did not, could not, look at them. A wind, very deep and far away, touched the flames and her face, damp and old, old.

The stairs ended in another vaulted corridor, but this time the rooms off it were not hidden by doors. Some rooms were torchlit. In one, Jaele saw stacks of metal cages, blacksmith's tools, anvils; in another, heaps of tapestries, jumbles of bowls, vases, many-necked jugs. Other rooms were dark, and she saw only brief glints off polished surfaces, or mounds black against blacker walls (these scenes too quick for iben-sight?). The passage snaked and Keeper disappeared around corners. She stopped glancing into the rooms and stumbled after him.

The chamber into which he finally led her was so vast that she could see no ceiling, no walls—only twists of ivy blowing thick and red-green, and wings disappearing into hazy distance. Jaele stood very still and turned her head slowly. Scattered in front of her were brick ovens and chimneys rising like stalagmites; squat iron cauldrons; giant slabs of tables littered with bottles and plants and furred or feathered animals; bushes or small trees; glass cases filled with emerald water and huge, distended, glittering fish. There were shadows as well, smoky at the outside of her vision, but when she turned her head, the air was clear. She sat down heavily on a massive log, and Dorin appeared beside her.

"Jaele, you shouldn't have left your room."

She smiled shakily and put up a hand to stop him from speaking again. "I wouldn't have, except that I was ravenous." *And alone.*

"I'm sorry," he said quickly, "I knew you would be. I've been trying to make you something delicious, something I learned far away." The eagerness in his voice almost made her smile.

He led her among the bushes and chimneys to a thick wooden table that curved at both ends like a boat. On it were red earthen platters, silver drinking cups and tiny bronze food spears. There was thick, steaming soup, dark green leaves wrapped in pastry and petals, fish in deep purple sauce, and globes of bread.

"How did you do this?" Jaele asked, and Dorin grinned.

"A secret," he said, gesturing to a massive chair. "Now sit, and enjoy."

After they had eaten, Jaele swung her legs back and forth and cupped her chin in her palms. She felt too slow and warm for speech or thoughts. She watched the winged creatures fluttering into darkness, the fish as they circled and breathed bubbles of reflected candles and leaves and iron heat. She watched Keeper moving silently around the room, stirring and feeding and bending low to touch with his large cold hands.

"I saw a woman," Jaele said at last. "In my room. And babies in another room. I don't think they were real."

Dorin turned to her with raised brows. "Ah, you saw . . . I am not surprised. You and Keeper and I are alone here—but as I told you, there is a strangeness about this place. I've heard people walking, once even talking. I've never seen them; you're lucky. What was the woman like?"

"Desperate, lovely. She said she was waiting for someone, even though the town was falling apart. Then she asked me how long she'd been waiting and I started talking and she disappeared."

Dorin rolled a speckled sourfruit over in his hands. "The One Wife, perhaps. Waiting for the Two Princes to come home from a battle where they died long ago. Or so I assume. There's no evidence at all of a town, or people. Living ones, anyway."

"And Keeper?" she asked in a low voice, looking into the kitchen. She could not see Keeper now. "He said he looks after the Princes and the One Wife. How could he if . . . ?"

"If they've been dead for too long to remember? I'm not sure."

Jaele shook her head. "Perhaps they're not really dead to him. Perhaps he tends their ghosts and they seem alive. I'm sure he showed me those visions. He showed me, then took them away. Or . . . I don't know. I don't understand." She put a hand to her forehead; her palm felt cool. Dorin was gazing at the plants and fish. She looked at him and noticed that his hair was longer and lighter than it had been on the silga mountain, and his skin was lined with tiny seams and cracks from the sun.

"Let me distract you," he said, turning back to her. "I'll take you to the most interesting place in the fortress." His arms guided her to the floor.

She was not certain how he found the edge of the cavern; the ivy and the bubbling, twittering space looked the same to her as they walked. But after a time they came to an arched doorway and passed through it into a narrow, glistening passage. Torches guttered and sighed around them; Jaele saw shadows fluttering between Dorin's shoulder blades and across his hair. They did not walk for long: within moments a stone door rose before them. Dorin leaned against it and strained until the cords in his neck leapt and stiffened like bones. It opened slowly. Jaele felt a thread of cool air against her skin, remembered a deep dark place beneath the sand, then shook the memory away.

It was a huge round room, seemingly empty except for torches and a large glittering platform on wheels. Jaele took a few steps forward, gaping as the sandstone walls spun into vivid colours around her. There were rows upon rows of figures and scenes—rivers of cut stone and paint that stretched up to the domed ceiling.

"Come over here first," Dorin said, standing to the left of the door. "This is where it starts."

"Where what starts?" she said, staring at the images, but before he could answer, she pointed and said, "Oh—there's Keeper! Without his neckring. And two men with axes . . ." Her voice trailed off as she moved closer.

"It's the history of the palace," Dorin said. "This could be considered the library. You have to climb up onto the platform to see it all. It's such a long history that I've only really looked at the beginning and end. Here," he went on, and she followed him to a place across from the door.

It was Keeper, again without his neckring, standing with a richly gowned woman; he was touching her cheek, and her hand was on his. In the next image he was kneeling before the Two Princes; both men were pointing at him, eyes wide and raging beneath circlets of bronze. In the next, Keeper was at an anvil, his arm raised high; then kneeling once more, while he and the woman fastened the black ring he himself had made around his thick tree neck.

"Ah," Jaele said, "it was a punishment—he loved the One Wife." The images enfolding, strange, warm.

"Is she the one you saw?" Dorin asked, and she shook her head.

"No. Maybe I could find her if I had time." She traced her finger along the lines of Keeper's bent head. "Poor man. They Bound him and he served them—all of them—for so long."

"And served them well," Dorin said, moving a bit to the right. "See? Keeper in battle with the same Two. He's so powerful that the bodies of those he's killed lie waist deep, and the rest are fleeing. But look at this: here he is with a cauldron. He's pulling out what looks like a tree, and there are birds flying up out of it. Here he's standing in a garden with a lizard in his hand."

Jaele glanced up at the colours that blurred above them. She felt very still. "He killed for them, and created life for them, and he probably carved all this, too, because he is still Bound, even though all of the Two Princes are long dead. Will it end?" She felt hope stirring, in a place beyond memory, and thought, *He is so strong— and there is no one else for me now.* She dragged a trembling hand across her eyes.

She went with Dorin to a curve in the wall near the door. The lines here were brighter and more delicately incised. Beside the door the stone was smooth and red and empty. She crouched to look at the last images and drew back with a start.

"Yes," he said, "uncanny, isn't it? The likenesses are perfect." Dorin's face looking away, a strand of hair curling into the wind.

Jaele's body crumpled over Keeper's shoulder as he carried her and Dorin toward the palace. Jaele asleep with her head turned into the pillow, short hair and knobbly stitches along her neck.

"It's beautiful," she whispered, and there was an aching dryness in her throat. The edges bled away and she almost saw them—the wagons, the horses. Nossi blazing; Alnon slumping forward into his own blood; Aldreth weeping as he opened his mouth to Tell. Sickness rose in Jaele's throat and she fell to her knees on the stone floor. Dorin put an arm around her and steadied her as she shook. He did not speak, not even when she stood and staggered out the door. She did not remember, later, how she returned to her room. Shadows and a high screaming in her ears, a feeling of falling and then darkness.

I must find them. Aldreth may be alive. There may still be enough of them to help me. But I am so weak—and I have been here so long that the wagons will be far ahead of me. And so many died.

"*This journey may be yours to make alone,*" Bienta had said to her by the river. Jaele had told him that she would travel slowly if he and Serani came with her. She had told Nossi that she would wait with the Alilan until the desert. Now she would also wait, here in a palace, her rage and blood-need shrunk beneath fear.

I am here now, with Dorin. He will come east with me. We will go together. When I am stronger.

"I want to do some exploring. Alone."

Dorin stared at her. Then he smiled, a twisted thing she had never seen before. "Of course," he said, and pulled a pink petal from a flower that was hanging by his head. "My company has begun to bore you."

"No—listen," Jaele said. "I just want to be quiet for a while—to concentrate on the people Keeper shows me. The visions. You know I can only seem to see them when I'm by myself—I've told you this." She looked past him at the sun-streaked leaves, the branches that bent and swayed with blossoms.

"Indeed," he said. He strode back to the fortress. She called after him once, as he disappeared head-bent into darkness, but he did not turn around.

She drew a deep breath and walked slowly along the red snake path. She did want the visions. Needed them, to layer hues and sounds over her many wounds; needed them because even Dorin was too close sometimes, too warm with breath and sunlight. But after she had walked alone, she always hastened, almost ran, to find him. *We will leave together. We will go east together, soon.*

Soon trees and ivy surrounded her, and she followed a burbling of water to a fountain. She sat there for a time as the water bloomed from the stone mouth of a fish. Real fish drifted beneath the surface, and she trailed her hands above their gold and blue. It was like her beach—the human silence, the colours, the water. These images endurable, now, because they were an older pain? She did not try to think. She was empty of thought and feeling and night terror.

She walked on, past benches and smaller fountains and birds with huge sweeping tails. As she came to yet another turn in the path, she heard voices. She peered around a low spreading tree.

Ahead of her was a flower-ringed clearing. In it were two young boys and a woman, all three holding double-headed axes. The woman kept hers steady, while the boys' weapons dipped and listed. Her laughter lit her face, but the boys were frowning, their tongues stuck firmly between their teeth. "Slowly, now," she said, "feel your arms as tree trunks and your hands as fish with jaws of metal. Grip, my sons! Swing the way the wind slices the leaves in its path. It is a kind of music."

"But," panted one boy, "there"

"will be blood," continued the other, and their mother lowered her axe smoothly to the ground.

"That is true," she replied quietly. "But that is for your fathers to teach you. It is for me to give you balance and form—and music," she went on as she watched them struggling, "even though you will someday forget it." She looked sad, although the boys continued to heave and swing.

Jaele was gazing at her as she stepped out from behind the tree. The One Wife saw her immediately. "Who?" she asked, hands tightening around the axe haft, and then they were gone.

Jaele knelt where they had been: no footprints, no blade-shaped furrow. "Keeper!" she called. "Keeper, where are you?" But there was only distant birdsong, insect hum, water falling nearby.

She walked again, her fingers trailing across hot stone and cooler green. When the arched windows of the fortress were again visible, she stepped from path to blossom-strewn grass. Insect drone, water song, the scent of flowers were almost— almost—solace.

When she rounded the bole of another tree and saw another figure before her, she thought, *Vision? Dorin?* But then she halted and looked and knew him. He was perhaps ten paces in front of her, hunched over a crimson fruit and a knife. His hands stained with juice; mouth stained as well, as it tore and sucked. She saw immediately that he was thinner: cheeks hollow, collarbone rising from drum-stretched skin. His hair was longer, tangled, and a beard smudged his chin. There was no streak of blood across his forehead. *Of course not, it has been so long, and he can wash and swim, even if he cannot drink . . .* Her heart roared in her ears like sea, like screaming (a tumble of rocks in water; this knife; her mother's throat blooming dark and wet).

He took one bite, another, and she whimpered. She raised her hand and bit her knuckles to keep herself from crying out, but he lifted his head and saw her. Juice dripped steadily from his chin to the ground. His eyes widened and his lips drew back and she knew that he remembered a beach and a girl and a burned-out fire. He rose slowly; the fruit fell with a soft sound to the grass. She held her hands out, trembling, waiting for him to vanish. He took a step back. Then he turned and stumbled through the trees and flowers toward the fortress.

The fruit still lay on the ground. She stared at it. It oozed juice and seeds—real, solid, present. Present. Jaele cried out and ran after him, knowing that she was too late again, too slow, dazed with shock and folding time. She fell into the shadow of a corridor. She turned, turned, and saw nothing but window-light on red stone, closed doors curving away and into silence. She ran on—along hallways she had never seen before, up stairs, into chambers that were empty or jumbled with cushions, axes, vases full of freshly cut flowers. There was no echo of him, beneath the noise of her heart and her sobbing; no trail of blood and webbed footprints in ash-blown sand.

At last she stopped running. She was in a star-shaped room and her feet were soaked to the ankles in water. She had slid down tiled stairs into a wide, shallow pool. Her breathing rang from the walls and water.

"Keeper!" She waded out of the pool, calling his name with every step, until she was in the corridor. "Keeper!"

He was behind her. She felt him there, though she had not heard him come. She turned and looked up into his sun-latticed face. "There is a man here," she said carefully as her limbs began to shake. "Not Dorin. A different man."

Keeper angled his head. The light on his face shifted, but she still could not see his eyes. "Keeper serves all, here," he said. "Dorin. Queensgirl Jaele. The other man from beyond a sea."

She shook her head back and forth. "How do you . . . what do you know of us? Tell me."

"Keeper serves and tends."

She lifted her hands to her cheeks. Felt warmth of skin as if it were not hers. "Keeper," she said slowly, "you must take me to this man. If you truly wish to serve me, you will do this."

There was a long silence. She almost did not breathe. "It is Keeper who must tend," he said at last. "Not Jaele."

She bit her lip so savagely that tears rose and Keeper quivered in her eyes. "You do not know enough," she said, her words quivering as he did. "You do not understand. This man is evil—he has killed . . ."

"He is here. Keeper serves him as he serves Dorin and Jaele. Keeper tends them as he tends his gardens."

She was dizzy. "Then I will find him on my own," she said, and turned away.

. She walked through the strange hallways until the sunlight dimmed and dusk birds began to call from the gardens. Her iben-sight led her back somehow, to the kitchen and then to the library.

Torchlight touched her own face in stone, and Dorin's beside hers. She looked from their images to one before theirs: a man, lying crumpled before the fortress's gates.

"Who is he?"

Jaele started. Dorin said, "I didn't mean to surprise you—and if you'd still like to be alone, I'll go."

"The Sea Raider," she said. "I have seen him. I thought at first that he was another one of Keeper's visions, but it was him—he is real. He is here, though I do not know where. He ran from me. Again."

"How is this possible?" Dorin asked quietly. "How is it that he was ahead of you in Luhr, and now here?"

She gazed again at the image of the Raider. "He is following an ancient path east. This is what the fishperson in Luhr told me he would do. He is tracing the steps of those other murderous Sea Raiders, as I am tracing those of Galha and her Queensfighters." She lifted a hand but did not touch the stone. "Perhaps if I looked at all these pictures, I would find that their armies stopped here before they reached the river. I do not know. But he is here. I may not have to go to the sea now." She felt a rush of relief, and then regret; she remembered Nossi's words, and the map Bienta had given her. "Keeper will not take me to him," she said after a moment, "even though I tried to tell him why I had to find him."

Dorin said, "You cannot expect Keeper to understand—"

"It is because he is Bound," she said, interrupting Dorin. "He has no choice: he *must* serve everyone who comes here. If he could choose, he might do otherwise." She smiled at Dorin, though she did not really see him. "I will look for him now. And if I do not find him, I will wait for him—by the fortress gates and in the kitchen and the gardens. He will need to eat."

"And so must you," Dorin said, and he took her hand and led her away from the rivers of stone.

CHAPTER ELEVEN

Jaele did not see the Sea Raider again in the days that followed. She walked through the gardens, through all the hallways she knew and many she did not. Often she nearly ran, slowing only to open doors and rip curtains away from windows and peer down shadowed stairways. Sometimes Dorin accompanied her; mostly she was alone.

"You believe me this time," she said once, looking over her shoulder at him. "You didn't in Luhr, but you do now. Don't you? You don't think I'm mad?"

He shook his head. "Of course not."

Every night and every morning she went to the library to look at the stone by the door. There were no fresh images cut there as the days passed. "He is still here," she said to Dorin. "I am sure of it. Keeper would carve his leaving."

When she did not find him in the palace's corridors and rooms, she waited for him. She sat in the shadows of the bushes in the kitchen; she stood in the courtyard, watching the double doors that would open into emptiness. She was so still sometimes that her blood became his footsteps, and she ran again, straining toward the sounds that she only later realized had been her own.

She saw Keeper, twice, three times, though always from a distance. She followed him every time, and every time she lost him in the turnings of the corridors or in the mazes of the rooms. She walked and waited and slept too lightly for dreams.

One day, in yet another strange corridor, she thought she heard footsteps on the floor above her. The hallway ended in a door, which she pulled open. She saw a stone staircase winding upward and began to climb, her feet slipping into cavernous indentations. After a few moments she no longer heard the footsteps, but she kept climbing. *I have not been here; I should see . . .* The rounded walls were broken by slits of windows, and when she rested, she gazed down at the gardens. She did not look out the windows on the other side; she knew that she would see red sand rolling away unbroken into a haze of sun. When she reached the top of the tower, the sound of her breath echoed around her, and she leaned her head against the cool metal of a massive door.

It opened silently onto a windowless chamber. The only light was from a circular brazier set in the floor; flames streamed along walls and ceiling. She closed her eyes and thought, *It is just fire— not torches, not swords . . .* She opened her eyes and stepped hesitantly into the room, and as the fire dazzle left her sight, she went cold. Stone pillars stood in a ring in front of her, and set in each one were bones: skulls and bulging ribs and downturned feet with long wrinkled toes. She looked from one pillar to the next to the next. She shrank beneath the hollow darkness of eye sockets. They were behind her as well, fused into the walls, and she tried to back away from their crooked fingers. Jewels flashed and she saw rings hanging, necklets sagging against spine-circles. She edged around a pillar and found skeletons on the other side too: the Two Princes, polished and grinning.

The sounds were very faint at first. Jaele turned her head and stood frozen. She heard a low pounding, a murmur of footsteps or voices. *Too many to be him,* she thought as her eyes darted to the rows of slightly parted teeth. The pounding came closer—a stamping up the stairs—and she looked desperately around the chamber before slipping behind the column farthest from the open door.

The feet stopped just outside the entrance to the room. "Open?" asked a low voice, and Jaele pressed her fingertips against her forehead. Bone gleamed beside her. There was silence, then the footsteps drew nearer and halted. They echoed for a moment, endless disappearings into stone darkness. Slowly, barely breathing, Jaele eased her head away from the pillar until she could see.

The One Wife appeared first. Jaele had not seen this one before, but she was similar to the others, tall and dark and seeping sadness. There were men behind her, their eyes lowered, bearing torches. The One Wife's head was turned to something beside her; Jaele angled her eyes and found Keeper. Cradled against his chest—small and curled as children against its hugeness—were the Two Princes. Jaele drew in her breath with a hiss and Keeper looked up.

She clung to the pillar, thrust her body against the stone despite the arm bone that lay against her own like an oar, she thought desperately—like a bleached yellow piece of wood. She closed her eyes and waited, but no footsteps approached, and the scene did not shift again into emptiness. After a time there was a rushing sound and a high, terrible screaming, and she whimpered because she knew it would not be heard. When there was silence once more, she peered around the column.

A new pillar stood by the door. Jaele's eyes widened as they met the stare of a Prince set in the stone but still clothed in jewels and tunic and flesh. Firelight seemed to lick his teeth and hair. As she watched, Keeper reached his hands around the column; the One Wife raised her arms, and the red cloth of her dress rippled away from her skin. A sickening flash of light—too bright, dead sand and air at desert noon—and flesh seared in fat sizzling, and now Jaele screamed, layers torn away to the fire, the stench, the sound of Nossi dying.

When the light and her own cries had faded, Jaele looked again at the place where they had stood. They were all gone; only bones and threads and the flashing breath of rings remained. She swallowed and pushed the sweat-curled hair away from her mouth, and before she could think more, remember more, she ran out among the columns and past the still-glowing pillar by the door. The smell clung to her skin. She cried out and flung herself down the dark stairs.

The red corridor was empty. Jaele leaned against a window frame and breathed until she could smell only Keeper's garden. "Please," she whimpered, "please—no more fire. No fire . . ." She watched petals falling, gentle as rain, catching on leaves and grass.

Jaele was screaming. She could see nothing through the blood in her eyes; she was struggling, choking for breath between dream and waking.

Nossi had swum with her beneath the boat. She was laughing, trailing a wide swath of red. Jaele's father had ripped a piece of cloth from her hand, crying *"Never"* while her brother clawed at her neck. She had spun into the open wound of the Perona woman. It was purple and wet and lined with teeth that chattered as they tore her flesh. Nossi laughed.

Dorin was shaking her. She saw his eyes in the darkness, and a shape looming behind him, and she put her hands in front of her face. She was sobbing now. He lowered himself down beside her and held her. Her cheek slid damp against his neck, tiny circles as she breathed. When he lifted his hand to wind it in her hair, she made a sound and he lowered it again, pulling her in, in, until she was wrapped against the hard, warm length of him. She heard and felt him humming a gentle song with no words. Her eyes were heavy and sore, but there was nothing behind them—only black laced lighter as her eyelids fluttered. She fell asleep.

She woke to sun lying across the stone and the edge of her bed. She was quiet and still and, for a time, without memory. When she did remember, it was slowly, in incoherent snatches of water, blood, screaming. She remembered Dorin and turned her head. There was no one, of course, and she thought briefly that she had been wrong. But then she noticed rumpled cloth beside her: his blue tunic, which she had held so firmly that he had slipped out of it rather than pry her fingers open.

"Jaele." She sat up slowly, despite the sudden surging of her blood. Keeper was standing in the doorway, stooping so that he could see her. "Jaele," he said again. "Come."

She stared up at him. "Where?" she asked, her voice small and dry.

"Come," he said.

She knelt and drew her father's dagger out of her pack. For a moment she thought that there would be blood—horse, woman, the red of sun and rage—but the blade was clean. Keeper looked at her, at it, and said nothing.

He led her through halls she knew, down stairs she knew. Torchlight and ancient wind and then a space of wings and glass-bound fish. She pulled herself up to stand on the huge table. *I will see him from here when he comes. I will be ready.* Keeper began to walk away. She cried, "Wait!" but he did not look back at her.

Animals stirred the ivy. She spun round, her hand clenched sweat-slick around the dagger's hilt. Spun and spun—and then glanced down and saw the Sea Raider leaning against a chimney, gazing up at her.

There was a moment of stillness again, as on her beach, and in the garden. She had expected him this time—but she could not move. She watched him wet his lips with his tongue, watched him swallow and blink. She saw the glint of his eyes—narrowed, hooded—and shivered.

She slipped down from the table without looking away from him. He shifted against the stones; ivy rustled, and a moth fluttered up behind his head. She felt herself blink and swallowed over the dust in her own throat. He straightened and took one small, careful step, holding his right hand out so that she could see its webs—and she leapt forward with her dagger raised.

Suddenly there was a blade in his own hand. She saw in one glance that it was dark and notched and much longer than hers. But she ran, closing the space between them, and was not afraid.

When she was only paces away, he lunged. She stumbled, and twisted to keep from falling, and he was past her. She wrenched herself around and saw the ivy stirring where he had been. She followed. This time she heard his footsteps and his breathing ahead of her, close, close. She could not see him—saw only the swinging plants and the darting of the creatures in his path. She cut at knotted creepers and could not remember such density before, such jungle profusion. Her foot hit something—stone or root— and she cried out again, in pain and desperation, because his sounds were farther away and she was losing him again.

When she came at last to a wall, she halted. She heard nothing but birdsong and her own breathing. *No,* she thought. *No no no.* Then she walked, tracing the curve of the wall until it led her to a door and a staircase. She sat on the bottom step. *Mother, Father. Elic.* She bent her head over her dagger and was still.

Jaele found Dorin in the Throne Room. He was sitting between the thrones—two identical constructions of black metal that were shocking against the familiar stone. They stood on a raised platform in the centre of the hexagonal chamber. Before them was a hollowed-out pit stacked with fresh wood—Keeper's wood, new wood that would smell of sap and earth below the ridged layer of bark.

There were no windows, but Dorin sat bathed in the blue and red light that streamed through the dome of coloured glass above.

Shifting shades of fire and water on the stone, the wood, their skin and hair. *Alnila,* Jaele had thought, too quickly to quell it, the first time she had seen the red glow. Now she did not. She walked toward him and watched his smile fade as the light showed him her face.

"Jaele?" he said as she sat down beside him on the platform. "What is it? Your dagger—what has happened?"

"Keeper brought me to him," she said. "Or brought him to me. In the kitchen." She cleared her throat as if words would be smoother. "I nearly had him, but he was standing so still and then he moved so suddenly—I tripped, and then he ran into the plants and I couldn't follow fast enough."

"So," Dorin said slowly, "he ran from you. Again."

She nodded. "Yes. But he had his knife, and I thought, when he jumped toward me . . . but he ran."

"Perhaps he was afraid," Dorin said, and she made a sound that was almost a laugh.

"Afraid? Of me? No. I saw his eyes." She paused, then said, "Keeper knows what is happening and why; he is causing it to happen. He took me there—he told me to come. Perhaps he was finally trying to help me, but could not do more because of his Binding."

"Or perhaps," Dorin said, each word measured, "Keeper only wanted you to see him."

Jaele did laugh, this time. "Ah, of course—to see him. I suppose I should also have asked the Sea Raider who murdered my mother to join me at the table. If only you had been there to suggest *this!*"

Her breath was ragged and rough, as if she had been running. She stared at her dagger, at the blade and jewels which caught the light and dazzled it back against the stone and their skin. She was cold, beneath these shifting waves of water and flame.

"We must free him," she said finally, quietly.

"Oh?" Dorin said, looking at her. "Why?"

She raised a hand to the bumps that were smoothing now along her neck. Keeper had cut the thread out, snipping it without a blade. "He is a slave. If he were free, he would not have to serve the Sea Raider. I am sure he wants to be free," she continued as Dorin opened his mouth to speak. "He shows me these visions, and they are nearly all images of sadness and need. He is asking me for his freedom."

"Why do you think that?" Dorin said, in his voice of edges. "How can you possibly assume that you know his mind? Look at him. At the gardens and the palace. What kind of slavery is this?" He paused, but only for a moment. "Jaele," he continued, and she shivered. "You don't think that he'd help you kill the Sea Raider if you freed him?"

She slipped from the platform; her feet struck echoes from floor and dome. She knelt by the sunken brazier and stretched her fingers toward it. She stared at her hand upon the warm, knotted wood. "Yes. He might. And if we could not do that here—if the Raider escaped, somehow—Keeper could come east with me. With us."

"Us?" His voice was very soft, but the word seemed to sound against the glass of the dome. "I told you in Luhr that I could not accompany you to the Raiders' Land—I told you I could not fight with you. *I do not have your anger*—I told you this."

"But you and Keeper and I—"

"Stop." His voice hard, louder now. "You cannot think this. Do you actually imagine that you could tear Keeper away from the only long life he's known? And just so that you will be able to cower in his shadow while he crushes Sea Raider bones, as you have not yet—"

"Cower?" Jaele felt taut, and she blinked to ease the scathing dryness of her eyes. It was a relief, this anger; another layer over fear and sorrow. "Who are you to speak of cowering? You run, you flee, rather than confront whatever it is that torments you—"

"And you hid, didn't you? You hid until the Sea Raiders were gone, until it was all over."

"It's not the same"—but her voice was splinter-thin now. "And I'm not hiding any more, am I? I'm going to avenge them, as Galha avenged Ladhra. I have sworn to do this, and I will."

Dorin leapt down. She fastened her eyes on his brown leggings, which were coarse except for the smooth-worn knees. "And feel comforted? Guiltless? You think it will be that easy, Jaele?"

She felt a crack, then, a criss-crossing like ice. She rose and looked at him, and as she spoke, she was far away and exultant. "Why is it that you are so afraid of me? Of my search? As if you are at peace. Bienta agreed that you were a fleeing one."

"Ah, Bienta," Dorin scoffed, "the perfect man, passing judgment. How thoughtful of you both to discuss me. A *fleeing* one?"

"Yes." She felt as if she had just remembered to breathe. "You cannot dispute that. You fled the Giant's Club, you fled the silga mountain—you fled from *me*. We're together again, Dorin—so when will you disappear next? Shall I prepare myself now?"

There was a silence. Words rattled in Jaele's head and sounded real, a deafening roar in the windowless room. A patch of crimson light lay over his right eye and cheek, and blue on his hair. He shifted and she refocused her gaze, searching for his strong outline beneath the light.

"Prepare yourself?" He laughed, like pebbles grating.

She was no longer far away and anger-dry. She put a hand out into the air as if to steady herself. She had been in the kitchen—she and the Sea Raider, with their daggers. It did not seem real.

"Yes. You must know this."

"But," he said with his twisted smile, "what about the man? The one with the voice, the one you loved?"

"I never said I loved him," she answered quickly. She was almost blind, withered with shame and sorrow—but the wagons had gone without her, and Dorin was here, and she could not be alone. "I never said that. And why does this matter to you?"

He laughed again and looked at her, although she could not see his eyes. She waited. He moved past her and she followed, but when he wrenched open the doors and went out into the corridor, she stood still. After a time she slid down the wall until she was sitting staring back at the dome. Sun from the hallway wove in the air beside her. She wrapped her arms around herself to stop the shaking which she could see but not feel. Her dagger lay beside her; she did not touch it.

She rose much later. The dais that had been light-soaked was dark; the thrones swept shadow toward her. As she walked slowly away from the chamber, the moon silvered her hair and skin like frost.

She saw Dorin sometimes in the days that followed, edging around stone and trees with his head bent, melting from corners into shade. She did not follow him or call out; it was enough that he was still there to be seen. The Raider was still there as well, though she did not see him. She looked at the library stone beside the door and found it empty, morning after morning, night after night. Still there.

She sought again, despite the helpless certainty that she would not find. As she wandered alone, the palace voices grew louder; they hummed and crackled, and she fell asleep with them ringing in her ears. She no longer saw distinct forms, as she had earlier—only trailing lines of colour and whorls like moving cloth or limbs. After a time she became accustomed to the confusion, and as she passed her days in solitude, it was more and more a comfort. Weeping and laughter that she did not recognize: she could drown in these voices.

Keeper also came to her, solid beneath the blurred muttering. He brought her sweetbread and fruit, and soft green tunics with belts and leggings—even, once, flat shoes with buttons. She would feel his shadow upon her in the sunlight and see him over her shoulder and smile her hope and her escape to his mountain face. She no longer asked him to lead her to the Sea Raider; instead she spoke to him of freedom.

"I could help you," she said once. "I could help to Unbind you somehow, if you allow me to. Then you could choose whom to serve." He looked down at her, then walked in long slow strides away.

He serves me now, she thought as the voices jabbered and cried. *He serves me. He will serve me better when he is free. He will help me. Dorin will see that I am right, Keeper will be our strength because I will save him, I will find a way to Unbind him.* And then she would catch sight of the black ring and remember the stone pictures of his Binding, and she would moan and close her eyes against the people she could almost see, and those others she would see too clearly.

She went to the library and gazed at the Sea Raider's image so intently that sometimes he seemed to move: breathing, blinking, lifting his eyes to look at her as he had in the garden. As he had on her beach, long ago, before a girl had danced, before daggers and flame had shone in the sky above a marsh. She ran her fingers lightly along Keeper's powerful arms and torso, his black neckring, his fingers curled around axe or bird. She looked at the pictures of Keeper and the Sea Raider and felt hope, rage, old and bruised.

One morning Jaele woke to silence. It was grey beyond her window, and she heard the sound of her own breathing above the rain. "Dorin?" she whispered, and "Keeper?" But she was alone, truly alone, and she gasped at the sound of her feet touching the floor.

The corridor was quiet except for water. She walked slowly, turning her head from side to side and widening her eyes so she would not blink away a drift of colour. She wandered around corners and beneath doorways, and the darkness thickened. When she finally heard a noise, she stopped. An unfamiliar hallway; a woman's voice. She began to walk again, following the voice beneath arches until she came to a closed door.

The woman was crying. Jaele put her ear against the wood and heard it quite clearly: muffled sobs, words broken between. A low, low sound as well, constant as singing. Jaele pushed slightly and the door opened.

She was blinded at first: there was sunlight in the room, dazzlingly white, and she pressed her palms against her eyes. When she could see more clearly, she eased her head around the frame.

The One Wife was standing by the window. Her fingers were on the ledge, pressing ivy leaves into hollow shapes. Jaele saw her instantly—her hand and dress and the glistening wetness of her cheeks. It was the man—the deep singing voice—she turned to next, and her own fingers dug splinters from the door.

Keeper was kneeling before the One Wife. Even on his knees, he was rock or tree. One hand was cupped around her cheek, curled into her hair. His face was close to hers, breathing, murmuring, and Jaele saw that he too was weeping. She saw as well, moments later, that his neck was bare.

"No," she heard the One Wife say, very clearly now, "there is too much danger for you, Maruuc," and then he rose and drew her up against his chest and lowered his face to hers so that she could no longer speak.

"Maruuc." Jaele whispered only, but their heads lifted and she froze beneath his eyes, which were dark and furious, and which she had never seen. The One Wife gazed at her; her mouth opened, but she was silent. They all stood still. The ivy rustled, a cloth wall hanging flapped; sunlight eddied over the bright cushions on the floor and corner bed.

When a hand clamped around her shoulder and neck, Jaele cried out. Keeper was behind her, above her, looming in the darkness of the corridor. She shrank from his face and the ring that gleamed black at his throat, and twisted again to the chamber. Maruuc and the One Wife were clutching each other, turned wide-eyed to the door. The woman reached out a hand. "Maruuc?" she said in a child's voice, and the man who held her shouted, "No!" Then their skin and clothing shimmered and thinned, and their outstretched hands and staring eyes trembled away, and there was just a sunlit room and Keeper standing with his head bowed.

"Maruuc," Jaele whispered again, and Keeper raised his head so quickly that she stepped back until her spine was flat against the door frame.

"No," he said, and his voice was the same as ever. "Only Keeper, who serves."

"I'm not afraid of you," she said—words wavering with her lie— "and I must speak. You have been creating these visions for me, then taking them away before I can do anything—except for the first time, the One Wife. Were you surprised that she could see me? Were you testing me? You show me these things—why not Dorin?" She looked up into his face. "And you brought me to the kitchen to find the Sea Raider. You want to help me, but you cannot while you are Bound. You cannot speak your heart. Your Binding is death. This place is death, despite your gardens and your birds." She drew a quick, shallow breath. "You know that I need you as much as you need me. Let me help you, Maruuc. Please." Her teeth were rattling, and she clenched them in what was almost a smile.

Keeper was looking at her—she was sure, even though she could not see his eyes (again, always the shadowed bone). "No," he said. "The birds and water and walls. The green garden and dark rain."

"Say *I*," Jaele interrupted, and her voice broke and leapt. "Say *my* black neckring, *my* solitude, *my* love."

His hands came down. He lifted her slowly, so that she hardly noticed until her eyes were on his great brown mouth. "Keeper is Bound," he said, and she felt his voice in her bones and skin. "Always." Jaele drew a breath and he shook her, though gently. "Strong girl—listen. Keeper serves Jaele, with time that flows backward and around. Serves Jaele." He lowered her to the floor and her legs were water. He kept his hands about her until she could stand. "Now," he went on, and pointed down the corridor, "go. Go now."

She went, walking at first, then running through a shifting, blinking haze of tears and rain. At last, when she came to the turning that would take her away, she looked back. He was still there, standing in the bright doorway, watching as a woman cried and called his name.

The stone by the library door had been cut. Jaele sank to her knees and felt dust and shavings on her skin. She touched the fresh carving and thought it was warm. The Sea Raider walking between the fortress gates. Out into the desert, beneath a low round moon. He was hunched over, clutching a bag to his chest. Fruit, she knew. Fruit from Keeper's gardens.

Her hand trembled on the sharp new ridges.

I know how deeply you understand the twinning of rage and helplessness. I felt this then—but even as I did, I was not surprised. The Sea Raider could not wait any longer; even Keeper's tending could not save him. The Eastern Sea still called, and he had to follow. And so, I thought, must we. Dorin and I. Keeper, freed. We would go east together, all of us. I would still have the revenge I had spoken of with Nossi.

Jaele thought of the map she had not taken out of her pouch since Nossi had commanded her to put it there; of Galha and the river with her daughter's name; of Fane, with its tall, pointed houses and its harbour. These thoughts, warm and effortless with the Alilan, were aching things now. *We will go east together, Dorin and Keeper and I . . .*

She looked for them after she left the library, but could not find them. Daylight thinned to dusk, and dusk thickened to night. *Tomorrow,* she thought, and slept as night birds sang in the garden outside her window.

"Jaele," Nossi hissed, "wake up. Wake up, Jaele."

Jaele opened her eyes. All visions—the Sea Raider in kitchen and garden and stone, boys with axes, tower fire—vanished like smoke before this one bright image of Nossi. "No," Jaele whispered, even as she rose shaking from the bed. But she followed when Nossi said "Come" and slipped out the door.

The corridor was dark. The full moon threw window-arches of white on the ground and on Nossi's hair. Jaele followed slowly at first, then more quickly as her shaking became hope. Nossi danced through the streaks of light; she whirled and sprang, and when she looked over her shoulder at Jaele, she smiled.

Jaele was silent. She wanted to call out but could not after that first "No." She thought, *She will dance me into the night and away over cool sand, to the wagons with their painted ivy flames.* But Nossi kept to the hallway's curves, and Jaele passed beneath one final arch to find her waiting at the massive double doors of the Throne Room.

"*Jaele,*" Nossi said urgently, one hand on the door. As Jaele moved forward and tried once more to speak, Nossi quivered like water and was gone.

"No!" Jaele cried, and her body snapped as if waking, and she blinked at her own hands on the wood. "Nossi," she whispered, and because she had begun to tremble again, she pushed at the door and looked into the chamber.

The wind was roaring, battering at the coloured dome which now only dribbled thin red-blue. Fire crackled: the wood in the brazier before the thrones was burning. Scented smoke rose in violet clouds and wreathed the Two Princes who stood above. They seemed very tall, and Jaele squinted against the blaze of colour that was their jewels and bronze. Between them was the One Wife, tiny before the clawing black thrones. Her head was raised, but her eyes were wide with fear, and Jaele looked to the front of the dais and knew with a sudden savage joy what she would see.

Maruuc was there, kneeling with his hands chained behind him. Blood beaded his wrists and fingers, and his naked back was patterned dark and glistening. Jaele could not see his face, which was turned up. She supposed he was looking at the One Wife, steadily and maybe smiling.

"Maruuc," one of the Princes cried, his voice wavering above the wind, "it is only because we"

"have need of you," the other continued, "that we will not kill you. You are"

"mighty in battle, and possess knowledge of rain and growing that is necessary to"

"our survival. But bear in mind that if we could, we would"

"crush you and throw your bones to the sand lizards. Therefore we have ordered your Binding with this collar of your own fashioning."

The Two Princes turned to the woman and waited. Slowly, still gazing at Maruuc, she lifted the black ring in both hands until it shone empty in the air between them.

"You will be Bound. You will hold one end of the ring, and the"

"One Wife will hold the other, and when it is done, she will be sent into the desert at noon in"

"garments of black, and she will wander and be picked clean by wind and sand and"

"teeth. But you will serve us and our sons and our long line until it is no more, and even then you will live and serve"

"any man or woman who enters this place, and you will live for all passings in your gardens and your empty rooms."

They were smiling. Jaele saw their teeth through the smoke and thought of the tower room and the yellow bone. Together the men grasped the One Wife's arms and lowered her to the floor beside Maruuc. Together they said "Rise," and he did, laboriously, so that the writings on his back twisted open like mouths. "The chains," they said, and she drew a key from her dress and fitted it, shaking, to his wrist chains, which fell to the floor in thunder above the wind.

"Do not try"

"to run, man of no name, or we will kill her now, before your eyes"—and the lovers stood together, very still, each holding one end of the neckring.

"You have forged well, at our command, and the metal is still living. It will"

"squirm like a snake when it is placed around your neck, and you will both pull it until the Binding is complete. You, beast-woman, will place it there now." And, when she did not move, "*Now.*"

It was like a fever, Jaele thought later: Nossi and the smoke and wind, the chamber that tipped in the heat, this scene for which she had longed. She raised a hand, infinitely slowly, and looked at it, watched its fingers bending back and forth at some command in her head that she could not remember giving. She looked again at the people who seemed too far away: Maruuc and the One Wife in front of the thrones, Nossi and Aldreth on their horses, her parents and brother on the sand. Keeper *would* serve, he would cut them down at her word—and the One Wife was drawing the ring around his bent head while the Two Princes laughed and cried "Now!" and Jaele screamed "No, Maruuc, Maruuc!" and ran toward them all.

She saw the woman's eyelashes clumped dark and wet, and the raw edges of Maruuc's wounds. They were looking at her, and for a moment everyone was motionless. In that moment her own fingers strained for the writhing band and fastened on it. There was a sound above the wind—a jagged crash, a first splintering—

but she knew only that the hot metal was scalding her skin and that she must hold on.

"No," she whimpered, and pulled the ring away from the One Wife. With her other hand she clawed at Maruuc's neck, where the collar had already sunk into his flesh. He cried out once, and then Keeper was there beside them, reaching for them and bellowing until Jaele could hear nothing else and see nothing except the cavern of his throat.

"It's too late!" she screamed as he towered. "I've touched it, I've stopped it, and you *let me do it!*" Maruuc was weeping and looking beyond her at the One Wife. "You let me do it, Maruuc—you are Unbound." And then he had her. He raised her lashing and she looked into his face, and he cried "Never!" and the word was hot wind against her cheeks. The sound of crumbling grew louder and she was liquid with fear, but just before he let her fall and the world broke apart, he tipped his face and she saw his eyes.

When she raised her head from the floor, they were all gone. As she lay still, the dome above her shattered and the wind caught red and blue glass and spun it like snow. Crimson stone began to fall, ripping in boulder pieces from the walls, and she rose and ran as they crumpled the ground and the thrones and the wood, which was grey. She ran, and the gardens and rooms bled together. She ran through a rain of blossoms that turned to ash before they settled on the earth; through an underground hallway, past rooms stacked with tipping jugs and crashing metal; through leaves shrivelling and dust. She ran along a darkening garden path, past birds swallowed by crumbling fountains, water spilled and drying to sand. She ran by her own room, where glass vials sang and flagstones gaped. Through a vast chamber: ivy stripped away and glass broken, fish drowning in air. People—thousands of them, on every path and in every hallway—cried out and fell suddenly, finally silent. She too cried out as she saw their colours die against the stone. At the last, before she ran out the double doors into the desert, she saw Keeper in the library, hacking into the stone by the door an image of a girl and an unbound man and the end of all things.

CHAPTER TWELVE

"Run!" cried Dorin. He was beside her, bending low to the ground and shielding his face with his arms; she saw him briefly before red dust howled into her eyes and mouth. He pulled her to her feet and they stumbled into the wind while the earth buckled and the palace spat rock at the black-red sky. There was a wailing—not wind, not Jaele—and she looked back as they slithered away.

"Dorin!" she cried, and lunged for him. He turned and they stood for a moment, trembling against one another, watching the storm advance.

An undulating column of darkness stretched from earth to sky. It moved in devouring circles toward the palace, which already lay like broken bones on the sand. The wailing grew so high that the inside of Jaele's head flamed deaf-white and her own voice burned her throat but was lost. Sand rose in sheets above their heads and the shadow fell over them until the light was underwater-ghostly. Dorin grasped her wrists and mouthed "Down," and they plunged to their stomachs.

There was grit in her mouth, on her lips, rough between lashes and lids. She felt Dorin's arm across her back and was safe—enough air beneath the living sand, numb darkness, and this weight of him. They lay together in the shrieking, lashing wind until the column spun its way around them and faded.

Jaele did not remember falling asleep, but when she lifted her head and rubbed her clogged eyes open, it was day. She sat up and squinted into the sunlight. After a moment she saw Dorin standing atop the dune hill. She rose and went toward him, her feet slipping along the sand as they had when she was a child. He did not turn, though he must have heard her. He was smiling slightly.

"I assume you have accomplished this, somehow," he said, and swept his arm before him. "There's nothing left, Jaele, not even a rock. Just *look*."

The sand was smooth, rolling softly in places, unbroken by stones. It stretched out before them like an empty sea: no gates, no gardens, no Maruuc striding across the sand to her. Jaele felt her throat close and open over tears—old tears of bitterness, sorrow, anger. She remembered the earth silga and thought, *I freed Keeper, yet he is not with me. He will not serve. Unbound and gone; another who will not be beside me to the ocean. My dagger gone as well, and my father's cloak, my seagreen bag*—and new tears rose and trembled in her eyes.

She shifted slightly and felt something against her skin, metal snagged on the underside of her tunic. "Dorin," she said, "wait—look," and she drew the twisted black of Keeper's neckring from where it had caught in the cloth he had stitched for her. Dorin did not touch it when she held it out to him. She looked at her hand—at the place where the metal had burned—but it, like the sand, was unmarked. Then she remembered Keeper's plants and red stone, and his birds and fish; she saw these images vividly, clearly, without the thread of her own pains beneath. She looked at the smooth, quiet sand and almost smiled over the regret that remained, like a song of insects or water.

"He looked at me," she said softly, "at the end—he lifted me. He is Unbound, as he wanted to be." She swallowed and said, "I know it was right. I know." The neckring lay open, broken, in her palm.

Dorin said, "I don't see your Raider—he must not have escaped in time. A neat finish: revenge and Unbinding at once."

She shook her head. "No. The Raider did escape—he left the night before . . . this. I saw the new image in the library. I tried to find you, afterward. He has gone on. East." *And so must we,* she thought but did not say.

Dorin gazed at her so long and steadily that she turned away. When he walked back down the slope, she stood for a moment, blinking and biting her lip. Then she tucked the neckring into her pouch and followed him to where the shapes of their bodies had already trickled away. He was standing above a large bundle. Before she had decided to speak, he said, "Provisions. Water and food. Should be enough for both of us."

"Water and food?" She cleared her throat. "How did you get this? Or were you intending to leave last night? To leave alone." She heard her laugh and its sharpness. He stared at a point above her head.

After a time he slung the pack over his back and began to walk away from the place where the Palace of the Two had been. East, she noticed, and wondered at this. Then she looked at the sand and the red rocks and the pulsing sun, and she cried, "Dorin— wait. We will not see that . . . other place?" The place she had not allowed herself to think about since her dizzy, fevered walk away from the palace.

He glanced over his shoulder at her. "The battlefield?" he asked, though it was not truly a question. "No. The storm may have cleaned it all away, in any case—though if you want to . . ."

There would not be wagon tracks or hoofprints; even the bones might be stripped bare and scattered. Rocks and dunes, shaped, reshaped, burying a palace and a place where blood, words, loves had fallen. "No," she said. She walked over to him and they continued on together. She did not turn back to see the melting footprints they had made beneath the cloudless space of sky.

That night the stars were white and blue, and the moon was so large that Jaele could see its lines, dark jagged threads weaving across the light. Dorin drew wood and flint from his pack and she snorted. "You had everything planned, didn't you? A perfect escape." He rose and reached again into the pack. He threw something and she caught it before she realized her hands had moved.

She knew the material as soon as her fingers closed around it: seagreen bag, folds of cloth within. Colours she could see in the night air, and a smell—almost a taste—of home. Iben slate and earth as well; Alilan fires and horses. She fumbled with her father's cloth and there was a brief glint and the dull sound of a shape hitting sand. The jewels of her dagger shone, and the blade curved gently silver.

She sat down heavily and stared at Dorin's fire-rippled face. "You weren't going to leave alone," she said at last into the silence. "You were going to ask me to come with you. You wanted us to leave together."

"And that's what we are," he said, snapping a twig in his fingers and tossing it into the flames. "Together. Though I was not intending for us to leave with such drama. You're just lucky that the wood I took didn't disappear like the rest of it."

"I'm sorry, I didn't know you were—"

"You know nothing," he interrupted, and he raised his eyes to hers across the firelight. "Nothing." The silence returned, thick beneath the crackling wood.

She woke in pink light to his hand on her shoulder. She was briefly confused and thought, *We mustn't wake Serani.* Then she shook her head and her eyes opened, and she took the hand he was holding out to her. "Come," he said, and smiled a shadow of his smile, "let's run now, when it's not too hot."

He leapt away before she did, but soon she was past him, feeling her body draw up and harden into strength she had forgotten. They ran beneath the ghost lines of the moon, and as they did, the sun appeared, a scarlet band above the flat. When they reached the top of a dune, he caught at her ankle and she fell with a shriek. They tumbled, twined together now, and when sky and earth had tilted into place again, she looked down at him. His face was pressed against her, just below her breasts, and she could not see it—only his hair and the brown of his neck. His arms were around her hips, locked behind her thighs. She lifted a hand and touched his hair so that the sand fell out of it like rain. She felt some of this sand beneath her fingernails and closed her eyes.

He eased himself up along the edges of her body, which trembled a bit. She could feel his breath, and hear it, but she kept her eyes shut. Only when his lips brushed hers did she open them. He was so close that he seemed blurred, skin and eyes and mouth large as if seen through glass. She smiled and reached up, and his mouth opened under hers with a taste of warmth and strangeness. For a moment she remembered Aldreth—vivid as crimson sun or the path of a scar—but Dorin's arms tightened and she wrapped her legs around him and forgot.

He slid his mouth down her neck, biting and kissing and tickling until she laughed and he raised his head and laughed and they rolled each other over and over in the sand. She tugged at his tunic and he at hers, and she arched her naked skin against the warming golden sunlight and his hands. She lowered herself until he was inside her, and he dug his fingers white-nailed into her hips and lay very still. She held his face between her hands and looked, looked, even when she began to move so quickly that the lines of him dissolved. She saw his mouth go wide; she saw the muscles of his stomach and chest clench when he groaned. Then he pulled her down, and at the last she saw his smile and they both shouted and laughed and lay twisted together until the sweat dried on their bodies.

They went back slowly, stumbling and giggling and pushing each other into the sand, clothing trailing behind them like ragged tail feathers. Jaele touched him as they walked—shoulder blades and knuckles and knobbled backbone. He stopped once and drew her to him. He curled his hand around the shell that hung against the hollow of her neck, and said, "Still." She nodded and replied, "Of course," and they clung to one another but did not speak of that place above the leaves. He sang and whirled her and she threw her head back and saw the sky, which was streaked spinning white. She saw the sky and Dorin and her own strong brown skin, and there was such a pain, pushing at her chest until she felt as if it should be bleeding.

BOOK TWO

CHAPTER THIRTEEN

The sun was shining on the river, and on the trees that lined the opposite bank. The leaves were silver; they gleamed and flashed in the light, and hung low over the water so that the tips touched their own reflections, sometimes with a ripple of wind. The trees' bark was dark, almost black, and seemed unusually smooth. Amid the silver, and bending the branches, was the fruit: blue globes which, when sliced open, revealed handfuls of black seeds and thick juice that would stream over hands and down arms like veins or the tracings of a river delta.

That was the other side of the river: silver rustling and ripeness and tall shoots of green that were very bright against the black of bark. This side of the river was different. No trees grew here—only small grain plants that had been coaxed from the damp earth beside the water. The ground was the dusty gold of desert fringe; the houses rose like rounded red hillocks of sun-baked river mud and brittle grasses. Flatboats lay pulled up onto the bank; they were dry, in the blinding daylight, but at dusk they would be poled out over the water, toward the blue fruit that hung ready each evening for cutting or bobbed, already fallen. For now the river was empty except for leaves and occasional wind-driven glimpses of cloud.

There was a deep silence; only, once or twice, a sound like sighing from the trees on the opposite bank, and gentle water on the earth. Jaele was alone, breathing as slowly as sleep. All of the villagers were inside their clay houses; in late afternoon they would stir and stretch and emerge to greet each other. They were large, solid people, dark as wet ground but with a sheen of blue that came from ages spent harvesting and opening the fruit they named "lynanyn." Themselves they named "shonyn," and as Jaele began to learn their language, she discovered that this meant "fruit of moment."

She and Dorin had arrived at the shonyn village exhausted, without food or water; these they had finished, although they had been careful to eat and drink only as much as was necessary. They had not expected the desert to go on as it had, limitless, blazing each day under a sky that held only dry white clouds. She had looked ahead for a mound of stones that could have been a well, but there was just an empty and unchanging sweep of sand. Her map remained in her pouch. *We are already lost,* she thought, remembering the formless red brush strokes of desert. The Sea Raider had been a day ahead—and now? They walked east, though they did not speak of this; east, though this was not as important as it had been.

One morning, as they ran toward the rising sun that was still pale, they saw a distant mass of cloud. They stopped and stared. It seemed to be rolling toward them like a wall of water. "Rain!" Jaele cried, but Dorin frowned.

"I don't think so."

They stood close together. She watched his face and could feel it beneath her fingers, even though she was not touching him. The cloud sped; it was spreading and red-brown, shot through with light.

"Dorin . . . ?" she said uncertainly, and he clutched her hands.

"Listen to me. We're going to go back to our packs. When we get there, we'll hold on to them and each other, very tightly. Now run."

As they raced back the way they had come, what little sunlight there was darkened again to night. Their packs were almost invisible against the ground. Dorin and Jaele fell to the sand. She drew the cloth bundles against her, and he wrapped his arms around her and said into her ear, "Try not to breathe through your mouth, and keep your face turned to the side." They lay together and she remembered that it was not so long ago that they had huddled away from the sky.

The cloud swept over them and the air around them broke open in lightning. Jaele saw driving sand and boiling layers of darkness before she bent her head to her chest. She pressed herself against Dorin, curled like a leaf or a fist. When she felt the first wild lurch, she looked up.

Grit stung her eyes, and she blinked it furiously away, then screamed until the inside of her mouth was choked with sand. They were spinning high over the ground, and the dune-crested earth was slanting away, and the cloud around them was warm and groping and splintered into red like eyes. She saw the tilting earth—and suddenly a figure behind and below them, blurred by cloud and wind. He was looking up at them; she saw the paleness of his face. She screamed again. Then Dorin's arms tightened so that her voice died and the sand clotting her tongue spat away. She twined her legs with his and watched—although she did not want to—as the darkness bore them upward and the ground disappeared.

Fingers grazed her skin; she was certain that if she looked, there would be wet, sinuous trails along her body, gummed in her hair. It was very warm and, when there was no lightning, as black as deep ocean, and there was a sound like snarling or teeth. The muscles of Dorin's stomach tensed as he shouted, but she could not hear him.

She felt very far away and still, and she later thought that she had closed her eyes.

Only when the descent began did Jaele shake herself again into consciousness. The fingers were digging now, kneading as the shadowed sand spun and dipped into sight through the thinning darkness. The red light blazed just before they fell, and she felt herself squeezed so sharply that her vision flattened to black. When she could see again, she was lying facing Dorin and the mass of cloud was flowing away above them.

They lay silent and unmoving for a time. She felt something on her skin and looked down. Desert creatures were streaming over her and Dorin—tiny lizards and scaly worms and blind, hairless rats, drawn in terror from their cool buried places and fleeing the sky. She and Dorin were coated in a gelatinous black wetness, and some of the animals stuck briefly, shrieking and waving their claws before they wrenched themselves free. But they melted away, and as they did, the sun began to shine faintly from the traces of cloud.

Dorin laid a hand on her cheek. After a moment she bent her fingers around it; when they moved to separate their hands, there was a loud liquid noise, and they smiled at each other. They sat up slowly and the black jelly fell off them in trembling lumps. Jaele spoke, though she did not want to.

"Dorin. While we were going up, and I could still see the ground, I saw someone below us. He was looking up at us. I think—I am almost certain—it was him."

Dorin bit the inside of his cheek. "Surely," he said after a moment, "the cloud was too thick and the height too great for you to be certain of this. Or perhaps it was your fear that made you see him?"

She looked at the sand behind them and noticed for the first time a thick black swath beneath where the cloud had carried them. A charred path. She shook her head slowly. She had seen an upturned face: pale, almost featureless with distance. But his face, his body shimmering flat against the dunes. She remembered the

Throne Room then—Dorin's anger and her own—and was afraid. *We must not fight again.* She wrapped her slippery arms around her knees.

"Yes," she said. "Perhaps."

Dorin wound his fingers in her hair and drew her to him. "It is us now, Jaele," he said after he had kissed her. "Not him. Not any more." *But there is still the sea,* she thought quickly, before she layered silence over protest and fear.

The sun climbed and burned, and as it did, the wetness on their skin and on the cloth of their packs dried and cracked away until it lay on the sand like shattered pottery. Dorin sang, "A man in the desert held out his hand, but it like me was made of sand . . ." She laughed, remembering the siri bird grove, the shining threads.

They began to walk. She did not think. She took small, unsteady steps and knew that Dorin's hand was around hers.

Even when only a trickle of water and a few dried bits of food remained in their sacks, Jaele moved in joy that stripped away her skin and made her nerve-endings pulse against the air. There was a beautiful searing clarity to the sun on her skin and Dorin's, and to the sweat that shone before it dried.

I forgot my journey: where I had been, where I had sworn to go. Everything I described to you, when first you asked for my words, and everything I have described this time—I forgot it all. I forgot you: your yearning, your ocean song, your kindness. You, and Murtha the earth silga. Aldreth's voice, Nossi's dying scream, the scar that puckered my own skin, beneath my hair. I forgot Keeper and the dome of coloured glass. And I forgot the Sea Raiders—even the one—and the ocean in the east. Rage and grief were silent beneath the singing of my new hunger.

She was powerful; she felt it as she walked, as they moved together. She watched his face when she was above him. He turned it to the side and closed his eyes, and he was so beautiful, so helpless, that she lifted her own face to the sky and laughed.

She would wake in night chill and find him leaning on one elbow, looking at her. In the moment before her eyes cleared, she saw such sadness; but when he bent to her, it was gone, and she was never sure, later, that she had seen it at all. She gazed at him as well, before dawn when he slept deeply. His eyelids fluttered as he dreamed.

"It amazes me," he said once, touching her forehead, "that you are there and I," touching his own, "am here." She forgot her questions.

They walked with torn-up strips of one of Dorin's shirts wrapped around their heads. They began to see water as the cloth tugged at their sweat-curled hair; it flashed dark and wet below the sun, and at first they cried out and tried to run. Even after they had watched these pools tuck into themselves and vanish, Jaele felt a thudding in her chest when the next appeared. She could smell it and taste it—she wouldn't swallow it right away, she would ease her tongue and teeth around it and swell green— and she could feel it beading on her, cool and quiet, as sweat and tears and sea were not. She whimpered at its imagined closeness to her mouth, to her angry red arms which were speckled with brown spots like someone else's. She did not know if she cried. "We dream of beds and snow, as tramping on we go," Dorin sang. Their bodies leaned into one another with a useless sodden weight. Only at night, when it was star-point clear and cold, did they wake and touch with desperate grasping speed. They did not look behind them.

They stood and gazed at each other, after they had tipped the last droplets of water into their mouths. "So," Dorin said with his crooked smile, "now we must hope."

"Yes," she replied, and there were dizzy suns behind her eyes which blurred his outline and made her retch into the sand as he held her.

She stumbled blind, for a time. Later, he carried her, and her head knocked against his collarbone in a bouncing rhythm that made her think of her father and her smaller, softer skin. He murmured to her, and sometimes she heard him. "Not long now . . . the sand is changing, I see brown plants and everything is golden . . . there is a wind that smells like water . . ."

And then he set her down and there was water on her face—but perhaps it was still just a yearning, like the pools that had melted on the sand. "Jaele," he said, "wake up. Do you feel it?" The water slid across her cheeks and down her neck, and more dribbled between her lips, which she moved like old cracked bones. She opened her eyes. There were white clouds and the sky was bright, but not anguished as before. His face bent to her and she saw that he was thinner, that there were shadows beneath his skin and deep lines around his eyes and mouth. He smiled and raised her head and laid the waterskin against her lips. "Drink," he said; "we are alive again. We have found a river."

"A river?" she repeated, after she had drunk. *The wide river that begins in the desert? We could take you to that river riding backward on our horses.* She shook her head to silence the voice, but the river was there, blue and smooth and low in its banks. *No,* she thought, *this is not it. We are lost and will find it later. Later.*

They spread their cloaks over a collection of boulders and slept in the shade from sun-up to dusk. Dorin slept without moving. Jaele woke often and watched him, as she had before, but now it was different; there had been a change as he carried her. She traced a finger along his jutting cheekbone and wanted to kiss him there, where he was sleeping beneath his sun-stretched skin.

They made love again, slowly now, and afterward they swam and slipped against each other and floated on their backs in silence. Jaele did not dive to see the silty bottom, did not hang suspended below the water's surface and look at the formless sun. She took short shallow strokes and reached for Dorin's arms.

When they were rested and the burning of their flesh had cooled somewhat, they began to walk. They followed the river as it twisted and bent; they drank ceaselessly but ate almost nothing. Short green plants grew on the riverbank, and occasionally they chewed on the small leaves, but these were sour and they always spat them out quickly.

"I'm so hungry," Dorin said one day, "that I can't feel it any more." Then he smiled. "Stew and fruit, salt and sweet, we can't have enough to eat / Bread and wine, hunger and thirst, we will gorge until we burst."

Jaele moaned and splashed him. "Stop," she said, "please stop."

On the fifth day they saw the shonyn village. They had been stumbling knee-deep in water, talking about food. "There was the sweetmoss in Luhr—do you remember?" Dorin asked, and Jaele sighed.

"Of course. And the bread Serani fed me that first day—so light and full of holes, it shrank into air on my tongue, but it tasted . . . What? What is it?"

"I'm not sure." He was shading his eyes. She looked too, but saw only the river flashing against brown and sky. "Do you see silver there, or maybe on the opposite bank?"

She frowned and rubbed her right foot up and down her other leg; sand trailed and clung. "I don't think so. Just the water, and we're half sunstruck, aren't we?"

They walked on, fingers tracing circles in each other's palms, until Jaele stopped and squinted. "You're right," she said, "I see it now. Something shining over there . . . and little hills?" Small red mounds, they saw later; they also saw the trees, and the deep blue shadows of fruit on the river.

As the sun slanted and their own darkness fell on the wet sand beside them, they watched brown figures emerge from the mounds. They gathered by the water, and Jaele and Dorin heard their voices, drifting along a sudden wind. The words were strange, and she turned to him, laying the back of her hand against his cheek. "Well?" she said, and he drew in his breath and let it out in a sigh.

"We're hungry," he said, "and we won't survive much longer like this. Let's approach them with our hands held out."

As they did approach and dark, seamed faces turned to them, Jaele remembered other hands outstretched and empty above sand, other words that were confusion, a plea that ended in blood.

There was silence as they drew closer. The openings of the mounds were hung with cloth. A child stood on a slab of black wood, holding a length of string in his hand. The wind blew their hair across their mouths; the water surged and rushed against its banks. Jaele and Dorin walked slowly. When they were near enough to see the people blinking steadily, they lowered their packs to the ground and took a few last paces forward.

She supposed she was smiling. She lifted her blister-scarred palms and tried to hold her fingers still. Her blood was thin with hunger, and she filled her lungs with air that was almost, but not quite, the sweetness of fruit. She could just see Dorin beside her; his hands wavered, and she realized that she would always know the creases inside his fingers, and the brown spot below the thumb of his right hand.

A man and a woman stepped toward them. Their mouths opened on words, and Jaele shook her head carefully, so that she would not be too dizzy. They came so close that she could feel the man's breath on her face. "Jaele," she said, turning a hand up to point at herself.

"Dorin," said his voice to her left, and after a moment the man and woman raised their own hands and turned them up. Jaele looked at the man's, tough and lined as snakeskin, and felt her knees buckle with relief and weakness. She knelt on the moist sand and someone reached for her, carried her, and the earth tipped beyond her swinging strands of hair.

They lowered her gently inside a small hut that stood just beyond the central cluster. Dorin crouched next to her and ran his hand along her arm so that she shivered and smiled and turned to him. The hut was cool, and the hanging cloth blew inward like a sail. At first they were alone. Then the same man and woman slipped through the door, holding plain earthen bowls. There was steam, and a smell which made Jaele's innards cringe with desire. They laid the bowls on the ground by the door and rested on their knees, waiting. Jaele and Dorin glanced at one another as they picked up the food. It was a kind of mash—green and reddish stems mixed into a creamy broth—which she sucked into her mouth with a clay cylinder. It was thick and warm. As they ate, Jaele noticed that, although the outside of the bowl was plain red clay, the inside was a deep blue. When she had finished, she turned it around in her hands.

After she and Dorin had placed the empty bowls on the ground, the two who still watched from the door passed them a wide-lipped jug. Jaele lifted it to her mouth. The water was achingly cold and slightly bitter. She handed it to Dorin and sat without moving.

The man and woman rose and stooped beneath the rounded doorway. Before they backed into the twilight, they pointed at each other and out to those gathered silently by the water. "Shonyn," they said together, and then the curtain whispered down and there was darkness.

Jaele and Dorin lay down together on a thick cloth mat and covered themselves with a blanket; these were the same dark blue as the insides of the bowls. There was nothing else in the hut. They murmured and kissed lightly as cloud. They fell asleep quickly, and so did not hear boats being pushed into the river and long poles plunging and lifting, ever fainter, toward the other shore.

When they woke, there was sunlight on the ground, wavering around the shape of the curtain. At first Jaele was surprised at her body, which felt warm and slow and satisfied; then she remembered the food, and she smiled and arched her skin against Dorin's. He held her hips and breathed into the hair by her ear until she giggled.

Two more bowls were lying outside their doorway when they parted the curtain. In them were slices of blue fruit and a collection of fat, round seeds. The fruit was thick and dribbled juice down their chins; the seeds were tough and meaty and bitter. They ate everything, then sat on the ground looking down at the village. The shonyn were gathered by the river, but none of them glanced at Jaele and Dorin, and none came to retrieve the bowls. Jaele and Dorin watched, close together, their backs against cool red clay.

"Look across the river," Jaele said, "by the silver trees. What are those shonyn doing?" A line of them stood or knelt on gently bobbing flats of wood. Jaele squinted. "I've never seen such boats before, if that's what they are."

"I don't know," Dorin said, "maybe they're fishing? Or gathering fruit?" The flatboats were too far away, and silver leaves flashed light from the water. Jaele and Dorin saw people stretch and bend and turn, but could make out nothing more.

The boats glided back as dawn sun slid to mid-morning white. Two people on each craft held long black poles which they swung smoothly into the river. Many shonyn lined the shore now; when the boats nudged aground, they lifted their arms for the glistening fruit that was handed down to them. There was some laughter and lazy whistling.

"Should we go down?" Jaele asked.

"No," Dorin replied, "not yet. Let's just keep watching—perhaps we'll learn something. They seem to have forgotten us."

Knives glinted; a child squeezed juice into a bowl; a woman reached back to bind her hair with a strip of cloth. Voices rose and fell against the dark, wet earth and the still water and the sky. "I'm sleepy," Jaele murmured, turning her face so that her cheek touched the rough wall. "I just woke up, but I'm so sleepy . . ."

When she opened her eyes, shadows threaded her skin and hair and Dorin's outflung arm. Two more bowls of food steamed beside them on the ground. Sunlight fell cloud-scattered on the village huts. There was no one by the river; the curtains blew gently around silence.

Jaele ate—something warm and sweet this time—and again noticed the blue within the clay. She did not wake Dorin, but after a few moments he stirred and sat up. There were the marks of tiny stones on one side of his face, and creases made by his own skin. "We slept?" he mumbled, and she reached over to touch his hair.

"So it seems."

He groaned. "We sleep and sleep, then sleep and sleep, and sleep and sleep some more . . ."

"And we've had visitors," Jaele said.

He looked at the food and shook his head. "Will we ever be able to talk to these people? Are they drugging us so we won't bother them?"

Jaele stood and stretched her arms. "I don't know, but I'm enjoying myself. And now I want to walk."

They did not go into the village; instead they walked south, over the hill where their hut stood. At first they followed a stream that branched off the river, but it soon wound into moist sand, and then they were once again in the openness of desert. Jaele shook Dorin's hand away and ran, shouting and spinning until he caught her and pulled her down to him.

They returned along the path of their own footprints when the west was red. "Look—we're home!" she cried when the rounded shape of their hut appeared on its hill. He gripped her wrist and drew her against him, and he held her there tightly and silently and she did not breathe.

The shonyn had risen and were again clustered by the flatboats. Jaele and Dorin watched from the hill as some of them climbed aboard and pushed off with the poles and others waved them away. They still did not look up at the hill; even the children's eyes were on the boats. "We'll wait, I suppose," Dorin sighed. "They must speak to us eventually. Until then, we'll eat their food and become intimately acquainted with their sleeping and boating."

"Mmm," Jaele said, and rubbed her eyes. "It's amazing, but I think I'm tired *again*."

They ducked into their hut and slept. When they woke, it was night and there was food, and they ate. River and trees shone with stars. The air outside was cold, and they huddled beneath their blanket and watched the shadows on shore and water through a mist of breath. They did not speak. Jaele slipped in and out of sleep with her head against Dorin's shoulder. Each time she opened her eyes, the scene was the same except for the sky, which was black then grey then coral.

He kissed her awake as the boats returned. "Another day?" she asked.

There was food, of course, and the shonyn below laughed and whistled until their morning's fruit had been delivered and prepared. Then they disappeared into their huts and all was still. Jaele and Dorin slept again. They ran into the desert as the sunlight darkened to bronze and walked back to watch the boats whispering toward the other bank.

It may have been the third day when they woke at dawn to the sounds of footsteps and wheezing. They dressed quickly and went to the curtain. The wheezing gave way to a loud and gusty coughing. They glanced at each other. "At last," mouthed Dorin, and drew the cloth aside.

A very old man was sitting on the ground a few steps from their door. When he did not turn to them, they sat as well. For a few moments there was silence, except for his breathing. He was small and delicate, his skin furrowed with dark blue creases. His hands and fingers were rounded, jutting bone; his body made angles beneath his tunic. He was moving slightly, swaying forward and back. When at last he looked at them, it was so slowly that they hardly noticed.

"Do you," he said in a deep, steady voice, "speak the Queenstongue?"

His accent was strange, but the words were clear and precise. Jaele answered, "Yes," without hesitation, then halted in surprise. "So," she continued after she had blinked at him a few times, "why did you not speak to us when we first came to you by the river?"

"Ah," he replied, "my old comrades and I heard only your names. We decided that you had Queenstongue accents, from what we could remember, but we were sitting too far away from you. We did not have the will to rise. Do I speak sufficiently? Good, then. Also, we expected that you would come to us, which you have not done, forcing me to labour to you myself." He smiled and turned his gaze back to the village.

"I will answer questions," he said, and Dorin spoke immediately.

"How is it that you know this language but do not use it? What are the silver trees and the fruit and the boats? When—"

The old man held up a gnarled hand. "Gently now. I will speak, although it tires me, and perhaps I will answer. And you will eat." He indicated the customary bowls, and they reached for them as he began.

"Queenspeople were the first visitors to this place. They came in their boats—great twisted things, unlike our own. Cloth that flew in the wind and the loud splashing of many sticks. The first time they came, they stopped these boats and trampled along our banks and pointed fingers at our dwellings. Only when they had eaten our lynanyn did they become polite. The Queen herself walked down to the river to taste one, and it impressed her so greatly that she proposed through signs an agreement of trade. We exchanged our lynanyn for clothing material and jars of metal. Some of it remains, in the homes of the oldest shonyn.

"A few of them stayed with us, and it was from them that we learned the Queenstongue. It was a harsh language, and puzzling in its time-describing, but it was necessary for good trading, and children were instructed, and on it went until the time of my own childhood." He paused and his eyes slid from the huts, up and along the river's curving length. "I can call back that first time of my own Queensboat seeing with such clearness. It came downriver during the rains. The day was dark, noisy with thunder. All shonyn were within their houses, yet I was awake and heard another noise above the rain, and I looked out at the river. I saw the strange boat amidst the lightning and water sheets, and for a moment I imagined that I was still sleeping, caught in a nightmare of strangeness. Then I saw the Queensfighters who lived with us running through the rain toward the river. They were shouting and laughing, greeting the boat. Even their laughter frightened me. But I was very small and overly sensitive, as all shonyn are during the rains." He sighed, looking back at the village and the empty river by the trees. "I only ever saw smaller boats, however—none of the great ones of before. Certainly none like those that swept down the river when Queen Galha and her army came."

Jaele felt her breath still for a moment. *This is the Ladhra River,* she thought numbly. She stared down at the dark water. *I am here. Without an army.* With Dorin only, who had said (she remembered now, in a rush she could not quell) that he would not journey with her to the sea. Dorin, whom she needed so fiercely.

"It was a vast army—we had never seen such a thing. We discovered that this army was sailing to the ocean to wage a war of revenge upon sea people." Jaele could not turn to Dorin. She took his hand in hers and felt the quick warm pressure of his fingers. The shonyn man fell silent then, and did not speak again for so long that they thought he was sleeping. But his eyes were open, and finally he sighed and smiled and touched an age-bent finger to his forehead.

"We shonyn live for a long time—much longer than most who walk on two legs. But our memories are deep and clear, and each day we return to them. We have so many memories, and they are so vivid, that we are sometimes unsure whether they are ours or others'. But that is not important. Memory is our language—and that is why the boats stopped their sweeping up the river. They did not understand us, those people from the tall white city. They traded with us through many queens, but always they chortled, and perhaps they imagined that the desire to trade and teach had been a whim and was best forgotten. So long a trip through the desert for some big fruit—this I heard one man say. So when I was a boy, it stopped. Our Queensfighter teachers departed. One of them, a kind one, came to us alone on her horse and told us that the Queen could no longer spare people or boats. This one stayed with us, and then she too went away. Myself and the other children were the last to use the Queenstongue. We still speak it to each other now and then—because it is memory and real, for us. This is why my speaking is so fine. But we have not taught it to the youngsters. If they know words or phrases, it is through clever listening only." He paused, then said, "And that is the story of language, as I know it."

He turned to them and saw Dorin's smile. "Am I now also amusing to *you*, Queensboy?" he asked, and Dorin said quickly, "No, no—it's only that for days no one has approached us, and we imagined that speaking would be difficult. But your speech is fine and . . . copious, and wonderful," he added.

The man nodded slowly. "It is difficult to know what we will find in strangeness. But there must be an attempt. Also, I am old and soft and, although they tire me, I enjoy my words—a shonyn trait, you will see. And now, youngsters, your names."

They told him, and he nodded again. "And yours?" Dorin inquired. "If that is not an impertinent question."

Their companion tipped his head to one side and peered at the trees, which were gradually edging into light. "It is a challenging thing, for our names are not one or two as yours are, but many and varied, encompassing all of our line and the colours of our thinkings. We attempted to simplify for the Queenspeople and other travellers—thusly the words *shonyn* and *lynanyn*—and as I recall, my name was *Saalless*. Much is lost, of course. But for your grasping, this is the only way: Saalless."

He stood up carefully, waving a hand at them when they rose to help. "*Tomorrow,*" he said, "is a strange word. Nonetheless—tomorrow there will be time for more questions. Yes, and *you* must come to *me* on that day, for I am too old for all this climbing of rough terrain and losing of sleep. And you must come only at dusk; until then I am rarely wakeful."

He began to step sideways down the sandscrub hill, and Dorin called out, "Tomorrow, then!"

Saalless paused and turned back briefly. "These words-after of yours," he called back, "are perhaps the oddest." Then he resumed his descent. They watched him in silence until he had disappeared among the others waiting for the flatboats' return.

"I think he likes us," Dorin said. Jaele did not reply. They looked at each other, long and silently, as the river flowed like singing below them.

CHAPTER FOURTEEN

Jaele and Dorin walked down to the village the next day when the sun was red on the leaves. As they wound among the houses, shonyn nodded to them from doorways, and a few lifted their hands. The two moved quietly through a deep and steady hum of words that were not for them.

Saalless was sitting on the clay bench by the river, talking to several men and women as bony and seamed as himself. Dorin and Jaele stood behind them. After a few moments Jaele cleared her throat loudly. The old shonyn turned to them slowly, and Saalless said, in the Queenstongue, "See now—my young comrades have indeed journeyed down to speak with me. Greetings, children. Come, sit by me—my ancient fellows will move aside, I am sure, though it may take some time, as you say . . . good, good . . . now settle here, and we shall enjoy the vista."

They sat on either side of him and gazed across at the trees and the boats that seemed to hang light-struck below them. "This is the time of surpassing beauty," Saalless said. "Some say the dawn is loveliest, but I do not agree."

"That is because you are aging," said an old woman, "and what once thrilled at dawn now seems hollow beside the fulsomeness of dusk."

"I think," another pointed out, "that it is because we now sleep at dawn. It is only at sundown that we truly see our world."

Saalless grunted. "As usual, friends, your speaking is lengthy and intrusive. Allow Jaele and Dorin to talk, and learn from their own fine speaking."

There was an expectant silence. "Well," Jaele began awkwardly, "I'm wondering why you live here on this dry bank when the other is so lush."

Saalless and his friends sighed together. "The most difficult of our memories," he said, touching a finger to his forehead. "There was a time when we *did* live there, beneath the silver trees. There was much greenery, and the lynanyn hung heavily from the branches; the fruit was more plentiful than it is now. I say *fruit* because there is no other word in your language that approaches its reality. We were few then, and we built small houses from the black wood that fell from the trees—at first only the wood that fell. But soon our numbers grew and the houses were not enough to hold us, and we began to cut and chop the wood that lived. We constructed larger dwellings and consumed fruit which had not dropped ripe to the ground. We cut it, like the bark, before its finished time."

Jaele noticed that the others were murmuring, low, strange words that were quiet singing beneath Saalless's voice. "We destroyed the bounty," he continued, "and for this we suffered. Lynanyn lay on the moss, shrivelled as old skin and oozing rank liquid. It was inedible, even cooked, and the juice was sour and caused us illness and loss of strength. The silver leaves grew dry. At night we lay in our houses and listened to the leaves knocking against the trunks and branches. Then they too fell, and there was only a twisted black emptiness above the green plants that were dying."

The murmuring was louder now, and it wove among Saalless's words until Jaele felt sleepy. She heard fruit and tangled silver—and then desert fires, a man speaking, and she shook herself away. She looked at Dorin's hands, lying still on his thighs.

". . . for we were desperate and starving. We used the wood from our houses to craft flatboats, and these we steered to the opposite bank, which for so long had been a spectre of grim dryness. We settled there and turned in grief to the naked trees and the ribs of our old homes, and wept in repentance. We had brought seeds with us, rescued before the widespread withering, and we planted them in the dampness by the water. At first many grew small and brown and died, but slowly there were plants and grains, and while we waited for them to mature, we searched for fish. It was a dark and difficult thing, this searching. Such pursuits are not natural to us. Now we do not eat fish until the rains, that terrible time of change. During this time the water pushes the fish over the banks and we can lift them out with our hands. But when first we came to this shore, we hunted and attempted survival, though many died and were buried beneath the sand.

"We could not bear to build houses in the form of those we had inhabited before. Instead, we moulded river clay and dried grasses into mounds which hardened in the sun. And so we lived and harvested our humble crops, and one day someone cried out that she saw a leaf growing on the deserted bank, and it was true. As we watched, the leaves returned, as silver and lustrous as before, and new trees grew and spread among our forgotten planks. And then we glimpsed the first lynanyn, and the second, hanging round and dark above the river.

"Although we were sorely tempted to return, we watched only, and waited until the lynanyn were so plentiful that they began to drop into the water. We rowed our boats across at dusk and pulled these out, glistening and ripe, and that dawn we tasted them again after all our depriving."

He turned first to Dorin, then to Jaele. "You cannot imagine the rejoicing that took place after the lynanyn meat and juice had been consumed. We are usually a quiet and calm people, but that morning we lifted our voices high and perhaps even danced. That same day we decided that, though we would not live again on that shore, we would ferry across each night to harvest lynanyn. We vowed that we would never again touch the wooden hearts of the trees. Thusly we have continued. We have not scarred the bark, and in return the trees produce such a quantity of fruit that we are well satisfied. We cook it, drink it, use its juice for dyes and its dried tough fibres for cloth. We are content on this dry bank."

The lilting sounds faded. "Superior," said one of the other shonyn. "Unrivalled," commented another. "Not enough!" cried a third. Someone grumbled, "I do not remember that there was dancing," but no one appeared to hear him.

Saalless smiled, and his head bobbed from side to side. "My thanks, companions," he said, and turned to Jaele and Dorin. "I have answered your question," he stated rather than asked.

"Oh, yes," Dorin said.

"Excellent." He spoke briefly in his own language, which seemed rounded and light. "Now we watch, once more in quiet, and soon we sleep."

Jaele rubbed a hand across her eyes. "I'm sleepy all the time in this place, but you seem to sleep more than anyone else."

Saalless nodded slowly. "Surely. As I told you, we shonyn live longer than most, but near the end of this time our bodies grow thin and reluctant, and we begin to sleep more, then more, until our sleeping is sun-up to dusk. We have a quiet finishing: we do not wake."

"And then?" asked Jaele.

"And then we are laid on flatboats and returned over the water to the place of our first living. There we are buried in the ground beneath the roots of the black trees, and we rest again below the leaves." The old shonyn stirred again, rustling and sighing. "Now," Saalless said, "no more speaking, for we are all tired."

Jaele said quickly, "Please explain one more thing to me." He turned to her and nodded, and she continued, "You have mentioned the rains several times. Why are they so unpleasant to you?"

Saalless gazed up into the cloudless sky. "This too will be strange to you, since you cannot know the terrible strength of change in shonyn life. There is no sun during these rains, and our bodies lose their usual patterns of sleep and waking. We are unable to use our boats; indeed, even venturing out of our houses is treacherous, for our dry, familiar sand turns to sliding mud. Nothing is the same. The rains themselves, which come always in the same season, are different each time. We fear their changing darkness and noise. It is perhaps our only fear."

The leaves across the river were not shining now: no sun, and still no moon. Saalless's words seemed to echo in this clear, quiet darkness. Jaele shivered and longed for daylight.

Jaele was alone, breathing as slowly as sleep. It was early afternoon; this she guessed from falling sun and shadow. She had left Dorin slumbering with his cheek pressed against his arm. They had made love as they did every day now, in the small cool hut or in the sand and wind of the desert. Often they were still half asleep, and she imagined that she was dreaming before he woke her with his hands, his hair in her mouth. She did not dream; she had not since their arrival in the village. She slept in darkness and opened her eyes as he trailed his fingers along her skin, singing, sometimes, under his breath. She did not remember the fear she had felt below the silga mountains as he had walked silently beside Serani's wagon, his eyes shadowed and far away from her.

They ran less and less as time passed, although they continued to walk down the hill away from the river. "Jaele Jaele, Dorin Dorin," he chanted one day, "running up a hill / Dorin Dorin, Jaele Jaele, catch her he never will." Occasionally he walked by himself, and she woke alone and felt breathless in the silence. When he returned later, he always wrapped his arms around her; he did not speak, and she clutched him and thought, *He's back, he's here.* She did not remember that she had once needed to run, to pursue, to seek out blood and vengeance.

Now she was sitting with her back against the clay bench where, days ago, Saalless had told his story; by the river which could not have a name—not until Dorin was ready to walk beside her to the sea. She angled one side of her face into the hot afternoon light. Perhaps she slept. She started when a voice beside her said, "Greetings."

A young voice, and the word was spoken thickly; she was strangely nervous as she turned to look at the person next to her. It was a girl, smooth-skinned and dark and smiling.

"Greetings," Jaele replied. "You also speak the Queenstongue?"

The girl shrugged and sat down cross-legged on the ground. "Not well, and my accent is also not well. But I listen to Saalless and others speaking, and I practise alone. I am Lallan."

Jaele smiled. "Lallan—although the name loses much in my language."

Lallan snorted. "Saalless speaks so much. But his thoughts are true. I know," she went on, "you are Jaele. Dorin is sleeping?"

"Yes. Like everyone else. I don't know why, but I couldn't sleep this morning, for the first time since we got here. The river is so beautiful when it's empty," she added, and Lallan nodded.

"I also feel awake today," she said. "I hope not to bother, but can you speak? So I can listen to your voice."

"Of course," Jaele said. "But then you must speak, and maybe teach me some of your language. It sounds like water to me."

They did speak while others slept, and their words were awkward and they laughed at each other and at themselves. Lallan taught Jaele river, tree, earth, house, man and woman. Jaele repeated these words, and even then, at the first, they felt round and cool in her mouth. She listened to Lallan and corrected her: "*Where* are the trees—begin with *where*," and the girl cried, "I see!" and they laughed and threw pebbles into the river.

As shadows lengthened toward the black trees, Lallan said, "No—this I do not truly see. This *was* and *swam* or *will be*. I never understand when Saalless speaks these words, and now you speak them. Please explain."

Jaele frowned. "I don't know. They're words for the past—and *will* is for the future—"

"Yes," Lallan interrupted, "*this* idea! Past and future. Explain."

Jaele opened her mouth, closed it. "I . . ." she began, then took a deep breath. "It is difficult. Past and future are so important in my language. The past was long ago—or only recently, but still finished. And the future is what has not yet begun: what we do not yet know. *Tomorrow* is the future."

Lallan's eyes narrowed as they slid over Jaele's face. "But this is strange. You think you know what is finished—or what is not, yet? You separate this time?"

Jaele held up her hands, then dropped them helplessly. "Yes. We do. Time is in parts, and so is our language. I cannot explain it well. But tell me: what do you say for a time that is finished? Like," she continued quickly, "Saalless's childhood."

"But that is not finished," the other girl said. "No time is finished."

"When someone dies? When someone is taken across the river to the trees?"

"No—not finished. Nothing."

"But Saalless speaks of memory; that is past, over."

"No. Not over: still. Your word *now*."

Lallan curled her right hand into a fist. "I also cannot explain," she said at last. "It is darkness to you."

They were silent. Lallan scratched at the dry red earth with a stone so that there were furrows; she filled these in with the palms of her hands, stroking until even the marks of her fingers were gone. Finally she sighed and threw the stone high and arching into the river, and it sank while waves became ripples and ripples clouds.

"I do not understand how Saalless knows," Lallan said after a time. "He and the others—they speak like you, without difficulty. Perhaps because in . . . childhood, they hear the words often. This childhood you speak of." She turned to Jaele and smiled slightly.

"Well," Jaele said, "it's obvious this will be demanding. But I wish to talk with you again. If you do."

"Oh, yes," Lallan said. "Even if I do not understand, and I am . . ."

"Frustrated?" Jaele finished, and Lallan nodded.

"Yes." She stood up and stretched into the sunlight. Jaele could not see her face. Then she moved away, ankle-deep and slow in the water.

CHAPTER FIFTEEN

There was a time of quiet, before the rains.

All my days with the shonyn were vivid, but this time was so much more brilliant. I remember it now as a slow unspooling of my father's brightest threads. I know how desperately you yearn for words of air and light and happiness. I must speak carefully when I describe this time to you. You must see.

Mornings with Saalless and others, watching the flatboats return, dark over silver.

✧   ✧   ✧

Lallan and a young man are standing together on a flatboat, poling water that looks like rain where it falls. They smile and talk sometimes, and sit very close onshore.

"Do you love Onnell?" Jaele asks, and Lallan raises an eyebrow.

"We do not speak of love so much, but I am with him now."

✧   ✧   ✧

Days and nights shift—the water starred or white blazing, swelling in sleep and dusk. Sleep, now as much as shonyn; sleep through sunlight, and stretching walking down in afternoon violet. The cadence of speech slowing until words roll and fade away.

"The river's beauty, and the blue of the fruit," Jaele says in her new language, and the roundness in her mouth very soon is not strange. She repeats the words, murmurs them beneath the low red ceiling as Dorin makes spirals on her skin and maybe listens.

✧   ✧   ✧

"Ah yes," Saalless replies, "we fashion our pottery from clay, dyed with the blue juices of lynanyn. We fashion and reap, only in this small town. You must be thinking this place primitive, being of the Queen's stock—you with your cities and towers."

"No," Jaele says, "not primitive," and her voice disappears. She no longer thinks about words for past and future: she is drawing in the new, Lallan's *still* and *now*.

✧   ✧   ✧

"Dorin, you are very quiet," Lallan says, peering into his face, which is turned away.

"Yes," Onnell says. "Why so?"

Dorin shrugs where he is sitting, on the edge of people and wet earth. "I do not like words," he says, not looking at them. Moments later he walks away. His hand slips through Jaele's hair and she smiles.

✧   ✧   ✧

Sometimes Jaele talks to Lallan or the old ones, and Dorin is alone. But always the circle back—to clay walls, to desert sand that skitters over their feet and fills their outspread, tangled hair. No fear and no urgency, and the circle seems closed, tenderness of eyes that do not look away.

✧   ✧   ✧

"Lallan is overly impatient," Saalless says, and shakes his head. Jaele watches the creases of his face open like dark, dry flowers, like gorges. There is slow detail to her vision, now. "She is quick. This is not a shonyn trait. I cannot match her to blood parents."

"Blood parents?" Dorin asks, and the old man turns to him.

"You will not be familiar with this. Our children belong to all, from the time of their birth. Many women sustain with milk. Babies grow among many parents."

Jaele sees that the skin of Saalless's throat and chest is not dry— more like the palm of a young hand. She raises a fistful of lynanyn seeds to her mouth and squeezes them slowly, teeth and tongue cool bitter blue.

✧   ✧   ✧

"Saalless has told me about the rains," Jaele says. Lallan is drawing a piece of fallen green along Onnell's wrist. He reaches up and grasps her hair, eyes half lidded and smiling. "Tell me what you think of these rains," Jaele continues.

Lallan frowns a bit, as if her words will be strange. "The river folds and rises. Sometimes our huts are wet inside. We do not use boats: lynanyn cross the river and flow over the banks. There are even fish. And it is dark, dark."

"We sleep less," Onnell adds in a heavy voice. "In darkness it is difficult."

"Yes," Lallan says, "it is a change. We think there is danger in it."

"Change," Jaele says. "Danger." She wants to go to Dorin, to climb into the warmth of his sleeping limbs.

✧   ✧   ✧

"Lallan—do animals live among the lynanyn trees?" The silver looks like copper now, in the light of dusk.

"Not many, and all small."

"And shonyn never walk on the other shore?"

Lallan turns to her with raised brows. "Never. Why these questions?"

Jaele lies down so that she sees only sky. "Today I thought I saw something moving in the trees. Perhaps it was just wind and cloud shadows."

✧   ✧   ✧

"Saalless's skin is blue, and Lallan's is blue too—but blue for us won't do . . ."

"It *does* do," Jaele murmurs, her cheek above his heart, so close to sleep.

✧   ✧   ✧

Moments unravelling formless, until the clouds.

"Dark," Lallan said in the Queen's language, and Jaele looked up past her pointing finger. The clouds were massed high and far away; they were like unformed clay, twisting and climbing and suddenly changed. "The wind comes soon," Lallan continued, and it did, thrusting at the murky steel sky and bodies that bent.

It was cold. Jaele flinched as her skin rose, as the river scurried white. Her eyes felt wide, and something—awake?—that was unfamiliar. "Will there be danger for me as well?" she asked.

"Perhaps," Lallan said. "Feel. It is different air. But wait—it passes. Only hold the sunlight and you are the same."

Jaele ran up the hill to wake Dorin. She felt her body's awkward speed, its aching. "Come!" she cried as she parted the curtain. He was sitting against a wall. For a moment both were very still.

"What is it?" he said at last.

"The rain," she replied hesitantly. "It's coming: the clouds are so fast. Everyone is gathering below to watch."

"Oh," said Dorin. He pulled a hand through his hair. When he kissed her, his lips slid away and into the strands beside her ear.

They walked down through shifting patches of silver and muddy gold. There was a crackling; Jaele lifted her arms and saw the down stretching, quivering desperately. Lallan beckoned to them from the bank and they waded toward her, through wind that ripped the breath from opening mouths and reached farther, down into glistening and bone.

The distance had disappeared behind black water. Jaele remembered rain in livid walls above the ocean, advancing over the headland rocks and reaching for them—she and Elic stumbling laughing for the hut, their father drawing them into a blanket, his arms. She closed her eyes; in this place of safety a memory, whole and bright. She clutched Dorin's hand and shrank before the wind.

They were soaked, flattened: clothing, skin and hair, eyelids. The faces upturned—blue running darkness—and fingers spread apart, cupped in fear or abandon. Jaele took a step forward. She felt a terrible pure recognition, and recoiled. Dorin's hands slipped like seagreen ribbons over her skin.

The river leapt as if beaten by pebbles. Soon it was roiling warm and white over their feet. Some of the brown plants by the shore tore silently, swept into someday sunlight and covering sand. The other bank—silver leaves and fruit and choked bones of houses—was lost.

The shonyn scrabbled away, small wet creatures bowed to the earth that shifted and coursed beneath them. Jaele and Dorin ran until they were inside, naked and grasping below the rain.

The dark water rose and fell, chewing at the sand until it collapsed in mud and washed roaring away. No flatboats set out over the churning river; after the first cloudburst no one sat or stood outside.

"This is our island," Dorin said one morning or evening as they gazed through a gap in the curtain. "Our island, and when the rain passes, there will be only us."

Jaele pressed her face to the hollow of his throat and breathed in deeply. His smell still hurt her.

"And we will be surrounded by all sorts of creatures," he continued, "short and tall and scaly and flat, who will smile at us and be our friends." They laughed.

They ate the lynanyn Lallan had told them to save for the rains. Their bodies stuck and slithered in juice, and they crawled outside and held up their arms and watched blue flowing like blood. Wet earth scent sank into their hair and the tiny threads of their fingertips.

Each day was distinct in light or sky or wind. Jaele saw white-grey clouds driven low; she saw others hanging still, bulbous and purple. There were no lengthening shadows—only a glowering that sometimes began to shine, perhaps with far-off day. The rain lashed or spattered on the clay. It was almost peace, almost a different kind of lulling.

Then she dreamed, one day or night, and woke trembling. She remembered nothing—no images, no sounds—only a sense of clawing, hands and limbs knotted and torn apart beseeching. She was moaning and curled tightly around some place in her stomach, her chest. Dorin was stroking her, but she could not feel him. "What? Jaele . . . what . . ." But he was already asleep, and she lay alone while he breathed and muttered and turned in the darkness.

"I hate this!" Jaele hissed. "I hate this sound, this rain."

Dorin wound his arms around her and pulled her toward him. "Why?" he asked, touching a finger to the smooth skin by her eye. "This is our island, yes?"

She wriggled; he drew his finger down her face to her chin, which he tilted up. "Yes," she said, and felt a loosening. "It is. I'm just restless, and I haven't been sleeping well."

"But you're happy?" A child's voice—but never before, never even at the Giant's Club, by the clear pool full of snails.

"Of course I am," she said, and held him, clutched him in remembered sun.

One morning Jaele woke to silence. She lay with her eyes closed, sinking, wrapped in air that was still and golden. Light seeping, burnishing the insides of her eyelids—and Dorin's breath in and out where before there had been only rain.

She was blind, kneeling in the doorway; there was sun and searing blue and leaves that pulsed, and she ground her fists into a blaze of tears. She waited a moment before waking him. Her hair stirred in a cool, dry wind. She could hear the swollen river lapping slowly as a heart against the bank.

"It's over," she whispered when she went back to him. He stretched up and into her arms. She spoke with her lips against the place where neck curved into shoulder. "The danger is past."

He shifted and leaned back on his elbows. "Danger? What does that mean?"

She shrugged; she could feel the sun on her bare skin. "Don't you remember what Saalless told us? Lallan said it too. There's danger during the rains. Some kind of change—perhaps for minds or hearts."

He sat without moving. "Change. Ah, yes—I remember. An interesting idea." He smiled—the twisting she had pushed away—and Jaele began to draw on her clothes.

"What's wrong?" she asked, looking at a green thread that was straggling from her tunic, over her thigh.

"Wrong?" he replied. "Why would you think that?"

She too smiled, crooked and disappearing. "I don't know," she said, thinking, *Your eyes at sunset above a sea of trees. The sadness that never leaves you.* She ducked out beneath the curtain.

There were shonyn outside now, walking carefully over the churned earth toward the water. Jaele and Dorin joined them; steps from the hut their fingers caught and twined. Lallan waved from where she was standing beside Onnell and Saalless. "How are you, rain stranger?" she cried.

Jaele called back, in the shonyn language, "I survive, I think." Saalless turned and looked at her, without smiling.

The river was high, and still murky brown from heaving of rain and wind. There were silver-green dartings in the brown. Jaele pointed and Lallan said, "Those are the fish. Watch." Young shonyn waded into the water, hands poised then plunging, and drew out fish that shone and wriggled and gaped.

"Yes," Saalless said, "we will cook the fish tonight and several nights after, then not again until the rains return."

"Saalless," Jaele said, "I still don't understand why you don't fish all the time. Especially if you enjoy the taste, which must be so different from lynanyn."

"It is this," he said. "We do not hunt out our food. The lynanyn ripen and we harvest them, and our grains we transported long ago. You might be saying that we shonyn are finders rather than seekers. Thusly are we different from most others."

"Oh, stop talking!" Lallan said as she rolled her eyes skyward. "There is too much to see."

Birds circled, high and dark and sometimes ghostly in the white shadows of cloud. Downriver they glided lower; they hovered briefly and dove, heads then wings then all submerged before they reappeared, beating heavily upward as two, three fish lashed in beaks and claws.

"Breathe, quiet one!" Lallan said to Dorin in his language. The smell was sharp and sweet, and Jaele half knew it, half named it before she realized it was not the sea.

"Long ago," Saalless began, ignoring Lallan's groan, "the Queensships were billowing in now, after the rains—when the water was yet dark from storming, and the air was clear and scented. Laughing and singing on new wind, and flashings of metal—so strange. Brown skin, cloth of red and green and gold. The ships were like great creatures we had heard of, which rise above the ocean and rock for a time before falling back to be hidden."

Jaele heard her father's voice, a layer of darkness and smiling over Saalless's. She shook her head and sat down on one of the riverside benches. Dorin sat with her. The clay was cool, still damp.

"Of course," Saalless continued, "after the rains there was foolishness—shonyn men and women who desired Queenspeople—although most remained true."

"True?" Dorin asked, and the old man nodded.

"Please imagine—but most probably you cannot. You and I are not the same, and this is why our people must be apart. Those shonyn who did desire went away on the large boats and were lost to us. Their children, I am sure, were never peaceful."

There was a sudden clenching in Jaele's chest and throat. "But that's a terrible thing to say!" she cried, and almost felt tears. "How can you be sure what those children felt? How do you know that the shonyn who left weren't happy?"

He looked at her and smiled a bit, and his eyes seemed very bright—or perhaps it was the sky, the unaccustomed sun. "Child," he said only, "child."

Another dream—the images clearer—a hand in hers, strung with hair and splinters of wood. She woke shaking again, and Dorin rolled over and put his arms around her. Murmuring until they both slept.

The flatboats set off once more toward the lynanyn that bobbed thick and ripe beneath the silver leaves. Shonyn slept and talked and cooked the last of the fish. Jaele avoided eating any of this fish, and Lallan frowned and shook her head. "I do not understand," she said as they sat again on dry earth. "It is so good, so different, as you say, and it is only for a short time—why do you not eat?"

Jaele looked away, into a blur of light and water. "Because," she replied, "I remember things." Now, here, after rain and dreams. *It is almost time. We must leave soon. We . . .* She remembered fear.

Lallan snorted and shifted onto her back. "You *remember*. And it is only fish."

Jaele slept more as well, though not as deeply as before. She woke often and lay with the weight of Dorin's arm across her chest. She lay very still, feeling her skin against his. In the silent latticed sunlight it was so important to be still.

She and Lallan laughed again, and tossed pebbles into the river. *Water cloud shore black wood looping time:* the words left Jaele's mouth like twilit air. Saalless and the other old shonyn talked and talked, their own words a low, steady blooming. Dorin occasionally came down to the bank and sat with them. He never looked at Onnell, and only rarely at Lallan. Sometimes he did talk or rhyme or sing, which made them giggle; Jaele was strangely proud.

"Your Dorin," Lallan said one day when he was not there, "is strange and quiet, but when he speaks, he is suddenly friend-like."

"Oh, Lallan," Jaele said, "just because you can't imagine being quiet doesn't mean it's strange. He's really not strange. Not at all."

Lallan peered at her. "I like him, dearest Queen's one. But he is not maybe for you."

"No—don't . . ." She heard her own sadness, beneath thin, useless anger. ". . . don't ever say such a thing, it's not true, he is for me."

Lallan was drawing a strand of hair through her mouth; it curled and glistened. "Maybe you do not see what is clear. Maybe you discover. Maybe not. If you are contented now, that is all."

"Why don't you come down with me more often? To the river, to talk to Lallan and Saalless and the others?" A long time since they had stumbled along the shore to the town; long since Saalless had laboured up the hill to speak to them. Since they had first whirled beneath the sky.

They were sitting now where the ground was flat and the river hidden. The rains had drawn colour from the sand: green shoots, pink and yellow petals, red stalks that swayed tall and dagger-tipped from knotted roots. The wind was rising cool with dusk.

"Because they're *your* friends."

"That's not true," Jaele said. "They like you; they wonder why you don't join us more."

Dorin dug his heels into the sand, savagely, with a dull sound that made her flinch. "They like me, do they? I wonder why. They have nothing at all in common with me." He paused. "Perhaps no one does."

"Oh," she cried, and leapt up and away from him, striding circles as sand flew. "You are so selfish, you have no idea what people are like—you dismiss them, you dismiss me—but I understand you, I do. I do and you won't believe it." She was crying, trembling, too far away to touch. He sat and gazed up at her—haunted, shrunken, incandescent with sadness. "Let me know you," she whispered, and dropped to her knees. "It is breaking me."

Dorin made a sound and stretched out a hand. "You can't know. What I am—it is too far from what you are, it would mean an ending for us."

"And you don't think," she said, "that this is an ending?" She added, "I thought you were happier, you seemed happier. But you are the same as ever." *And I?* she thought quickly.

He looked down at his knuckles, straining pale while the rest was so still. "I don't know why you would think otherwise—why you hope as you do."

"So you're not happy. Not at all." She was hot, stinging salt and dust.

He drew a breath. "I am. Sometimes so much that I think I am reborn. So happy that I don't even fear. But."

They sat. She was not sure who began to laugh first. Quietly, as they crawled toward each other. Laughing tears and touching as if skin were new.

Aldreth is Telling blood, easing his mouth along her stomach. Her fingers are knotted in his hair and she is screaming. Horses are rearing around her, flailing and spewing flame, and she cannot see Nossi although she can hear her cries through smoke and sand and heavy thud of bodies, strange boats.

Dorin was sitting up, dark against the shifting curtain. "Not again." She realized she was clutching his hands. "I can't share this with you, Jaele. Whatever it is. Whoever." He pulled his hands free and slipped outside.

She listened to her own thin whimpering as she rocked herself gently, sore bones and flesh.

So fragile, now—reflections of sun or cloud in water that moved and broke into scatterings of colour. Tender, clear air. His arm lying terrible, golden across her breasts. The ladder of his naked curved back. Bent head; sleeping, softly open mouth. She lay motionless and watched. Raged against danger and hope and the beauty of his face; against the dreams that opened her like a scar.

The plants by the bank were waist-high and feverishly green. Lallan had drawn a frond down to her face and was tickling it; she brushed it over Jaele's cheeks. Jaele laughed. It was almost dawn. The flatboats were returning slowly, heavy with lynanyn.

"You sometimes look like someone else to me," Jaele said in the shonyn language. "You remind me of someone else," she repeated in her own.

Lallan raised her eyebrows. "Explain."

"A friend I had. Nossi." Speaking it a sigh, a slow thread of blood. "She was a dancer. Her eyes were blue. And she rode a horse named Sarla."

Lallan said, "Why are you sad now, thinking of this friend Nossi?"

Jaele rubbed the back of her hand across her eyes. "Because she's dead. She was killed in a battle. I had travelled with her, and we were like sisters." After a moment she went on, "But in many ways you are not like her. Perhaps I'm just thinking about her now, so I see her in you. I don't know."

Lallan groaned. "Again I do not understand. You are sad that she is dead? That she is your sister? That I am like her but not like her?"

"Yes. All of those." She concentrated on the silver, blurred dip and spray of the poles.

"Do you have family?" Lallan asked, and Jaele laughed shakily.

"Strange you should ask. They are also dead. My mother, my father and brother. Also killed." Not spoken of since she had lain next to Nossi, beneath stars. She looked down at the river with a princess's name and felt the stirrings of an old and desperate need.

Lallan sat up. "Stop. Stop this sadness I do not comprehend."

"I can't," Jaele said.

"So listen to me: these people are in your mind, your life. They are here, present."

"No. They are gone, past. I will never see them again, so I will forget. Slowly, but it will happen." Her voice was high and tremulous, and she cleared her throat roughly.

"We shonyn do not forget."

"Well, then, you are *lucky*," Jaele almost spat, "because I do—I will. That is why this past of mine is so important, so sad and lonely: because no one wants to hear about it. Not Dorin. Not you. It sits in me and rots."

The muscles in her neck and shoulders were humming. Lallan touched her again with the plant: along her forehead, green shadows over her eyes. "You are angry now. Different."

"Yes. I was happy when we came—more than that. And this place was so peaceful. Sleepy and slow."

"Too slow for a Queenswoman, as Saalless says?"

Jaele shook her head. "Not that. I don't think so. It was perfect. Days unfolding, all the same. It was safety. But long before I came here, I had a . . . purpose. A journey to make. This peace is not for me." She tried to smile. "You may have been right about the rains."

"For us they are dangerous because they separate us. They change our days, as Saalless tells you."

"But," Jaele said, leaning forward, "maybe change is good? Saalless says you are impatient. Do you never want to go away, see other places? Do something different, even if you end up where you started?"

Lallan was frowning. "No. I am here. I do not change my feeling, like you. I seek nothing more."

"Then perhaps it *is* because I am a Queenswoman. I think—" she said, and felt tears, "I think that this time is almost over."

They were quiet. The boats were ashore. Hands held gleaming, dripping fruit, voices murmured as ever, other time and all time, all children and all old. When Lallan spoke again, golden light was streaming through the cloud, and the trees were glinting day.

"Though I do not understand," she said, "I can aid you. With lynanyn and whatever more you need."

Jaele nodded and closed her eyes. After a time she rose and walked slowly away through water that was still cold.

They were sitting outside the hut, Jaele against the wall and Dorin against her. The hottest, brightest, emptiest part of the day. "Let's leave," she said, her lips touching the skin behind his ear. "Move on toward the sea . . ."

He stirred and drew away, half turning to face her. She crossed her arms over her chest. "The sea? You're not still thinking about your plan, are you?"

"No," she said, and the lie came clipped and fast, "no, not at all. I only said that because I still find the ocean beautiful, I miss it. But we could go anywhere, anywhere you can think of." Her voice echoed like the heat, pulsing and fading, and afterward an exhausted dampness.

"No." His eyes were almost closed. His hair was golden, some strands white, others red. "I don't think we should do that. I'm happier here now than before."

"But you don't really speak to anyone, you're not a part—"

"I'm fine here. Better than elsewhere. I think we should stay." He paused, then said more quietly, "We have an island here, remember? We can run in the desert or sleep with the sun on the ground. We are alone together." Another silence. "But if you want to leave, please do. It would hurry the inevitable, which might be merciful."

Jaele shook her head. "The inevitable. Listen to your own words. You're happy now?"

Dorin snorted. "Difficult to believe, isn't it?" He slipped his hand into her hair, cupped her head. "Jaele. Please stay. I will try to be happier." He drew her in. He was shaking, and she held him, smoothed her palms across his back.

"I'm so sorry," he whispered, and she said, "No, no—don't cry, love, we'll try," and she kissed him, the salt beneath his eyes, his brown stomach, as insects droned in the sunlight above the river and the silver trees.

She dreamed and woke crying out; reached for fingers, even if torn away, but there was nothing except air, cloudy and cool.

"Saalless," Jaele said, "would you understand if I explained my past to you?"

The old man sighed. "I speak the Queenstongue surpassingly well," he said, "and now and then I feel an entering into the mind of this language—thanks to the great boats and visitors of my own 'past.' Nonetheless, I am unable to truly enter its heart. So I might listen to you and offer certainly wise and meaningful words, but I would not feel your pain. If it is pain you are wishing to communicate."

She smiled at him and could not speak. He laid a blue hand on her knee. "Oh, child," he said, "I see it. But if I felt it, I would no longer be shonyn. You must seek out another for this understanding."

"Yes," she said, "but I am afraid." Again. She covered his hand with hers; the bones of it were solid and round, like stones.

Jaele woke with a start one afternoon. She was shivering, although she could not recall having dreamed. She sat up and gazed at Dorin, sleeping curled and slightly smiling. The river's song was loud in the silence, and she went out to it, down to sit against the bench. Alone in the sunlight as a hot wind hissed in the silver leaves. She wanted to stay awake—wanted to feel again the rhythm of her body in sunlight—but could not. She lay down in the shade on the side of the bench that faced the houses, not the river. Slept in shallow darkness until the sounds woke her.

One splash, two—quiet noises at dusk, but now, in the deep stillness of shonyn day, Jaele opened her eyes and sat up. She looked
around the bench and across the river—and she saw the Sea Raider.
He was wading into the water beneath the lynanyn trees; reaching
for a bobbing fruit with fingers that she saw were already stained
with blue. *"Perhaps just wind and cloud shadows"*: she remembered
her own lazy words as she watched him walk deeper, deeper, until
only his head and arms and the upper part of his chest were visible.
His shadow among the trees. *His* face upturned beneath a cloud of
darkness and red eyes. She breathed once, ragged as tears—another
noise that seemed to echo—but he did not lift his own head as he
had in the garden, long ago. Jaele breathed again, quietly. Watched
him, because she could not yet move.

His hair was much longer than before, and it clung to his neck
and cheeks. Hollower cheeks, beneath the straggle of beard; leaner,
paler than in Keeper's garden and kitchen and carvings. His lips
and fingers were soaked with fresh blue, and blue coiled darkly in
the water around him. There had been crimson before, dripping
from mouth to chin to grass. She heard the wetness of his mouth
on the fruit and imagined teeth, sinking and discoloured. The
lynanyn husk floated away on the water. He swam in one stroke to
the sweeping branches of a tree and reached up. She watched his
fingers grip and twist, watched him gnaw and heard him suck. She
was shaking now. Her teeth chattered; she bit down on her lip and
did not taste the blood that welled. *No dagger,* she thought as he
edged deeper into the shadows of the branches. The dagger
wrapped in folds of cloth, in her bundle. In a hut where Dorin was
sleeping—far behind her, up a hill brilliant with sun.

She did not stand and run up the hill. She slid down instead—
silently down the bank and into the river. Each limb eased into
water with such care that there were no bubbles, no ripples—only,
in her own ears, a sound like sighing. She did not think of purpose
or need or fury; she felt them, deep as the source of breath. She

thought of nothing as she drew herself gently, gently across the river toward the shadows of the branches and the man beneath.

She stopped swimming when she could see him clearly. She saw water beading on his neck, patches of white skin beneath his beard, his blue-grimed webs and nails and fingertips. Three strokes more and she could have touched him—but she remained three strokes away; watching still, hungry for the close, sharp details of him.

He was looking up into the trees. She watched him wrench another fruit down, watched him wipe savagely at the water that fell from his lifted arm to his mouth. Then a ripe lynanyn dropped from a tree farther along the bank. The splash was sudden; there was no time for her to breathe deeply and sink away beneath. He raised his head from the torn lynanyn he held and turned toward the sound, toward her.

He saw her. Blinked rapidly, several times, and narrowed his eyes. His lips drew back over his yellow-blue teeth. Beach, garden, kitchen, river—in each place a moment of stillness. Stillness of mind and limbs and eyes; even the water and leaves unmoving. Then he lunged, both hands straining forward, his body slicing the water into waves. She choked and flailed, twisting away from him and from the waves. She spun, beneath, her eyes open on churning brown, and waited for his hands to find her.

The water cleared and she surfaced, coughing. She looked at the place where he had been, at the bank, the river around and behind her. She slipped beneath once more, sure that he would be there now, reaching. She swam in widening circles through the empty water and began again to think. He had lunged toward her, as he had in the chamber of ivy and stone. He had run from her there; he had swum here, as she had choked and lashed. He had swum from her, webbed hands and feet pushing him swiftly away. Now there was only water, and a blue fruit bleeding slowly beneath the trees.

Jaele swam as well—back to the shonyn bank, where she lay and shuddered before she pulled herself up to sit. She looked downriver, waiting for a glimpse of his head or back, though she knew there would be none. He was far away already, and she was weak, sleep-laden as a shonyn, her seagreen strength forgotten as a vow, a map, a smell of burning. She remembered stumbling from her beach as he vanished into tree shadow, and the memory was so clear that she moaned. Sand and smoke, blood on his forehead and in the water of her bay. Then the forest, the jungle, the wide road to Luhr. Dorin's hair stirring against his cheek as she told him she would follow the Ladhra River to the sea. The iben's song of birds and waves, sung beneath barrow stones. She sat beside the Ladhra River and trembled at the knotted pain that had returned to her.

When she stood—later, her clothes and hair dry—she looked at the plants by the shore, the flatboats, the quiet red houses and the desert behind. Her safety, for a time. Now she looked and almost did not recognize the place. A long sleep shaken off; dream scattering in sunlight.

She left the river and walked among the houses until she came to the one where Dorin lay. She knelt beside him and spoke his name—quickly, because she could not bear to watch him sleeping. "Dorin." And again, because the first had been too soft: "Dorin."

He groaned and opened one eye. "Jaele, what are you—look, it's still sunny—what are you *doing*, waking me . . ." Both eyes open now, his own voice fading, like a body disappearing into water.

"The Sea Raider was here. I saw him just now, in the river."

He sat up. "Oh, Jaele," he said, and they gazed at each other as the river sang and the silver leaves hissed in wind. They did not touch. She felt the deep waiting calm that comes before a dive. "I am so sorry," he said at last. "Are you all right?"

She drew a deep breath. "No," she said, and the calm dissipated. "No. He came from the trees—he has been watching me, I am sure of it. And it *was* him I saw in that storm. He was behind us, Dorin. Following me." She tasted drying blood. "I do not understand. Why following? Lingering, when he must be sick?" *He stayed at the fortress as well,* she thought rapidly, dizzily. *Maybe he can resist the pull of the ocean for a time.*

Dorin said, in his even, careful voice, "He may need you somehow. As you need him. He too may be haunted." She wanted to scoff but could not. He went on, "He could have killed you in the desert or here—even at the Palace of Yagol. But he didn't."

"He had his dagger," she said, "at the palace. And he lunged at me this time—and his eyes, Dorin—I cannot explain how they looked." His eyes, his teeth, his stained fingers and mouth.

Dorin said, "Perhaps he was afraid."

She did laugh then. "You said that before, in the Throne Room. But he is not afraid—not of me." She bent her head into her hands. "I have to leave," she said, over an old fear. "I have to follow him, again. He will go to Fane now—he has already been here too long. I must follow. This is the Ladhra River." She looked at him. "Please come with me, Dorin."

"I cannot." Quiet voice, a ripple beneath. He smiled his crooked, twisting smile. "Must we say all this again? I cannot share this journey with you. And I cannot live with people. With their pain and their need and their noise. I thought I could be happy here with you—perhaps the only place this might be possible. But of course I was wrong; this is not enough for you."

Jaele shook her head; tears blurred his face. "No. Not now—not any more." They were silent again. The curtain blew gently in, out, changing their shadows on the red earthen floor.

"Stay with me," he said, and she lifted her eyes to his. "The Sea Raider may die before you find him again. And you would be a fool to cross the ocean alone. Stay with me," he said, softly. "I am sure that in time you would forget the strength of this need."

She tried to smile, though there was anger, now, prickling through fear and sadness. "Now *you* try to convince *me* to change my mind?" She shook her head. "I need to go right away—I have already stayed too long."

He looked sharply up at her and she flinched from his words before he spoke them. "You have stayed too long? Forgive me: I did not realize—"

"Stop," she said. "Please."

He pulled his fingers through his hair, savagely. She saw tears rise in his eyes before he ground them away with his palms. "No—you are right," he said in a low voice. "You are right to leave me here."

She shook her head again but did not speak. Reached out and pulled her bundle and pouch toward her—other things forgotten, for a time. Windblown sand hissed from the cloth and settled on the russet of Keeper's tunic. She wrapped herself around the colours; she could feel the dagger, and almost bits of green that would crumble like the sand, no smell of sea.

"Farewell, then, Dorin," she said, and smiled her own smile of sorrow and bitterness. She knelt with her sack and her pouch and could not move. They had lain here together, touching, this morning only. Now a dream scattering.

He put his hand to her cheek and she kissed it—the deep threads of his palm, skin cool and shaking. "Farewell to you, love," he said, so quietly that she could hardly hear him. She rose then, before she could see him clear again, and stay.

Outside, the same silence and sun, distant cold silver. Footprints leading to the water and back, endless smudges, smoothed and remade. She walked among the houses and did not look around, though she half expected, even now, his step behind her, his voice crying, "Wait!"

Lallan was sitting by the river. She looked up at Jaele, shading her eyes. "I do not know why—I cannot sleep," she said, and in a different voice, "Jaele. Queenswoman-friend."

"You were right," Jaele said, slowly, so that she would not dissolve beneath the urgency of her leaving. "This . . . he is not for me. I must go."

"There are lynanyn in my house," Lallan said. "You take them. Do you want more from me?"

Jaele nodded. "Please—could you say farewell to Saalless for me? I cannot stay to tell him myself."

"Of course," Lallan said. "Though you know that we shonyn do not have a word for this. I will speak it in your language."

Jaele smiled. "Thank you, shonyn-friend."

Moments later her frayed seagreen bag was full of lynanyn; she held it briefly to her chest before she tied it to her belt. Stillness and no one, not even Lallan. Jaele was on the bank, stumbling through mud that sucked at her feet. Then she was in the river, swimming with her head above the water so that when she turned—once— she saw the huts and the black-barked trees shrinking behind her. The river bent and she was beneath, far from the surface, her arms and legs cutting her away and nothing in her eyes except golden- brown and remembered trails of fish.

CHAPTER SIXTEEN

Jaele walked and swam, and her fingers were stained with blue. She followed the river as it wrapped through sand, shining to a distant flat place of earth and air. Drifts of crimson and gold lit her face at sundown, and still she walked. Beneath star-flung darkness, when the water made another sky. She swam, and floated on her back, so still that she felt her blood, and heard it. Sometimes plants hung over the river and she touched them, and the leaves were smooth or sharp or dusted with down.

Her skin felt bruised by the wind, by sun and dusk. With the shonyn she had seen soft, comforting details: the child's flesh at Saalless's throat, the ridged curve of a lynanyn stem. Now she saw with a vividness that shocked her. She saw the water around her ankles and the minuscule forked tracks of unknown creatures in the wet sand of the bank. Shadows and light on skin, deep and shallow river. The order and texture of stars or clouds. She rarely slept.

At first she watched the river for movement beneath: shadows, waves behind webbed hands and feet. Once or twice splashes woke her from light sleep, and she knelt, looking into the darkness. Each time she saw only the moon-limned spines of fish, or nothing at all. In daylight she often felt eyes on her as she walked, and would turn slowly or swiftly, gaze leaping from water to rock to sand. Emptiness, only. Emptiness ahead and behind. She thought again, *He is far ahead of me by now*—but she remembered the desert and the lynanyn trees, and she slept with her hand on her father's dagger.

One night she found some sticks and small logs stacked on beaten dry grass by the river. The wood was a bit blackened but still intact—gathered carefully from the sparse riverside trees, a cook fire that had been hastily abandoned. She knelt and scraped her fingernail along one of the sticks: black ash, but good dry wood beneath. She looked at the sticks and logs, then out into the desert, where there were dark hills of rock, terraced and looming in moonlight. Suddenly there were Alilan hoof beats in her ears, and Aldreth's voice and Nossi's, clear and pure. Jaele struck sparks from the flint in her pack and cupped her hands around the thin flame that sputtered and rose. When it had caught, she stood up.

At first she did not move. She watched the fire until it blurred; she saw twigs curl and fall and logs blister, and she felt heat on the sand and through her gripping toes. She closed her eyes. Her fingers began: they opened and closed around flame air, stroking its weight, its shape. Her arms wove, swept water and wind and strained up to rocky sky. Her toes and feet arched and her knees bent. She pounded the earth, slowly then faster, and her eyes were wide as she began to turn.

The fire climbed and swayed. She whirled away from it onto the cool sand; whirled tiny in the shadows of the stone. Her head was echoing, throbbing with her own cries, and the hills sent them back to her: *Mother Father Elic Serani Llana Murtha Aldreth Maruuc Nossi.*

When she fell to the earth beside the fire, she was shaking, and sand clung to the smudges of tears on her cheeks. She cried until the flames had begun to gutter; she cried for the names and for her journey, and could not remember having cried for them before.

She slept at last with a knuckle of anger pressing against her ribs; when she woke, it was a clenched fist, bones and flesh feverishly hot. The sky was still blue-black, but there was a sickle of red wavering along the far-off line of sand and maybe water. She untied her necklace and thrust it into her pack. Her eyes were swollen and burning. *What I did, didn't do, because of him. How far I could have gone. The sea, by now. Instead, this.*

The rage was like a skin, and she stretched into it with relief. She knelt for a moment and touched the wood, powder on her fingertips. Then she rose and ran. She ran along the bank, each footfall away, the air still cold and smelling of somewhere and everywhere. The rock hills dwindled behind her. She leapt, sometimes, for breaths a bird or an arrow. She ran until her lungs were white. Then she slowed, dropped dizzily and panting. *I am here. I am going to the sea.*

She looked at her map that day, for the first time since Nossi had laughed and told her to put it away. Now she unfolded it slowly, certain despite Bienta's assurances that it would fall to ragged pieces in her fingers. It did not. She touched the parchment, feeling the smoothness, the surface like scales or fins. She saw no Palace of Yagol, no shonyn village—nothing but the river that widened and widened as it swept east.

An old map, Bienta had said. There might be other villages before Fane; other people who would listen to her, walk with her to the river's last widening. She stared down at the map, tracing the river's lines, and could not imagine or even want these people. *Nossi*, she thought, and *Aldreth*, and she wept again, with her head bowed over the map.

She held her dagger balanced lengthwise on her fingertips. It was clean and cold. She pointed its blade away from her, toward the Eastern Sea.

She followed the dagger with her steps. *"The Eastern Sea is crested and grey, children, even when the sky is blue. Perhaps you will never see it."* She was light with unburied rage.

The river was spreading now, spooling tributaries like silver-blue thread. Sometimes pools bubbled up from below, fresh water that tasted of stone. Jaele lay on her stomach and watched her face: eyes and nose broken apart and joined and smiling. "Water-girl," she murmured in the shonyn language, and thought of Lallan for the first time since she had swum away. The banks rolled scattered green and there were flowers, so tiny that she had to stoop to see them.

One day she found people, in a place without green. She was running; they quivered out of heat and sweat, and she slowed. Her eyes darted and sought—but she knew immediately that he was not among them. The figures were bent and small, hunched over the water. She realized as she approached that they were holding cloth, swirling it before they wrung it out, drops like shattered glass raining down around their arms and ankles. Others were holding children. Rough hands scrubbed dark, wet hair, smoothed it back from foreheads and eyes. The children made no sound. There were no voices at all—nothing except the dip and fall of water.

They had not seen her; they were leaning over, strung loosely along the shallow middle of the river. They wore short, shapeless white; the children wore nothing. Jaele looked away from them and saw the houses: gaping rocks with no roofs, some with only three walls, two. Crumbling bricks of sand slowly returning. Smoke curled into breath against the sky and its gauze of cloud. A smell of old meat and dry, bitter grass.

She began to walk again, between the houses and the riverbank. She and Dorin had approached the shonyn at dusk—but this was different. The shallow, dirty river, people straightening to gaze at her from black eyes. Silence that was heavy and sore.

She had intended to speak, to smile, but her mouth was dry and their faces shocked her with bones. Even the children's cheeks were hollows where lips would slide away. Their eyes were huge, round with hunger or dread that made them ancient. They stood very still and stared—and Jaele walked carefully past them as a smoky rotting wind choked her and lynanyn hung like stones against her back.

"Jaele, my daughter, my breath, be still and listen and do not disturb your brother! Now, if you follow the Ladhra River to the Eastern Sea, you will come to Fane. When Queen Galha rode down its streets with her army behind her, it was a bright, rich port, and its harbour was so full of ships that it looked like a forest. Now it is a place of ruffians and filth; a low, sad place, like the rough grey sea it overlooks. A forgotten place."

She smelled it first: salt and foam and fish, seagreen lying tangled and dark on tide-washed sand.

Grasses and plants had returned, after she left the crumbling huts and the silent children. Small trees bent before the wind. She looked at her map and knew that she was close, closer.

The river began to broaden. It rushed now, rippling with the gleaming, graceful backs of fish. All following the same course, pulled by sunrise. Jaele ran while they flickered just below the surface; her feet felt slow and clumsy. She yearned for and feared the shape of the town, the ocean whose scent was rage and aching.

She came within sight of the sea at night. She climbed a gentle hill and stood still where it sloped away. She knew, despite the darkness: her iben-sight showed her the vast, star-picked shifting of sea water. The river roared, but beneath it she heard the booming of waves. They would be white and laced with birds; but quiet, only a heartbeat from below, where eyes opened wide on bone-chill and fingers brushed spinning green and stone. She clenched her fists and cried out.

When the sun rose, her father's words were false, just for a moment: crimson-gold light flooded the water, calm and still and waiting before the wind that she could smell. She gazed along the path of the river and saw the place where it darkened and disappeared. She looked along the river and saw Fane: pointed roofs and plumes of smoke and, edging along the coast, a thin, empty road. She was far enough away that there was no sound but the sea; no sound, no movement except for the smoke which struck the golden sky and turned it grey.

As she watched, the wind rose in cold, wild gusts and the sunlight wavered behind cloud that was driven thick from somewhere, from the water or beyond. *"A low, sad place, like the rough grey sea it overlooks."* She looked at the dull, smoky stone of Fane, the white-capped, choppy slate, the cloudy distance where another land raised its rock from the ocean. She thought of Queen Galha's fleet blackening the waves, thought of herself, and shrank from the solitude that had been filled with Queensfighters, silga, fishfolk, Alilan riders, a giant, a boy: at least a boy.

I am here, she thought. She breathed the sea and gazed at the roofs of Fane and remembered the army that had massed enormous and invisible behind her on the sand of her harbour. She remembered the ocean song of the iben. *I am here.* And then she went down toward Fane and the Eastern Sea, trembling, bobbing alone in the dark, salty wind.

FANE

CHAPTER SEVENTEEN

Jaele walked into Fane at night. There had been a beaten path by the river—not a road, although perhaps once, long ago. Now the roads led from the town along the coast; the scrub and desert lay distant, connected only by an overgrown dirt track. Jaele followed it down; and as her feet fell on the weedy path, she did not look around her, and so moved past small creatures and flowers and eddying water that she did not see and would not recall.

The waves were deafening and black by the time she reached the first buildings of Fane. There were other noises beneath the sea roar: screams of laughter, a baby's wail, a woman singing—all caught thin and vanishing as spray on her eyelashes and lips. She felt the path harden into stone and realized that her shoes and clothing were rags—rent, bleached bits of fabric that fluttered as she walked. She hesitated beneath an archway. For a moment she remembered the arches and fountains of Luhr and a fist of loss, pushing her to numbness. It was very dark here, despite the points of fire that wavered in the thin windows above her.

There was no one on the cobbled street. She stepped out beyond the arch.

She wandered what seemed to be the main road. It wound down beside the river, branching into smaller streets that disappeared around corners or hillsides into gloom. Voices echoed and died. Carved faces leered above towering wooden doors. Occasionally there were smells: the salt, always, and rot, and cooking that made her stomach clench—fish, and once or twice seagreen. She breathed it in and felt sore.

The wind raised bumps on her flesh. She remembered, trying not to, all places of warmth—even a winter clearing, snow on Aldreth's hair in the morning. She stood still as voices and footsteps behind her grew louder and shadows loomed on the walls. They sped past her, perhaps eight, black-clothed and open-mouthed. *Not him—of course not,* she thought; but as in the marketplace of Luhr and the Palace of Yagol, every shadow would be him.

Street and river sloped toward the ocean. The buildings were lower now, and she could see that they were brightly painted, though bare in places. She heard creaking timbers and almost ran, her feet slipping over the cobbles. Ahead of her she saw the river's mouth, and a crumbling tower beside it—and then she burst from the street and onto harbour planks.

It was a wide harbour, not as sheltered as her own. Across the river, Jaele saw nothing but empty water and dark shore. To her right was a row of houses and shuttered shops; before her were the docks.

"Its harbour was so full of ships that it looked like a forest." She walked slowly toward the four ships that rose and dipped with the waves. They were large, peeling, splintered, and their lashed sails flapped pale and gentle as distant wings. She leaned down to touch one. The ribbed salt wood was not the same—old and rotten—but still her breath caught in her throat. She put her fingers to her mouth and tasted sea. Then she lay on the knotholed deck, felt it

hard against her backbone as she looked up at the stars and half-clouded moon that were so white and so arm's-length clear: in the desert, yes, on the silga mountain, yes, but more and truer here. *I have followed the Ladhra River to Fane.* No need to look at her map, except to trace distance and wonder.

She slept beneath the jutting window ledge of a tall house. It was set apart from the others, and its door opened onto the far end of the wharf. Slept, and woke to shouting and the red sun, huge over the rim of sea. The water shone flat and scarlet and she blinked, groaned as she moved. The shouting came from a few men who stood on the docks and boat decks, untying sails and knotting rope as thick as the trunks of young trees. As Jaele watched, crates and barrels were passed up by bulging arms already slick with sweat. These men called to one another in words she would have understood had she been closer. She thought it strange that there were only six or seven of them; stranger still that after all their bustling, only one of the ramshackle ships cast off and crawled northward out of the harbour.

She crouched beneath the window after the ship had creaked out of sight. The remaining men clustered together, then drifted back into the town. She was again alone. As had happened the day before, she saw the dazzle of sun and water fade into blue sky that soon darkened. Only dawn and deepest night were vivid, she would discover; the rest was a shifting grey gauze that just sometimes was touched by brightness.

As she was preparing to rise, easing her limbs outward, the door beside her swung open. A brightly clad man emerged and stared down at her. She squinted at his shades of red, green, yellow, and turned her gaze to his face. This was all nose and lips, framed by white-golden hair that stood out in short spikes from his head. He scowled down at her. Before she could shift or speak, he was gone, striding away with his blinding cloak blown like a sail behind him.

Jaele stood up and went after him. He was so vivid, and he had looked at her, however briefly; she suddenly needed to keep him in sight, to follow him into the dark, tangled town. She walked behind him up a small alley, stopping to glance at the painted stores she had seen the night before. Pink with white lettering, silver with black, blue with gold: "Rope & Tw" "Fish Gre ns Shells" ".Priceless Treasures From." Words partially erased or gone which she read haltingly, trying to remember what her parents had taught her on cold, foggy nights. *"Say this word now, Jaele. And again. See the shapes and hear them . . ."* People sat in the open doorways; old people mostly, leaning against the stone and looking at the harbour. They did not look at her.

She ducked beneath low archways and squeezed herself between close-set walls, and always she saw the man ahead, shimmering his own daylight. After a time she emerged into a wider street. The buildings here were also painted, but they were all houses. As she passed them, she caught glimpses of flowering vines splayed across stone, chipped dry fountains, other deeper columns and arches. She saw children leaping and screeching, racing around the fountains. She looked away from them to jump over runnels of filth that bubbled among the cobbles, and held her nose against the stench. Still she had him in view, above the other people who now thronged the street. They called to one another and hurried through the grey salt mist, clutching baskets, babies, loops of fishing net. And as she saw all this, she watched, still, for another man, tall and lean and bearded.

The man with the cloak disappeared at last into a dark doorway between houses. When she stepped inside, she realized it was a tunnel: the stones of the roof curved only a short distance above her—he would have to be ducking—and a row of torches spat along both walls. The air was smotheringly damp; when she laid her fingers against the rock, they slid over spongy green moss.

Footsteps clattered toward her and she pressed herself to the slippery, beaded wall. At first there was nothing but the sound—

then a sudden pale face, and a bulk that was body and perhaps cloth, bound upon a shoulder. The man or woman nodded at her and there was a stale, dank brushing of wind. Retreat and echo and silence.

She continued on, iben-sight grazing rock seams, brown curling among green—but shrinking from the flames. She could not look directly at the torches, and thought of Llana fleeing lightning in the red ring of the barrows. Words skittered in her head: *Perhaps there is more in dark, puckered stone than torchlight?*

Her breath was hissing when she saw daylight. Another person brushed by her: a woman, also carrying a folded bolt of cloth on her back. She nodded as well, and Jaele stepped past her and out of the tunnel.

The view here was the same: a narrow cobbled street that swung out of sight between rows of painted buildings. She stood for a moment, vaguely disappointed. Then she heard the noise: a low, steady clacking—dancing, stabbing, mocking so that she was hollow. She went forward, past the first few houses. The same courtyards, half hidden by flower-spotted creepers and partly open doors; but no fountains, no leaping children. Looms instead, four, six in each shadowed space. Bent heads, flying hands, shuttles and whirling threads. She walked on and saw that there was cloth hanging from outer walls—cloaks spread wide, blankets, sweeping lengths so vivid against the grey.

She stopped where the street turned and found that it was a dead end: an ivy-thick wall rose from the cobbles. She looked back and watched people fingering cloth, crying out prices, arguing and laughing—and above it all, the looms. She was dizzy and cold, straining for voice and hands, sensing these things so briefly before they came gently, terribly apart in the noise and weaving of here.

The cloaked man was holding a brilliantly blue and golden tunic. She fastened her eyes on him, so focused that the colours bled. He emptied a pouch into another man's palm; silver and copper beads spilled out and were accepted. He slung the tunic over his shoulder and walked again toward the tunnel. Jaele could not move after he had gone; she felt as if she had been swimming, her limbs heavy and awkward. When she did rise and enter the tunnel, the sputtering darkness was empty. She traced the streets outside blindly, wending up and down and seeing nothing. Wood of walls and boat, mouths that smiled like smoke and words that sounded, but only in her own voice.

Stars were pricking the sea when she walked again onto the planks of the wharf. The waves rolled slowly; she sat beneath his window and listened, willing them to lull her away from her hunger. She wondered whether Nossi had seen the ocean as well as the river. Whether Aldreth had tried to Tell water and lowering sky. Wondered where he was—where Dorin was. Quickly back to Nossi, whom she missed so much, a silent gaping that she could trust. If she dreamed, she did not remember it.

When the man glowered at her the next morning, she tried to speak, but the dryness in her mouth was stifling. He swept away, each step and twitch of his new tunic emanating annoyance. She did not follow him this time. She crouched in front of his house all day, waiting, because again—as in Luhr, kneeling beside pottery shards—she did not know how to continue; how to seek, now that the man who had drawn her to this place was so close. *Get up, look for him*—but fear and uncertainty kept her still. She stared at the deserted harbour. There were no sailors now, and none of the scraggly boats put out groaning toward the open water. Her stomach grumbled, and she scrabbled through her bundle and even her pouch. Her teeth gnashed imagined seagreen.

In the late afternoon the wind rose. The waves crashed, rearing high before thundering over stone and docks, then ebbing in foam. The sky was a dense, lightning-punched yellow that thickened as she cowered against the wall. The rain began almost immediately; splinters lashed her body and the ships shrieked in their moorings.

He emerged from the murky distance. She watched the colours of him ripple and run. She did not see his face until he was directly above her. For a moment he gazed down at her; she felt herself trembling but did not otherwise move. Then one of his hands plunged toward her and hoisted her up, and he dragged her into the house.

The heavy door slammed and jarred her eyes, her jaw, her streaming, pooling limbs. He called, "Annial!" and turned to her, hands squarely on his hips. "Well, I have no idea who you are, or why you are so taken with my house, but I'm certainly not going to let you sicken and shiver on my doorstep like a pathetic beast. Wait here." He spun away from her and she stood alone, collapsed against the smoothness of the door.

Lanterns hung from stakes in the walls; they flickered over a mess of wine-coloured chairs, a huge round table, goblets, scythes and spears, and carved heads like the ones above several door frames in Fane. Among, on top of and beneath everything else were books: thick leather-bound books, and scrolls curled like new leaves, littered everywhere so that surfaces (floor and table, even chairs) could be seen only in patches. A wooden staircase spiralled up from all of this, to a second level that was dark.

Jaele did not move. An old woman shuffled toward her, through bands of fire and shadow. Her sandalled feet slapped the flagstones, the crimson carpet, and somehow avoided the books. Scrolls angled slowly as she passed.

"Don't mind him," she said in a voice that grated like sand and rocks. She was standing paces in front of Jaele, peering up at her from wizened smallness. "He seems rough as the breakers off the cliffs," she continued, "but isn't."

They regarded one another, and Jaele was again aware of her clothes. Keeper's fingers on thread and leather; stains of desert, river, lynanyn.

"He's let you in," the old woman said at last. "Now I suppose I shall try to mend your damages—as I do his."

"Annial?" Jaele said, and cleared her throat. Her voice uneasy, as it had been so often since Luhr.

"To be certain," Annial replied. "And he is Ilario. I am not, as you may be imagining, his servant—" She was walking, leading Jaele surprisingly swiftly up the stairs and speaking over her shoulder. "—although I do cook for him, as I did for his parents and theirs and theirs, in my girlhood. No, I am a friend—always have been, since my girlhood. Did I mention that? A friend of his great-grand-mother's. We couldn't bear to be separated, and I lived here with them when Fane was prosperous and the tall ships crossed from the islands." They had turned the last curve and were standing in a hallway that was torchlit at the end, where there were three closed doors. Thunder rocked the house.

"The time of tall ships that crowded the harbour, and Queens-fighters who galloped down our streets, so colourful and hand-some—the women too—and me a girl living by the sea with Hania and her man." Jaele's breath caught; here, after so long, words which warmed and welcomed her. "Then their children, and theirs. Then Ilario, and he will be the last."

Jaele sensed a pause and spoke quickly. "The last of his line? Or the last you will take care of?"

Annial's white brows drew together, and she laid her palm against the burnished handle in the centre of the farthest door. "Both, child, for he will father no sons or daughters, and I am far from girlhood, though girlhood is very clear to me. Clear as water, the pictures of myself and Hania and the handsome Queensfighter who slid from his horse to give me flowers bound with golden thread. The tall ships. I have not seen you before?"

"No," Jaele said, and the tiny woman's eyes were clouded green and puzzled. "You have not. I am Jaele."

"Good. Very good. Perhaps we shall meet for sweets with the children later, when the storm has passed. I fear for sailors on such nights—tossed and bent off course, too close to the Raiders' Land."

Jaele almost stumbled as she stepped past Annial and into the room. Lightning-raked but otherwise dark; a cushioned seat below the glass-paned window. Heartbeat glimpses of devouring black ocean. A small grated fireplace lined with drifts of ashes. A low bed with carved claw feet; before it a carpet which, when lit, revealed a map: islands, coastline, jagged black and pale creased water. Like her own map, but not; she did not look closely. *Tomorrow*, she thought, dizzy with exhaustion and relief.

"Sleep here, Jaele. You seem cold, but then winter is coming—you can see it in the colour of the air. You may light a fire in your hearth if you like. Rest well." Annial thrust her face back around the door frame as she left. "Your hair is the same as hers." The door closed with a click.

Jaele did not light a fire. She drank cold water, poured from a red-glazed pitcher into a shallow cup. The pottery was smooth and somehow warm, and she held it to her lips, thinking for a thunder-space of food eaten in a chamber beneath the sand, and then of a bowl that had been blue within. She slipped into bed—a bed, not since the desert—and her body's quivering warmed her under the blanket.

Lightning, hunger or water's roar, looms and the blurring edges of the map.

CHAPTER EIGHTEEN

The morning was silver, and there were flames swaying against the old black chimney stone. Jaele sat up and dragged her fingers through her knotted hair. She looked out the window and remembered that Annial had mentioned winter.

A tunic and leggings lay folded beside the water jug, and she eased herself into them, sighing skin and blue cloth. She stood for a moment by the window, gazing through bubbled glass at white sea, low, thick cloud, the dark line of cliffs that curved away, ringing the harbour to her right. The same empty boats tossed and creaked.

The stairs groaned when her feet touched them; she hesitated on each, listening for sounds from below and hearing none. What she did hear, when she finally reached the book-filled room, was singing. A young woman's voice, indistinct words: wind, shadowed eyes, ribbons of wine. She followed the voice along a back corridor which led into a cluttered kitchen. She stood in the doorway and stared.

Copper pots of all sizes hung from a low central beam and dangled perilously close to Jaele's head. There were earthen jugs and bowls, some glazed and others river-brown. Wooden spoons and baking paddles as long as oars, knives with metal hilts that gleamed like swords. Baskets brimming with green fronds, fruit, jutting ends of bread. Small pots, large ones, packed with earth that sprouted green and yellow shoots. A row of stone-lined ovens with heavy iron doors, neat stacks of wood beside them. There were scattered stools and chairs, and several cushion-strewn ledges that seemed to have been formed out of the walls themselves. Four round windows were set in the far wall, each slightly higher than the one before ("the rising moon," Annial said later). There was a small door beside these, and it stood open on a walled space of frenzied leaves and blossoms.

Jaele sat down heavily on a stool by the hall door. She felt transparent, hunger-stretched, breathless with warmth and scent and the bumpy crusts of bread. The lovely singing stopped and Annial exclaimed, "Who's there?" as she emerged from the clutter brandishing a huge pair of clippers. She gazed at Jaele, wide-eyed, then smiled. "The girl Jaele. From the storm. Ilario brought you in, and I took you upstairs. You are hungry now, I have no doubt. Here, child," she said, and whirled among the cutting tables and low straining shelves, then spun back to the stool with her brittle arms stretched around bread and sweetmoss and even seagreen. "Wait, now," she cried, and soon a cup of herb water was steaming between Jaele's hands.

Jaele trembled as she raised the food to her mouth and felt it there, ridged or yielding, and so familiar that she shut her eyes.

Annial moved off, her head a finger's span from the pots. "I know I should close the door," she was saying, "but too soon it will be bitter cold, and the icemounts will be crawling past the harbour, and we will yearn for this time of temperate air. Even Ilario, who now moans and complains about the chill creeping around his cloak."

"Where is he?" Jaele asked, mumbling around seagreen and hardly hearing herself. A part of her grieving, sunk in taste and ocean darkness.

"Oh, somewhere about; he does travel in a day. Walks the streets or cliffs or other places he does not speak of. Walks and walks like no other of his family, although I know he has reason." She stood still, her head turned to the open door.

"May I help you?" Jaele asked when she had finished eating—standing, moving to somehow fill her hands. As she ducked below the pots, Annial smiled.

"A fine idea. It has been a long time since anyone shared this kitchen with me—even Ilario, who used to sing as he chopped seagreen. A fine idea." She handed Jaele a small knife and gestured toward a vegetable-laden table. "You may cut those into strips for tonight's soup. This kitchen was so full, in the days of many ships: Hania and I, Boren her husband, their children, usually a sailor or two, perhaps a Queensfighter. Yes, our kitchen was famed, praised by all, and our rooms were always slept in. Even the top floor. Even the ledges in this room, and the carpets in the library. Ilario's library. How he searches. There was singing and laughter, and we drank wine."

Jaele chopped and cut slowly, slipping into the rhythm of Annial's voice. There was a cool breeze from outside, and a smell of vanishing rain. Time passed. She spoke a bit, and nodded agreement to words she immediately forgot. Safety again, found and clutched.

When Ilario swept in from the hallway, she started. He stopped mid-step.

"Ilario!" Annial cried. "Come sit! Hania and I—I have been telling Jaele about the days when you played here."

He glanced at the old woman, then looked again at Jaele. "The storm is over, yes? May I inquire why you are in my kitchen?"

She fastened her eyes on the wild spikes of his hair and spoke to him clearly, for the first time. "I am helping Annial. We have been talking. I am sorry this offends you. I will be gone by nightfall."

"Nonsense!" chirped Annial. "Ilario, what would your parents say? This poor girl has nowhere to stay—she is a traveller, and this house has always been open to travellers. You ungrateful, terrible boy. Tell her she may stay."

He turned to Annial, and Jaele caught her breath at the smile she saw light and disappear. He said nothing, but spun back into the corridor.

"Jaele," Annial began, "you must excuse him. I love him as I have loved the others—perhaps more, for we always love the most difficult, yes?" and Jaele said, very quietly, "Yes," as Annial continued, "But he is a good boy, a good man, and he will soon be friendly. It is just his way. We must wait."

Jaele set her knife down and wiped her hands on a rough brown cloth. "Thank you," she said, "for your kindness to me. I will leave your home."

She heard Annial's protest behind her as she walked into the darkness beyond the kitchen; back through the scrolls and up the stairs, into her room with its grey window and lowering fire. She sat on the bed and stared at the floor until slowly, almost unnoticed, the map eased into focus.

In the daylight it was layered with colour and shade, so intricate that it seemed she could touch the wrinkled mountains, the desert's sandy gold, the blue-green twining of river and trees. Bienta's map, woven—but not, for dark and flowering among these landscapes were words; words spiralling like uncoiling serpents, gleaming up the rugged slopes of hills, shrinking to tiny perfect rain in mountain passes. Some she understood: she saw "Luhr" and "Galha," letters ringing the crystal spires, and she ached; "Telon" and "Fane," as well. The other words curled in her eyes unknown. Names stretched over the silga mountains, the desert, the river and jungle—names she had never heard of and did not recognize. There should have been echoes, perhaps; there should have been sounds that reminded her of sky and a lake in winter.

She hugged her knees to her chest and wandered the road from Luhr to a patch of jungle to a small edge of beach that lay still, encircled by water and rocks, the colours pure because there were no words to darken them. Quickly back, leaping over desert where she saw "Perona" but not the other—to Fane, whose cobbles and court-yards were riddled with script, and then the grey, heaving ocean. There were a few words here, folded between waves, and islands fastened to one another with writing like impossible bridges. On until, shrinking, she slowed at a coastline that was jagged with empti-ness. No words, no names, no rock or hills; only a flat, dark dagger-strip at the corner of the map, fading into fog and then floorboards.

Jaele shivered, looked up and out of the window at the gathering clouds.

She did not leave the steep harbour house. She slept, then sat watching sea and sky: crimson-gold dawn, night that convulsed with lightning. The ships creaked, empty and bound. She thought, *I will speak to the sailors about passage east when they return*—but they did not, and she was more relieved than sorry. Too tired to imagine another departure, despite the man she had seen in the shonyn river; the man who would surely be swimming now, across. She lay propped on an elbow, tracing the carpet map in silence, thinking, *Soon I will be stronger.*

Every morning, she heard the front door below her crash shut. She crouched on the window ledge and watched Ilario stride along the wharf and vanish. He rarely returned before dusk. She would go downstairs to the kitchen, where Annial would be waiting. "Jaele dear," she said the day after Ilario told her to leave, "you are wise to stay. He will soon be kind."

Jaele drew her fingertips along the books and smelled age and crumbling. Golden letters twisted like vine; hidden beneath scrolls were stone tablets, cold and grey and porous as dead coral. Deep-coloured rugs prickled her feet.

Sometimes she went into the town after Ilario had left. Annial wrapped her in a long woollen cloak the first morning, clucking and smoothing with her old crab hands. "The wind is bitter," she said, "especially where the buildings crowd close together. The winter is breathing on our skin. The boats will not leave their moorings now—not until spring." *It is too late, then,* Jaele thought, and again felt thankfulness and regret. *He has already swum, and I will follow him later; I will cross the Eastern Sea in spring*—and there was something so comforting about these words that she smiled.

"Far from the glorious comings and goings when I was young," Annial was saying. "Poor Fane, so dull, only a shadow of before, like myself." She paused and stepped back to look at Jaele. "How well the cloak suits you: dark like your eyes. It was mine when I stood taller. Now go on and explore, and we will drink some steaming herb water when you return."

That day—and on those that followed—she walked without choosing a way, angling her body into the salt sting of the wind. She rounded corners into places she would not see again: sudden bowers of blue leaves and moss-damp cobbles; a square with a central fountain, cracked and fallen and spilling violet dust; a steep, wide avenue flanked by houses whose doors gaped on weed-shattered sky.

There were other places that she did see often, without effort. She ducked one day into a cramped, cloth-hung marketplace and sucked in her breath at the stench of meat. Meat everywhere: dangling from wooden spikes, layered deep in blood on trays, stripped and slabbed and oozing in piles on the stone ground. Children sat on their haunches, fanning away flies, flicking at maggots with dagger points. Jaele threaded her way around the stalls and spikes as people thrust past her with eager, outstretched arms. She did not see the end, but unexpectedly it was there: space above her head, lungs gasping relief and daylight. Somehow her unguided steps led her back to this market, and she stood still for a moment each time, gazing before she turned back.

She also came frequently to a short lane that blossomed into a vast spreading tree. Its boughs bent almost to the street; from beneath they were belled like the rib cage of a great ocean creature, and they fluttered with slender white leaves. The first time Jaele saw the tree, she stopped walking and gaped, for the air seemed dazzled with sunlight or snow. She sat against the strange smooth wood, feeling the long leaves stirring against her hair, though there was no wind here. *A harbour tree,* she thought. Although she never tried to, she returned to it often by day and once or twice by night, when it shone the falling paths of stars.

The place she found most easily was the tunnel and the weavers' quarter beyond. She knew the dank, pitted walls and the echoes, the shadowed courtyards and the figures that were never familiar enough. The ivy was golden and russet now, tendrils curling over the cloaks and carpets. At first she sat at the end of the alley and sank slowly, deliberately, until the many clatterings became one: one shuttle flying, one head thrown back in laughter. Each time she sat there, the backward-circling became more difficult. There were faces around her that she began to recognize, and rhythms of coins, singing, occasional silence that she came to know. Each time, she yearned and grasped and felt a new distance, a slippery transparency at which she raged. But still she went often to sit there, and did not want to leave.

Everything was twinned: a bright image and a darkening one. The smell of the sea; the fishing boats pulled up on the beach beneath the cliffs; women with long thick hair; boys slender and sharp; the sounds of an inn drifting out into the street at dusk. All of this was so close that memory buckled away from her. She thought that someday it would die.

She dreamed, not of her parents, but of Dorin. In these dreams she stood before him and screamed, swelling to fill the sky above him, and she woke voiceless with fury.

Days went by and still Jaele did not meet Ilario again. "He is occupied," Annial said once, as she and Jaele stirred cauldrons of broth and seagreen. "He is searching, I believe, although I think there is no hope."

"No hope?" Jaele asked, and the old woman whispered, "Shh, child, in case he hears you. As I said, I know nothing for certain. Hania often said so, as did Ellrac, the Queensfighter—I have told you about him? He gave me flowers."

Jaele woke one night, shaking from a dream. She pressed her forehead against the window; the sea was skittering rain, and the glass was very cold. She was widely, inescapably awake.

The stairs creaked beneath her feet, and she cringed; she had never wandered the house so late. Accustomed shapes loomed strangely in her iben-vision, and she trailed her hands over them to make them real: books, chair backs, the jutting edge of the table. The kitchen door was closed; there was no light below it. She pushed it open.

Ilario was sitting on a stool, leaning over a counter with his head gripped in his hands. A single candle-flame fluttered in the tiny wind from the door. Jaele wiped away the tears of her vanished iben-sight and found that he was looking at her.

"You are still here." His voice was low, and she could hear no anger in it.

"Yes," she replied, her own voice rough with sleep. He raked his fingers through his already tousled hair and was silent.

"Ilario," she said, whispering because of the night, "I am sorry that my presence galls you, but I have nowhere else to go—and now the winter is coming, and I will have to stay in Fane until the spring. I will have to wait."

Ilario glanced up at her, and the shadows twisted his lips into a half-smile. "Girl, your speech is windy and meaningless. Please breathe. Several times." She did. He continued, "As it is so late, my customary unpleasantness is dulled. You could sit, if you liked."

She sat down carefully on one of the cushioned wall ledges and looked around the kitchen: smudged clumps of vegetables, towers of bread, the silver-beaded windows. He growled a laugh. "You may look directly at me. How well I intimidate! Better than I had imagined."

Jaele looked at him. He seemed pale, between the darkness and the candlelight. "Yes, you intimidate," she said, not whispering this time. "You are miserable. I hide from you. I know when you go out in the morning, and I scurry around at dusk so that I can eat and be back in my room by the time you return. Am I talking too much?"

He answered, "Surprisingly, I am enjoying your blethering. Proceed."

Jaele cleared her throat and ran her fingernail along a knife groove in the wall beside her. "I don't know what else to say. I have no money. I must wait until the spring to continue on my way."

"Why?" He was lounging against the wall opposite her, but she could sense interest in the lines of him.

"I do not know if I can explain it to you. It is a . . . sensitive thing."

"Ah," he said. "So you wish to stay in my house and eat my food until the spring, at which time you will be off again without telling me where or why. I see. That is considerate of you."

"Very well," she said, clenching her fists, "tell me why you sit here alone in the middle of the night. Why you go alone every day. Why you are so unpleasant." She was breathless with the memory of her brother, and the vivid, heated twining of their words.

Ilario gazed at her steadily. After a time he smiled, and she remembered how he had smiled at Annial. "These too are sensitive things. I concede your victory. Although," he added, "to be fair, I am not foisting myself upon *your* household."

They sat for a while without speaking. The rain made slow dancing shapes on the floor and walls. When he stood, she followed him with her eyes.

"I thank you for your fascinating tale," he said. "Perhaps you will tell me more some other night." At the door he turned back. "Please blow out the candle before you return to your bed. A fire would do little to endear you to me."

Jaele grinned at the closed door, then rose and quenched the candle. She fell asleep on the ledge and woke at dawn to Annial singing of fishfolk and gold.

The day after her talk with Ilario, Jaele went with Annial to a fruit market. It was muddy, darkening afternoon when the old woman stood among the pots and declared, "We *must* have speckled sourfruit. This is most desperate. Come with me, child—I may require the aid of younger arms."

When they reached the end of the wharf, Jaele stopped before the crumbling tower that overlooked the river. So much of the tower had fallen that she could almost touch its topmost stones. Its round base was very wide. "This tower must have been enormous," she said. Her fingernails pressed into the moss that grew in the fissures between the stones. "Do you know what it was?"

Annial smiled. "Of course I do, sweetlet. There was a bridge here, long, long ago, when my grandmother was a girl. She told me that when the ships came down from Luhr, the keepers of this tower and the other across the river would raise the bridge with great wheels and chains. The boats would then pass through to the sea." She sighed. "When I was a child, there were still links of chain inside, all rusted and bent. But the bridge itself was gone—and now the chain is gone too. There is only the stone, and I suppose it will vanish soon enough."

Jaele looked across the river at the ruin of the other bridge tower. Beyond it were roofless houses with shattered, yawning windows, and doors that hung from single hinges. She saw the road, which began where the bridge must once have rested. It widened past the houses and climbed until it reached the emptiness of the coast.

She said, "Your grandmother must have told wonderful stories."

Annial nodded. "Oh, yes. Wonderful stories—I could almost hear the chains screaming and the Queensfighters calling from the ship. The children say I am like her." She frowned down at the basket in her hand.

"Speckled sourfruit," Jaele reminded her.

Annial cried, "Of course! How we have dawdled. Come, come!"

It was raining slightly now: mist on eyelashes and hair, an odour of wet stone and crimson-brown decay. Jaele hastened to keep pace with Annial, who bobbed quickly along. After many turns and slippery stairs they arrived again at the river, which thundered between steep walls of grey rock. Annial led Jaele over an arching bridge; the railing was carved with faces and shapes that looked like leaping fish. The water below was white.

"Follow, follow, follow . . ." Annial was singing, her voice like spray. ". . . the river bends and cries . . . come my love to find me . . ."

The market was not what Jaele had expected: the open space of Luhr, perhaps, or even the hanging ropes and awnings of Fane's meat quarter. She and Annial came to a low stone building and passed beneath its squat entryway. Beyond was a courtyard, empty except for a dirty, sleeping child and a rotting wagon lurched onto its side. Annial turned right and continued through another door into a roofless room that smelled of overripe sweetness. There was a woman there, huddled on the flagstones among piles of sunfruit, which glistened with rain. Annial moved swiftly on, down some stairs to a deep earth-scented chamber where a man stood with grapes gleaming silver in his palms. He chanted, "Smooth and cool, silver and cool," but Annial did not pause.

There were more underground chambers, more steps and corridors and rooms that lay open to the darkness and rain. In each place was a different kind of fruit. People with baskets bent and sniffed, shook or gripped the fruit before moving on or dropping payment into waiting hands. Jaele saw all this as she scurried to follow Annial.

"Why," she panted, hoping Annial would hear her, "are these fruit so fresh when it is almost winter?"

The old woman called back over her shoulder, "Much of it is grown indoors, under glass. Some grows for much of the year in the jungle which lies to the north. A valiant few harvest this jungle fruit. We are lucky, here in Fane, to have the freshest fruit until the snow. Then we must wait again for spring."

Annial stopped at last in a tiny room lit by a lantern which swayed gently, blurred with trails of water. By now it was very dark; the orange and blue of the speckled sourfruit were muted. Two figures stood in the corner. As Annial and Jaele approached, a male voice cried, "My lady Annial! I thought you had forgotten me," and she laughed gaily in reply.

"Serdic," she said, "you are ever pining, and I am glad that you miss me. You are as gallant as my Queensfighter . . . But see, I have brought someone with me today—a friend."

The young man was swathed in a cloak. Jaele saw his face, which was very slender, and a bit of dark hair, but little else. The woman beside him was similarly covered against the rain. She was very short, and her cheeks were round and flushed. Both were smiling.

"Jaele," Annial said, extending her arm toward the two, "please meet Serdic and his sister Tylla: my old friends, and staunch providers of speckled sourfruit, like their parents and grandparents before them."

"Staunch," Serdic agreed. "Greetings, Jaele."

"Greetings," she said, and thought that the skin of his cheeks was so white-smooth that it would bruise at a touch.

"Serdic," Annial began, "we require two armfuls of the small ones, the ones not yet completely ripe." Jaele watched Annial's fingers skimming the fruit, lingering, curling somehow in their brittle case of skin. Then she turned and found Serdic gazing at her.

He glanced away at once, flushing, and she felt a tightness in her chest, as if she had drawn a breath she could not let out again.

". . . but this one is too soft and smells too sweet. Hania used to chide me for bringing these home, they are *impossible* to peel . . ."

She was acutely aware of the water like veins on her hands, the folds of cloak damp against her legs. His head was bent now, his own long fingers picking at the fruit.

"Thank you, Serdic—that one is perfect. Now I think we are finished. And my, what foolishness: I have forgotten the herbs I usually bring as payment. Jaele or little Ilario will have to deliver them to you tomorrow. I am too old for such rigour."

He looked up again and said, "That will be fine," as he and Jaele smiled at each other.

That night the moon blazed through the vanishing rain, and she lay on her side tracing the stones and river of Fane. *He is beautiful, so pale and smiling,* she thought, and was certain, and shivered with strength.

The next day was cold, and the boards of the dock were slick and snapped with frost. She stood for a time gazing at the boats and the fall of the waves. Her arms were full of Annial's bitter wet herbs, piled there with a "Go now, and repay my charming friend Serdic," and a knowing smile.

She found the fruit market without effort. Serdic and Tylla's open chamber was thronged with people. She hovered just inside the doorway and watched him. His head was uncovered today; black hair spilled over his face, and he tucked it behind his ears as he bent to lift the sourfruit. One by one the buyers passed her, obscuring him, until she was the only one left and he was looking at her.

"Greetings, Serdic," she said. She stepped forward. "And Tylla." The girl nodded at her, grinning. "Here are the herbs Annial promised you." She dropped a few strands and Serdic knelt with her and they laughed, their breath streaming white.

"Thank you, Jaele," he said when he had put the herbs in a basket. "Thank you." He paused. "I am repeating myself." They all laughed, so easily, into the air that was now spinning slow, fat snow. "Will you stay?" he asked quickly, and flushed again. The snow melted against his cheeks. "Stay and help us. If you wish. If Tylla wishes," he added hastily, and his sister put her hands on her hips.

"Serdic," she said in a low, rough voice, "I wish for nothing but your happiness." She glanced at Jaele and her eyes glinted a chuckle—like other eyes, another sister smiling.

Jaele stayed. She sat on a stool, counting coins and sorting shells, flowers, bread—everything that was exchanged for fruit. Serdic was beside her, crouching and stretching and smiling at those who called his name. He spoke to her now and then as Tylla busied herself paces away.

"Do you live in Fane?"

"No. I come from a harbour—a beach. To the west and south of here."

"Your family is still there?"

"No. They are dead."

He turned to her and said quietly, "I am sorry. I did not mean to upset you."

Jaele shook her head and did not look at him. "And your family?" she asked after a moment.

"Up the coast, in a smaller town. Tylla and I live here until the sourfruit trees stop bearing—then we return home."

"And when do the trees stop?" She was surprised at her dread of "soon."

"After the ice begins forming. Not long now. Winter is beautiful in our town: the icemounts pass so close, and the sky shines at night. Fane is never so beautiful."

✧   ✧   ✧

"Why are you here?"

"I'm waiting for the spring. Then I will continue my journey."

"Journey?" he asked.

She said only, "Yes," and he was silent.

✧   ✧   ✧

"Have you met Ilario?"

"Oh, yes. He is . . ." She held up her hands, and Serdic laughed.

"I know—he and Annial both. You are lucky to have found them."

✧   ✧   ✧

At midday they ate bread and cold seagreen. Jaele tasted nothing but felt the stiff, porous edges of the bread and the crisp seagreen spines.

✧   ✧   ✧

The snow stopped falling. Jaele and Tylla rubbed the sourfruit until they glistened, then dried them in their cloaks. "Oh," Tylla said as something fell glinting from the cloth, "I meant to give you this to put with the rest of the payment"—and she dropped a brooch into Jaele's palm.

For a long, long moment Jaele could not speak. At last she said, "When—who gave you this?"

Tylla turned to her, frowning. "A man—he came before you did today. What is wrong?"

"It—" Jaele said, and breathed over the tightness of tears. "This was my mother's. My mother's brooch." She closed her eyes and held it to her cheek: cool bronze, slender lines that were fishing net, a single raised ruby that was a fishing boat. *"Oh, Reddac"*—*Lyalla*

blushing, wordless, as Jaele and Elic gaped at her. "It's pretty, isn't it?"
Reddac said eagerly. "I had it made by a jeweller in town—you have
so few pretty things. Do not dare reprimand me for its cost," he went
on as Lyalla opened her mouth. "It is not important. Put it on . . ."
"Someday it will be yours," Lyalla said later to Jaele. And now, in a
crumbling stone chamber in Fane, it was. Jaele held it to her cheek.

"Jaele?" Serdic touched her shoulder and she opened her eyes.

"The man who killed my mother gave this to you," she said, and
her voice surprised her with steadiness. Tylla and Serdic looked at
each other.

"The tall one who seemed ill," he said slowly. "I remember him,
of course: I told him this was too valuable, but he pressed it into my
hand. I gave him a bag of sourfruit and tried again to return the
brooch to him, but he turned and left. He was limping. His hands
were wrapped in strips of cloth—I thought he must be cold."

Jaele swallowed and clenched her fingers around the brooch.
"He took it from our hut before—after—I don't know when, I
wasn't seeing clearly . . ."

"I will go with you to Ilario and Annial's," Serdic said.

"No," Jaele said, "I am fine, truly"—but when she stood, her legs
shook and she had to lean against the wall behind her.

He walked with her, touching her elbow lightly. They went down
through the narrow streets and she watched her feet on the cobbles.
She could not look up—would have had to reach for, shrink from,
every face. *He is still here; he is still watching.*

"Thank you," she said to Serdic when he had led her to the
house.

"Do you want me to come in?" he asked, and she said, "No. I just
want to sleep for a bit." Then she slipped inside, without turning
back—for she felt eyes upon her, as she had in the desert: eyes
burning with hatred fever thirst.

She climbed the creaking stairs and lay curled on the bed, her
mother's brooch sharp and warm in her cupped hands.

CHAPTER NINETEEN

Fear turned, with sleep, to desperation. In the days after finding her mother's brooch, Jaele walked the streets again, searching, yearning to turn and look into the Sea Raider's face. She walked with the dagger thrust into her belt, her hand on the metal, beneath her cloak. She traced all the paths of the town: its markets and lanes, the weaving quarter, the outer edges where stone and wood crumbled into snow-dusted earth. Often she returned to the house only when dawn was touching the sea. Her iben-sight showed her different places at night: empty markets where wind stirred cloth, and dogs snarled over scraps of food; arched doorways where children huddled together in hole-thin cloaks; taverns where people sang, their voices seeping like ocean fog beneath doors and around windows. She did not see him.

When she woke each morning, she looked from her window at the water, straining to see a shadow moving below the surface. She thought, *Surely he will not be able to stay much longer—surely he will not wait for spring?* Her vision blurred as she looked and looked and saw nothing but far shifting grey.

Her daylight steps always took her back to the sourfruit chamber. She did not tell Tylla and Serdic anything more, and they did not press her; only shook their heads, day after day, when she asked them if he had returned. She sank into silence there, and in the house where she went only to sleep. Annial left trays of food outside her bedroom door. Once she spoke: "Jaele? Are you there? I have not seen you in days—we are all worried, sweetlet—please come out. Whenever you are ready, of course. I will wait for you in the kitchen."

"Thank you," Jaele said, her voice thick with exhaustion. "I will come down soon, but now I must rest . . ." She did not see or hear Ilario.

She had not found the Sea Raider during her first days in Fane; she did not find him now. Desperation dulled slowly. She began to walk without seeking out every face, and she took the dagger from her belt and left it in her room. She slept long and deeply. She thought, *I will find him here, later—or in his own land. And if it is there, I will take my revenge on all of them, as Galha did.* She felt patience settling, gentle and thick as snow.

"Serdic," she said one day in the sourfruit chamber, "I have been meaning to ask—where do you and Tylla live while you're in Fane?"

He flushed again. "I could do better than tell you: I could show you. Would you like to join us for dinner tonight?"

She nodded. Tylla also smiled at her, as she gathered the day's unsold sourfruit into a red bag. "You needn't wait for me," she said to Serdic, and grinned. "Go on ahead. I'll meet you at home."

She waved over her shoulder as she left, and Serdic said hastily, "Every day, she takes the rest of the fruit to Lorim, and he gives her his leftover mang." He cleared his throat. "We make juice with it."

They were standing quite close together in the empty room; Jaele could see the shadows of his eyelashes. She said, "I'll come home with you. For a meal . . . You already said that," she added, and laughed.

She followed him, her snowy footprints small in his—through the sky-roofed rooms, over the bridge with its wooden fish, down winding steps and along a narrow ledge. He glanced at her and they spoke words that were so vivid yet would not be remembered, and they laughed. Until, only spray's height away from the river, there was a steep wall and a jagged stone door with a handle, round and braided with rust.

Jaele looked back at the ledge and the distant steps, then down into the foaming river. "This is your door?" she cried, her voice swallowed by booming, and he nodded.

"Of course," he shouted, "there is another door. Much safer and quieter, leading into a street. I like this one more." He smiled and brushed a strand of hair away from his eyes. Then he tugged at the ring and the door opened.

The air was dark and heavy with damp and the scent of sourfruit. "Be careful," he called, and she felt herself sinking, reaching until her fingers touched old, smooth bark.

The trees rose around her, with roots that arched—some as tall as her waist—and twisted back again to the earth, and boughs that grew high from the trunks and wove together in a stillness of tiny red leaves. Lanterns hung from some of the branches; fire danced and slid over the leaves like wind. Sourfruit dangled below the crimson. She stretched up and brushed one, small and yellow, not yet speckled.

The river was a muted throbbing now. Her voice seemed quiet. "Tell me about the trees."

They walked together among the roots and he said, "They grow without sunlight, almost without air. They need only water, which oozes up from the river and perhaps even from the ocean: sometimes I think the earth here smells of salt. This is an ancient grove. The walls were built in Queen Dalhan's time, and the first trees were growing long before that, in what was then a cave by the sea."

There was something she desperately wanted to hold—his voice, his head lowered and raised, his arm lifted to touch a lantern or a branch. But not him: more herself, and the windless, earthy calm.

"My grandmother discovered this place when she was a girl. Her parents had a house on the street above. One day she found a small door in the floor of the cold-building. There were worn, dusty steps down to what is now our kitchen, and a path to the grove, which was thick with dead and rotting sourfruit and fallen trunks. Now it is our livelihood, but also nearly sacred. We leave it only for the winter, when the trees do not bear fruit. I will live here until my children are old enough to tend the trees. My future children." He stopped walking and ran his fingers through his hair. "I am certainly talking too much," he said, and she laughed again, so easily.

"No. Tell me about your future children."

They walked on, and he said, "Ah well, I don't know. They may be thin and verbose, as I am. Tylla's will no doubt be strapping warriors, even if there are no wars. But these children are only shadows yet." He turned to his right and led her out of the trees; they passed from earth to stone.

"And this is the kitchen," he declared as Jaele gawked.

This was another place of air and colour, shocking after darkness— like the earth silga forge, the blue chamber beneath the sand, Keeper's kitchen. Perhaps your own dark space will someday be flooded and filled, as these others were.

Serdic's kitchen was a cavern. Rough, crystal-limned walls rose to a roof that glittered with violet, green, golden cascades of stalactites. There were ovens like Annial's, set deep in the walls; tables—stone blossoming from stone—like flat-topped, frozen waterfalls; crooked footholds that crawled along the walls and ended as cushioned niches, some dizzyingly high, all lit with lanterns. Serdic darted up one of these precarious stairways and knelt, looking down at her. "It is lovely and spacious up here," he called. "Would you join me?"

She climbed up and pulled herself onto the ledge. The cushion was the colour of dark wine.

They sat so that their legs swung over the edge. Once or twice their knees touched. From their height Jaele could see the silent red leaves of the sourfruit grove.

"This is a dark cavern," she said, "but it seems so open, as if you could fly. Perhaps to the sea, and beyond."

He said, "Your journey," and even though it was not a question, she replied, "Yes."

She felt him turn to her; there was a breath of gentle scent—maybe his hair. "But across the sea is the Raiders' Land. Although I'm sure you know this."

She laughed softly. "A foolish quest, and my father and mother would not have approved. They always counselled against rage and revenge, said these were best left to stories. Though it was easy for them to say such things, when our life was so safe. So happy. My brother . . ." She remembered Elic whispering, *"We are both brave."* Tears stung her eyes but did not fall; her vision blurred so that lanternlight and crystal veins and stalactites were one.

Serdic said, "That man was a Sea Raider, wasn't he? I couldn't tell: he had wrapped his hands in cloth and I couldn't see his fingers. So . . . he is trying to get back to his land, and you will follow him there and confront him."

"Or," she said, "I may yet find him here, in Fane. Our paths have been so entwined." She paused. "I did not speak of him to you," she continued, "because at first it was so terrible, knowing he'd been there with you. And then I simply did not want to." She made a low sound that was almost a chuckle. "But it does not seem to have mattered that I did not tell you. You apparently know me so well, already, that you do not need to ask me questions."

"Your brother?" Jaele glanced at him, and he smiled. "This is a question. What did your brother think about revenge?"

She smiled as well. "He was young. Of course he thought revenge was noble and glorious, all those stories . . . He would have come with me. He would have cursed them as Galha did." She almost asked Serdic then, almost said, "I am alone—will you come with me? You and Tylla?" But she did not want to speak the words in this place of warmth and shining. She kicked her heels against the rock until he put a hand on her knee.

She lowered her fingers slowly, carefully, to his. His skin was translucent-soft, as she had imagined; she stroked it, fingertips to wrist, and heard him catch his breath. She kissed his neck, just below his jaw, and he slid his own lips over hers. She watched him: the veins on eyelids that fluttered, hair fallen dark along his cheekbone. *He looks lost,* she thought as his hand fumbled through her hair.

Tylla chuckled in the kitchen below, and Jaele and Serdic drew apart, laughing and flushing, and descended. He touched her lightly—on neck, cheek, hair—as he and his sister prepared their dinner of seagreen and fish. Jaele's flesh seemed prickled and scarlet; she was coiled, watching him.

They spoke and ate and drank wine from huge glazed goblets, and she was vast, her skin looming up toward the crystal and the invisible sky. Then they were among the trees, the two of them alone, kissing and clinging, falling sometimes to thrust against the trunks. Later they lay together on a mat of thick cloth, set atop a wide, level tangle of roots. The leaves blurred above his straining naked shoulders; she arched against him and heard herself groan.

Sounds and motions that were not hers—and in the slick stilling of their bodies she began to cry.

"Jaele?" he asked, smoothing the hair from her forehead, and she rolled away, covering herself with arms and knees.

"I'm sorry," she said. His hand was motionless on her hip. When her breath had steadied, and with her face still hidden from him, she spoke. "I shouldn't have. There is—was—someone, and I left him, but it's so close. I didn't really realize until you ,. . ." She dragged her wrist under her nose. "I'm so sorry. I will leave."

He stirred. "No," he whispered, and the word was hot against her shoulder. "I won't touch you again, but please don't go."

She lay quiet. After a moment he pulled a blanket over them both. She was quickly warmed; it had to be his warmth spreading over her, although she could not feel his skin. She followed the flame through the leaves until her stinging eyes closed.

His arm was curled over her when she woke. It was heavy and almost familiar, but she remembered immediately that there would be a dark sourfruit grove. She eased herself onto her back. Serdic sat up beside her and gazed at the still-burning lantern. She knew that he had been lying awake, his arm draped carefully still.

"What time is it?" she asked.

"It's morning. You won't be able to feel it, but I can."

She wanted to lay her fingers against his cheek, or the slender clenched hand by her head; as she had wanted to touch a scar once, in a forest of winter, not red.

"You'll leave now," he said, so bleakly that she flinched.

"Yes," she replied. She did not move, yet, to put on her clothes.

"And I won't see you again."

"No more questions that aren't!" she laughed, almost. "Of course we'll see each other again. If you want. As long as you don't . . ." There was silence, until she went on, "But that's unfair, of course." *Curse you, Dorin,* she thought, as Serdic turned his face away.

She drew on her leggings and tunic and laced her hide boots. While her back was still to him, he said, "It's not unfair, really. I would much rather see you without touching you, if that's what's needed, than not at all. You have been here with me, and now . . ." He paused. "And now I like you very much."

She slipped off the pallet and sank into the spongy earth. He reached for his own clothes. When he was ready, they walked back through the trees. They talked: he was probably late; Tylla would be furious; Annial would be unaware that Jaele had been gone; the day was doubtless grey, as usual, maybe snowing . . .

At the door, the river was loud. "Stormy," he cried, and reached for the ring.

She touched his fingers. "I will see you. I promise." She was not sure if the water had taken her voice, but he nodded before he pushed the door open.

Jaele flung her arms over her eyes. River and sky were searingly white. Serdic held her waist as she reeled. When she finally opened her eyes, she saw snow gusting in a fierce wind, water lashing against the stone. She clung to the wall. He shouted, "I will help!" and they began to creep along the ledge.

"It was the strangest feeling," she said later to Annial as the old woman hurried about the kitchen, preparing broth. Jaele was wrapped in several blankets, shivering in one of the wall niches. "It was like a storm I was in once in the hills—but this was different. I knew there was a wall, I could feel it and his arm around me; but I couldn't see anything except the water and the snow. He led me up the stairs after what seemed like forever, and I screamed at him to go back. It's such a terrible day—no one should be out in it."

Annial pointed a spoon at her. "And he agreed? My estimation of young Serdic has decreased. He should have escorted you home— particularly because the night which preceded this storm was surely so tender. Yes?"

Jaele shrank into her blankets. "Well . . ." she said, but Annial was no longer listening. She put a steaming bowl in Jaele's hands.

"I had only one night with my Queensfighter. The next day he set sail for the Raiders' Land with several others—young men and women, all. None returned. I sat every day and gazed at the sea, but never was it anything but water and cloud. Hania urged me to seek out another love, but I could not. I have tended you children ever since. Generations of you. And it has pleased me, in its way."

The storm went on for days, and Jaele watched it—livid, churning waves glimpsed through rents in the snow. On the evening before the clearing, she and Ilario again found each other in the kitchen. "Lucky wench," he commented, with one eyebrow arched. "Winter has truly arrived. Now I will be sure not to cast you out upon the cruel, cold streets of Fane." He coughed, bending his chin into his chest.

"I thank you for your generosity," she retorted, and he bowed his way from the room with exaggerated flourishes and a grimace of a smile.

Sunshine woke her the next morning. She squinted as she padded to the window, and it was a few moments before she could see. The water was golden, the sky a brilliant sweep of blue. The boats in the harbour were still and quiet. She thought she saw—far, far out—a plume of spray. Such clarity—and yet there were edges, already, muddy cloud seeping toward the sun.

"Sweetlet," Annial called as Jaele stepped into the kitchen, "see the miraculous clear! A perfect day for you to go to the market for some speckled sourfruit. We've had none for days, and Ilario is so *testy* without it."

"Well," Jaele began as Annial thrust a basket into her hands, "—well, no. I can't. I'll do all the cooking if you want—and it's a lovely day for you to go walking . . ."

The old woman regarded her without blinking. "I see. You are afraid of poor Serdic, who is as generous and kind as any you will meet. Poor Serdic, who is my friend. You are afraid—"

"No!" Jaele cried. "Please stop. I know that he is kind and generous, and I know that he wants to see me, but I can't—not yet. I can't explain." A lie, since it would be so easy to explain revulsion, pity, shame.

"And if he asks after you?" Annial said as she stood by the back door with the basket over her arm. The snow outside was sparkling.

"He won't," Jaele said, and Annial pulled the door shut behind her.

"I smell a love story gone awry!" boomed Ilario as he gusted into the kitchen. Jaele winced and sat down. "Tell all," he continued as he tore off a piece of soft, steaming bread. "Leave nothing out. This is by way of thanking me—woefully late—for my house and victuals."

Jaele groaned and rubbed her eyes. "I can't. It's too base. Although I'm sure you'd appreciate that."

He chuckled. "Ah, my girl, it's all so easy to see. I shall humour you, though, by posing questions. You are pining for someone?" She nodded. "And you have recently allowed yourself to be blinded by passion with another?"

She glared at him. "You've been listening to Annial and me; I am not impressed."

He held up an imperious hand. "To continue. This other is simply an inadequate distraction—you now feel remorseful and revolted?" He sat down at the table opposite her. "You need not answer. After all, I speak from long and tawdry experience."

Jaele laughed ruefully. "A flawless analysis, whether or not you listened at the door. Annial thinks I'm cruel."

"Mmm," Ilario responded. "And so you may be. But remember that, to her, the love of one good man is sacred. She who spent her young life and old pining for a fisherman who perished on high seas."

There was a moment of silence, which Ilario broke. His voice was now quite soft. "You, of course, think that she loved a Queensfighter who died on an ill-fated expedition to the Raiders' Land. A gentlemanly, handsome fellow on a horse who no doubt recited poetry. And perhaps Ellrac the fisher *was* these things."

"So," Jaele said, after a time, "there was no expedition to the Raiders' Land?"

"Oh, yes—there was one, during Annial's girlhood. The Raiders had been driving at the coast, sometimes killing, mostly stealing livestock. A band of Queensfighters set off in pursuit and never returned. Strangely, though, the Raiders did not return either."

"Yes," Jaele said quickly, "they did."

She felt Ilario looking at her. He said, "Perhaps—but never here." He stood then, and stretched his long arms above his head. "It is now time for my daily skulk. I am disappointed that I seem to have done more storytelling than you have, but one can always hope."

"Ilario," Jaele said, and he lingered in the doorway. "There's nothing wrong with fishermen."

"My girl, my girl," he replied, rolling his eyes, "I never suggested there was. You must not be so tender. As I've always said, the tender parts are inevitably eaten."

Jaele went out as well. She walked through Fane, over ice and snow that crackled loudly enough to fill her ears. When she returned to the house, the kitchen was warm with firelight and Annial was preparing dinner.

Jaele sat in one of the wall nooks and watched her. The old woman was silent, her back rigidly turned. A pile of speckled sourfruit gleamed in the basket by the door.

"It's strange not to hear you singing," Jaele said after a time. Annial did not reply. "I love it when you sing: you have such a young—"

"You were right," Annial interrupted. "He did not ask for you. Not in words." She swept a pile of vegetables off the counter and into a pot. "But in his eyes, my girl, and in the lovely lines of his face, you could see his yearning, plain as plain. Yearning that will become sorrow. He spoke not a word about you, but it was all I heard."

"Annial, please," Jaele said, and her voice trembled. "I am not as good, as true, as you are."

"Well, I don't understand it. You and Ilario are the last, and neither of you gives me anything but heartache. I have seen generations, and now I have only heartache."

CHAPTER TWENTY

Jaele woke to an insistent knocking. "Awake, sluggard girl!" Ilario cried from behind her door. "Awake and come with me!"

She groaned and stretched until her skin ached. "When have you ever requested my presence?" she called, and heard his chuckle.

"A rare opportunity indeed! I will await you by the front door."

By the time she had dressed and descended, he was standing outside, gazing at the harbour with his hands clasped behind his back. She stood beside him.

"Peer out toward the ocean," he said without looking at her, "and listen. Above all, listen."

Jaele stared past the ragged boats to the white-streaked cliffs that encircled the water. "What am I looking for?" she asked after a moment.

"Addle-head!" Ilario hissed. "Not looking. Listening."

"But—" Jaele protested, and Ilario held up an imperious hand. "Stop prattling. *Listen.*"

At first she heard only waves and wood and the distant keening of birds. Ilario was very still beside her. She was about to say that she had not imagined he could be so tranquil when she heard the sound. It was a humming; it began gently, barely touching the bottoms of her feet. Within minutes she could feel it in her teeth, on her tongue, the lids of her eyes—but still the harbour mouth lay empty. She glanced along the wharf and saw that it was thronged with people. An infant wailed. Beside Jaele a man with burnt-leather skin smiled toothlessly and squinted at the open sea.

The next sounds were so close together that they were almost one: splintering, groaning, creaking; high, sweet notes that sang clear above the rest. As Jaele shrank from the clamour, she saw a twisted spire of ice moving slowly behind the cliff. She clenched her fists; there was something terrible about its size, its grace and crashing song. Ilario sighed.

She saw the icemount more clearly when it glided to rest at the mouth of the harbour. Under the sunless sky it was pale green, almost transparent, and it glittered slightly—drawing light from where?—as it turned gently around. Its sides were toothed and massive, curving and sheer; arches leapt toward the air; bubbles breathed and died within frozen cascades. The icemount roared, and waves surged against the wharf. Jaele felt the water on her feet and legs, so cold that she stood on nothing; but she did not look down.

When there was silence at last—the waves pounding, beating, lapping—she heard other icemounts. Their calls were still distant, but the humming ran like an earth tremor beneath stone and ocean. Jaele imagined fish darting in fear, seagreen fronds straining away from the rumble which would send cracks lancing along the harbour floor.

People began to move back among the tattered buildings. "But," Jaele said, looking at Ilario, "there are more coming! Listen!"

He arched an eyebrow as he too turned away. "Now *you* urge *me* to listen? Yes, more will arrive soon, and over the next many days, but it is the first that draws us." He opened the door and gestured her inside. "You also will hardly notice them."

Days later, Jaele was still noticing them. She woke each morning to a new vista of peaks, and the sun—when it shone—glanced off ice of green, blue, lightest pink. The icemounts crowded the harbour and jutted out past the cliffs. She watched them for hours as they turned, their spires and buttresses shifting almost imperceptibly.

She also huddled in her cloak on the dock, for it was only outside that the notes and clangings could be easily heard. Sometimes there was long silence, when even the waves and timbers were still; sometimes there was crooning or sudden, deafening thunder. Jaele sat shivering and remembered that her father had said *"low, sad place,"* and she longed to tell him of colours and singing.

She was sitting at the round table in the front room, tracing a vine-like sweep of words, when there was a knock on the kitchen door. She continued trying to read, and the knock came again.

"Annial?" Jaele called as she rose. There was no reply, and the old woman was not in the kitchen. Jaele pulled open the door. "Serdic." She spoke before he could; the word sprang away from her in a tiny, disappearing breath of happiness.

He was damp with snow, and his hair clung to the slender white of his neck. In his hands was a clay bowl full of gleaming scarlet leaves. Jaele looked at this only briefly (already recoiling) and said, "Come in, please—you're so wet—it's snowing."

He stood by a counter. Jaele stood by the door, her back against one of the round windows. His bowl made a gentle sound when he set it down. She stared at the rise and fall of the bump in his throat.

"I knew you wouldn't come back." The bump a small thing, struggling in skin. "I have been sad, which is strange, since I hardly know you. I thought that if I saw you, I could ask . . ."

She looked away, down at a basket of dried fish. Salt lay like unmelted snow among the scales.

"You can't even look at me." He laughed breathlessly. "And I thought I would come here and ask you to travel with me to my home. Just for a time. To see how much more beautiful the ice-mounts are there, and to help you forget—at least until the spring."

She raised her eyes and said, "I can't, Serdic." They looked at each other steadily. He walked around the counter toward her until her head was tilted up toward his face. *No,* she thought, *it must be passion always, even rage.*

Serdic closed the door quietly; only when she felt a cold brush of air, then returned warmth, was she sure he had gone. She went to the counter and cupped her hands around the earthen bowl. The leaves were glistening, slightly curled at the edges. She sank her fingers into them, and the wet-sweet scent that rose made her wince.

Jaele went up to her room. She lay on her stomach and followed the wind-carved ridges of desert. Felt an aching emptiness where before there had been a pulse of anger, blood smeared dark across a forehead, moving skin, seagreen hair. Breath and spires in candle glow.

The next day the leaves from the sourfruit tree lay like ashes in the bowl. They smudged her fingers with black; she wiped them clean and retreated to a corner of the kitchen.

It was very early. She had hardly slept; had watched the sky instead, as it spun stars then cloud then almost-dawn slate. Once or twice the icemounts called: a note, two, a quiet shifting creak. No thoughts, after the first grappling with memory. Only a hollowness beneath her ribs.

Her fire shivered as she stood and drew on her clothes. Iben-sight led her along the hallway. Once down the stairs, she blinked, and her own vision took her on in grey, to the kitchen.

"So you're awake," Annial said later, when she entered and saw Jaele in the corner. Now the light was clearer, tinged with pink.

Annial picked up Serdic's bowl; she opened the door and tossed the ashes away.

"Does Ilario go to the same place every day?" Jaele wanted to know, wanted Annial to smile and answer and chatter about wine and Hania.

"I've no idea," the old woman replied. After a moment she added, "I do not think so. His search may take him near and far. As Hania used to say, the most heartbroken searches lead you away from the hearth and back again."

Jaele almost smiled. "Thank you, Annial," she said.

"Mmm," Annial muttered.

When Ilario left the house that morning, Jaele followed. She walked silently behind him, though she knew she should have called out, should have hurried to walk with him. She watched him through lightly falling snow, saw him pull his hood over his face as he strode along the wharf. At first there were a few people between them, gazing at the icemounts, but after he stepped from the wharf's edge to the cliff path, there was no one. Jaele hesitated, then turned back to the harbour. The icemounts circled and hummed. She saw her window below the steep tiled roof of Ilario's house.

When she looked for him again, he had disappeared around the cliff face. She ventured onto the path, which was ridged and crusted with snow. Clenching her fists, she went quickly after him.

The path bent gradually up, clinging to the jagged stone. It was wide enough for two people to walk side by side, but she pressed her body against the rock and stared at her boots. She heard water and ice and sudden bird cries—and, somewhere ahead, Ilario's feet and the cracking of his cloak in the wind. She glanced up once and there was a green-white flashing of waves on rock. She huddled for a moment against the cliff.

When Ilario came into sight again, the path was beginning to wind down toward the water. She ran, almost tripped. His cloak darted blue and yellow, and she could see snow clustered like berries in the spikes of his hair. The waves were louder, and she felt spray needling her skin. She saw, peripherally, the glittering side of an icemount. She slithered and gasped; and he was gone.

When Jaele reached the point on the path at which he had vanished, she found a slender fissure in the rock. Grey stone flecked with silver; the dry stalks and leaves of cliff-sprung plants straining in the wind; darkness and echo. She drew a breath and slipped inside.

There was no air or light. Rock dragged at her hair and scraped against her knees and toes. She crept along sideways, and as she did, her iben-sight bloomed and she saw glistening whorls of moisture and crystal, long-legged insects that skittered away from her, deep red moss in shapes of land or faces. Her ears rang with breathing, and she was sure that Ilario would hear her and wait and reach out to grasp her arm—but she shuffled on alone, down and down again. As usual in small dark places, she could not feel time pass; only by her heartbeat did she know, and by the changing patterns of moss.

The passage opened so abruptly that she twisted and fell, blinking against light—streaming, pulsing light of every shade, coming not from sky but from a great forest of stalagmites that jutted from a sea of thick, waveless white. Jaele knelt on a rocky ledge and thought, *No, they are too tall, taller than the cliff. They are icemounts, trapped away from the ocean.* She clutched at the stone, afraid of the motionless white liquid below her and of the shapes that sent their colours glancing like lightning off the walls.

Ilario was climbing up a violet stalagmite a leap's distance from the passage. He was stretched wide, as slender and tiny as one of the insects. He passed through swaths of different colours; sometimes she could not see him in the blaze. At last he came to a particularly wide ledge and stopped. For a moment he hung there. Then, in a shimmer, a ripple, he slipped away. *Inside,* she thought in terror; *it is water and he is within, bubbles whirling and breaking at a surface he cannot reach.*

She knelt and did not move. There was no sound, though there should have been a steady dripping. She knew that her knees would be patterned with the marks of stones. Fear—such fear that she had lost the flint grey winter sky and the wind that tore her voice—but still she did not move.

Ilario emerged from the stalagmite as suddenly as he had entered it. This time he slid, almost fell, down the polished side. He crouched for a time at its base before leaping to the path. She heard his breath then: it rasped from one wall to the next until she was surrounded, cowering. As he stumbled toward her, she tried to stand. His bent head lifted and he saw her.

He stood motionless; even his breathing was quiet. His face was white except for a smudge of blood on either cheek. Jaele opened her mouth—his name, or a wordless sound—and he moved again, limping around her into the passageway.

She was not sure how much time passed before she forced herself to follow him. The narrow tunnel was silent but for her own scrabbling. Her fingers pushed against the moss, the slippery stone, willing them to be yielding earth or water.

I felt desperate, trapped. How must you have felt, when you were first prisoners? Did you press yourselves against the earthen walls and rip your talons, your flesh, with clawing?

She burst into the air, her eyes dazzled and filling with tears. Icemounts and snow-crusted path; wind that stirred her hair against her cheeks. Thunder of waves.

She ran this time—sent herself flying along the trail, desperate for a glimpse of him. Only when she turned the final corner into the harbour did she see him. He was walking swiftly, head held high as ever. She slowed and watched him stride along the wharf and into the house. When she reached the door, she hesitated. When she opened it, he was there.

"I cannot find the words I need," he said from his seat at the round table. His voice was low and measured. "You have trespassed. You have meddled. You are a *fool!*" Now he was shouting, straining up from his chair to loom over her. "Away! Get away from here before I do you harm!"

She stumbled up the stairs and along the corridor to her room; lay on her bed and trembled as the daylight faded. Annial came in with a tray of food. She set it down by the bed and stood looking at her. "What has happened?" she demanded. "Ilario paces and you lie moody as a child. Tell me."

"I cannot," Jaele answered, without turning her head. "I do not know. Truly, I do not."

"Well, then," Annial said, and left the room.

Jaele slept for a time, dreaming of a milk-white ocean roiling, reaching spume and heat. She woke in darkness to the low hum of icemount song and Ilario, sitting on the floor beneath her window.

She struggled to sit up, tugging at a blanket until it covered her knees. "Don't be afraid," he said in a strange, rough voice, and she let out a gust of breath.

"I *am* afraid, and sorry—so sorry. I don't know why I followed you . . . I should have called to you. I am so thoughtless."

There was light—silver, star—shifting on his face. She saw him smile. "I do enjoy your nattering, you know. You have made me want to listen, again, to words."

She snorted, pushed tangled hair behind her ear. "You enjoy? Of course—I've noticed how you seek me out and linger to speak to me."

"You do not understand, Jaele. Listen to me now, when it is night and I am weary or helpless enough to speak." He was silent then, for so long that she thought he had forgotten her. When he finally continued, it was barely above a whisper. "I am dying."

She opened her mouth, closed it. The air, their skin, so still.

"Annial hasn't told you?" he went on. "How alarming, or reassuring, that her tales have not wandered to my plight. Yes, so young, and now the last of a venerable line."

"How?" Jaele asked. Perhaps a dream, like the white sea, like Nossi's hair.

"How." He laughed hollowly. "That I cannot tell you. Only that I am sure."

She noticed that there was snow outside, spinning like points of whitest flame in the path of the moon she could not see. She watched it, and his face blurred at the corners of her eyes. She bit at her lower lip until it stung. Then she said, "Sea Raiders murdered my parents and brother. I followed one of them here—or he followed me. If I do not find him, I will go across the sea to the Raiders' Land. In the spring." She thought that Ilario's eyebrows arched, and felt relief like warmth in her blood.

"So we trade confidences at last, my unexpected guest." After a moment he said, "Where did you live, you and your family?"

"A small harbour—tiny, really—only us, in a wooden hut." She talked on as she had not done since she lay beside Nossi, watching sparks and the slow swinging of the stars. But this time she did not tell of Dorin; this time she spoke of the sheen of washed sand, the clacking of the loom, the path that led through scrub and trees to the town whose name she never knew. Her brother, chubby and unsteady on the beach, holding out his arms to her. Her mother's hair, dark and thick, sweeping the water as she bent with her net. All of these images leading to the end—of course. The end. Throats opening beneath blades; a man who had run into darkness and trees. "And he is here," she said at last, her hand closing over the brooch that lay beside her pillow. "Or he was. Perhaps he has had to cross already. I know nothing—nothing at all. I began by following him, and then for a time he seemed to be following me—and now I do not know. Sometimes I feel that I am mad. Or dreaming."

"Ah," Ilario said, "you see? We are alike, you and I." In the silence the icemounts' song rose to sweetness. The snow drifted and wove. "I am sorry for your pain," he said finally.

She replied, suddenly awkward, "And I for yours," and continued, rushing, "Where do you go each morning, then? If I may know. You need not—".

Ilario held up a hand, and her clenched muscles relaxed. "You may know the gist of it, my girl. Each day, I rise and strike out on some pilgrimage, as I have for what seems an age. I read, you see; I comb my books for ancient lore, and it lifts my heart, for a time. I go in search of herbs and roots and sacred trees; hermit healers and mad children said to cure all with one long look from their wild eyes. And this morning, as you saw, I attempted to tap the power of the deep earth. Each day a quest, even though my friends draw away and vanish. Even though I know that the sickness continues and grows, and I am weaker with every dawn."

"You do not seem weak," Jaele said. "You walk with such vigour I can hardly keep pace with you."

"As does Annial. Yet she is old—older than I can guess—and when she is alone, I know that she bows with pain. She and I are also alike, in this."

Jaele leaned against the wall, which was cold. She felt the fading of their voices and thought they spoke so differently, she and Ilario. Her words and his, effortless, warm. She could almost hear a loom and the dip of oars.

She started awake, not aware that she had been sleeping. The light had changed—now greyness, dawn, cobwebs strung over Ilario's open eyes. She stirred, and he slid over the floor to the carpet.

"Look," he said softly, and pointed. "Look, and show me your harbour."

"Mmm," she replied, "I can show you, but there's nothing . . ."

The water of her bay was dark with seagreen, and there were names—Reddac, Lyalla, Elic—curling over the shore. She touched them, remembering her mother's slender fingers drawing the letters in sand, saying, *"Look—this is your name, and Elic's; these are sounds you can see"*—and she bent her head so that the tears fell hot on the backs of her hands.

Ilario was sitting at the round table when Jaele finally emerged from her room. She had slept again, her closed eyes stinging. When she woke, it was all even more of a dream, except for the lovely black curves of the names.

He glanced up at her, then returned to his reading. "I'm sorry," she said. "You came to tell me something last night, and *I* ended up talking, crying. It was insensitive."

"Perhaps," he said, and set his book down on the table. "Or perhaps it is not so simple as one pain. And you, my girl, are decidedly too sensitive. I have no idea how you've come so far, with all your shrinking and apologizing." He smiled, but there were edges in his voice, a strange sharp discomfort.

"Tell me about the carpet," she said, and sat down with him.

He shifted in his chair. "I have told you—I do not speak well during the day."

"Ah, I see. You will creep up to my room in the middle of the night and wake me whenever you wish to talk. Shall I expect you tonight, around moonrise?"

He chuckled, and she finally saw his eyes. "There, you see? I was wrong. You are entirely *insensitive*." He paused, tracing with four fingers the sweep of an embossed letter. "The carpet. I don't know much. It's been here for so long, and your room has always been for travellers who told of journeys and homes. I used to crouch by the fireplace and listen, and when each guest had moved on, I scurried upstairs to gawk at the new names and try to say them myself. I don't know where the carpet came from. Perhaps, long ago, one of these travellers brought it and left it as a gift." He raised his eyebrows at her, in mock surprise. "Why, I can speak! Daylight, and I can speak! You are a foul sorceress to loosen my tongue thus." They smiled at each other.

When they entered the kitchen, Annial was drawing fresh loaves from the ovens. She placed them on wooden racks, then looked up quizzically. "Together for breakfast, I see," she began uncertainly, almost hopefully.

Ilario went to her and bent down to kiss the top of her head. "She knows, Anni," he said quietly, "I've told her."

The old woman said nothing. She gazed at Jaele, and her eyes were dark with tears.

The days and nights of deep winter passed tormented. The wind shrieked and clutched the sea into ice-topped swells; sleet lashed the windows and clung there, frozen into lattice so thick that it was impossible to see out. The markets were closed, the streets empty even of children. Fane hunkered grey and still except for dirty smoke that was swallowed by storm. The words of Jaele's father were truth, now that there was no dawn and the icemounts lay smothered and dull.

Jaele rarely left the house, though sometimes she did wind herself in cloaks and scarves and walk into the town. She did not see the Sea Raider; she did not truly expect to. *He will be somewhere deep and warm, if he is still here at all. If he did not swim, before the snow.* Despite this thought, she wished that she could see out her window to the docks and the harbour. As if he might be standing there, looking up.

Ilario too slowly ceased his daily journeyings. He had continued them for a time, also venturing out with his head and body wrapped in glowing cloaks. Jaele and Annial would hear him return, blowing and cursing, and they made no comments as they passed him hot herb water. He soon left the house for shorter periods; eventually, not at all. "I have never been impeded by winter before," he snapped one day, "but this one is too much, even for me."

"This is half-truth," Annial said to Jaele later, when they were alone in the kitchen.

"Oh?" Jaele asked. "And what is the other half?"

Annial peeled the husk from a green lyna in one deft motion and laid it beside the rest. "This house is not his prison now that you are here. He is more content."

Jaele snorted and said, "Content? He is a short-tempered misery!" She knew that there was happiness in her voice, and that Annial heard it.

Ilario woke early every day and stomped down the stairs to the kitchen, where he clanged pots and dropped spoons and uttered loud oaths. He then paced: around the front room, through the kitchen, back again. Up the stairs, along the hallway, into his room, down the stairs. "Sit!" Jaele would cry, and he would growl from the floor above.

"Please," she begged him once, from her seat at the round table. "I am trying to read this history of Fane, and I am a poor enough reader without your stamping and blustering."

He looked down at her with narrowed eyes. The silence where his steps had been was like a roar. "Poor reader, are you? And you're attempting *Magon's Account of Fane*? No, no—I will not accept this. If your reading skills are inadequate, that book will surely murder you with tedium." He went to the shelves and examined them; he knelt on the floor and swept his hands through parchment and leather. At last he held up a thin volume whose pages were edged with green and blue. "A meditation on the sea, by one of my ancestors. A bit delirious, but it will interest you." Jaele took it, and he rose to pace again.

"Wait," she said, and he turned. "Help me. Teach me. Sit down."

So began their reading and writing time, which saved them from the winter and made walls and ceiling into firelit safety. They started on that first day with *The Sea, My Home*. Ilario opened it gently and smoothed its pages. "By Elmorden Flint. An unlikely name. She also produced the artwork."

Jaele reached out to touch what looked like gold-encrusted waves, cascades of murky green, a rocky headland half obscured by spray.

"Now read," he commanded, "and I will see how much work we require."

She began shyly, so that the words twisted from her mouth like living creatures, surprised. After a few phrases she grew calmer and slower. Ilario corrected her softly, interjecting with a word or syllable but never stopping her. There was a flow; even as she strained to read, she felt it.

"The sea, my home
My home is salt and fury
Is crest and bleak
Is sudden gold and still."

When she came to the end of the page, Jaele halted. Ilario said, "You see—it's gaudy stuff. But you read well: a credit to your first teacher. It is words like this, though, that give you trouble . . ."

Jaele's reading improved swiftly, as did her writing. She and Ilario soon took turns choosing poems or histories or longer tales that spun out over the evenings. Annial began to join them at the round table. She was quiet, nodding sometimes as she listened. When they were finished, she would sigh and stir and say "Beautiful"—even, as Ilario laughed to Jaele, if they had been reading from *Warfare of Ancient Societies* or *Scourges and Diseases of the Lower Desert*.

The winter passed, and the three of them read and listened and cooked together as snow thickened on the round windows. Ilario grew thinner. His bright clothing hung from his shoulders and hips; his collarbone seemed to be jutting, thrusting at skin until it whitened. He coughed—at first a tickle, then a stubborn rasp, then a racking that bent him over and brought blood like fine mist to his fingers. Sometimes, while Jaele read, he would go to the window and look out at the harbour, leaning his forehead against the glass. She paused the first time he did this, and he snapped, "Over-vigilant girl! I am still listening." He was shaking; his tunic shifted, as if in a breath of wind.

"You should write a story," Ilario said. He was sitting on a stool, peeling sourfruit skins delicately away with the tips of his fingers.

"What do you mean?" Jaele asked, handing the fruit to Annial.

He coughed, pressing his mouth against his shoulder. "A story—surely you understand this? I thought you moderately quick-witted. A tale of some sort. Fantastic or true or both, as you wish. It would occupy your mind after we have finished reading. Spring is still distant, as you know."

Later he gave her a thick sheaf of paper and a black writing stick. She sat cross-legged on her bed and gazed at the snow drifted on her windowsill. A fire crackled in the grate; a candle stood on the floor below her. She wrote, "The sun blazed down on the sand. Queen Galha rode from the gates of Luhr on her white horse, and her army followed. Her people stood silent and afraid, because she was going across the wide sea in the east."

She reread the words, then put the page face down on the floor. She could feel tears. Quickly, on a new sheet, "I rage when I think of you. I do not know where you are now," and then she wept, jagged and unfinished.

Ilario struggled to stand. "I am going mad. I must leave, I must get out." He tottered for a moment. Jaele and Annial wound their arms around him and he sagged between them. Jaele's fingers slipped into the spaces between his ribs. "Get my cloak—open the door. I need the wind."

They led him slowly out and onto the wharf. "It is icy—please be careful," Annial said. "Hania will be so distressed if she finds you out here—and your mother . . ."

"Hush," Ilario said, not too roughly. "Please." They stood together, and Jaele heard and felt his breathing—saw it, even, as white and filmy as her own. "The icemounts are retreating," he said. "You may not be able to see it. But it's happening. Their song will change now, too. A farewell. Sad, I think, because of spring."

That night Jaele woke from a featureless dream to find Ilario sitting beneath her window. "Again?" she mumbled, and he chuckled, then coughed.

"Again. It is difficult to sleep. Nights are terrible now. And I remember our last such meeting . . . with great fondness."

She was fully awake now. "Ilario. I don't have to leave here in the spring." She felt the unexpected truth of this like a blossoming, a flame.

He spluttered—she thought with laughter. "Ridiculous girl! You must. You absolutely must."

She leaned forward and spoke rapidly. "I will stay, and Annial and I will take care of you. I can continue my journey when you're well again. I'm sure you'd be well by summer."

He coughed and coughed, curling into himself until he seemed very small. When he finally lifted his head, he said, "No. *Dying*, I said. Not just sick. You don't need to be here . . . for that. Go. It is what you must do."

After a moment Jaele said, "I'll help you—you should lie down," and she half carried him to her bed. He lay on his side, and she sat on the map-carpet, holding one of his brittle hands between both her own.

They did not speak again. Near morning, he slept. She listened to the rattling in his throat and wished that she could take him gently down where bones were light and breath was bubbled silver.

Jaele walked out more as Ilario dozed and the icemounts began their creaking journey away. The streets dripped and cracked with falling ice, and there was a smell of unburied earth and stone. She sat and stared at the river—shapes in the foam disappearing, borne away to the sea at which she could not bear to look.

It was a bit like my last days in the shonyn village. My eyes caught at details and held them in fear and wonder—fear, now, because I knew that this was an ending. With the shonyn I had only dreamed it.

Shards of ice shrinking to runnels around her sodden shoes. The dried blood of Ilario's sores—on his neck, his forehead, his lower lip. The grooves in Annial's biggest wooden spoon. Three books stacked on the floor; the words "of Air" on the one turned toward her. The dark names of her family, looming up until she was surrounded by a forest of wool and weaving. The hollows of Ilario's cheeks. The way his teeth and nose protruded from his drum-skin. His eyes, gazing at her from the bed they had made for him in the reading-room. His eyes hot fevered grasping blue.

Once, he lay reading aloud; he still insisted on doing so, said that he only had to learn how to breathe differently, to get the words out. "There was lace . . . at her throat and he . . . drank long of its white against . . . her darkness. She . . ." He was wheezing, his shrunken chest fluttering with effort.

Annial rose and went to his pallet. She took the book slowly from his fingers and sat beside him. "She too gazed at him—a Queensfighter, tall and slender, with coils of green silk around his arms and neck. They stood alone by the tower, where the banners sang in night wind."

Annial fell silent. She was looking out the window at the moonless harbour. She was so still that Jaele thought, *She is remembering.* Ilario gazed at her, then at Jaele. She felt lashed by his breathing, and by the smile that shone untarnished grief from the wreckage of his face.

Annial, Ilario—she knew that she should be with them, that she should read them asleep and tender, but she was aghast. Aghast at the snow that now fell as rain, at the groaning farewell of the icemounts, at the waves rough and hollow against the boards. She stared at the edge of carpet where the map vanished. She clung to memories of the man who had drawn his knife across her mother's throat, the webbed hand she had sent arching into the sea—but they were not enough. Blood, ash, nails against rock were not enough. The Alilan, Serani and Bienta, Luhr—the shonyn village above all—she could have stayed in the round red hut with Dorin's arm heavy on her breast.

At last, when mud caked the paths and the harbour was empty except for the three pitiful boats, Jaele looked again at the sea. She examined it from her bedroom window, from the reading-room window, from the wharf. As she looked, she knew that she would not wait to see him again here, that she would not wait for the sailors' return. She crossed another wooden bridge and stood before the empty harbour houses. She walked past them along the road, following it until the coast lay stretched before her. The road here was empty, grey and brown, wind-bent. She turned away from it. *I will find the way from here, somehow,* she thought. *Another time, when all will be clear.*

She and Ilario and Annial were very jolly during their last few nights together. Annial told stories of Ilario's boyhood, then meandered—as ever—to tales of her own youth. The words, the images, so sad—but they sat and laughed. Giddy without despera-tion. They drank wine as well, even Ilario, who said it usually sick-ened him. He was flushed and breathlessly loud; Jaele imagined that he was speaking more easily. Annial's hair slipped out of its pins. She tossed them into the air, and they watched the silver glinting in candlelight and carpet. They all slept in the big front room. Jaele fell asleep to Annial's voice, stories and songs covering her so that she did not dream.

One night she woke when the sky was still dark—a deep blue, perhaps close to dawn. She did not move, but Ilario whispered, "Tomorrow, my girl. For you, I think, tomorrow." She felt ill from wine and half-sleep. She said nothing.

When she was certain that Ilario was asleep, she rose and wrapped a cloak around her shoulders. She eased the front door open and stepped outside. There was a moon and a dense ring of stars, and the water lay sparkling smooth. She had brought her pouch and bundle. The dock was slick with dew or rain. She walked slowly and wadded her cloak beneath her when she sat. There was no end to the water—no line or crest or wave to indicate distance. Distance—or depth. She shuddered, remembering the murky black she had never dared to enter. Her lungs were not strong enough— and it had been safer diving in her bay, where the seagreen stretched toward watered sunlight.

Jaele opened her pouch and bundle: fishfolk stone, shell necklace, Murtha's green rock, twisted black neckring, Bienta's map, her dagger and brooch. She thought of her almost-companions and looked at their tokens, small and still before her on the glistening wood. The wind was blowing fresh from the east; it stirred her hair and lifted the corners of her cloak. The smell of it ached in her nostrils, on her skin. "Now. Alone." Her whispered words echoed with fear and regret.

Later, the front room was soaked in light. "Ah—Fane in . . . the morning," Ilario said. Annial held a cup of herb water to his mouth; his lips and tongue could not seem to find it, slithered and sought like a baby's. Jaele looked away.

"Almost market time again," Annial said, "and time to see young Serdic. Perhaps you will want to greet him, Jaele, when he returns?"

Jaele shifted and felt something thicken in her throat. "No, Annial. I do not think I will. I must leave today. Ilario knows it—I must go now." She glanced at him; he was smiling (ghastly lovely skeleton smile).

Annial said slowly, "As you wish, of course—but everyone leaves us, and it is so sad sometimes. We used to sit at the window, Hania and I, and he would walk by and put his fingers against the glass, just lightly."

Jaele put her arms around the old woman. Bread and wood and skin like folded paper. Annial held her very tightly. As she let her go, she whispered, "Be safe, child. I am afraid for you."

Jaele laughed shakily. "I will be back. I am sure." Words spaces of wind between her teeth.

She bent over Ilario and kissed the top of his head. His hair was thin and tasted of salt. "Here," he hissed, and she felt him pressing her hand. "You may . . . yet need one. A better one."

She looked at the new black writing stick, at his fingers. "Thank you," she said.

"Now," he continued, "be off. About time . . . lingering girl!"

She laughed—heard it clear around them, a current or a pulse.

When she pulled the door closed, she did not hear it above the waves. The sunlight had disappeared into seeping cloud; gusts of wind peaked the water and turned it grey. Grey water and air, a smell of brine. Jaele stood and looked at the harbour, for just a moment. She saw the jagged towers and the river's mouth. The failing boats, the hunched cliffs, missing planks and ooze-slicked stone. Then she began to walk.

She turned back once and saw the house, which now seemed small and threatened by the sky. She was not sure if there were figures in the window. She lifted her arm, then moved on, slipping among the silent, peeling buildings of Fane.

THE EASTERN SEA

CHAPTER TWENTY-ONE

There was no one on the coastal road. Jaele followed it until the last houses were winks of colour, bent behind her. After a time she left the road and went down the scrubby slope to the sea; down, the road lost, to waves that roared spray against her body, so cold it clung to her like ice. She sat at the water's edge, shivering in her cloak. She waited. Annial had given her a speckled sourfruit and an end of bread. She ate, wondering when she might eat again, and what, and thinking that she had not wondered this since she stumbled down to Fane in the autumn.

She stood once and paced the strip of tumbled rock and dark, clotted sand. A child searching for the marks of Queen Galha's boats, the print of some other foot. She gazed into the slate distance, thinking, *I should be remembering all that has brought me here, but I am empty* . . . Ilario, alone in the emptiness, and Annial rocking him like a little boy.

The massed clouds began to break apart, and there was a flood of burnished evening light. The wind had died as well, and the ocean lay calm. Jaele squinted into the blaze at a place where the water seemed lifted and broken; it smoothed again, but her eyes flickered to another spot. Closer. The sea was rising and falling, splintered by gold. Glint of water and scales, and a long, low hissing, and suddenly a head, rising and rising.

Jaele resisted the urge to fall to her knees on the sand. She thought, *I will not run from this,* and held her hands out, trembling. The sea snake uncoiled itself from the waves like a pillar of golden smoke and hovered, huge head angled toward her. She looked up and saw the hard green of its eyes and the scarlet of its three-pronged tongue; then she closed her own eyes. *Dorin was right,* she thought, the memory swift and vivid, almost calming. *He stood beside the Giant's Club—a little boy—and told me what he would see someday.* She waited.

The sea snake shifted; water churned and foamed onto the sand by Jaele's feet. She heard the hissing again, high above her. She opened her eyes and saw the shadow of its head as it swept toward her. She felt its breath, hot, moist wind in her hair and on her neck. It lowered its head until it was touching the pouch at her belt. She looked into one small green eye; it blinked as the great nose nudged her twice, gently. She carefully lifted a hand to the pouch and quickly drew it back again. The leather was warm; it was also, she noticed, glowing red. She remembered the fishfolk lake in winter and the oceanweed-firm hands that had led her down; she remembered her fishfolk stone, trickling light into the murky water.

The sea snake's eye widened as she drew out the stone. It blazed in her palm and the light glanced like flame from the golden-scaled head beside her. The sea snake blinked again and rumbled deep in its throat. Its tongue jabbed quickly in and out, just above her head. It rose to its full height and held itself briefly still, stretched against the crimson sky. Then it folded slowly down, so that it lay flat on the sand with its wedge-shaped head at Jaele's feet.

A gust of wind twisted her hair across her face. "The fishfolk gave me this stone," she said, wincing as her voice scraped and

leapt. "Do you know them? Will you . . . are you going to take me
to them?" The sea snake regarded her, its tongue flickering.

She returned the shining stone to her pouch and tied her bundle to
her belt so that the shape of the dagger rested against her thigh. "I will
go with you," she said, and took a hesitant step. The snake lay still. It
did not even move when she grasped one of its upright scales and
pulled herself to sit on the flat place behind its head. She watched the
darting of its tongue and felt dizzy. When she shifted her gaze, sunset
leapt from the golden scales, and she covered her eyes with one hand.

The sea snake turned slowly, slipping from sand to ocean so
smoothly that she hardly felt it. Water parted silently around them.
She craned back and saw the rocks of the shore, smaller, smaller,
shadows. Everything shrinking except the sea—the sea alight for
another breath, and then one soundless crushing plunge away.

*Darkness, they moan, no more darkness, we beg you, and she says, I
know how you long for light—but there was darkness then, and
airlessness. I remembered the fishfolk lake and did not struggle. I
gripped the sea snake's scales with my hands and its sides with my legs,
and I did not close my eyes, even when fear began to rise like breath
in my throat. Perhaps I had been wrong, I thought; perhaps this beast
was taking me nowhere, taking me to a place of death—but as I
thought this, I saw light blossoming below us, a glow such as I had
never seen, streaming into my eyes and my lungs. I thought again of
the winter lake, and it seemed that everything there had been dimmer,
smaller—that it had not prepared me for this joy.*

Fishfolk circled and darted and sketched welcome in the water with
their long webbed hands. She bubbled at them, attempting to

respond with her own heavy fingers, trying to show them her stone at the same time. The sea snake slipped out from under her and surged away; other fish scattered, some changing direction together in a solid silver wall. Fish glowed in gigantic sprays of purple fern, curling tendrils of orange and pink that looked like fur; living rock soared in arches that dripped dark blue moss. She could not see a bottom to anything. Fish and plants and rock were suspended in currents of light that were not from any sun.

Two of the fishfolk beckoned to her and she followed them. She laughed into the water-air, spinning like a child, so quickly that colours blurred.

The gleaming green largest fishperson was floating in a forest of twisted coral. Jaele swam under an arm of it—vivid yellow—and held herself straight before the creature. Her two fishfolk companions were behind her, just visible. They spoke to their leader, who regarded her steadily. A moment of waiting—silence, if there had been clouds and grassy hill—and then she tried to speak as they did, as she had beneath the lake.

She outlined the spires of Luhr, clumsily, too quickly—but they drew closer to her, held out their hands in understanding, and she continued. The lake country in winter, the fingers of ice, darkness, the fishperson who had gripped her until the light. The fishfolk motioned to each other; she could not follow but knew somehow that they were excited, happy, remembering. When they had finished, she went on more slowly. She did not attempt to describe or repeat the words she had sketched to those others. She did not ask if they had seen a man swimming. She was ashamed of the way she had left the ones under the lake, lashing their hands away in anger; and she knew now that she was alone. She drew the sun, the east, herself swimming, hauling herself up on a shore.

The fishfolk were still. She cupped her hands so that the water was heavy in her palms. Light eddied over the large fishperson's body, and its scales pulsed with colours she had not seen before. At last it spoke, sketching hands like its own, steel, a queen's curse. Perhaps a question. She nodded, suddenly afraid. "No—do not," it said.

"Yes," she motioned, and yearned to tell it *mother father brother ashes,* in the words of her own language. After a moment she slashed at her throat, fluttered her hands in a slow spreading of blood, lowered her head. She unwrapped the dagger from the bundle at her belt and held it steady, east.

There was another silence. At last the large fishperson nodded. "We understand," it said. "But rest, now, before you go on."

The two fishfolk led her back under coral loops to a moss-covered rock screened by violet creepers. She started when she saw eyes, tiny and green, blinking from the vines. But she lay down somehow, the moss so soft that she sighed wreaths of bubbles. The fishfolk were gone. The light dimmed to reddish gold. She thought, *Only this morning with Ilario and Annial.* She reached for them. He wrinkled his face in pretended reproach as the water spun him gently. Annial's eyes lit with delight, her grey hair soft as a girl's around her face and shoulders.

The tiny eyes were turned to her when she woke. They blinked, stretched, retreated, blinked again. She smiled at them, digging her fingers and toes into the moss. "Farewell," she motioned as she slipped among them. The purple whispered on her back and legs.

There was a stand of seagreen below the rock. She picked an armful of strands and wound them around her belt. Not since her bay—she closed her eyes for a moment, feeling the seagreen rising, twining in her hair.

She had intended to seek out the large fishperson and the sea snake, but they were waiting for her by the coral. She remembered Serani and Bienta, their eyes tender before she could speak. Looking at the sea snake's slow coiling and the sheen of the fishperson's scales, the ache returned. Layers of sorrow, rage, fear, parting.

"Your strokes will lead you back," said the fishperson. Others had gathered; their hands were echoes. Jaele tried to draw "yes" in the honeyed water. A slender fishperson swam up to her; it held a blue bag. "Water and breath inside," the head fishperson said. "Clean, to drink when you are far from our lands."

Jaele took the bag, which was smooth, made of sea plants, perhaps. There were two fronds at its short neck; she tied them to her belt. She felt borne up by her old bundle, by the bag on the other side. *Now*, she thought.

The sea snake slid beneath her. She could feel its muscles bunching, and held tightly to the upturned scales. She looked at the fishfolk who were ranged around her in rings, below, beside, above, shining into the distance. "Thank you," she said. Their hands cried out, "Your strokes will lead you back"—all of them, so that her ears and eyes were dazzled as the sea snake leapt upward to the darkness.

Three spaces under the sea, she says later. *The fishfolk realm with its shining sunlit plants and coral, rock that breathed and sprouted moss. Then a dark, ruined space*—so dark that Jaele could hardly see the serpent below her, her iben-sight quenched as it had been beneath the fishfolk lake before the light. She clung, occasionally taking great gulps of air from the bag at her side. She felt crushed by water and the weight of silence.

The blackness was broken by sudden bursts, weals of colour that lit the water. At first she cringed, ducking her head; after a time she squinted and tried to see. They were creatures, their bodies illuminated from within. Some were shaped like overturned bowls, trailing glowing streamers; others were thin, striped and whorled with veins. There would be utter darkness for an age, then a series of flashes and the hiss of bodies brushing by them like wind. The sea snake did not falter.

Jaele learned to look below when the light ripped away blindness. She saw rows of volcanoes pluming smoke, ridging vast slopes and valleys. Crumbling stone buildings, arches fallen and scattered. A tower, once; they passed through its window and she saw a round table, a greened bronze pitcher on its side. Forests of bare trees still standing, covered in crescents of red fungus as large as her head. All this glimpsed in fragments so vivid that they burned against her eyes long after the creatures' light had passed.

There was no time. She tried to imagine Fane—spring around the harbour, the kitchen door propped open to the sun—but the images bled away, so far below. She and the sea snake, alone, and the strange, brilliant moments that might be long or short—she was not even sure of this. Seagreen, when she thought of it; air now and then. She knew that they would not stop moving, that they would not break the surface of the ocean. It was swifter below, undisturbed by waves, circles of twilight, stars, dawn.

She felt them change direction once. The next lightning flash revealed a hulking shelf of land on their left. *An island*, she thought, but they did not slow.

And then the sea snake did stop. She felt the difference, but was not sure until the creatures' light had flared twice. The same landscape of craters and dark mould and once molten chasms. The sea snake was shaking; she bent toward its head. Sensed then, despite the dull roar of ocean and body, a presence gathering behind them; a swelling, shrieking darkness untouched by the glow, which did not come again. She clutched the sea snake's scales, willing the drifting membranous creatures to show *what*— but there was nothing. The advancing darkness; a smothering press of cold.

When the sea snake burst away, she almost lost her grip. She was lifted off its back, her screaming filling her ears. Speed cracked her skin, her bones fissured and melted away; perhaps she was no longer on the sea snake but dissolving backward. The thing was still behind them, so close that smoke roiled the water. She needed breath—but no bag, no fingers, her lungs would be throbbing scarlet if she could look down—and just as she whimpered surrender, there was a light.

A sigh—they know what this means.

But not light as there was in the fishfolk realm. Not even the dim green light of the water in my bay. She falls silent, reaching for words.

As soon as they plunged into the new place, she could sense that the pursuing force had not followed them. They were stunned into stillness, hovering on the other side of a curtain. Wincing against the light. *But not light,* Jaele thought as she drank breath from the bag. Her head, skin, blood bloomed until she wriggled.

In the brown clarity she could see the sand bottom, flat and smooth. She tilted her head back and saw the water, which did not glint or shift. No movement at all, except where the sea snake's tail was gently winding: tiny ripples, instantly swallowed. *A tomb,* she thought, and knew how close they were.

The sea snake swam almost hesitantly. She felt its uneasiness, watched it turn its head to the barely ruffled water. "Who gave you this mission?" she asked it, trying to form the words with her mouth so that she would not forget. "Unlucky creature. So kind to help me—but if you had no choice?" The holes of its ears opened on her burbled sounds.

At last they saw a shape in the distance. Jaele and the serpent strained together, closer, until it lay below them. The rib cage of a boat, belled white almost gleaming. They passed above it, Jaele hunkering closer to the gold. Another boat, a length away; another.

A forest of bones. Search vessels, fishers' coracles, Raiders' crafts. So close.

Then—days, invisible moons later—the sea snake would not go forward. She waited, stubborn and hopeless. When it angled its head, she slid off. Her arms and legs churned at leaden water. She and the beast gazed at each other. She put a hand to its wedge-shaped cheek and watched its tongue flicker. *No, take me back. I'm sorry to have brought you this far, but I cannot . . . Come onto the shore with me; rise up on the end of your tail and strike. Be my army of silga and Queensfighters and Alilan, be Keeper and Bienta and Nossi and Aldreth and Dorin—beside me, touching me so my skin is warm as if brave.*

When she turned and swam away, she knew that the sea snake was still there, suspended above the skeleton ships. She flailed and thrust herself forward, so immediately exhausted that she could not remember diaphanous spinning. She thought she was moving upward—but maybe not. The water was unbroken, unchanging, and there seemed to be sand on all sides; sand under her eyelids, silting her throat. She was choking, thrashing as she never had, not even as a baby set free beside her mother's boat. Writhing until pain lanced through her skull.

There was stone—jagged as a blade, but she had to grasp it, had to pull. Through half-open eyes she saw blood branching from her fingers, blurring to cloud in the water. Sleepwalker scrabble up the rock. *Alneth, Alnila, Mother in your boat, Father at your loom help me, I am slipping.*

The ocean broke around her head, but she did not breathe. She dragged herself farther, to where the dagger stone became earth—gritty, sticky, sealing her eyes shut. Then she breathed, spewing water salt choking, bile tears that only seeped.

Jaele, bleeding and blind, curled on the shore of the Raiders' Land.

BOOK THREE

CHAPTER TWENTY-TWO

Thrust up on the sand, tender and bloodied as a baby, or something newly dead.

The land outside Jaele's closed eyes darkened and lightened several times; she knew this with her skin, which was sleeping. Sleeping on a beach drizzled with sunlight and ashes and wind-scattered smoke. A severed hand, a pain that turned her body white. A man gazing at her, with shifting leaves behind him.

One day her eyes opened, but she could not see. One day she told her arm to move and it did not; another day it did, and began to scrape the muck away. Her fingers were like stones sinking through water—except that the air was heavier than the sea. Flesh and innards grated, screamed swollen against the wind. A hot wind, the first thing she felt; nerve endings like the tiny ocean creatures she had seen, advancing in pink wisps from their shells, retreating in fear or unreadiness from the current. Hot as the desert, but different. Even in the desert there was whispered green.

Next the keening—the furnace wind driven over empty spaces, as she later knew. Then, just beginning to hear again, it was a sound of spines: piercing, embedded where she was most bruised. She began to quiver.

Her eyelashes cracked apart, first one by one, then together, wrenched by tears and fingers. She wept, so much salt because the light was harsh and scalding,

they hiss in pain, and she feels their hands reaching to cover her, to touch her face and their own—*We are sorry that our sight did not help—the lake, the enchanted fortress, the deep ocean—our vision weak in these places—and later you suffered as we do, in brightness*

then blinked her eyes clear. At first she could not understand— there was a maddened tilt of sky and hills. Then she knew that she was lying down, and that the hills were mounds of dirt a finger's breadth from her face. As soon as she realized this, the wind gave way to stones, to knubbled contours of earth that pressed into her woken body. She was bathed in heat and sores, awake, awake.

When she sat up, her gut heaved; she vomited sea and mucus, wiped her eyes, stared at the wet ground. Earth that was yellow-brown, coated in black dust. A few stones—rounded or broken-apart sharp. Only stones, but she looked away from them. Stood before she could think, rising into a smell of old burning.

Yellow-brown dirt and rock angled down to the sea. Rock slightly sloping, like the empty shells of sea creatures. She saw jagged and shattered shale where the waves rasped, the water so dark she could not imagine being beneath. She wrapped her torn arms around herself, gripping the sodden pieces of the tunic which had seen the desert and Keeper's hands. Her head was full of air, lifting her slowly away.

The sea was ridged with walls of water taller than she was, but the thunderclap noise of their breaking was dampened by the wind. She turned her head into this wind—turned herself around so that she was facing the land. It was flat except for the mounds of rock. The black dust still blew, soot and dirt shifting like rivers over the stone. There was nothing in the distance except sky, dun-coloured and crushingly empty. No paths, no boats pulled up on the shale, no webbed prints in the dust. She too was empty. Numb, now that she was standing on this shore. She tried to summon rage, grief, blood-need that would drive her inland—but could not. Even fear was still.

You are here—now walk. Her own voice, distant—and she did walk. Her feet dragged over the ground, over the lumped stone. She felt desperately clumsy; her bones had rent and fused again at alien angles, the ocean had warped her, she was carrying other bodies through the dust. She did not look up, concentrated on her shredded shoes and rip-nailed toes and the patches of earth around them. The wind whipped her hair into her eyes and mouth, and she stopped to bind it with a strip of her leggings. Hair still damp and clotted with sea.

She trudged for a long time with her gaze trained below. Gradually, there were more rocks, sharper, and different notes in the wind. She could no longer hear the sea, and looked up when she stopped walking.

Behind her was the flat expanse she had crossed, no view of ocean. In front was a line of hills, ragged piles of rock over which she could not see. She began to climb. Her hands wrists knees opened instantly, the barely knit wounds of her shore crawl coursing fresh blood. She crawled here too, struggling over rocks that fell away beneath her and clattered hollowly down. Her head echoed. There was darkness in her eyes; when she rested, she realized that the sky was deepening. Stars flickered among the soot that still hung in the air like mist.

She slept, stretched out on the stones. Her body jerked and twisted, heart quiet then hammering, and she woke in half-night. Her skin was tiny white pebbles under the wind. She shifted and crouched, reaching to climb again.

It was day. She did not remember the change, but the wind was stifling and the sky yellow, and the side of the rock hill fell away below her. She could see the summit, wobbling in the dust that was suddenly thicker, and in moments she was there. She knelt and coughed until her lungs burned. Then she rose.

There were countless stones here as well, but flatter and packed more closely together. She walked a few steps before halting. Bent to look, uncertain because of the soot—but it was there, a shallow pool of water, what had to be water, though it lay among the stones like squid's ink. It was warm and still; even her fingers breathed no ripples.

There would be water, stagnant, just enough to sustain them. They could voyage across the sea, but would die if they drank the water of other lands. Tepid black pool, then, motionless in rock, without reflection of sky or faces.

She remembered the fishfolk bag; for the first time since reaching the Raiders' Land, she felt it resting against her leg. She raised it to her mouth. Her lips were broken and edged as earth; water flowed over and in. The honeyed, clear water that had also been breath. She felt sunlit veins and blossoming, and moaned as she drank. She stopped herself—too soon, her thirst vast—because perhaps there would be an end, a bottom to the magic.

She ate seagreen—strands and strands, still tasting of fresh ocean. With each bite she felt a sharpening. The sky, distinct behind the dust; firm knobs of earth; her hands and limbs and skin and heart hardening like iron, but so light. She stood after her meal and began to slither down the slope beyond the pool—propelled, throbbing with rage and direction. *I am here for vengeance.* The words glittered with joy and knowledge. She was unafraid. Please: a village, a line of faces above webbed hands, *him*. She would run toward them all, crying *Reddac Lyalla Elic*. Sea Raider blood would soak this dust. Her father's dagger was cool in her palm; the cloak he had woven hung heavy, filthy, dazzling from her shoulders, held there by her mother's brooch of net and boat.

By the time she reached the bottom of the hill, darkness had fallen. A sallow moon rose, but its glow did not touch the ground. She had glimpsed nothing, while she was descending (black dust thick as rain); now a fog was obscuring hill and earth and her own feet. She sat with her arms around her knees and did not sleep.

Daylight thinned the fog to mist. She saw a runnel of water beading the rock face, gathering in another dark pool; she heard a steady dripping when the wind was quiet. There was a smell of vegetation rotted and dead, though she could see only water.

She moved and a large stone tumbled away from her foot. She winced, then leaned forward to look more closely at the stone. It was a deep, polished amber, smooth on all sides except one, which was covered with raised black lines. Thin and thick, spiralling, curling. She stared at the shape. After a moment she knew: a creature that had swum—the tiny, slender bones of fins, skull, tail. A fish from the green and blue before Queen Galha's curse.

She touched the marks and sadness threaded unexpectedly through the weaving of her strength. She rose and began to walk swiftly, the mist parting around her (perhaps they closed their mouths on this fog, yearning). She was looking at her feet again; other fossils lay gleaming on the ground. A trail, deliberately made: each of the fossil-bearing sides had been laid up, so that she saw their dark shapes as she passed. There were bones and scales—also fern, fronds pressed and moulded, ghostly in black.

When she lifted her eyes, the last of the mist had burned away. She halted: in the clarity she saw a garden. It was many long paces

ahead of her, so lifelike that at first she did not notice the absence
of colour. A stand of trees, boughs heavy with fruit and vines;
flowers with petals wide and soft; tall grasses gently bent by a
breeze.

She stepped toward the place and saw that it was stone. She
heard herself whimper, but kept walking. The stone was cool,
smoothed white; somehow there was no black dust. Veins of leaves
and stems, folds of bark, roughness of moss and lichen, grass tufts
covered in the fuzz of seed: all bleached and silent, yet living—until
her fingers met rock. She stood in the waist-high grass and turned
so that she could see the rock hill behind her, the angled, empty
land ahead. *Their webbed hands have carved and stroked in memory*.
Stories of vibrant leaves and streams, told by grandparents who had
never seen, to children who would never see?

She walked on and emerged from the grass at a lake, wide and
long. Most of the surface was puckered with imagined rain; near
the shore was the tail fin of a plunging fish. At the far end, though,
water again became rock and dirt, and there was no more carving.
She could see the place where the work had stopped—suddenly, a
ripple half done. She sat down there.

No numbness, no rage and eagerness—gone, swallowed like
bones by rock. Soundlessly, graspingly, she cried out to remember.
As if the force of the noise in her head could show it to her again:
the boats, the blood, the leader's hands, fire streaking through the
thatch. The faces of her family. *Bring me their faces at least—let me
see again*. But no. No.

It was night, so soon. She slept by the unfinished lake. Dreamed
of sounds: pound, pulse, trickle, drip. Rustle as well, and hiss. When
she woke, her mouth was gaping and the hot wind was howling
through the stones.

She left the garden and walked on because it seemed she must.
She ate some seagreen and drank two swallows of water. Soot and
shattered rock on yellow ground—she did not turn back to look at

the trees and plants. That night she dreamed she was floating, suspended in water warmer than any she had ever felt. Even the fishfolk water had not been like this. Like liquid sun—her bones soft beneath her skin.

She drank deeply after she woke, no longer caring if she reached the bottom of the fishfolk bag. When she was finished, she tilted it, wincing at the cold coursing of the water over her breasts and stomach. She followed the water with her eyes: wet and dark down her body, drops of it falling from the hem of her tunic to the earth, where they hissed and vanished. She poured a stream from the bag—the hiss was louder, and it seemed for a moment as if there was smoke—and the ground remained dry.

Later that day she came to a jumble of massive boulders, with the shadow of a hole beneath them. She did not hesitate.

You know that darkness is slow and weak, for us. Our prison. Their voices seem clogged with earth.

Wait—it is not what you think. Listen.

Her iben-sight showed her a broad sloping path free of stones. The walls were high; the roof far above was veined with silver. Ten people could have walked beside her. She knew that if she spoke, her words would leap and return and leap and return.

The path curved down and around so gently that she was surprised when she looked back and found the entrance gone. She touched the walls, almost expecting them to be damp, but they were coarse and crumbling; her fingers smelled of ash. The air was grey, not completely dark as she had anticipated. Down and around, her footsteps muffled, her ribs echoing heart.

After a time she came to a sharper bend, and saw the reflected shimmer of light beyond it. She stopped and stared. There was no sound—but her feet stuck. Such fear, humming in the silence.

She closed her eyes and stepped around the corner. Halted immediately as light bathed her eyelids and iben-sight receded. Then she looked, moved forward, saw.

It was a river-chiselled cavern, streaming with water and sunlight. Rain on the river, gold on the river, dazzled, dappled motion like music which washed her eyes with tears. But no. No, no—and she dropped to her knees, looking down at the dry bed and up at the rock roof etched with holes. Long slender holes like ripples; tiny clustered holes like rain; large round holes like suns, moons. Others—small, scattered, perhaps random, perhaps constellations.

They have laboured, they have made this place so beautiful it is real, it is sacred.

She covered her eyes and wept. Cracks, ribbon-thin at the stone garden, lanced wide. *I am sorry—so sorry—I have failed you all, I did not run at their backs so that they faltered, I did not run after him, not fast enough—and now I cry in this place that is theirs.*

When she opened her eyes, she was lying on her back. Light and rain eddied over her skin. Sun edged to silver and stars spun; she was tossed among them like driftwood. She knew these stars—or maybe time was folding. She heard the river, and dreamed.

✧   ✧   ✧

It is deep green. Somehow everything is green, soft, laden with water. Vines and blossoms brush the river, which foams and sings and whittles at the rock. Whittles and surges, rises from the earth in spray and flows down to pools, down to jugs, down to mouths, down to the sea. Children with the hands and feet of seabirds follow the river, singing and breathing and stretching older, liquid

green. They walk as well, and speak with sounds like ground
pebbles, and they gather and cut wood into boats for carrying food,
fresh water, strange, unimaginable things borne back from beyond
the pools and flowers. The ocean is wider than the river; the ocean
is forever. Their voices clamour, more and more above, and only
the children follow the river. They sink to the silence of their blood,
lie still among thick creepers and coiled trunks until night darkens
the water. They lie still because this will become memory later, in a
desert. Memory that will keen in the webbed hands that carve or
kill. But now the green—deeply green.

✧   ✧   ✧

She was awake and running, her cries wrapped around her in wind.
Something following her—pebble voices, the shadow of a boy—as
she fled over broken earth, over sand, over sodden jungle leaves.
Stars burned through the dust as she ran, and the Raiders' Land lay
gilded and stark, though she did not see it. She saw nothing—not
even the webbed footprints, not the stone that caught her foot and
sent her sprawling. Her eyes closed again, though not in green-
drenched sleep.

Silence woke her. Wind and distant water were still, and she sat
up, frowning and uncertain. A moment later she remembered:
fossils, a frozen garden, a lake and a light-filled riverbed. She rose
and saw the garden far behind her, and the black-toothed hills
behind it.

She walked toward the vines and blossoms and the almost-
finished lake. The silence all around her; she heard only her own
breath and the thud of her feet, and they were someone else's. She
was beyond empty, beyond the numbness of her arrival: she was
apart, away, nowhere. Absent in a wide and barren place.

As she drew nearer to the carvings, she finally saw the footprints.
For a few paces she watched her own feet scuffing them, scattering

them back to formless dust. Then she stopped and knelt, her fingers reaching out to follow the lines of webs and flesh and bone. She lifted her eyes and traced the steps until she could not see them. Then she looked at the garden and saw him sitting against the stone.

Her dagger slid smoothly out. She held it before her as she rose and walked on, her feet in the marks of his. Closer, as the wind began to blow; closer, as he sat and did not move. At first she thought his stillness must be sleep, and her steps quickened. Closer—she saw ragged cloth, paleness of legs and arms; she saw blood on his face and she saw his eyes, open and raised to hers.

She stood above him. Blood on his hollow cheeks, on his arms, his hands. His skin oozing, cracked, the webs between his fingers hanging jagged and torn. His lips drawn blistered over blackened teeth. There was a smell—rotten leaves, wet before crumbling. His chest heaved with shallow, moist, grating breaths. His eyes were wide and unblinking and golden brown.

She stood above him with her father's dagger in her hand and her mother's brooch at her throat. His eyes moved to the brooch and back to her face. She remembered him on her beach, in Keeper's palace, across the shonyn river. Remembered him ahead of her, behind her, shaping and wounding. And now here. She gazed down on him and saw his helplessness and knew that the dagger would not be enough.

She sat, watching his eyes. When she untied the neck of the fish-folk bag, she saw him flinch (widening cracks, new blood) and blink once, slowly. Water flowed from the bag into her mouth, down her face, along her arms; it beaded on her skin and hissed away to nothing on the ground. She drank, and still she watched him. His eyes, which burned as she had known they would; his lips drawn up in a silent snarl.

After she had drunk, she sat with her dagger balanced atop her crossed legs. Light faded, and they were sunk in the garden's shadow—but she could see the white glint of his eyes, the black weeping of his skin. She held herself very straight and did not sleep. When the darkness began to thin, she lifted the dagger from her lap and rose.

He watched her stand. Then he moved: his right hand and arm groped along the earth behind him. She clenched her muscles, bunched them ready and aching. He dragged his hand back again and she saw a knife. His knife, longer than hers, blade curved and notched. He held his knife up to her, hilt first, trembling.

Her mother's throat as it gaped; her mother's eyes. Blood like rivers snaking to the sea. This blade. She watched her own white fingers reaching, taking it in her hand so that she was holding two daggers. He gazed at her and did not blink.

She took a stumbling step back, then another. For a moment she could not see him: saw instead her father's hands, upturned, outstretched, empty. A throat splintering beneath her own dagger as horses reared against desert sky and torchfire, as her eyes and flesh blazed red. The earth was hard with stones; she did not remember sitting. One dagger lay on either side of her. Her hands were wet and she looked down. Sweat, not blood. A breath came swift with relief. Not blood.

She looked at him and he at her, across a space of shifting dust. The sky darkened until he was a featureless shape against the vines. Her breathing was as loud as his, as loud as Ilario's. Blood and bones, plucking at skin. Ilario sitting against the wall beneath her window, snow so thick behind him that she could not see the sky.

Voices muttered and she almost recognized them. *I like those stories . . . I ran, I hid . . . Maybe you discover, maybe not . . . But there weren't many of them . . . Comforted? Do you think it will be that easy, Jaele? . . . They began to sicken, for the water they had brought with them was gone . . . In her heart was desert and blood . . . Perhaps it is only a story . . .*

When she woke at sallow dawn, he was slumped to one side with his head resting on a rounded stone fruit. His eyes were closed. She leaned forward and heard his breathing, quieter now, and saw that his chest barely lifted. Fresh blood seeped from the cracks in his flesh and wound slowly down, into the dust.

He did not move when she rose. She stood for a moment; then she left her bundle, the fishfolk bag, the daggers, and walked. She walked to the foot of the hill and drank black water from a puddle, and she was surprised that it did not dissolve in her mouth like jungle fungus, yellow with its own dust. She bent her head and drank from the pool without reflection or ripple. The water was thick and salty, and she retched before she drank again.

He was lying twisted on his back when she returned to the garden. His eyes were still closed. She went to the far end of the carving and drew her fingers along the edges of vine and blossom, along the foaming crests of waves on the stone lake beside. *This beauty that is theirs,* she thought—and then, like breath after deep water, she *did* see. The Raiders in their ragged animal skins: tattered, frightened men and women who had thrown their own leader's body into the fire. The fear in the eyes of the one who had held her mother—the man who had not wanted to kill her mother. The man who had run into forest, into red stone corridors and ivy; the man who had swum rather than use his dagger again.

A shocking new pain held her still. Faces, motions, were changed. Memory was changed. She closed her eyes, wrapped herself in breath and the winding, shifting colours of before and now. Willingly, as the pain spread like flame or ivy beneath her skin.

When she opened her eyes, she saw stars. She walked to the black pool to drink again, then returned for the last time to the garden. She sat beside him through a night that seemed to deepen and deepen. She spun in darkness, holding to the thread of his breathing. An ocean of darkness, endless and cold. The black salt water rose again in her throat. Then light seeped, sluggish as his blood, and smoothed at the stars until they vanished into ash.

When she touched the jutting bone of his shoulder, his eyes fluttered open. Golden brown, burning with thirst and death. She raised the fishfolk bag so that he could see it; she watched his eyes focus and widen. She took a long swallow of water and closed her own eyes against tears. Then she held the bag out to him.

Dust eddied in the scalding wind. His lank hair stirred against the ground, leaving lines as delicate as the imprints of fins in rock. She still watched his eyes, his face; she knew what he had decided before she saw his nod.

Although she only touched him gently, behind his head, his skin chipped like bark beneath her fingers. She felt a rush of hot blood, and the fishfolk bag shook in her hand. She cupped his head and angled the mouth of the bag toward his.

Water fell, clear and light. His blistered lips glistened. He swallowed, swallowed again, and raised his eyes to the sky. His chest lifted in one deep clean breath. For a moment she thought that the fishfolk water might be different, that there would be another breath, and another. But there was one, only. His head eased back into her hand and she laid it carefully down against the earth.

Later, as the sky began once more to darken, she straightened his limbs and pressed his eyelids closed. She walked to the lake and shivered into sleep beside the frozen waves. She woke in daylight and looked down at him. His body was already crumbling, its edges sifting away over the dry, bloodied ground.

She knelt beside her bundle and laid its contents out before her, as she had done on the dock, the night Annial's hairpins had fallen shining to the carpet. Jaele looked at the stones, the map, the broken neckring. She had seen the faces of the Sea Raiders and found them changed; now she saw other faces. Murtha's.

Murtha, who did not want revenge. Not against the tree silga, not against the Sea Raiders, of whom he probably knew nothing. Bienta—he gave me an ancient map and I looked only at my own path. You—you sang to me and I felt only bitterness, even when you gave me your gift of light in dark places. And Keeper. Keeper Told me his life, and I saw only his towering servitude—except for that moment when he showed me his eyes and I knew my own smallness. And then, briefly, when I looked at the sand where the palace had been. But only briefly, and soon forgotten. So much forgotten. And so much running. Flying through these lives, when perhaps it was they who lit, so fleetingly, in mine?

Aldreth and Nossi, skinny Alin and Grandmother Alna. Serani and Bienta. Saalless and Lallan. Ilario and Annial, Serdic and Tylla. The Perona woman. And him, his people—people of blood and ragged skins, vanished green and water. I remembered all of them then. Remembered them as I could not, before this place, and wept.

When I had no more tears, I looked inland. I saw nothing, of course. No distant huts, no webbed prints in the dust, no raging red behind my eyes. I could have walked on, past the place where he lay. I had come so far to seek among these stones.

"There is choice for you, child." Grandmother Alna's words, and tears in the creases of her face—and I had kissed her, grasped my dagger, leapt down the wagon steps. My choice to kill a Perona woman? To look for a desert battlefield and then turn back? To run through a jungle? My choice—now, only now. A knot unbound, and a tender aching place beneath.

Jaele put the stones and map back in her pouch. The twisted neck-ring she left on the ground beside him. Then she picked up the two daggers and walked. Away from the stone garden and past the fossils, up and over the hill with its thick black water. Through blowing ash to the shale at the edge of the ocean.

Fog rose from the water into the dun sky, into her face as she stood on a tumble of boulders. Waves soaked her and sucked at her feet, but she stood firmly, even when she drew back her arms. She threw her father's dagger and the Sea Raider's and they flew. Her vision bloomed briefly outward like blood in the tide, staining, spreading again to clear. After a moment she dove out beyond the rocks. She swam in long, steady strokes, westward and away.

RETURN

CHAPTER TWENTY-THREE

My companion sea snake was waiting for me, circling in the dead water, twining among the bones of the ships. It carried me again, and there were stars everywhere, in the sky and in the water. We did not dive. I thought: I understand—it is a different journey now.

There was a storm, after the first calm, conscious night. Jaele clung to the sea snake's familiar ridges, numb with cold and weariness. Waves pitched, rose black against the sky, screamed down upon them with such force that her nerves died. Lightning split, horizontal and red.

Ah—remember when you came to us, time ago. There was skylight above, and Llana fled and found you among the stones. You were small and crumpled.

She was withered, empty, battered by water and noise; she clung to the scales with hands she could not feel. Only when the clouds parted on blue did she lift her head.

The sea snake was not moving—only drifting, carried by the swells. Birds perched atop the water—up up, gently down. Birds. Shreds of seagreen and moss, torn by the storm. Fish spinning, glancing beaded light. Sudden returning life. Jaele craned forward.

Land rose from the rolling ocean. At first she thought it was her land, that she had slept so long—but she knew in a breath that it was not. The sea snake began to swim again, and details sharpened: trees spread thick and dark; a sweeping violet beach; massive wooden rafts lashed to what seemed to be tree trunks, growing bald from the water. She bent her head, queasy, and concentrated on scales.

The violet sand hissed as the sea snake's belly touched it. She gazed at this sand, which was fine, with scatterings that looked like gems. Unclenching her hands, she slid off the creature's back. She slept immediately, curled in the serpent's shadow as the sun climbed and sank.

She woke blazing with thirst. Sat up and waited until the dizziness had faded, then rose, leaning on the sea snake's flank. She did not drink from the fishfolk bag. "Still here, friend?" she asked, and her words rasped. It angled an eye at her and blinked, and she tried to smile.

The trees began about thirty paces from the shoreline. They soared into the light, sheathed in huge four-pointed leaves and clusters of berries or larger fruit. She walked slowly, until sunlight only dappled her skin and ragged tunic. She reached up and grasped a silver-white bunch. Round, three in her palm, crimson within, soft golden seeds so sweet her teeth ached. She moaned as she ate, as the juice coursed and dried and stained her fingers, deeper than blood. (Had he moaned, eating Murtha's berries, Keeper's fruit, Serdic's?) She walked on, eating until her arms were numb from stretching. She found a pool, clean and still, dark with tree shapes. She bent and sipped. It was fresh water—fresher, even, than that in the fishfolk bag lying on the shore.

When her mouth and stomach rang—enough—she sat with her back against one of the great trunks. The sea snake's gold shone against the sand; the ocean lay seamless and clear. No wind, no waves. The rafts shifted soft as whisper.

She slept again, after the sun had fallen away in scarlet. Almost dreamed, but wrested herself away, further into darkness. Voices woke her.

They were loud, laughing, singing. She heard a clacking as well, and knew what it was. She remembered Dorin leading her among the wonders of Luhr, remembered the fishfolk and their mats, and the half-giants' clacking songs. *Eels' scales,* she thought as the half-giants came clamouring onto the beach.

She crouched beneath her tree, hidden by its shadow. They were to her right, many paces away, but she saw them clearly. There were three women and three men, all at least twice her height, perhaps more. Fishing nets swung from their shoulders and jogged against their hide-wrapped legs; three also carried wooden poles. A few half-giant steps back from the water, the poles were dug into the sand. Jaele saw that they were connected with rope, which stood taut when the poles had been secured.

The sea snake had disappeared, Jaele noticed as the half-giants strode into the ocean. They walked out and out, singing; she understood nothing but glee. When they reached the rafts, the water was at their necks. She watched them haul their glistening bodies onto the wood, watched them throw the nets shining as spiders' webs, or birds', against the sky.

Their nets and arms were enormous; the fishing did not take long. The rafts remained tethered to their tree trunks; the half-giants simply tossed the nets and pulled them slowly back. Tails and fins and mouths thrust above the surface so that it was stormy. The fishers laughed and clacked above the noise. When all six nets lay alongside the rafts, the half-giants leapt into the water and surged back to the shore.

They sliced and gutted their catch so swiftly that Jaele could hardly see their hands. By the time the sun was directly overhead, the nets sagged empty and the ropes were thick with split, cleaned fish. The half-giants stood together for a few moments, talking and gesturing; then they turned and walked again toward the trees.

She did not move. She remained beneath the tree, hidden until long after they had passed. Unready—still too tender.

She ate more of the silver fruit as the sun dipped again toward the sea. She also found berries, fat and blue among vines, and these were bitter. At dusk she walked among the slanting outlines of fish, poles, rope, but touched nothing. Invisible, her footprints already skimmed away by night wind.

The sea snake had returned, and lay with its head and neck raised out of the water, regarding her unblinkingly. She placed her fingers lightly on the smaller, smoother scales beneath its jaw. "Time again," she said, and cleared the rough strangeness from her throat. Then stood with her feet washed in waves, yearning for new direction.

The sea was stranger on top than underneath—stranger in light, distance, time. Maybe because of the sky. The space around us was so endless that I saw clouds above and away—but farther, a flood of white-gold, or a column of spinning rose. I could never tell how far. The water we swam in was calm, but I could see waves advancing, so distant that sometimes they never reached us. Once or twice the sea snake arched us up into the air, but we were still so tiny. I wanted to

be lost, but we weren't. Just tiny. I think of Ilario's carpet now, and Bienta's map, although I didn't then. I thought of nothing, in those first days—felt nothing except hunger and thirst. It is only now, telling this to you, that I try to know what I saw.

Once, a waterspout thundered upward, shattered by dawn sun. The sea snake slowed, and they passed so close that Jaele's body was soaked as if by rain. Colours leapt and wove, and her ears pounded. They glided into clear water beyond the spout. When she turned back, it was gone. They swam on, out of, into silence.

Just before the first shorebirds appeared, they met a group of sea snakes. The creatures rose from the waves, cascading water and grunting, chirping, bellowing. Some were very small; others were huge, and could have carried many of Jaele. For a time they travelled together, the others leaping around them so playfully that she smiled. Then, with final noises and a slapping of tails, they sank. Bubbles frothed and stilled. "You are nearly free," she said to her sea snake, and knew that this was so.

As they drifted and swam, Jaele remembered. Not fire in thatch or blood-clotted sand; not her own fingers scraping stone, in silence. Those would return—but later, and perhaps changed. Now she remembered holding her brother on her lap, smelling sun and salt in his silken baby hair. Remembered her parents' voices late at night, laughing and low. *"Don't talk so loudly, Reddac,"* her mother whispered, *"Jaele's sleeping,"* and her father whispered back, *"No she isn't,"* with such a smile in his voice that Jaele almost giggled. And then she thought of Lallan by the river, saying, *"They are here, present."* "River tree earth house man woman," Jaele murmured in Lallan's language. "Water cloud shore black wood looping time."

Images bruised but not raw, unburied and shining in the Eastern Sea.

Rain was falling when she heard the bird calls. This was the first rain. It was flesh-strippingly cold, and her hands were slithering nerveless from the sea snake's ridges. She lifted her head; the noise came again, raucous and close. Bird cries—and suddenly she smelled the land: wet, moss-covered rocks, dripping leaves, woodsmoke, roasting meat and peeled sourfruit. She closed her eyes.

The coast advanced in pieces, edges, shadows through the downpour. She felt the sea snake slowing; felt its belly grind against pebbly sand. Neither of them moved for a long while. When her eyes opened, she saw a flicker of hillside, and knew that it had brought her to the place where they had begun.

The serpent lowered its head, and its body vibrated; somewhere deep within was a thrumming, a warm urging voice. She slipped smoothly down and stood on her shore. Scales were slick against her forehead; perhaps if she leaned long enough, she would carry their imprint away with her. She straightened and stroked the great neck, the wedge-shaped nose, and its tongue darted dry along her hand. She smiled.

"Please," she said, and held the fishfolk bag out to it, "take this back to them. I do not need it now." The sea snake opened its mouth; hand-sized teeth closed gently around the bag. "Farewell," she said more quietly, the word lost in rain. Then she turned. She walked, even though she could not yet feel her feet or the earth— walked up the slope and did not look back.

Fane's streets were deserted but for the rain, which coursed brown and choppy as the branches of a river. It was warmer water than the sea; Jaele began to sense blood again, a sluggish prickling through her veins. There was stone beneath her, peeling paint and buildings beside, arches and tunnels, damp, drifting smoke. A person passed her once, hunched and hooded; she shrank against a wall and did not breathe until she was again alone.

Only two boats rolled in the harbour now. She stood on the wharf and gazed at them so that she would not have to turn her eyes elsewhere. Time had passed, and there were only two boats. She could not remember what the missing one had looked like. Ragged and splintering—but exactly?

The house was grey as rain, except for the darker smudge of door. She could not tell if there was smoke, or shapes behind the windows. She walked slowly.

It was warm: the lanterns were lit, and although the fires in the front hearth and in the kitchen were very low—almost out—the wood was still deep red with heat. The door was unlocked. There was a smell of slightly burning bread. I knew as soon as I stepped inside that the house was empty. I stood by the round table and stared at the scrolls and books, scattered as if I had just missed the hand that had moved them.

I pulled the bread from the oven using Annial's wooden paddles. There were black, cracked-open bubbles on the top of each small loaf. I was so faint that I could hardly put them on the cooling rack. I ate, scalding my fingers and mouth, consumed by guilt because how could I eat Annial's bread when she was gone?

She ate bread and seagreen and speckled sourfruit that was palely unripe. Drank water from the barrel outside the kitchen door. Sat in a wall niche, limp with sleep, following the rain on the moon windows.

She woke in the night and called out for Ilario before she remembered. The silence made her shiver. She rose and went through the reading-room to the stairs. They creaked, of course. The hallway lanterns were also lit, but were flickering more faintly than the ones below. She did not turn to the left to her room—right instead, to a door she had never opened.

The walls were bright with cloaks, with tapestries, with glancing firelight. The bed was high off the carpeted floor, covered in a many-coloured blanket. There was a wooden cabinet with glass doors; inside were leggings and tunics, carefully folded.

There were only four books here, all slender and bound in dark green. They were stacked on a small square table beside the bed. Jaele sat on the blanket and reached for them. She opened the uppermost book with trembling fingers; the pages rustled and creased. They were cream-coloured pages, the ones at the end clean and fresh. She turned to the beginning.

Ilario's writing was beautiful. The letters looped and twined, and the lines were spaced as if he had measured the distance between them. He had used a dark red writing stick. There were no smudges, no words scratched out and begun again. "There is a roughness in my throat that is not the winter—I am sure of it, although Annial steeps me in herb water and scolds me as if I were merely a boy with a chill."

She closed this book and drew out the bottom one. Black writing stick this time, and words that slanted gently at the edges of the page. "Tonight the man with the wooden flute spoke of Luhr, and I watched the name appear in the weaving of the carpet. He was young and tall and fair, and sang to me when the others had gone to sleep. I was so small when father took me to Luhr, but this traveller made me remember."

I could not read more. The cloak I had watched him buy was shining—the cloak I would bury my face in before leaving the

*room, seeking his scent and the years and years of his warmth
which I had not known. I grieved for him before I knew for certain—
and I had thought, so recently, that this keen grief was past.*

No fire burned in her hearth, and the room was chilly. (Was it
spring, still, or early summer? Or autumn? Her body twinged,
almost throbbed its confusion.) She knelt by the carpet and could
not speak; the darkened shore lay empty. She glanced at her bed,
which was neatly made, and rose to look out the window. Rain
pattered, then pounded as the wind lashed. She could hardly see the
boats; the cliffs had vanished.

She stripped off her tattered clothing and slept with the blanket
drawn up to her chin. Dreamed of piping, horses, pitching stars.
The rain had stopped when she opened her eyes. Voices rose from
the docks. She washed her face and stretched into a tunic that lay
folded on the table. Soft, blue, newly stitched. It felt unbearably
light against her skin.

Jaele threaded her way among people and streets.

*I had been away—far away, alone and in silence—for so long: I felt
myself blinking, waking in these streets. Imagine how you will feel,
walking again in your mountain air. I thought, "I wept in a stone
garden by a lake," and I was filled with that place and this one, both.*

She came to the fruit market almost without thinking, and
walked quickly past the rotting wagon. Tylla was working alone
in the sourfruit chamber. Her hair shone red in the weak

sunlight. She saw Jaele among the other customers and turned her face away.

"Tylla," Jaele said, and for the first time in so long heard an answering voice.

"I am surprised that you are here. Forgive me if I do not seem happy to see you."

Jaele breathed deeply. "I did not expect a warm welcome—nor do I deserve one." A plump man dropped five shells into Tylla's palm and reached for three small sourfruit. Jaele said, "I have been away, as you know. Annial and Ilario are gone, but everything in their house is warm, even the bread."

There was a long silence. Tylla walked over to a pile of sourfruit, rearranged it. When she returned, she spoke steadily. "Go to our sourfruit grove. Go now, before I decide you should not."

"Thank you," said Jaele.

The river was swollen, deafening. She found and followed it until she saw the hewn steps, the ledge, the rust-handled door. She did not slow or stop; a new fear was waiting.

Her feet sank into the earth of the grove and she stood still for a moment, bathed in leaves. She heard Annial singing: a young girl's voice, caught and reflected by scarlet branches. Jaele followed it as she had the river.

Serdic turned to her when she came through the trees. He was sitting on the ground beside Annial. Her hair was loose and tangled over her thin shoulders; her eyes were wide and soft. Hands upturned and motionless in her lap. Lips cracked, open on this song that had no words, only lovely piercing waves.

Serdic was smiling so sadly that Jaele dropped to her knees in front of him. She held out her hand, which shook; he grasped it in his, which did not. His cheeks and neck still curved white bruised.

"Annial." Jaele repeated her name until the singing faltered and died.

Annial's eyes darkened with focus, leapt from Jaele's face to the leaves and back. "He is gone," she said in a brittle voice, "and I am gone. In my way. Young Serdic has kindly brought me here. And you are safe, sweetlet. Jaele."

Jaele reached for her, took the tiny sharp hands in her own—but they lay still, and the song began again. After a moment Serdic drew her up and led her into the trees.

They stood apart. She rubbed the backs of her hands across her eyes, and he spoke, low and quickly. "Ilario died about four days ago. I had been visiting him—them—every day since my return from my village. Four days ago I arrived at the house. I could hear Annial screaming while I was still outside. She was holding him so tightly that I had to hurt her, I think, to separate them. She quieted, and I carried her here. Then him. It was like carrying a baby—not a child, a baby." He paused; she watched him swallow. "Tylla and I buried him among the roots. Yesterday at dawn Annial wandered away and I found her at the house, baking bread and tending the fires. She held out her hand when she saw me, and after I had damped down the fires, we came back here. She has been singing since then. Not eating or drinking or sleeping—only singing."

"Could you tell," Jaele said after a moment, "if there was pain for him?" She wanted to say more but did not.

Serdic touched the line of her jaw, very lightly. "I cannot say. Not without guessing. But he looked as if he were trying to sleep."

They went back to Annial and sat with her as she sang. She paused once and said to Jaele, "He is a good boy," then sang again, as if she had not spoken. Jaele closed her eyes. She had been to the Raiders' Land, where everything had changed; now here, among the crimson trees where Ilario also was, enfolded by earth and roots.

"It is late," Serdic said at last. "Tylla will be back soon." He and Jaele smiled at each other.

"Ah," she said. "Then I suppose I should leave." She rose and kissed Annial's hair. The old woman lifted a hand to touch her.

Serdic and Jaele walked slowly toward the door. "It is so good to see you, Jaele," he said, not looking at her. "Did you find what you sought?"

She took a few steps. "I do not know. Yet." Then, swiftly, "And you? How was the winter in your town?"

They faced each other, the door and distant river roar beside them. "It was beautiful," he said with another small smile, "as it always is." Annial's song was a thread, now, winding and thin.

"Serdic, I am sorry—so sorry. For . . . before."

He shook his head. "Never mind before." She stepped into his arms and felt him breathe once, twice.

"I am here to stay this time," she said as she drew away.

Serdic put his hand to the door ring and she slipped out of the grove.

CHAPTER TWENTY-FOUR

"Here to stay." I imagined that it was true, at first.

The days and nights were warm after the rain had passed. The fires in the house burned to ash, except in the kitchen. Jaele returned to the sourfruit grove on an afternoon that smelled of spices and blossoms. She leaned over the bridge and watched the muddy river; the scales of the carved fish were slippery beneath her palms.

Annial was sleeping on a pallet against one of the kitchen walls. Tylla and Serdic were at the table, which was covered with freshly picked sourfruit. Jaele smiled at Tylla's look of surprise. "Yes," she said, "this time I came back."

The girl smiled slowly in return. "I—we are glad of it."

Jaele sat next to Annial and touched one of her bone-ridged hands. She remembered Saalless and thought, *They could have filled*

313

each other up with memories. "I am happy to see her sleeping," she whispered, and Serdic nodded.

"It was days before she would—and now she sleeps more than she wakes."

"And does she still sing?" Jaele asked.

"Sing when you are far from me, sing when you are near." Jaele looked down into Annial's eyes, which were clear and bright as fish-folk sea. It was a song they all knew. They sang it together, Annial's voice rising above the rest, and then they sang others—children's ditties, ballads of love and battle—until the sourfruit had all been cleaned and put into baskets and bags.

"I am not sleepy," Annial declared when there seemed to be no more songs. She was still lying down, her stiff fingers bent around Jaele's.

"That is good," Jaele said, "because I wanted to talk to you. I wanted to tell you that you can come back to the house and live with me there. I will stay with you. If you like."

Annial regarded her—they all did. Jaele could hear the crimson leaves rustling; could hear, almost, roots twining above and below the earth. At last Annial said quietly, "Hania is gone, and her children, and theirs, and now my Ilario. I knew I would be alone—but not there, where we lived together. I cannot go back there. And," she continued, her eyes sharpening on Jaele's face, "you are a traveller, like all the others."

"But I *will* stay," Jaele said, then fell silent. She gazed at the crystal, which shone as brightly as she remembered. Tylla disappeared into the trees with bags of sourfruit slung over her shoulder.

Annial hummed a tune Jaele did not know. Then she unclasped her hands from Jaele's and said, "I will be happy, in Lirella's grove."

"Who is Lirella?" Jaele asked Serdic later, as they sat on one of the docks, in the shadow of the two ships.

"My grandmother. She and Annial were friends, especially after Hania died."

Jaele lifted her face to the sky, which was tumbled with white clouds. Sunlight lanced between them—white-gold in the water that rolled only softly.

"This wind makes me want to travel," Serdic said. "To follow the road as far as it goes." He paused. "I suppose you've had your fill of travel."

She smiled. "That is more than true." She looked past the boats, eastward into emptiness. "I am sorry I cannot tell you what I found there, Serdic." She remembered Nossi's words then, and her fierce smile as she spoke them. *"It would be glorious. A tale Told by generations of Alilan."*

Oh, Nossi, it was not that way.

"I do not ask you to tell me," Serdic said quietly. "It is enough that you are safe, that you have come back." After a moment he said, "And that you plan to stay."

She laughed. "Another question that isn't. And yes—I meant what I said, to you and to Annial."

They both looked back at the house—tall and pointed, smudged with grime of storms and smoke. "It will need painting," he said.

"Indeed," she answered, "and I thank you for offering."

They painted the house blue: *the blue of the sky above Luhr, of Nossi's eyes.* Serdic arrived from the market in time for the evening meal and left long after sundown, which was later every day. At first they ate awkwardly, quickly, eager to retreat to the ladders and the wobbly glimpses of tile and cloud. As the days passed, they lingered in the kitchen; Serdic showed Jaele how to make sourfruit cakes, and she read to him from the books and parchments. They laughed and talked and cooked—and every evening he returned to his grove, and she climbed the winding wooden staircase to her bedroom.

When the painting was done, they sat at the very end of the outer dock with their backs to the darkening sea. "A fine job," Serdic declared. "It is an entirely different house."

"Yes," Jaele agreed, and looked down at her blue-freckled hands with a twinge of sadness. She smiled, though, when she glanced at him.

"What are you smiling at?" he asked, without turning to her.

"You," she replied. "You're blue. I think it may suit you."

He did turn to her then, and they sat very still. Jaele said at last, "Thank you. For your friendship."

"You make me happy," he said, and again she felt a shadow, a breath of footsteps that led away.

"I was very angry before," she said. "About many things."

"And now?"

"And now I do not know. There has been a change—but I am still not sure. I am still unready, somehow." "*So much unfinished in me,*" she had wanted to say to Nossi, so long ago. Still true, though everything else had changed.

Serdic smiled, and she noticed that his skin was golden now, not white: drizzle of sunlight on the market, and on the roof of the blue house. "Jaele," he said, "were you not listening? You make me happy."

That night I dreamed of a morning blue and mild, so bright that I had to close my eyes, after I had stepped out the door onto the wharf. I halted, and my vision returned, and he was there. There, so close to me, maybe six paces away. The masts and rigging of the ships were behind his head. I looked up at the sky, around at the scrubby cliffs, back to him. I saw the wind stirring the hair on his arms. I saw myself in his eyes—I must have stepped closer. I saw a tiny cut on his lower lip, and his teeth as he began to smile—I had forgotten.

He was holding me, clutching me, "Jaele Jaele Jaele" warm in my hair. I pressed my mouth to the slope of his neck and cried. His scent was the same. He kissed me, and I could feel his smile, slippery

with tears. "Dorin Dorin Dorin," I sang, and he lifted me, spun us
both around on the dock until the water was the sky. He was laughing.
There was light everywhere—look at it circling us and the house
and the cliffs, and now you—even though it was just the light of
dream.

She woke slowly, reaching for him, then lay gazing out at the
morning sky. After she had risen and dressed, she pulled a sheaf of
parchment from under the bed. A page near the bottom curled
away from the rest; there was already writing on it. "I rage when I
think of you." She looked down at the words and they were echoes,
only. She had intended to write something—about the house,
about Serdic—but in the end she put the papers on the floor
beside her bed and laid the writing stick carefully on top.

Jaele walked far that day. She sat beneath the slender falling-star
leaves of her tree; against the stone wall in the weavers' quarter;
within the dusty, empty circle of the bridge tower by the docks.
Touching her mother's brooch, she remembered her night wan-
derings: the dagger in her belt, her eyes keen, fevered with his
closeness. Another echo—different, vanishing, dizzying.

She ate the midday meal at an inn she had never noticed before.
Its walls and low ceiling and benches were damp, and the smoke
from the torches stung her eyes. There was only one other person
there: a woman wearing a travel-tattered cloak, a dirty pack beside
her. She smiled at Jaele as she rose to leave. Jaele smiled back,
although again she felt a sadness, a gentle, twisting pain.

It was evening when she came to the fruit market. Serdic, Tylla
and Annial were in the sourfruit chamber, and Jaele stood looking
at them before she entered. Annial was sitting on a cushioned chair
behind the other two. Jaele could hear her humming, even from
this distance, even over the voices of the customers. Occasionally,

Tylla and Serdic turned to her and spoke, and she smiled up at them sweetly as a girl.

"She knows us, and then a moment later she doesn't," Tylla murmured to Jaele when she had joined them. "She speaks of Ilario and Hania and Ellrac—or she speaks *to* them, as if they were beside her. But she seems happy."

"The last time I was here with you, it was snowing," Jaele said to Serdic later. She thought, *And you were pale and beautiful, and I knew what would happen—but not all.* She saw his own remembering in his gaze and did not look away.

Still later he said to her, "You seem quiet. Restless." The walls were jagged dark against the sky, and there was a star in the south; it would be shimmering in the sea, above an island, through a shifting pall of black dust.

"I *am* restless," she said, and was surprised at her own words. "I am—I don't know why."

Serdic peeled a sourfruit with a tiny knife and chuckled. "You'd think I wouldn't be able to eat these any more, but they're still as delicious as ever." After a moment he said quietly, "You won't stay here, Jaele. You can't. That's why you're restless."

"No," she said, "I've told you I'll stay, and I will. I love it here— the house, and your grove. And Annial needs me."

"Look at her," he said softly, and she did. Annial was whispering, her head turned to the air beside her.

"She may get better," Jaele said, but as she spoke, she remembered Ilario.

She left them as they packed the unsold sourfruit away. She almost ran through the narrow streets. She sat in the kitchen, which no longer smelled like bread, and later she slept there, curled in a wall niche. She woke in deep night. The fire had burned to a muttering glow. The stairs creaked beneath her bare feet.

In her room, she knelt beside her pouch, which was lying with her belt and bundle by the door. She drew out her shell pendant.

The thread shone between her fingers, though the light was dim. The shell was cool against her skin—cool as leaf, as wind, high on a mountainside.

I am certain that it was right, leaving him to follow the Ladhra River. Certain—but there is such longing. Where is he now? What is he doing? Would he know me, in these words I speak to you?

They lean close to her, and she feels their steady breathing as she cries.

It is done. You are here. Think on that: you are here.

Noise from the wharf woke her. She looked out and saw sailors on one of the boats. They shouted and sang; one of them hung upside down from the rigging. She heard the screech of chain and watched the anchor rise, dripping green weed and harbour slime. Rows of oars dipped and canvas snapped. The ship pulled away from the dock and sailed out beyond the cliffs.

"There were two ships in Fane's harbour,
They groaned outside my door.
Then there was one, and someday none
And silence will me bore."

Jaele smiled at her own murmured words. Echoes, only, and her bruises.

There was no one in the sourfruit grove when she arrived, and no one in the kitchen. She climbed up to sit where once she and Serdic had sat together, talking of vengeance. She leaned her head on the rock and closed her eyes.

"Jaele." She started. Serdic was sitting beside her.

"I didn't realize I was asleep," she mumbled. "I didn't sleep well last night. And it's so quiet here. Where are Tylla and Annial?"

"At the market. I came back because it was a slow day, and they wanted to stay. Annial was drifting in and out of sleep—and when she was awake, she was urging Tylla to find a husband. I'm fairly sure she thought she was speaking to our grandmother." He paused. "Jaele," he said slowly, "I finally have a question for you. Will you leave?"

She closed her eyes briefly, then looked out once more on the stalactites and the leaves. "Annial spoke the truth when she said, 'You are a traveller, like all the others.' Someone else who was very dear to me said almost the same thing once: 'She is also a traveller.'" She paused. Nossi grinning, Aldreth leaning on the door frame, looking down. "They were right, both of them. But I do love this place."

"Is it—" Serdic began, and cleared his throat. "Will you leave because of . . . that person you love? Will you try to find him?"

Jaele shook her head, thinking for a moment of her dream: Dorin's smile, his arms wrapping her tight in sunlight. "No. As another of my friends said, he is not for me. I am not for him." She drew a deep breath. "I will not be looking for him or anyone else this time. It will just be me. I want this."

Serdic said, "You are very brave, you know," and she laughed quietly, without bitterness, and touched the back of his hand with her fingertips.

"Another question. That night when you ate dinner with us and I touched you, I felt something—a scar, I think. At the base of your skull. I've wanted to know how you got it but was afraid to ask."

Jaele said, "And now that I'm leaving . . . ?" and they smiled at each other. She put her hand up under her hair and drew her fingers along the jagged ridge. "I travelled for a time with a tribe called the Alilan. I was with them when they fought the Perona, their ancient enemies. I assume it was a Perona rider who injured me, but I'm not sure. I was watching someone. Listening to someone. I didn't know the blow was coming." Her words were smooth and warm, unbound. "When I woke up, I was somewhere else. I'd been carried away from the battlefield by a huge man, nearly a giant. He stitched my wound before I awoke. And I think he also helped to distract me, for a time, from other wounds which neither of us could heal. Much later I left—and he left— and travelled on."

"And when you leave here, where will you go?" Serdic's voice was low, but it sprang from the stone and filled the cavern.

"I don't know. Anywhere. There are so many places—and perhaps it will be good to travel without a destination."

"I promise that this will be my last question. *When* will you go?"—and she laughed again, this time wryly.

"When I decide I need to leave, I tend to do so immediately. I will not linger here—I cannot."

The silence was long. At last Jaele touched his hand again, very lightly, and he stirred. "Well," he said, "in that case, I will walk with you to the market."

Their feet sank into the warm earth beneath the trees. They stood at the river door and lingered for a moment, smiling at each other, before it opened on roar and spray.

They walked without speaking. Jaele looked at the stone of tunnels and houses, the peeling paint and crumbling plaster, the coils of ivy, the faces of children. Serdic's face, turned away from her. His hair curled in the wind, which no longer smelled of spring—now smoke and rotting fish. *I tried to remember—to remember before the end—but knew that I could not.*

There were no customers in the sourfruit chamber. Tylla glanced from Serdic to Jaele. Before either of them could speak, she said, "I am sorry that you are leaving, Jaele—but glad that you came to say farewell this time." Then she smiled and held out her arms, and Jaele stooped to hug her. "Will you stay and help us until nightfall?" Tylla asked, and Jaele shook her head.

"No—I can't, I mustn't—" and no more words came over the tears in her throat.

Annial's hands were cool and rough in hers. "Farewell, Annial," Jaele said, and the old woman's eyes wandered to her face and stilled.

"Jaele with Hania's hair," she said in a voice like singing, "or Hania with Jaele's," and she reached out to stroke it with her crooked twig fingers.

"Farewell," Jaele whispered again, and rose.

Serdic walked with her to the entrance chamber, which was also empty. The wagon was gone, though the marks of its wheels remained, scored deeply into the dirt. The walls stretched into shadow with the steady darkening of the sky; dusk, and this time no star. Their hands met and clasped, very tightly.

"If you ever come back this way," Serdic said, "and we are not here, follow the road up the coast until you reach the first town. It is beautiful there—as I may have mentioned before." She lifted one of his hands to her cheek. "If," he said, and she nodded.

The first tears came as he held her; she felt their dampness on his tunic when she moved her head. Then she was standing apart, wiping her face on her palms; then smiling; then walking alone down the sloping, narrow streets to an empty house by the sea.

She stayed for a few more days in the house, straightening books, sweeping the kitchen floor, cleaning ashes from the fireplaces. She paused often, gazing at a page or a wooden spoon. Once, in deep night, she woke and found Ilario sitting beneath her window. She smiled at him and saw the stars, shining through his skin. His face and form blurred, like Nossi's and Aldreth's, like her brother's, mother's, father's—and she felt a pain, now, that had not been in her upon the Eastern Sea, with the first glow of returned memory. Blurring and distance, despite her longing. Ilario beneath her window. *You are as faded to me as all the others, my dear.*

She filled her sack with the last of the seagreen and some small burnt loaves that she had made with Serdic. Placed Ilario's journals in her cloak and tied its corners together. For a while, kneeling beside it, she thought she would take the carpet—to have the names at least, the words that she could see. In the end she did not. She arranged the blanket on her bed.

Close the door, down the creaking stairs, seven paces, close the door. Out into the pale summer sun of Fane, to follow the river away from the sea.

Eagerness lances among them, though all but Llana are silent.

Yes! Be strong in your words and thought. You are so near. We are so near—speak and be strong.

Jaele hesitates, then continues.

There is not much more to tell—not really. I travelled slowly, and my path was different than the one I had taken before. It was early summer, and shallow pools were spread over the sand, joined by rivulets of water; in the sunlight, from a distance, this looked like the thread and jewels of a necklace. Sometimes it rained, but not enough to cloak the sun. The drops flashed as they fell, and they were warm on my skin. As I watched, tiny flowers curled out of the sand—pink stars, light blue.

At first there were whole days that I did not see. My ocean return and Fane had been a balm, a salve; now, walking and alone, my thoughts spun. I thought of Dorin and my father's stories and Ilario's books. The Sea Raider: I remembered him on my beach, in Keeper's palace, across the shonyn river, then in his own land, lying with his face turned up to the sky. It wounded me again, in a way I could not understand. I unfolded Bienta's map and gazed at the lines and colours that had been my guides, the desires of my heart, and I yearned for them. Luhr, the silga mountain, the Ladhra River, Fane.

Queen Galha's footsteps, his, mine—but now? Nothing felt rounded or closed. So much unfinished.

I left the desert and found hills, covered in leaves and needles. I walked beneath arches and columns of sun-soaked green. I came upon some towns and cottages after this, and slept by several hearths. The people were friendly; maybe they pitied me. They gave me food and wine, and one woman cut my hair and exclaimed over my scar. Children climbed into my lap while their parents asked me where I had come from and where I was going. I told them I wasn't sure—and I wasn't, until I saw your stones.

I dreamed, but not every night: shadows that I strained toward, knowing I would recognize the faces. I always woke on the point of seeing and holding, and lay empty. "This is what I have learned," I thought. "I cannot truly hold anyone—cannot even see them once they are gone."

I walked through meadows of tall grass and flowers on swaying stalks. The heat was overwhelming, and there were days when I could not travel except at dusk or dawn. I swam in a lake so wide I could not see the other shore. The water was still and cool and not quite clear, and my feet sank in the ooze at the bottom. Once, I saw a city set in a valley floor. I walked around it, using an animal path that climbed up the mountainside then down again to farmers' fields. The corn had been harvested, and I threaded my way through its stubble. I realized that the days were a bit cooler and nights almost cold. Autumn had arrived, and I had not noticed.

My feet remembered the lichen and slate before my eyes did. I had been hungry and ill before, and there had been a storm, lightning above the red rocks. This time I saw the barrows in daylight. "Now this part is done"—you said that to me, long ago, and I did not understand. Now I looked at the sun on the stones and knew that I had come to my ending, my circle closed. That night Llana appeared and led me into heavy earth, and you were waiting for me.

They shift, seem to stretch in the black cavern. *We were expecting you. We knew you would return. We felt our change beginning when you spoke light to us before. We hoped. We knew.*

Jaele breathes in and out. Her body is aching, but she is not faint as she was the last time. *What change? What have I done?*

Listen, they say, *and open your eyes even when they pain. Speak as you listen—speak, because the change is not yet complete.*

The change . . . I have told you everything—all that I saw. Even Lallan throwing pebbles. Even clothes in a river, raised up and weeping glass. What remains?

They speak, all eight. *Tell us your freedom, and ours.*

My freedom, she repeats; *my change.* She knows, then, with a surge of warmth and tears. It is almost too clear, too bright: light on water, a bird's thread. She does not speak for a time. *I know,* she finally says. *I know, now that I have run and swum and danced. Now that I have told you everything, from beach to Fane to these red barrows. You have listened and sung and asked, and they have lived. My mother and father and brother, my friends, my companions. They are here.*

She pauses and breathes and finds that she is trembling. Then, slowly, she speaks their names—each one, every one, as the iben stretch in the darkness. The names a weaving, smooth and whole, vivid as sun or flame; words she feels in her mouth like joy. *You are here,* she says at last, and smiles as Llana wipes her tears away.

She feels trickles of dirt on her skin, hears it hissing as it falls. Points of light prickle the thick, deep earth. The iben's horns and talons glint as they look upward. They are silent.

You are still waiting, she says. *But all that remains is what will be, above. What I did not know until now. I will leave here: I will run in sunlight—*

There is a rending crash, then another, another. The points of light crack wide as the earth tears apart. A searing glare—Jaele cries out as her dark sight is ripped away, but she does not hear herself, her voice is lost in the ringing, keening joy of theirs. Singing of sand and mountain cloud, running in dawn-bright grass—singing and calling, then, one or all: *Our freedom from yours. We have waited so long, thinking only of darkness and past, endlessly following grief. Endlessly—until you, and your tale. Others sometimes came to us, but none told us what you have. Yours is a tale of before and now and someday all together and one. Like us, child Jaele. We will not forget.*

The iben reach and cry, and Jaele speaks again, for somehow they are still listening, still need her words:

I will run through the silver rain and corn to where Serani and Bienta dance I will pass beneath the gleaming portcullis of Luhr and look up at palace spires I will follow the tracks of Alilan wagons in red sand I will I will go home.

There is no cavern. Shattered stone and spinning sweep of sky so blue, so unexpected, that it is almost white—the iben crouched then leaping. She sees them arched into the sun; sees their faces as they turn to her.

The hut is drifting ash and frame of blackened ends—but there is the bay, the Giant's Club, the snails and layers of water, seagreen weaving. Ilario's words breathing in my hands. My fingers curled around the writing stick: my words another circle closed or open, as shonyn now still always.

I can see the stars, shining through their skin.